La Rosa Chronicles

Spiderling

BY

K Spirito

To Lynne Doherty, Enjoy! K Spirito

PETER E. RANDALL PUBLISHER LLC
Portsmouth, New Hampshire 03802
2006

This book is a work of fiction. Places, events and situations in this story are purely fictional and any resemblance to actual persons, living or dead, is coincidental.

© 2006 by K Spirito
All Rights Reserved.

No part of this book may be reproduced, stored in a retrieval system, or transmitted by any means without the written permission of the author.

First published by:

PETER E. RANDALL PUBLISHER LLC
Box 4726
Portsmouth, New Hampshire 03802
www.perpublisher.com

Book design: Grace Peirce

ISBN: 1-931807-53-1
ISBN13: 978-1-931807-53-1

Library of Congress Control No.: 2006905228

Printed in the United States of America

For Sal:
Loving you is like turning toward the morning sun.

Acknowledgments

A special thanks to all those indubitably fine people who have supported me along the writer's path, especially:

Sal Spirito, Sr., and Sal Spirito, Jr.

Poet, songwriter, and daughter Cynthia Godin

Editors: Corinne Wait, Lisa D'Angelo, and Carol Brooks

Peter and Deidre Randall

Grace Peirce

La Rosa Chronicles

Father Sandro's Money

Kathleen (work in progress)

Roses Falling (work in progress)

Time Has A Way

Everything Happens To Margi (work in progress)

Yesterday, Tommy Gray Drowned

Tomorrow Is Promised To No One (work in progress)

Candy-Colored Clown

Spiderling

Chas (working title)

Visit: www.kspirito.com

Prologue

"Mohammad Achmed al Hadi is wise to recognize that a man in his position breathes precarious existence," murmured Rashid al Sadun, lowering his head and eyes to confirm the utmost of respect. Their discourse, he knew, was low; still it seemed to rumble like distant thunder among the late-night shadows discarded by marble pillars. Even the lush, hand-woven carpet unfurled on the tiled floor and the blue and gold brocade pillows upon which Rashid and his master sat, failed to suppress their voices.

"I am prepared for the black day," murmured al Hadi, gazing up at the gold leaf ceiling aglitter like the desert sky at midnight.

Rashid eyed his master. His heart thumped against his breastbone, resounding like a great gong. "My master is too resigned to fate."

Fear of detachment had been Rashid's since being taken from his parents as a child; although servitude to Mohammad Achmed al Hadi and the royal family had allayed that fear. Al Hadi had become a father to the protector, a protector of the protector; and therefore, worthy of protecting, worthy of dying for; and here laid Rashid's complicated fear of detachment.

"A father's need to protect his seed requires sacrifice," murmured al Hadi. The sleeve of his white samite aba swayed as his left palm gestured to the rhythm of his words. His right hand lay flat upon the fine embroidery trim that cascaded down the breast of the garment. On his third finger the signet ring, which had been handed down through generations of rule, glistened in the low light as did the agal that held his keffiyeh in place. "Without trepidation I accept the forthcoming cloudburst of evil, for the ensuing flood cannot be outrun."

Position stipulated that Rashid was not to question, so he fiddled with the signet ring on his left hand, a smaller version of al Hadi's. *At the first sign of trouble,* he thought, *I shall shed this white linen robe for the more practical outfit beneath. Occasion has called for me to do so before. But these sandals…. Despite the fact that they are made of the finest of camel hide—most certainly, not as fine as the goatskin sandals worn by my master—they limit mobility.*

"Certain African countries offer safe harbors for those in my position," continued al Hadi. "However, I do not underestimate the vulnerability that bribery begets."

"Bribery is a useful tool," whispered Rashid. "I myself use bribery as a means to an end."

Al Hadi gave a light nod. "Sharp-wittedness and devotion have made Rashid my most trusted protector. Alas, all that Rashid is will be of no use when the black moment is at hand. Therefore, Rashid is no longer my protector."

"Master?"

Al Hadi elevated his left palm. "Rashid must survive…at all costs…survive to protect my survivors."

A tremor wracked Rashid's five-foot-nine frame. *Thankfully, my master is too busy with that map to notice my weakness.*

Spreading a world map on the floor, al Hadi said, "Muted Middle Eastern features render Rashid ideal for the task at hand."

"Mohammad Achmed al Hadi honors this humble servant," murmured Rashid, again bowing head and eyes. Curiosity pricked him like thorns. *My Master withholds the rage of a volcano nearing eruption, strangled by a higher power.*

Al Hadi took a pocket-sized pointer from beneath his aba and unfolded it. "Rashid will smuggle my survivors along this route." The pointer crept upon the map like slow-moving lava. "Across the great breast of Africa to Liberia, the bastard colony of the United States. At Robertsfield Airport, you are to board a plane." The pointer arced across the Atlantic. "This is the destination." As the pointer rapped on a spot on the North American Continent, Rashid gasped.

"I believe that capitalistic interests motivate my assassination," murmured al Hadi.

"As do I," agreed Rashid, much too hasty, much too loud for decorum, much too loud for this night.

Al Hadi's left eye narrowed upon Rashid and then scanned the shadows. Once again, focus fell upon Rashid. An anxious moment passed. Al Hadi nodded. And relief sheeted over Rashid.

"No better spider hole exists," said al Hadi, "in which to hide my survivors than beneath the bloated infidel's nose."

Pace response, Rashid admonished himself. He sucked in a breath then said, "I am in agreement."

Al Hadi pulled a white folder from beneath his aba. "Memorize this information, now, in my presence."

Rashid hesitated then took the folder, opened it, and removed the contents one piece at a time. "Assets. Diamonds. Gold. Precious commodities." He looked up at al Hadi. "All untraceable."

Al Hadi nodded. "As are the listed charities, which I created to provide additional funds should the need arise."

Rashid tapped his right index finger on his bottom lip. "Mohammad Achmed al Hadi has cornered the market."

"A bountiful life for those who survive me," murmured al Hadi. "When Rashid is certain the information is forever his, I will destroy all trace of it. Rashid will begin at once to gather supplies into backpacks and bury them here." He tapped the pointer on a spot at the border of his kingdom. "Rashid and the al Hadi dynasty must become skilled in the language of the infidels. Upon my death, ancestral robes will be cast off. Raven locks that make our kind pious will be cropped." He handed Rashid a black leather briefcase with gold features, which included the name Aranea. "Keep this at your fingertips at all times. Necessary travel papers are in it. Rashid will become American Timothy Aranea, uncle to my survivors who will also carry the surname Aranea. I have given each an American first and middle name."

And so the dawning of Mohammad Achmed al Hadi's fiftieth year, the nineteenth day of the third month in 1972, the assassination came to pass, a carnage beyond measure, meant to send the Middle East the message: submit to the Great Eagle or else. Rashid eluded death by taking refuge behind a pillar. A blade to an assassin's throat provided a sand-colored cloak, antelope hide trousers, and desert boots—and the means to escape the palace and the sandstone village.

Camouflaged within the worst sandstorm in decades, Rashid hastened to a boarding school in a far-off southern republic and retrieved his master's only survivor, a son whose brazenness and insolence had made him less favored not only in his father's eyes but also Rashid's. Brazenness and insolence was the reason the boy had been sent away. Rashid was of the mind that the boy was inherently evil. Evil revealed itself in the boy's eyes since first opening at birth. Whenever in the boy's presence, unsettledness roiled in Rashid's belly. *All that must now be put aside,* he commanded of himself.

The ceasing of the sandstorm plus a full moon forced night travel in the shade of dunes. At the border Rashid dug up the backpacks. After consolidating supplies into two packs, he reburied the surplus, including his and the boy's signet rings. Nearing Liberia, he shaved his beard, cut his and the boy's hair, and used a stripping agent to lighten their hair. Rashid traded desert attire for a button-down shirt, tie, and pleated pants. The boy donned jeans, light blue polo shirt, and loafers. Wearing glasses, though neither needed them, Timothy and Jonathan Aranea appeared to be Americans flying into Canada, purchasing a red Detroit economy car, and driving across the border into New Hampshire.

Chapter 1

*E*nrollment at an out-of-the-way private school on Granite Mountain came easy—bribery being a useful tool that compensated for incomplete paperwork and missing the majority of the academic year. Upon graduation Jonathan Aranea matriculated in Granite Mountain College, a converted rehabilitation center that had provided hands-on education in the building trades for shell-shocked veterans of World War II and Korea. Budget constraints had forced the utilization of the environment for materials to complete a majority of projects; consequently, ex-GIs had chiseled out of the east-facing vertical ledge a Grecian-style edifice complete with granite columns. Such magnificence deserved status; hence, a petition requesting college level accreditation had gone off to Washington where, without argument, Granite Mountain College had come to be. The edifice had become the Administration Building; veteran housing had become dorms.

Academia overlooked the fledgling college isolated within the White Mountains. It struggled for existence until the flower children of the sixties discovered its remoteness and enlivened the technical curriculum with ecological and humanitarian studies.

"Jonathan Aranea makes Mohammad Achmed al Hadi proud this first year at Granite Mountain College," remarked Timothy on the anniversary of al Hadi's birth and demise. "You have grown to be a towering, long-limbed man whose voice carries little trace of ancestry—just what your father prayed for."

"The eradication of my father and family goes beyond insult," spat Jonathan.

Timothy bowed his head reverently. Sadness laced his voice. "This is true."

Jonathan's misleadingly gentle brown eyes flashed with deadly intentions. "The blood of my father—my entire blood-line—is upon my neck!"

"Be wise to control passions," warned Timothy. "If left unchecked, undesirable consequences could befall you."

"I possess no fear," shot back Jonathan, his hands flailing in the protector's face. "These very hands will avenge Mohammad Achmed al Hadi!"

Timothy lowered his head and eyes and turned into stone. Withholding reaction was an ability he had acquired with the passing of time and practice, especially in the company of Jonathan Aranea, a foolhardy yet dangerous young man.

"Be that I alone survived while the rest of my family rots in desert sand," raved Jonathan, "it is my belief that through Great Decree, I am omnipotent! Invincible!" He put his back to Rashid and added, "A prophet! Victory over the infidels! Martyrdom!"

Timothy read between the lines. *My young ward proclaims that any counsel given from this day forward will be taken with a grain of salt. Alas, bitter regret and devotion to Mohammed Achmed al Hadi, a sacrificial lamb, sours my belly and threatens to twist my face. I must concentrate. Control myself. To do otherwise will bring about my own demise.*

Cunning, a strong arm, and wealth oozing from fields rich in black crude gained Jonathan Aranea control of Granite Mountain College by graduation in 1984. After naming himself top gun, he handpicked a well-rounded staff that was secretly sympathetic to radical beliefs. Others who did not follow his vision but were necessary to achieve his goals were intimidated into submission and brainwashed. If that didn't work, they were eradicated. He replaced the local police force, elected officials, and others who might someday come in handy. To make himself look more domestic, he chose a Mainer, Meredith Blevins, to be his bride. She was tall, athletic, like he, though paler, attractive enough for his purposes. On the surface she was a barren mother figure to students, trustworthy, kind-hearted with a keen sense of humor. But beneath the surface lay a traitorous, vindictive, deadly villainess—and that made Meredith attractive to Jonathan beyond measure.

Akin to vigilant spiders, the Araneas identified delectable achievers from high schools across the globe and lured them into the web expanding around Granite Mountain. Poisoned minds sucked free of independent thought began to make their way throughout imperialist society. All carried mental activation buttons that assured future loyalty and assistance. The political implications gave Jonathan head trips. His plan to drive the Great Eagle to its knees, make it infect and devour itself, surged like a flood upon the desert.

"The lifeblood of Democracy drains without notice," boasted Jonathan, braced upon knuckles while standing behind his office desk in the Administration Building. Light from the window behind him shrouded him in unearthliness as he made eye contact with each and every associate that was dressed as he and Timothy: sport coats, matching pants and shoes, button-down shirts open at the neck, and ties rolled up in pockets. "The stink of the unfaithful, disobedient ones upon this earth is coming to an end."

Timothy noticed Jonathan's right eye twitching. *When exactly did that ignoble tic begin?* He shifted in the chair in front of the bookcase that ran corner to corner along the wall opposite the desk. The chair was the last to fit his bulk, which had gotten out of hand over the years. Food was his vice, fork-to-mouth his exercise. *Ah yes,* mused Timothy, *the tic cropped up the day Jonathan was caught cheating on college entry exams. Fussing over the tic gained endless sympathy—not to mention a heavy greasing of the palms. "An eye given to such malady is bound to wander," agreed exam monitors.*

"The appearance of the norm is kept at all cost," said Jonathan in a controlled but dangerous voice. He turned toward the window. "That is imperative. Security will be lax, for to do otherwise will only serve to attract attention. However! That does not mean we are not watchful!"

"These Americans are so trusting," said Timothy, admiring the ever-increasing collection of vivariums that lined the adjacent wall. Labels affixed at the top right hand corners identified creatures within: Haplopelma Lividus. Heteroscodra Maculata. Haplovelma Albostriatum.

"That is to our advantage," snickered Jonathan. "A glorious future is ours."

"Although…" cautioned Timothy, "…one solitary error could mean the worst."

Jonathan shot a dark look over his shoulder. His eye twitched.

Timothy pretended not to notice. Gesturing to the vivariums, he said, "Jonathan Aranea certainly has a knack for making the species prosper." He sent an indulging grin that made Jonathan's face sparkle like lightning in the desert at midnight.

Jonathan acknowledged the compliment with a closing of eyes and a slight nod. Stepping to the vivariums, he said, "Dogs will be the main security."

"One in each dorm for students to dote over," suggested Timothy. "Soft, cuddly, and harmless-looking."

"I will implant a command into each dog," said Jonathan, "that will turn gentle pet into predator of the worst kind, and give to one convert the knowledge of the command."

On one afternoon during the hot, drawn-out, and especially humid summer of 1985, Jonathan insisted that Timothy tag along with him to the summit of Granite Mountain. By now, Timothy was aware that he was nothing more than a whipping boy for Jonathan's discontent; however, commitment to Mohammad Achmed al Hadi lessened the burden.

"We take rest," panted Jonathan, bracing an arm against the bulbous trunk of an oak tree. The branches had been gnarled by high winds continually blasting up the ravine.

Timothy squinted at the sky while mopping perspiration off his brow with a handkerchief grimy from doing so too often this day. "Not a breath of air," he heaved, "even at this elevation." Sweat fouled his khaki shirt and cargo shorts, and his hairy legs rutted in slimy cotton socks and hiking shoes.

"Even birds refuse to fly in such heat," groused Jonathan.

Timothy pulled his shirt out of his cargo shorts and unfastened buttons. His gut rolled out like rising bread dough over his belt.

"You grow too rotund," carped Jonathan, his voice edged like broken glass. "And you sweat like a pig. Smell like one, too. If not for your keen mind, I would have you roasted."

If indeed the day of roasting comes to pass, prayed Timothy while running the grimy handkerchief around his neck, *I will be content in paradise not to be in servitude to this impudent cur.* He swabbed his breastbone and then stuffed the handkerchief into a pocket of his shorts. *Not only does a keen mind prolong my days on this earth. More importantly, it is the locations of assets that this keen mind possesses.* He squatted like ancestors of the desert had done since the beginning of time and feigned empathy. "Something weighs heavy on the mind of Jonathan Aranea, this day."

"Summers," snapped Jonathan, the tic seizing his eye. "Protracted, stagnant summers. They aggravate me to no end."

Timothy watched Jonathan unbutton his shirt. *He will not remove his shirt. My ward never removes his shirt in public. Bare chests repulse him. He claims bare chests robbed man of dignity. And serve no purpose. So unlike the female breast.*

"Spring breaks!" raved on Jonathan, clutching the sides of his shirt in his right hand. His left fist wielded at the cosmos. "Holiday breaks!"

Timothy plucked a drifting leaf from the air. "Ah. These Americans do come up with many excuses to shop and play."

"I consider such interruptions to be a waste of time and brain enrichment," snorted Jonathan. "An unconscionable stymie of progress."

Timothy studied the leaf's network of veins: large main veins, small veins, some nearly imperceptible. *Imperceptible as I in this great scheme called life.* He squinted at Mount Washington looming over the southern end of the Presidential Range. Water vapor, uplifted from the windward side, interacted with mountainous terrain and temperature to form the orographic cloud that capped the summit. *It rains on the Rock Pile.* He heaved a sigh. "Progress is ahead of schedule," he said in a soothing tone. "Few hiccups have occurred along the way. Factions outside the United States are sitting up and taking notice of Jonathan Aranea."

"Ugh," grunted Jonathan with a wave of the hand. "Who needs them?"

"Ironic," said Timothy, gazing upon the granite edifice below. "Infidel legions giving rise to such a place. They never conceived that true believers such as we were destined to come along and turn misguided ideals against them and…"

"The common house spider constructs a funnel web with flat silk sheets," purred Jonathan.

Timothy gawked at Jonathan letting go of the sides of his shirt and pulling away from the oak tree. His eyes rounded to the size of eight balls. His face brightened like a full moon on a desert night. His palms extended, and he rotated as if a prophet ascending into the afterlife. An aura hung about him, not angelic, but dark, menacing, demonic. Convinced that his charge had lost his mind, Timothy stood up, reaching out to help.

"A narrow entry leads into a raised tube in the corner, a retreat or place to hide in the cool dark crevices in rocks," crooned Jonathan. "The spider chooses its hapless victim, rushes out, grabs it, then delivers the poison. Within the retreat, the spider feeds."

Timothy followed Jonathan's line of sight to the north face of Granite Mountain and then to the east face. Eyes skied down the slope then vaulted as if off a great imaginary ramp and soared westward. "What do you see that I do not?"

Jonathan stamped his foot. "The future lies beneath this granite pedestal upon which we stand." He clasped his hands. "And such an unlimited future it will be!" He threw back his head and howled with laughter that resounded across the Mount Washington Valley.

Trepidation spiked the hair on the back of Timothy's neck.

"Oh, you naïve New Hampshirites," wailed Jonathan, "if you only knew!"

"What is there to know?" cried Timothy.

Jonathan hooked his hands on his hips and said in sing-song sarcasm, "My vision."

"Vision?"

"A subterranean community within the bowels of Granite Mountain."

Timothy scratched his head. "My mind struggles to conjure up the vision."

"A warren much like those in which our desert brothers dwell," insisted Jonathan. "We will strategically locate structures that resemble abandoned mine shafts and then burrow into the mountain. Opportunity to strike the Great Eagle with the maximum impact is ours!"

"Drilling will most certainly attract attention," argued Timothy.

Jonathan pulled the sides of his shirt together. "Night will cloak activity…and thunderstorms when blasting. Before long the mountain itself will cushion construction."

Excitement zinged through Timothy as his mind weaved the framework of a circular descending warren that controlled activity, inside and out of Granite Mountain. *Perhaps,* he thought, *I am too hasty in judging this impudent cur.*

"Vehicles and personnel will bud out from the core of Granite Mountain like delicate spiderlings in the middle of the night, virtually unnoticed," said Jonathan while buttoning his shirt. "Granite chunked from tunnels and burrows will become buildings for scores of businesses seemingly unconnected in any way, shape, or manner to each other or to Granite Mountain College."

"Or to you," added Timothy.

"All will girdle the mountain," said Jonathan, "to provide hidden entries."

Timothy eyed the western slope. Halfway down, white birch saplings sprouted between cracks in baldheaded boulders. *Nature overcomes many obstacles to get a toehold.* He pointed to the boulders. "Perhaps there? An ecology studies camp?"

"Youth working on trails will keep authorities off-guard," agreed Jonathan.

Timothy sucked a food particle out of his top front teeth. "And a mile off to the left, an engineering camp?"

Jonathan nodded.

"What about the current landowners?" asked Timothy.

"Easily disposed of," said Jonathan. One side of his upper lip quivered. "We shall import new owners who in no way can be connected to us or the college."

"A great task," said Timothy.

Jonathan pursed his lips and deliberated the predicament. "Ah, well," he said. He drew a deep breath of satisfaction. "All in due course. We must first brainstorm methods to covertly select susceptible yet intelligent junior high and elementary school students, the sole purpose to mold the most lethal angelic-looking terrorists ever known to mankind and enhance our college alumni."

"But camps come to an end," said Timothy. "All return home."

"A way must be found to draw back our spiderlings to reinforce conditioning," said Jonathan.

"Perhaps a residential academy," said Timothy. "A place for snotty Americans to board over-indulged offspring to be educated and refined."

"Timothy Aranea, you are a genius!" shrieked Jonathan.

Timothy tossed his head back as though his face had just been brushed by a fresh breeze.

"For that I appoint you headmaster," said Jonathan. "Ah, yes, on the surface, Granite Mountain Academy and College will display academic excellence, expand youthful minds, while in the marrow of the earth, our clandestine culture exploits technology, cultivates biological and chemical agents, and conditions youthful minds. My very own spiderlings. All under my control. Can you not hear backwoods Hampshirites, my dear Timothy? 'Things like this just don't happen in our neck of the woods.'"

Chapter 2

"Where in the world have you been?" squawked Ken Waters, yanking open the front door of the turn-of-the-century home in Brighton, Massachusetts.

Here we go again, thought Katrina, rolling her eyes. *Dad's in one of his grouchy moods—again.*

Edging past his five-foot-ten frame, she kept an eye trained on him as he stuck his head out the door and scanned the neighborhood then the low, scowling sky. She felt like sniping, *For crying out loud, Dad, nobody's out there!* But then, the aroma of simmering tomato sauce and freshly baked chocolate layer cake bowled her over. She stuck her nose into the air in the direction of the kitchen.

"Well, young lady?" demanded her father.

She glanced over her shoulder at him. His hands were hooked on his hips and dragging down his blue jogging pants. The Patriots sweatshirt he wore was a gift from her, last Christmas. She sucked in a deep breath. "Ecology Club, Dad!" Slight traces of a southern accent lingered in her voice after four years of speech lessons. "Every Wednesday. Remember?"

His bottom lip slackened. His eyes rounded. Twisting his wrist to eyelevel, he gawked at his watch. "This late?"

"Face it, Dad! You blew it!" she spat, keeping a steady gaze on him. Inside though, guilt stalked her. *I got too caught up talking to Miss Matthias. Should've called home. But it completely slipped my mind, 'cause Miss Matthias, well, she's ever so nice. I'd like to hang around her all the time! She's got a way of lifting my spirits every time life drags me down. So petite and agile, and I love her short bouncy hair! It's dark as midnight. Shimmering—like her eyes do whenever she laughs. And Miss Matthias laughs a lot!*

Katrina plunked her backpack on the bottom step of the winding staircase, hooked her foot over the back of one sneaker, and kicked it off. Doing the same to the other sneaker, she shook an arm out of her pink sweat suit jacket and flung it off her other arm at the coat rack. She straightened her purple tee shirt that had fluorescent yellow block lettering, Brighton Junior High School, arcing across the front like the morning sun. Despite emerging womanhood, childhood clung to her five-foot-five frame. Being kidnapped and spending four years in a terrorist training camp in Judgment, Mississippi had matured her mind beyond her age; yet her elliptical blue eyes viewed life too inno-cently. She squinted at her father. *There he goes again, running his hand through his hair—a sure sign he's worried sick. I'm just too grown up for his comfort. All he sees is his baby girl.* "Why don't you worry about Addie for a change!"

"My baby girl's too naïve for her own good," he stormed, doing an about face and slamming the door. He rotated the lock and then slid the deadbolt into place. "Too cute and fiery! Qualities the male gender strives to tame!"

She pursed her sulky pink lips, not in defiance, though she knew he would take it that way. She did it to stop herself from bringing up the kidnapping. *It freaks him out too much. But I did get out of it…somehow.*

The nightmares had all but disappeared: her biological mother, whom she adamantly referred to as Regina; the cold, black eyes and backhand of that stinking idiot Jake who had claimed to be Dad's brother; the brainwashing at that camp in Judgment, Mississippi. Upon bolting awake, sweating, urine seeping, she always found comfort in her father's arms. "Regina and Jake are dead," he soothed her, "and the Feds got rid of the camp those two jerks sold you to."

But Dad's so paranoid about some jerk snatching me away again, even after Doctor Edie Fitzgerald (the shrink Uncle Curt recommended) got all our feelings sorted out. I just want the chance to be the person I want to be—whoever that is.

Retrieving two butterfly barrettes, which her father had given her just before the kidnapping, from a pocket of her jacket, she jabbed, "I can take care of myself!" Gripping the barrettes between her teeth, she fluffed her shoulder-length blond spirals that in younger days had been a mass of ringlets. She weaved one barrette into a tuft on one side of her head and the other barrette into a tuft on the opposite side of her head. "Every free moment, I practice that stuff I learn in those silly self-defense classes you make me take. I'm the most cautious person on planet earth!"

"Demons charm with a smile," he countered, shifting from one foot to the other. He elevated his palms. "These days, evil…"

"Here comes the lecture," she jeered, again rolling her eyes. "These days, evil prowls everywhere!"

He eyeballed her, perplexity shading his face.

"Now the spiel about how you wait up whenever I'm out," she continued. "You do more than just worry. You pray. Doesn't matter a particle if I'm out with Mom, Nana Elizabeth and Pop Pop, Gammy Getchen…"

"I…" he stammered.

"Oh, sure," she ranted. "You trust me. I'm smart as a whip, thoughtful, caring, so many great qualities that matter less than a hill of beans, because no matter what, you still worry—not because once you were a boy and I'm such a beauty…well…" She glanced down and scuffed a stocking foot on the hardwood floor. "…maybe the beauty part's right on…" Her brows came together. Glaring at him, she stomped her foot. "You're never *ever* satisfied I get the message! Just because you're my father you think it's up to you to protect me every second of the day!" She waved her hands high in the air. "Nothing is ever going to harm me again! Nope. Not as long as you draw breath!"

"Kat! Kat," squealed Adriano, bolting out of the dining room. The royal blue pajamas the five-year-old wore had a spaceman over the heart, embroidered by Gammy Getchen,

Katrina's maternal grandmother. His eyes, the color of chocolate sprinkles, came from Ken. His cheekbones blushing like ripe peaches came from his mother Julie. His hair was a mixture of both parents, chestnut streaked with honey blond.

"Hey, there's my Addie," puffed Katrina, bending at the knees. She scooped up her stepbrother and savored the smell of the baby shampoo that lingered on his hair. *Oh, to bottle that smell!* "My goodness," she yipped. "You're getting so heavy!"

"I hafta be a prize fighter when I grow up," puffed Adriano. "Daddy says so. So I can beat up any guy that bothers you!"

She gave her father the hairy eyeball. He shriveled and said, "You should've called."

"Mama's on the phone all the time," pouted Adriano. His soulful eyes pined for sympathy. "An' I'm not s'posed ta int'rupt."

"There you go, Dad," said Katrina. "The line was busy!"

"Sorry, guys," hollered Julie from the dining room. "You know how it is when Emma and I get to talking."

Ken tisked.

Katrina planted a kiss on her brother's pudgy cheek and asked, "Know how much I love Addie?"

Adriano grabbed her chin in his little hands and squinted into her eyes. "Too much!" He gave a decisive hitch of the chin.

"No such thing as too much," she said. Spinning the boy around, she caught a glimpse of her father. *I see him smiling. Worry's fizzling. Impossible for Dad to stay mad at me! Or Addie. Or Julie, for that matter.*

"Get a move on, my sweeties," hollered Julie. "Supper's getting cold."

"By the smell," said Katrina, heading toward the dining room, "Mom's latched onto another one of good ol' Emma's recipes." She stopped short. Lowering Adriano onto the floor, she winked at him. "You go ahead. Kat will be there in a sec'." She blew a kiss at him. He blew one back. Spinning around as if his kiss impacted her hard, she smacked into her father.

"Good Lord," exploded Ken, snagging Katrina by the shoulders. He held her at arm's length. "Where on earth are you off to?"

Shaking free of him, she muttered, "Forgot something." Her stocking feet made floppy sounds as she charged back to the stairway. Feeling his eyes on her, she plopped on the bottom step, back to him, and rummaged through her backpack. *Where is it?* She opened the left pocket. *There it is!*

"What do you have there?" clucked Ken.

"Nothing," she mumbled. Chucking the backpack, zipper and flaps left undone, into the corner of the step, she fretted, *I have to find the perfect moment to show him this.*

In the spacious rose-colored dining room, Julie stood at the buffet in front of the bay window, filling water glasses. A pale blue apron emblazoned with black-faced sunflowers, which was a gift from Emma LaRosa, protected brown pants and a peach-colored blouse. Honeysuckle perfume surrounded Julie as she put out a cheek for a kiss. Katrina acquiesced with a quick peck and a jab, "You get shorter with each passing day."

"Don't start," scolded Julie, a glint in her cocoa eyes. "Hands?"

"Oh, Mom," whined Katrina, flicking the brochure on the table.

"I did me, see?" said Adriano, holding up his hands and swiveling them front to back.

Ken entered the dining room, rotating his computer wiz hands and clearing his throat to attract attention.

"Daddy never gets dirty," bragged Adriano.

Katrina stalked past the three-season porch on the way to the kitchen. "Hey, Ralph," she said to the cat that had an intense eye on some sort of backyard prey. His tail twitched. "Well, don't say hi!"

"Another letter came back," said Julie.

"Why do you persist in sending them?" grumbled Ken.

"Uncle Curt's vanished from the face of the earth," muttered Katrina while turning on the water at the kitchen sink. "Freaky." She soaped up her hands, eyeing the rain sluicing down the atrium window. "Gosh, I got home just in time." She smiled at the grocery store flowers crowded into jelly jars perched upon the sill. *Won't be long before dandelions, lily-of-the-valley, and yellow-eyed daisies picked by the littlest hands of this family pack those jars, again. Leaving Toffee Castle is going to be hard—even for a couple of weeks.*

"Doctors don't up and leave their practices every day," said Julie, dashing into the kitchen.

"Curt's mother is about to croak," bawled Ken from the dining room. "He's an only kid. He had to go."

Julie opened the butler's pantry and shouted, "Yeah, but still. You're his best friend, his childhood friend. You two have been through so much. You'd think he'd keep in touch."

"Maybe he's dead," shot back Ken.

Katrina's eyes popped. Her hands hung within the warm torrent.

Julie slammed the pantry door. "That's a terrible thing to say!"

"Listen," snorted Ken. "Curt got sick and tired of putting up with me and all my problems. That's all."

Katrina shut off the tap, thinking, *Bet if Uncle Curt was here, he'd tell Dad to back off me a bit.* She tore off a paper towel from the roll hanging from beneath the cabinet and wiped her hands. Tossing the used towel into the trash, she headed back to the dining room, but as she rounded the archway, she stopped short. Her father was seated at the table, studying the cover of the brochure. Her teeth clamped onto her bottom lip. Crossing her arms over her chest, she rubbed her biceps. *Gosh, my skin's crawling as if millions of spiderlings were scootching over me.*

"What's this about?" demanded Ken, but didn't wait for an answer, instead, reading the title aloud, "Granite Mountain College Presents Education with Nature in Mind."

Her eyes shot to the floor. *Don't look at him,* she told herself. Skulking to the table, she slid onto a chair.

"Emphasizing ecological sensitivity and diversity," he said.

She peeked out the corner of her eye. His brow wrinkled. *Not a good sign.* His eyes focused on the image of a snow-capped mountain soaring against a crystal sky. She pursed her lips. *That's the most gorgeous picture I've ever seen!* She grabbed a piece of bread and bit off a hunk. *Just when I think there's nothing new under the sun, another off-the-wall experience smacks me in the face. Voila! Instant audience! That's what happened when Miss Matthias handed out those brochures about that place in New Hampshire called Granite Mountain. Long after everybody else left, I stayed. Miss Matthias rambled on and on about the benefits kids get out of going there. I got excited to the core when she said I'm cut out for that place. She really wants me to fill out the application inside the brochure! But she doesn't understand Dad. All the way home, my heart was racing. I thought I was going to have a heart attack! Almost did when Dad ripped open the door, overprotective as usual, and pissed off about me being late and not calling. He's just never going to let me go!*

Ken opened the brochure. His face scrunched. "Look at that turbine mounted on the roof of this building!" His head jerked to one side.

"What building?" Julie asked, returning from the kitchen. Potholders protected her hands against the steaming casserole she carried. She set the casserole on a trivet then bent to squint at the brochure. "O-h-h," she said, tucking a pesky honey-blond strand behind her ear and straightening. "Not too safe, I'd imagine."

Those two are wrecking my nerves, fretted Katrina. She snatched up the salad bowl and then set it down harder than she meant to between her and Adriano. As she doled out salad into his plate then hers, her hands shook so badly that vegetables dropped on the flowered tablecloth.

"Pass your father the salad, dear," said Julie, brushing her hands together.

"Imagine," said Ken, ignoring the salad bowl that Katrina offered, "daisywheels dotting Boston skyscrapers. Not efficient. Imagine working near those huge turbines? The noise? The vibration?"

Katrina watched her stepmother gnaw on the inside of her lip. *Mom knows I'm never going to live up to Dad's expectations. She'll get him to let me go. She's got a knack at diffusing situations. Dad is putty in her hands.*

"Where'd you get this?" he asked as Julie reached in front of him, grabbed the bowl, and sat down. She dished salad into his plate then into hers.

"Eco adviser handed them out," said Katrina as blasé as she could. "We get extra credit for going, and Miss Matthias says we can make up anything we miss when we get back."

Ken tossed the brochure onto the table. Picking up the cruet of the salad dressing, he shook it then uncapped it and drizzled bleu cheese dressing over his and Julie's salads. He picked up his fork, jabbed it into his salad, and chucked the forkful into his mouth. Chomping, he eyed Katrina who thought, *He's not falling for my aloof manner. He's seen it too many times before.* She grabbed the cruet and poured dressing on her salad.

"You're not thinking of going to this place," he said, watching blue cheese dressing overflow her plate.

Avoiding eye contact like the plague, she put down the cruet, grabbed her water glass, and gulped. Water dribbled out the side of her mouth. She set down the glass, snagged a napkin, and dabbed the seepage.

"Not a good idea," he said flatly.

"Here you go," said Julie, passing the casserole dish to him.

His eyes bugged out. "Now what do we have here?"

Julie cleared her throat then hooted, *"Braciuolini di vitello!"*

"You've been practicing your Italian," commented Ken.

Julie scooped a portion into his plate. "All afternoon."

Adriano cocked his head to one side and scrunched his button nose. "What's bashadivello?"

Julie and Ken exchanged glances then burst out laughing. "Rollettes," said Julie.

Katrina stared, bug-eyed. *Are these people from Planet Xenon?* As her father mowed down *braciuolini di vitello*, she ventured, "You are going to let me go."

Julie and Addie shot looks at Katrina then at Ken.

Katrina's eyes narrowed. Anger surfacing, her palm slammed the table. Silverware jounced. "Dad! Stop being so paranoid!"

"What's par'noid?" asked Adriano.

Julie reached over and smoothed the child's locks in a motherly fashion. "Swallow what you have in your mouth before speaking, dear. Food might get stuck in your windpipe and you'll choke."

"Windpipe?" asked Adriano.

"Shush," said Julie, stroking his cheek.

"M-o-m," whined Katrina. "All my friends are going."

Agonizing moments passed. Julie nudged a pesky strand behind her ear then reached over and patted Ken's hand. "Katrina should go to the camp, dear."

Chapter 3

*P*lagued by another night of Julie Waters roaming his dreams, Doctor Curt Shirlington coerced his blue eyes into opening. He turned his head and focused on a slender, five-foot-two imprint on the sheets beside him. *Penny's off to work,* he thought. *The smell of her, jasmine, still floats upon the air: sweet, flippant, but not honeysuckle—not M'lady.* He rolled into a sitting position and hung his legs over the edge of the bed.

The Black Forest cuckoo clock in the dining room ticked.

He scraped morning stubble, shaded deeper than his carrot-colored pate. "This place is stagnant as a mortuary after viewing hours." Despite his Bostonian birth and upbringing, his speech reflected a Scottish-English bearing. "Got tartared up again. Curt, old boy, you're a case. Your best chap's wench weighs you down worse than a blasted anvil. Get some muscle, for pity's sake. Be rid of her. Dote on Penny, a rock, never complains. Until she came along, life was beyond the pale." He swiped moisture from his brow and dragged it down the side of his face, neck, and broad chest. "Life's just pale now."

The cuckoo clock chirped. Curt wasn't counting. *Penny sets the spirit free—at least to a tolerable degree.* Guilt slithered over him. *This dodgy heart of mine should not be larking about another world with M'lady.*

A long time ago, Curt had vowed that the soft spot in his heart for Julie Waters would never escape his lips—and it hadn't—so far. Still, there were times when he nearly fell apart at the seams and scattered at Penny's feet, confessing like a blathering idiot that he was in love with M'lady. The two women had a budding friendship when he left Brighton just before Adriano was born. They hadn't been in touch—as far as he knew—since Penny got the job at the Centers for Disease Control and discovered him working at the same facility.

Getting to his feet and shuffling to the window, he mused, *Penny must never know that she walks in the shadow of M'lady.* He didn't pull back the curtains. He knew a thunderous torrent was raging. It raged every day without Julie Waters—in his mind.

An hour later, clad in a blue-striped, button-down shirt open at the collar, navy pants and socks, and black loafers, Curt closed the front door behind him. Not a single cloud interrupted the azure sky. Sprinklers hissed, adding moisture to the lawn and foliage that hadn't seen rain in days.

In his office, Curt offered his hand to Emily, the Cat, lounging on the mouse pad. Her mantra soothed and sweetened his soul as she arched into an all inclusive stretch then head-butted his belly. Big-hearted Penny had discovered the tri-colored cat in the dumpster about ten months ago and had come up with the name Emily, which was a character in the play Our Town. Upon asking her mother if she was pretty, Emily had received the reply, "Pretty enough for all normal purposes." And that was the cat's lot in life, ugly enough to be beautiful, unnaturally-marked, one pumpkin-colored eye, and one steel blue eye. The first time Curt set eyes on the creature, he jibed, "You call that a cat?"

"Fate brought this sweetie to the CDC," spouted Penny while giving Curt a playful shove. "Emily, the Cat, is just what we need to ease tension around this joint."

The moniker stuck. True to her calling, nothing fazed Emily, the Cat, no matter how riotous the occasion. She took up residence in his office and had a real sense of his routine, always there when he returned—just like Penny, always there for him.

He nudged aside the cat, donned his white clinic jacket, and sat down to sort the memos that had accumulated during the night. *An update of al Qaeda movements. London officials arrest a sympathizer, charging him with operating a website that recruits Muslims for a jihad. That's about all terrorists can do in Britain,* mused Curt. *Shooting ranges like those in the United States—military training of any sort—are illegal in England. What's this? Another rogue terror organization? And it's put together a website for kids? Honors martyrs and encourages kids to kill for Allah's cause. Cute animations.* Curt shook his head. *Covers up reality. The wee one must be plugged into the Internet. Hope the ol' chap's on top of it. She's twelve by now.* He did some quick calculations. *Thirteen? No, fourteen. Whatever. Wonder if she suffers any ill effects of her Mississippi ordeal?* He pushed back his chair. *May be prudent to ring up the ol' chap.* He glanced at Emily, the Cat, performing her morning ablution. "It's been a long time," he muttered. The cat stopped her ritual and her pupils dilated upon him. "Ol' chap's no idiot. Plus he's the anal sort. The wee one probably can't go to the lavatory without him holding her hand." His stomach flip-flopped. *What if M'lady answers?* Anxiety built in the pit of his stomach and bubbled up to his throat. A hard swallow choked it back. *Make the call,* urged a part of him. *The wee one might be scared and grasping at the security that those like the ones who had used her still offer.* Another part of him warned, *Getting in touch would be worse than poking the badger with a spoon.* His thumb and forefinger squeezed his bottom lip. *The curly-mopped eight-year-old detailed quite vividly the day Regina and Jake squirreled her off. "Jake kicked and punched Daddy." Her voice was laced with an acquired southern drawl. "Daddy fell on the floor." A quiver wracked her body. "Daddy! Wake up! Why doesn't Daddy wake up?" Her face turned dark. "I was four then, but I'm eight! I understand now. And it makes me very, very angry!" She sucked in a lungful of air. "Jake pulled me off Daddy and dragged me over to Regina. She slapped me across the face to stop me from kicking and screaming, but I didn't."*

"Regina," seethed Curt. "High dollar tart in low collar garb. Abhorred the wee one and the ol' chap. They had the father-daughter relationship that had been denied of her as a child, herself brainwashed by self-serving fanatics. Regina profited greatly from the sale of her only offspring, but in the end… Humph."

The last thing the wee one recalled of Regina, Curt mused, *was the back of her head above the front passenger seat of Jake's sports car and a gold earring dangling in and out of her blond hair. Jake and Regina were having a spat. She wanted him to go somewhere with her, but he said he had something to do first—that was rigging the Cessna to crash with her on it. Everyone assumed the wee one was on that plane, but that was not the case—Jake had dropped her at a terrorist camp in Judgment, Mississippi. Ol' chap had repressed the entire happenstance until M'lady got pregnant, which spurred him to recall Jake's electronic trail on the Internet, in particular, a site of a small town in Mississippi called Judgment.* "Imagine," muttered Curt. "Terrorists kidnapping and buying wee ones. Brainwashing them, turning them into weapons. A pox on their houses! Foolish gun laws. Paramilitary training is a picnic without the ants in America."

Emily, the Cat, arched against him. He fiddled with her ear, staring unfocused at scribbled notes he had stuck on the monitor. "Wonder if the mention of Regina still causes the wee one to pull into herself like a turtle into a shell?" He and the cat made eye contact. "That had gone on since infancy. Saints preserve, the wee one bears little resemblance to that tart." He picked up Emily, the Cat. "Oh, how M'lady fretted about the unborn one looking like Regina—as if that's possible." He rubbed his fresh-shaven chin across silky fur. "Hmm, she does bear a bit of resemblance to the ol' chap…but…what if she's not his? He told me that he figured the wee one was conceived one night when Regina arrived home, quite inebriated, and seduced him in the garage. They hadn't been sleeping together, since Regina had kicked him out of the master bedroom for snoring long before that night. She could've earlier shagged another bloke. A blood test would clear up paternity, but why bother? It's water over the dam, what with Jake being dead and all. Besides, Ol' Chap loves the wee one too much to be hit with such unsavoriness. Plus there's Adriano to think of." Curt tried to picture the boy as Emily, the Cat jumped out of his arms. The image remained unfocused. "Wish the lad looked like me. But if indeed that were possible, would he have red hair? Blond? Or a curious variation of both?" Curt squinted at the clock. 11:02. "Time for a caffeine fix." He braced his hands on the desk and got to his feet. "Back in a few, Em."

In the conference room a trio of lab techs were gawking at the twenty-five inch television perched on a steel shelf bracketed into the far corner. General Colin Thornton's face filled the screen. *Blowhard,* thought Curt. *Rambling on and on about the progress of the war in the Middle East as usual.*

Thornton used to brief every day, at least once in the morning and once in the evening—sometimes more. That's when the war got underway, but after the first wave to liberate Kuwait and bring Iraq to its knees met with disaster, he briefed once a day—that is, if the public or disjointed government agencies were lucky. Curt rarely caught broadcasts, receiving intelligence via official notices and Analyst Leander Holt.

Curt tsked. *Too much bloody information getting lost. Too many body bags. Vietnam revisited.* Too young to have any part in the Vietnam War, he was aware of the suffering it had caused to others of his generation, namely Julie Waters. Through Ken, Curt had come to know nearly everything about Julie—more than he should've known. To her, he was just a friend, but to him, it was a whole lot more. In fitful dreams she whispered love in his ear. Her touch was gentle and warm upon his skin, but daylight forbade her fingertips from brushing his cheek in that tender way that lovers do. Her lips remained a world apart from his.

It would be wrong to think that Curt had wanted to leave Brighton and his lucrative practice, but one too many patients had nudged his shoulder, asking, "Doctor Shirlington? You all right?" Not to think of Julie was like asking the sun not to rise or the sea not to surge and ebb. To want her for his own felt as natural as breathing. So it was time to go, cut and run, preserve friendships. His excuse: "My dear Mum's at death's door in Florida. As an only child, I'm obliged to hold her hand."

Yet everything that was, is, and ever will be New England coursed through his veins. He tried not to think of the changing seasons—her cheeks blushing like the first rose of spring, her hair streaked with summer, her eyes glowing like autumn, her voice pure as winter. The seed had been sown at the creation of time itself, no use to resist, though indeed he tried. He pitched unopened mail from friends into the trash, including Julie's. He screened phone calls via the answering machine. Ken had left messages. So did Penny, whom Curt had dated a few times. They had a nice time, but nothing ever came of it. He blamed himself for that, convinced that it was his fate to always love M'lady. Julie's voice never came through the machine. So many times he wished it had. *All for the best,* he supposed. But like an endless sunset, M'lady lingered on his mind.

His mother had died within months; although Curt didn't inform a soul. He laid her to rest without delay or fanfare and then fled to San Diego, leaving no forwarding address. Bumming around, he learned of a lab in Seattle, seeking researchers with biological and chemical backgrounds, and hired on. It was better than dealing with patients and easier to put behind him if necessary. That road led to another lab in Oklahoma City where his keen insights earned him several quick promotions and then a transfer to the Centers for Disease Control in Atlanta. On the outside his life looked picture-perfect. Others viewed him as confident, happy with whom and what he was, competing with life and most times, winning even when considered the underdog. Nobody saw the distress that Julie's memory caused him, though he often felt he was about to lose his mind, merely doing time, a workaholic in need of liberation. Drowning in work was the only way to be rid of her. Then the war in the Middle East came along, got bogged down, a political and military quagmire, another Vietnam. He hated war, but it relieved him of M'lady.

Time and miles had come between Curt and the woman he loved, though no matter the season or his geographical location, winter stormed within his soul. Nights, alone and cold, he crawled beneath blankets to clutch a pillow that embodied her. He tried not to dream, but his heart insisted, stirring up tropical breezes that toyed with her honey blond tresses. Her smile took his breath away. She reached out to him. He pulled her to him. Her skin warmed his. He couldn't hold her any closer, being everything she could ever want him to be. She gave herself to him, freely, seeping into his veins, intoxicating him like fine wine. He possessed her to the depths of his soul. Pent-up emotion poured out of him. "I love you, I love you." Her head lay upon his chest, her breath coming and going, soft, warm. "Tell me you love me, M'lady." The words he had longed to hear were never said. As stars slipped away, so did the beating of her heart, fading like the end of a great melody. He fought to hold onto her, keep the night from another cruel dawn that spread across the wall.

At the rear of the conference room, Curt poured coffee into a Styrofoam cup, leaned against the counter, and took a sip. "M-m-m. Strong and black," he muttered. "Just like M'lady's parents make it."

"You speaking to us, sir?" asked one of the techs who had been watching Thornton on the tube. Shifted sideways in his chair, the tech stared at Curt.

Embarrassment washed over Curt. He cleared his throat and blustered, "As you were."

The tech exchanged looks with his companion, shifted back in his chair, and focused on the television. The screen flashing like a strobe light drew Curt's attention. Laser and cluster bombs were sparking pyres of tremendous heat and incinerating targets. "During investigations of claims made by defecting scientists," said Thornton, "that chemical and biological sites are disguised as civilian businesses, it was affirmed that duel-use businesses are producing both lethal and non-lethal goods. Therefore, civilians in these situations were warned repeatedly to vacate or be killed."

Meanwhile, Curt mused while taking a sip of coffee, *duel businesses continue to produce more chemical and biological agents in a robustness, layering, and duplication more profound than thought. Is it any wonder that camps like the one in Judgment, Mississippi spring to life? Surely others are pressing on undetected.*

Curt refilled his coffee cup and sauntered out of the conference room. He stopped in the head to eliminate the buildup of coffee and to wash his face.

Emily, the Cat, greeted him at his office door, arching against his leg. She weaved in and out of his legs as he stepped to his desk. She jumped up on the desk when he sat down. She kneaded a new memo lying atop the amassing paperwork. He pulled the memo out from under her paws and read it aloud, "Need to discuss the connection between a camp named Ground Zero America, the al Qaeda terror network, and other training camps. Back in an hour. Holt."

"Ground Zero," said Curt.

Emily, the Cat, meowed. Her pumpkin eye and her blue eye heavy-lidded him.

He gnawed the inside of his cheek the way Julie always did. *Ground Zero: area directly beneath or above where the detonation of a nuclear bomb has taken place—the ground beneath M'lady.*

Chapter 4

*C*areful not to let her father see her gloating in the backseat, Katrina calculated, *It's going to take two hours to get to Granite Mountain. So what? I'm spending two weeks on my own, the first since Mississippi!* She wriggled out of the jacket that matched her blue jeans and picked gray fur off her red knitted tank top, a result of hugging Ralph good-bye. Her sneakers were new and white. Her butterfly barrettes, which kept blond spirals parted down the middle and out of her face, were old, most of the color worn off.

"Address unknown," muttered Julie, seated in the front seat and holding an envelope at eye level to read a message stamped in red. She was dressed in a pale yellow peasant blouse, brown stretch shorts, and white sandals. Makeup consisted of light pink lipstick. Her honeysuckle perfume sweetened the air.

"How many times do I have to tell you?" squawked Ken. "Curt will show up when he's good and ready. Quit dwelling on him."

Julie flipped over the envelope and squinted at the unbroken seal. Then she wedged the envelope under the pile of mail on her lap and opened another envelope.

Katrina had thanked Julie again and again for convincing Ken to let her go to Ecology Camp. Still, whenever other ears were presumed out of range, heated debates continued. "You've got to lighten up on Katrina," insisted Julie. "If you don't, she's going to rebel, and if that happens, it'll destroy our entire family. What about Addie? Katrina means the world to that little boy."

Katrina glanced at Adriano who was dressed in a black and gold Bruins sweatshirt and pants and black walking shoes, which matched the outfit Ken was wearing. His elbow braced the armrest and his fist braced his chin. "You look so bored, Addie," she said.

"Uh-huh," he said.

"Look at that gold dome," she said, finger pointing. "That's the State House—Concord—the capital of New Hampshire. The Concord Coach comes from there."

"What's a coach?" he asked, his nose twisting up.

"A stage coach," she said, picking more cat hair off her red tank top. "A carriage pulled by horses. People used to ride in them before cars were invented."

"The first teacher in space came from Concord," said Julie with a bit of sadness tainting her voice.

"Christa McAuliffe," added Katrina. "Her first name was Sharon, you know."

"Kat knows lots about N' Hampsha," boasted Adriano.

"Too much," grunted Ken. Muscles flexed on the side of his neck. His jaw hinges tightened.

Katrina pursed her lips. *Dad's not even trying to hide he's against me going to Ecology Camp. A godforsaken tent-out in the middle of nowhere, he calls it. Well, I'm not letting him wreck this for me. No way. No how.*

Julie patted Ken's right thigh. He glanced at her. She smiled and batted her eyelashes that picked up the golden hue of a summer's morn. He grunted.

Katrina rolled her eyes. *Nothing's going to improve his mood, not this warm April sunshine, not the light traffic heading north, nothing.* Her eyes narrowed on the highway ahead, weaving in and out of carved ledges. The greenest of hills rose and fell. *I feel as if I'm riding on ocean swells capped by the bluest of skies and whitest of clouds I've ever seen. The grass rolls out of the thick woods like emerald carpets. And the road's a ribbon, tying it all together—a present just for me!*

"Tilt'n Diner," yipped Julie, pointing to a billboard. "Exit 20! A quarter of a mile ahead!"

"Too early for lunch," sputtered Ken.

"But we stopped here on our honeymoon," whined Julie, head bowed, lips puckered, eyes coy.

Ken shot her a now-that's-a-low-blow leer.

"My tummy's hungry," griped Adriano.

"Poor Addie," soft-soaped Julie. "You have to stretch your little legs, don't you? How about you, Katrina?"

Katrina smiled thinly and nudged a blond spiral out of her face. The exit ramp loomed. Nobody spoke. Her father ran a hand through his hair. Julie gnawed the inside of her cheek. Adriano fidgeted. "Oh, for crying out loud," snapped her father. Tires screeched as he veered onto the exit ramp. Julie clapped with glee. Katrina winked at Adriano whose cheeks dimpled. Approaching the stoplight, her father hit the brakes and Katrina hurtled into the back of his seat.

"Why aren't you buckled up, young lady?" scolded Julie.

"This is New Hampshire," replied Katrina. "Live free or die."

"And this is your father," barked Ken. "Buckle up!"

Katrina pursed her lips then yanked the seatbelt across her chest. As she snapped the end into the buckle, Adriano strained against his seatbelt, demanding, "Where's we eatin'?"

"There," said Julie, pointing across the street to the left.

Adriano craned his neck. "Can't see!"

"We'll be there in two shakes of a lamb's tail," said Julie.

Ken glanced at her. "Two shakes of a lamb's tail?" he jibed. "You hang around Emma too much." Just then, the car behind tooted. His brows came together as he shot a look into the rearview mirror. "Hold your horses, bub!"

"Hold your horses?" taunted Julie. "Bub? Now who hangs around Em too much?"

Katrina led the way into the Tilt'n Diner, a stainless steel eatery frozen in the rock and roll era. The hostess was bent over a booth, chatting. Her butt jounced to the beat of Jailhouse Rock that was playing on the jukebox. Her jet black hair was teased into a twist.

"Look," whispered Julie. "She's wearing a poodle skirt. Bobby socks and penny loafers, too!"

"Park it anywhere," hollered the hostess, waving them in.

"Order me the liver and onions," said Ken. "Addie and I are hitting the head."

"I want spasgetti," cried Adriano, being hauled away. "I want spasgetti!"

Heading to a booth in the front window, Katrina noticed a heavy-set man behind the blue Formica lunch counter. He had on a white apron and chef hat. *Why's that guy looking at me like that?* She slid into the booth, picked up a menu, and peered over the top. The man diverted his eyes. He snagged an order clipped to a rotating device and hurried off into the kitchen.

"What'll it be?" asked a waitress, chewing and snapping a wad of gum. She was wearing black Capri pants and penny loafers, white blouse and bobby socks, and her blond ponytail swayed to the Coasters now playing on the jukebox.

"Mommy," shrieked Adriano, galloping along the line of booths. "Pictures of old cars are all over the bathroom walls!"

"Classic cars," clarified Ken. His mood seemed lighter as he jostled the boy into the booth.

"A funny looking truck's on the toilet," bellowed Adriano.

"Inside voices," said Julie, pressing an index finger to her lips.

"A *picture* of a truck is on the *wall—over* the toilet," clarified Ken, humor lighting his face. "And that *funny-looking truck* is a milk delivery truck. Before my day, people got their milk, butter, eggs, lots of stuff delivered to their houses."

Julie snickered, "Before your day. What were you saying about Emma again?"

Buddy Holly set the joint jumping with Peggy Sue as the waitress set a juicy burger and perfectly formed fries in front of Katrina. A cherry coke complete with bobbing cherries washed it all down.

An hour later, the Waters' family climbed back into the car and headed north on Route 93. Shortly thereafter, Plymouth appeared in a valley on the left. *Sure would be nice to go to college there,* mused Katrina. *Fat chance. I'll be taking classes online at home, so Dad can keep me under his thumb. Gosh. I'm going to be an old maid.*

"Brake for moose," said Julie, reading a roadside sign.

Katrina craned her neck to scan the rocky wash of the Pemigewasset River that snaked back and forth beneath the highway all the way to Lincoln. *Not one moose.*

At the Flume Gorge Visitor's Center, Ken parked the car. After a potty break, they gawked at the Old Man of the Mountains that jutted out of Cannon Mountain twelve hundred feet above Profile Lake. "He's made of five slabs of granite," explained Katrina. "All stacked up on each other like this." Her hands flattened horizontally atop one another and traded places, indicating the levels. "Forty feet from chin to forehead and twenty-five feet wide. He's twenty million years old."

"I'm five," bragged Adriano, his thumb jabbing his chest.

"Five," echoed Julie with a sidelong gaze at Ken. "Imagine that?"

"Time flies," said Ken, squinting at Adriano and then at Katrina.

Anxiety washed over Katrina. From the look on her father's face, the weight of the world had once again landed on his shoulders. He turned and clumped back to the car.

Katrina took Adriano by the hand and followed. Straining against seatbelts, they twisted in their seats and stared through the rear window at the Old Man of the Mountains. As the road curved, Adriano waved. "Bye, Mr. Man."

At Exit 35 Ken steered onto Route 3 then nine miles later, onto Route 302 east. Six miles passed. "Look at that!" exclaimed Julie, her finger pointing across Ken's face.

"That's the Mount Washington Hotel," said Katrina. "It opened in 1902."

Ken pulled the car onto the shoulder of the road and shifted into park. In silence they gawked at the hotel. Julie sighed. "Stunning," she said while winding a honey-blond strand around her ear. "Simply stunning."

"Someday," said Ken in a mellow voice, "I'm taking all of us there for vacation."

"Now!" spouted Adriano. "Let's go now!"

"Next year," said Ken.

Adriano crossed his arms over his chest. "I wanna go now!"

"Can we get going?" asked Katrina.

Ken frowned at her in the mirror. "My baby girl's a bit antsy, isn't she?"

Katrina diverted her eyes back to the hotel. *I'm not a baby*, she felt like hollering. She heard him suck in a breath. Then the car inched back onto the highway and accelerated. When the sign for Granite Mountain College came into view, she caught him glancing at her in the mirror. A sinking feeling came over her. *He's changed his mind. He's going to turn around, just wait and see.*

When her father turned down the hemlock-lined lane, she broke into a smile. An intersection came into view and beyond a granite arch marking the entrance to the main campus of Granite Mountain College. On the other side was the Grecian-style Administration Building. "That picture on the brochure must've been taken from this angle," commented Julie.

Ken harrumphed.

Katrina zeroed in on hand-scrolled lettering painted on rough-hewn wooden arrows nailed to a pole. *Ecology and Engineering Camps.* "Go left, Dad!" she spouted.

He frowned at her in the mirror.

If he does that one more time, she fumed, *I'm going to scream!*

He turned the wheel and stepped on the gas. The road cut through oak, birch, maples, and pine then narrowed. "Here, Dad," hooted Katrina.

All eyes focused on a dirt lane on the right as he stepped on the brakes.

"This place sure blends into the natural surroundings," said Julie.

Nobody would notice this place unless they were looking for it, mused Katrina.

"Too remote," grumbled Ken. "I don't like it one bit."

Katrina pursed her lips. She tried to look tough, but inside, something remote and threatening festered. *Maybe Dad's right. Maybe this isn't a good idea.*

Second thoughts turned to dust the instant a cluster of bungalows bedecked with flowery window boxes appeared over the hood of the car and high-spirited laughter reached her ears. A folding table doubled as a sentry post. Behind it, a ginger-haired teenager took a bite out of the middle of an oozing jelly sandwich and got to her feet. She was wearing red cargo pants and a white tee shirt that proclaimed in red, white, and blue script, Granite Mountain—Planning Our World. A nametag askew on the girl's shirt declared: Hello! My name is Camille! She grabbed a clipboard off the table and skipped shoeless around the table and up to the car. "Here for Ecology Camp?" she bubbled.

A stiff wind could blow Camille away, thought Katrina, covering her mouth to hide her mirth.

Camille stopped chewing. Her almond-shaped, hazel eyes that sharpened at the outer corners impaled Katrina. So did the ruby eyes of a pewter spider pinned to her collar. *Creepy,* shivered Katrina.

"Waters," grunted Ken.

Hair curtained her face as Camille looked down to scan the list of names on the clipboard. Her pinkie finger pushed hair out of her face as she looked up and asked, "Katrina?"

"That's her," snorted Ken.

Camille squinted at Ken. She grinned, teeth smeared with masticated bread and jelly. Backing away, she used the sandwich as a pointer. "Park over there."

As her father drove off, Katrina peered through the rear window. Camille was taking another bite of sandwich. As she chewed, she stared back. So did the eyes of that spider pin clinging to her shirt.

Fresh mountain air made for a deep night's sleep. The next morning, Katrina awoke disoriented when Meredith Aranea, the Camp Director, barged into the dorm, shrieking, "Spring proclaims its arrival! Come out! Smell the mountains!"

Katrina got up on one elbow. *Where in the world am I?*

Standing against the screen door with blinding sunlight flooding in, Meredith looked like an apparition dressed in white safari garb.

Burning logs, coffee, pancakes, bacon, and eggs filled Katrina's senses. Her stomach growled.

"Things are happening," shrieked Meredith. "Crows are cawing! Waterfalls are spilling! Spiders are weaving webs over brooks free of their shackles of ice! Soon, spiderlings will burst upon the world!" She tossed back her head of bobbed straw and released a long, arching wail reminiscent of the loon surfacing at the brink of darkness, and bringing forth the memory of Regina that spiked gooseflesh all over Katrina.

Chapter 5

*K*atrina was in her glory. Ecology Camp flowered her life with amazing experiences and newfound friends. Clad like other campers (red cargo pants and white tee shirts proclaiming Granite Mountain—Planning Our World) she tackled trail work like it was going out of style and jumped at every chance to learn basic outdoor skills. She built campfires, used compasses, interpreted topographic and road maps, and predicted climate. *I'm not about to lose my way or be stymied by quick changes in elevation or weather,* she thought. *How embarrassing is that? Plus Dad would use it as an excuse to take me back to Brighton.*

Those tacky hello-my-name-is tags were stuck to just about every shirt, including Katrina's. The ruby-eyed, pewter spider pins worn on collars singled out counselors. Other people wore the pins, too, but only once in a while or on what seemed to be staged occasions, which she assumed to be some kind of rituals or holidays.

Group leader Bert Moro caught her eye. His sexy, brooding, enigmatic presence struck her like a force of nature, straight to the heart, giving her fever beyond which no thermometer ever recorded. His bronze-toned hair, skin, and eyes made him look like the male models on tanning oil billboards. Lean but muscular, the five-foot-ten junior at Granite Mountain Academy was angular for his seventeen years. The first time he called her Trina, she squelched a giggle with her hands and squinched her eyelids. The known bad boy was right on top of everything except for wearing his spider pin. Meredith constantly chewed him out about it. "I lost it," he claimed.

"Again?" asked Meredith. "That's it! No more spider pins for you, bud."

New best friend, Brita Fry, had her enchanting green eyes on Vic Sag, also a group leader. Rugged and sturdily built, he towered over her five-foot-four tomboy presence. His wavy hair, light brown like his eyes, was always meticulously combed, while hers, short, wavy, and brown, was in constant disarray. His eyes routinely slid up and down Katrina's body, and he made no attempt to hide it. The slow smile that spread across his face and the aura of testosterone that swathed him may have brought others under his spell, but not Katrina. *He thinks he's a real babe magnet*, she fumed. *But one doesn't mess with a best friend's squeeze.* So she made light of him, all the while worrying, *Brita might get jealous. Not only that, Vic doesn't like it when things don't go his way and somebody usually pays the price.*

Chas Riley was the size of the average five-year-old and had a childlike voice, though he was fifteen. He reminded Katrina of Adriano, even though he had a primordial look about him: crinkled, tawny face, thick lips, flat, turned up nose, dark curly hair the same color as his small, distrustful eyes. Chas acted traumatized, shut down on the world, hanging back, nearly invisible while munching sweets. He rarely wore camp garb, choosing instead a brown plaid, flannel shirt and baggy painter's pants. His feet went sockless inside unfastened tan work boots.

The third day of camp, Katrina was selecting stones for the cairn she was constructing near a stand of poplars when she discovered a Jack in the Pulpit bathed in dappled sunlight. Waving off a mosquito, she crouched down to study its tubular form. When unfastened tan boots entered her peripheral vision, she knew right away Chas Riley was standing over her. Instinct told her not to hurry his trust. One hard word and he'd take flight. She cleared her throat and glanced up. "How about giving me a hand?"

His eyes widened. His hands formed balls, opening and closing. He scanned the area. He stuck a finger in his ear, wiggled it, then pulled it out of his ear and without a word, began to gather up rocks. When she picked up a stray pop top and put it into her pocket, he asked, "Why did you do that?"

"Three pieces of trash removed from Mother Nature each day," she replied while picking up a gum wrapper, "and she'll reward you in many ways."

Chas slapped grime off his hands. A dubious look shaded his face.

"Let's rip out all that overgrown vegetation around that tree," she said while folding the gum wrapper into a tiny square then sliding it into the same pocket as the pop top. "After that, you can paint the blaze."

He appeared to be eying the paint can and brush. He went to them and bent at the knees. He stood up, his thumb and forefinger clamping a rotten cigarette butt. He held it up for her to see. When she smiled and nodded approval, a thin smile wrinkled his lips. He slipped it into his pants pocket then swatted a mosquito on his forearm. "Over one hundred fifty-seven species of skeeters in North America," he said.

She slid him a look. "What are you, some kind of entomologist or something?"

"This region harbors the biggest variety," he said, trying to hide the growing smile. He flicked off the carcass. "A skeeter can suck a hundred times his weight in blood."

She shooed away a mosquito buzzing her ear.

"Clean clothes attract them," he said.

"Remind me to never do my laundry," she said.

From that day on, Chas stuck close to Katrina. *Looking for a friend*, she figured. *He doesn't seem to have any. Or is it inherent curiosity that keeps him close to me?*

Though sociable to most, Katrina steered clear of a few—like Camille Jennes. *Camille tends to be a leech. She never does her share of the work. She isn't shy about complaining either—whines all the time over the silliest things. Her hair's constantly in her face.* Sustenance came from jelly sandwiches on the run, reminiscent of the day Katrina arrived. Camille had a pipe dream about living in a mansion high on a hill. *An unrealistic likelihood,* mused

Katrina, *given that Camille's got stars in her eyes for super-sized Joe Ault, a self-destructive sort with a potty mouth.*

Ault's heritage was mixed: white, black, and Asian. His eyes were as black as his straight hair that flowed long and at will. Easily frustrated, he had a hair-trigger temper and loyalty to none. Manliness to Joe equated to one-upmanship, cruelty, and bragging that Camille was bed sport—even in front of her. He made obnoxious comments that counselors shouldn't: Suck it up! No pain, no gain! Be a man! Put your back into it! He circled campers—reminiscent of a great white shark getting ready to feed. He pelted food at them or slammed them against walls or trees. He issued challenges, "Gonna complain about me, peewee?" So, campers made wide arcs to avoid Joe Ault.

Alice Milton showed her true colors the first night of camp. "What?" she blasted. "Sit on the floor in front of a freakin' potbelly woodstove? Sip hot cocoa? I wouldn't be caught dead doing that crap!" The hazel-eyed, leggy redhead had a tall, solid-bearing, a boyish face, and broad shoulders. She wore camp garb and a spider pin all the time—and screamed a lot. Self-appointed authority came from Mr. Jack Daniels. She downed antacids as if they were candy. Katrina often wondered why Meredith looked the other way. *Maybe because Alice knows about computers, machines, geography, and all that kind of stuff. That's got to be the reason. Still, that know-it-all uses anything and every-thing to her advantage and is quick to take glory when things go right and adept at casting blame when things go wrong. And what a temper! Oo-whee! I'll never forget that day out on the Saco River Trail when Alice went psycho just because Brita popped her bubblegum.*

"You're such an idiot!" Alice had hollered. As usual, her voice was husky from booze.

"Bug off!" blasted Brita. Sucking in the dregs of the bubble, she put her back to Alice.

"Nobody tells me to bug off," growled Alice, locking an arm around Brita's neck. She jammed a leg into the back of Brita's knees, swung her around, and then let go. Brita ended up in the mire that flanked the trail.

"Stop!" cried Katrina, grabbing Alice's arm. She spun Alice around and eyeball to eyeball, demanded, "Why do you have to make big deals out of silly little things?"

"You ain't my Mama!" Alice bawled, driving the heels of her hands into Katrina's shoulders.

Propelled backward, Katrina landed near Brita who screeched, "Look out!"

Katrina looked up. Alice was soaring through the air, straight at Katrina! Rolling to the left, Katrina heard Alice do a belly flop in the muck. As she scrambled to her feet she heard Alice bellow, "Eat this, punk!" Katrina turned. A hand oozing with muck was coming at her face. She intercepted Alice's wrist, almost too slippery to hold, as she twisted and plastered the muck into Alice's face.

Alice fell back, but instantly recovered, sitting up and swiping muck off her eyes. Blobs of muck clung to her scraggly hair as she got ready to spring.

"Cut it out!" shouted Katrina, raising her palms. "We're supposed to be friends!"

"Friendship is overrated," scoffed Alice, raising her hands, fingers crooked, threatening. She took a step and then another.

Katrina giggled.

Alice stopped in her tracks. "What's so freakin' funny?"

Katrina pointed at Alice, squealing, "You look like the Creature from the Black Lagoon!"

Alice turned beet red. "Monsters are way cool," she raged. "They're ugly. Always misunderstood!" She lunged. "Rejected! Picked on! Dejected!" Muck flew as the two girls wrestled. "Monsters are not victims! They control situations! They make victims! So do I!"

Katrina's well placed knee sent Alice backward into the mud.

"Aarraach…" yowled Chas, charging into the fray like a rabid dog and wielding a rock.

Alice shielded her face with her forearm.

"Chas, no!" hollered Katrina. Jumping at the rock as though it was a volley ball, she smacked it into the woods on the other side of the trail.

Alice lowered her forearm. Resembling a statue made out of muck, she gawked at Chas then at Katrina then at Chas again. "Why you little…" she snarled while bracing a foot under her to get up.

"Cut the crap!" barked Meredith, stomping into the fray.

Alice laughed in defiance, which caused visions of Regina to loom in Katrina's mind. Waves of nausea washed over Katrina. Stomach muscles knotted. Knees buckled. A hand grabbed her arm, stopping her fall. The hand belonged to Alice.

"I said, 'Cut the crap!'" hollered Meredith as her hand weighed on Alice's shoulder.

Releasing Katrina, Alice flopped on all fours and escaped to the trail where she got to her feet. She sent Katrina a look that hinted of admiration then strutted off, proud as a peacock.

"You okay?" asked Meredith, putting an arm around Katrina. "Look at you! You're filthy!"

Katrina scrutinized herself then said, "Yeah."

⌒

Days later, hours of eighty-degree sun drained Katrina. Hungry and in need of a pee break, she hated to complain. Home-sickness skulked her. So like other campers, she sought out Meredith Aranea, a true friend, easy to talk to.

"My dear, Katrina," said Meredith in a motherly way, sooth-ing, metrical. "Don't allow outside influences to derail the goals we here at Granite Mountain have helped you to set. You have a healthy appetite for new challenges. Go for it."

"Yeah, but," whined Katrina, "hauling around tent rolls, pick axes, and spades is hard."

"Tests the mettle," cooed Meredith. "You thought you were physically fit."

Katrina hung her head and nodded.

Meredith gripped Katrina's chin in her hand and forced eye contact. "You are physically fit. You proved that the other day when you put Alice in her place. You're also mentally fit. You can take on whatever your heart desires—whatever we here at Granite Mountain ask."

Katrina felt like a million spiders were crawling all over her. A song surfaced in her head. Her father had taught it to her when she was a toddler, before the kidnapping. *"Mary's Song" got me through four years in Judgment, protected me from the brain-washing.* Katrina pulled away from Meredith.

"Brush-clearing and drainage is tedious and time-consuming," said Meredith. "But it's important and in the end rewarding."

Katrina swiped sweat off her sunburned face.

"You never pictured yourself away from home," said Meredith.

I never pictured myself away from Dad, either, thought Katrina.

"But here you are," said Meredith. "Learning. Tenting in Forest Service shelters. Leaving no trace. Not spoiling what nature intended."

"I never knew about water bars," said Katrina, "or how to build a bog bridge."

Meredith poked Katrina's shoulder. "No more thoughts of home."

⌒

The last Monday of Ecology Camp, Katrina's group set out on a five-day tent-out along the Webster Cliff Trail. An hour or so into the trek, Katrina said, "I love the rhythm of long-distance hiking, don't you?"

Brita grunted. "Let's take a breather," she said and plopped on a fallen tree at the edge of the trail.

Alice clomped past, grumbling, "Freakin' hot."

Katrina unhooked her gear then took off a layer of clothing. She listened to footsteps fading. "I hear a waterfall," she said and then pointed. "It's up on that ridge."

Brita's foolish bubble gum barged in on the remote stillness.

"Hey, there's a bald eagle," said Katrina, again pointing. "Wouldn't it be great to be able to soar like that? Listen! Its mate is calling. Oh, there's a nest on the top of that dead tree! Gosh, Ralph would have a field day way out here."

"Who's Ralph?" asked Brita.

"My cat," said Katrina, watching the eagle swoop down to the nest. "He sits on windowsills and zeroes in on birds and squirrels. I don't know what he'd do if he ever caught one."

"I never had a pet," muttered Brita. "Bet you live in a nice house, huh?"

Suddenly, Katrina missed Ralph and Toffee Castle. Meredith's advice echoed in her head, *No more thoughts of home.*

Brita blew a bubble. It popped.

Katrina heaved a sigh and said, "Maybe you can come and visit me sometime."

"Sometime," echoed Brita.

"Wish we could get closer to that nest," said Katrina, "and see those fuzzy fledglings and watch the papa eagle regurgitate food into their upturned beaks." When Brita failed to reply, Katrina glanced at her. Brita was looking at Katrina as though she were some sort of freak. "Better get going," said Katrina, gathering up her gear.

The third evening, Katrina stood jaw agape atop Mount Jackson, watching the sun set upon the most striking terrain she had ever seen. A voice spun her around, "You should see the sunset from here in the winter time."

"Bert!" she yelped.

Offering no apology for startling her, he said, "The mountains define themselves like proud patriots, huh?"

He was only inches away. She heard him breathing. It felt dangerous being alone with him. *Dad would never approve.*

"A bit nippy," said Bert. "Don't stop spring peepers from calling out their lust."

She turned away, so he couldn't see her flush. The breeze tussled her hair. He fiddled with a spiral. She turned to him, and for a moment, their eyes drank up each other. "Your freckles remind me of gold dust," he said.

"Angel kisses," she said.

He looked at her kind of strange.

"Dad used to call my freckles angel kisses," she said.

"He sounds like a cool guy," he said.

She said a lukewarm, "Yeah."

Just then, bubble gum popped. Katrina and Bert exchanged glances, disappointed that their intimate moment had been intruded upon. Pursing her lips, she glared at Brita who was picking pink matter off her face. Vic was with her. "Lots of huts in the backcountry to shack up in," he said, his eyes flirting with Katrina. "Some within easy reach of camp."

"Put a sock in it," spat Bert.

Katrina peered sidelong at Brita who was taking the wrapper off another piece of gum. *How in the world can she be so oblivious to Vic's flirting?*

"In winter," slushed Brita in the midst of popping the gum into her mouth and her teeth breaking it in, "we snowshoe out here. Camping on snow is way cool."

Katrina took a throw-away camera out of her pocket and took a picture of the fading sunset.

"Great spot for a picture," said Brita, glancing at Vic. "How about one of you and me?"

"No way," spouted Vic, backing away.

Brita grabbed the camera. "Okay then, I'll take one of Katrina and Bert."

Suddenly, Bert had his arm around Katrina, pulling her close. Long after Brita had taken the picture, they stood that way.

"These mountains teem with wildlife," said Vic. "Tracks everywhere."

Brita handed the camera to Katrina and said, "Wish you could go."

"Me too," muttered Katrina. *It was hard enough to get Dad to approve of this camp,* she thought. *How do I talk him into camping in the dead of winter? I just have to prove that nobody's out to get me. I'm safe. Group safety's always an issue around here. Oh, forget about it. He'll never consider that angle.*

"You are coming back for summer camp," said Vic, grinning wide and toothy.

"We do overnights at Franconia Notch," said Brita.

"Near the Flume?" asked Katrina.

"Never been there?" murmured Vic, reaching out for a blond spiral.

Bert pulled Katrina around to face the last remnants of sunset. He held her in front of him, their backs to Vic.

"The Flume's a blast when it's real hot," said Brita.

Vic cleared his throat and said, "Nothing like nature's air conditioning."

Summer camp's too soon, Katrina fretted. *Dad's never going to okay it. Next summer…maybe. Or next year…if I'm lucky. Oh, where in the scheme of this big wide universe do I belong?* Bert rocked her side to side, making her feel like a butterfly in a protective cocoon. As his breath fanned her earlobe, she sucked in the mountain air. *Oh well. Right now, I'm happy to be here with Bert.*

By the light of the campfire, Katrina helped Brita to sling a tarp between trees. The dark, starry sky turned everything into silhouettes. *Wish I was zipped up in this sleeping bag with Bert*, she mused as loons called in the distance. She dreamt of being alone with Bert, kayaking on flat water. She felt the oar strokes. She heard the water lapping.

The next morning, dew dripped off the trees as Katrina packed up along with other campers and headed out. They came upon a ridge. One side dropped off into a valley where mist roiled as though being stirred by a giant invisible spoon. The other side, ferns and scrub vegetation edged a steep granite cliff that ascended into the sapphire sky. Adrenaline zinged through Katrina. Her stomach clacked, sounding like billiard balls broken out of a triangle during an opening shot.

"Climb or turn back?" taunted Bert.

"Climb!" shouted campers. Their voices echoed back from the valley.

Climb, urged her insides.

She swung her gear off her shoulders and dropped to the ground. She yanked off her hiking boots and put on her climbing shoes.

Climb! Climb!

"Time to put all those bouldering techniques you learned in the gym to good use," hollered Bert. "Get the crash pads down! Let's tackle this sucker!"

Forget about a group leader going first! Climb!

She strapped on her helmet then chalked her hands, concentrating on every minute detail of the cliff. Upon solving the conundrum, she took handholds then anchored her right foot then her left. At one with rock, she climbed.

"Hey," yelped Brita, "Look at Kitty!"

"Trina!" cried Bert.

Katrina stopped at dead point. Her helmet bumped against the ledge as she peered down. Treetops swayed. Faces stared up at her. "Bert's digging his foot into the ledge," she mumbled. "Shoot, what in the world was I thinking? I'm making a fool out of myself. Anybody with half a brain wouldn't be stuck against this rock like a postage stamp, holding on for dear life."

Don't be a sissy! Climb!

She licked her dry lips. "One slip and I'm a goner. How did I ever get myself into this mess?"

Hurry! Bert climbs like a lizard!

Her heart pounded. Her knees shook. "I'm scared."

Precisely the reason to continue!

"The greatest limitation exists only in the mind," she muttered then let go of rock with one hand and reached up. Her fingers locked around a rocky knob. She did the same with the other hand then she lifted her right foot and wedged her toes into a gap in the rock. Then the toes of her left foot. Every move she rethought, again and again, as she boosted herself toward the summit.

Experience is on Bert's side. He's on your heels! Climb!

Just then a toehold disintegrated beneath her weight. She let out a gasp. Clinging to stone, she jabbed her foot at ledge. "Come on," she groaned, searching for a toehold. "Come on!"

Bert grabbed her foot, bracing it, yelling, "Go!"

She shook her head. *Don't look at him,* she told herself. *One look and I'm a goner.*

"Quit sweating bullets and get going!" he bellowed.

She licked her dry lips then put her weight on his hand. She was on her own again. She scrambled over the top and several yards in, crumpled, exhausted, gasping for air, exhilarated.

"Hot dog," panted Bert, crawling up next to her and collapsing. "You beat me!" His chest heaved. "This cliff's notoriously tricky to tackle!"

She gave him a tiny no-sweat grin, afraid to speak. Her lips were so parched she thought for sure they'd crack and chip into pieces.

Suddenly, his zeal vanished. "I'm going to have to tell Meredith about this."

He's jealous, she thought. *Yet his voice seems to hold more concern than jealousy.*

He sat up, unclipped a canteen from his belt, and took several gulps. He offered the canteen to her.

She shook her head no and sat up. She unclipped her canteen and took a swig. *He doesn't want to admit I beat him.*

He got to his feet and offered her a hand.

Again, she shook her head. Gazing at Mount Washington cloaked in clouds, she was slow in standing up.

"You're buying time," he said. "I don't want to descend this lofty pulpit either."

Lofty pulpit, she thought while studying the sea of mountain peaks. *Kind of like in Moby Dick. Wish I was Father Mapple. I'd pull up the rope ladder and make this pulpit impregnable. But there's no rope ladder. Too bad.*

To say that Meredith was impressed was an understatement. Hands fluttering, she spewed, "You're way above the rest in learning, social skills, and now climbing!"

With a mixture of humility and pride, Katrina glanced at Bert skulking at the screen door. *What is wrong with him? He won't even look at me. All the way back, too.*

"Listen," said Meredith. "I'll put together a packet for you to take home and study. Then take the test and mail it to me. I want you back here this summer, a full-time counselor in training."

Katrina shied away. "I-I don't think so."

Bert stiffened. His eyes zeroed in on her.

"I don't understand," said Meredith, her voice hinting of irritation.

Katrina glanced at Meredith and said, "My Dad won't let me."

Meredith's arms dropped to her sides. Her brows tightened. She sent a piercing frown at Bert and then drew up as if checking annoyance. Vague similarities between Meredith and Regina chafed at the scars forever etched in Katrina's soul. The passing of time had eased the anguish, which enabled Katrina to view the ordeal at times with curiosity. Like a shell on the beach, she could pick up the memory, touch it, and then toss it into the ocean of her mind.

"It's okay, sweetie," said Meredith in a sticky sweet voice. "I didn't mean to upset you." She patted Katrina's hand. "How come your Dad's against your coming back?"

Never, ever, tell anybody about Judgment, filled Katrina's head. She withdrew her hand.

Meredith wrung her hands, wetting her lips as though scheming. "Is it something I can help you with?"

Katrina sensed that Meredith was bent on clarification. She shifted from one foot to the other then adjusted her backpack. "I don't think so," she said, heading for the door. Bert stood in her way. She looked into his searching eyes. She pursed her lips and stepped around him. Outside, she startled Chas whose face reeked of guilt.

"My offer stands," called Meredith.

Halfway back to the cabin, Bert caught up, panting, "Trina! Hold on a sec'!" When she kept going, he grabbed her arm. "What happened back there?"

She shook him off. "Can't talk about it," she huffed then started off.

He skipped around her and toddled backward, asking, "Did I do something wrong?"

"It's got nothing to do with you," she spat.

"It's got everything to do with me!" he cried, grabbing her arms. He stopped. She landed against his chest, head thrown back. His eyes peered into hers as in a low voice, he said, "I-I like you…a lot. Haven't you noticed I pay more attention to you than anybody else?"

For an electric moment, she was sure he was going to kiss her. Rationality lost, her body pulsed with excitement. But then, his eyes flickered toward the trail. His brow creased in the middle. Bubble gum popped. He put her upright and let go. In a tailspin, she watched him run off. Jamming her hands into her hips, she spun around and glared at Brita jouncing up the trail, picking pink matter off her face. "You always show up at the wrong time!"

Brita sidled up to Katrina. "Bert's two-faced, you know, and does what he pleases."

"Not another word," snapped Katrina, waving off Brita and stomping away.

"But supper's just about ready," whined Brita. "I need a hand with the tables."

Katrina stopped. She clenched her fists. Spinning around, she leered at Brita standing there, looking dumb as all get out, fingers laced, lips pouting, eyes pining. Katrina crossed her arms. Another moment passed. She rolled her eyes and gestured with her right hand. "Lead the way."

☞

Last night of Ecology Camp, a soft breeze stoked the crackling campfire while insects joined the music of the night. Katrina sat beside Bert. *Gosh, I hope I look good to him in this blue jeans outfit. Maybe I should take off the jacket. I look better in this red tank top. Sure is nice to be out of camp uniform, but I wish Meredith let me keep mine. Wonder why Bert's wearing his? Maybe because he goes to the Academy.*

"You're sweet as apple-berry wine," he murmured, fingering a butterfly barrette.

Her hand covered her mouth to squelch a giggle. She squeezed her eyes shut. *Nobody ever says things like that to me.*

He leaned his head against hers and said, "I'm so going to miss you." His lips brushed her cheek and then her ear. "Am I ever going to see you again?"

Tears filled her eyes. *How am I ever going to live without Bert?*

"I'll always care about you," he said. "No matter what."

She gazed into his eyes. Guilt weighed on her heavier than the greatest Granite Mountain boulder. *It's so obvious that he's head over heels in love with me,* she thought, *and I with him. It's totally not right not to trust him with my past.*

Her father's voice rumbled in her head. *Never, ever, tell anybody about Judgment.*

Bert toyed with a wayward blond spiral and then cupped her chin in his hand. He turned her to face him.

Butterflies tickled her belly. *If only this moment would last forever.*

His lips sought hers.

Never, ever, tell anybody about Judgment.

She leapt to her feet. She took several steps. She stopped. She rubbed her palms up and down her thighs. She turned to him. His face was full of questions. "I can't stand it," she said. "I...I...I have to tell you..."

Never, ever, tell anybody about Judgment.

Her arms swung loose as she wavered side to side. *He's studying me like an encyclopedia!*

"Trina?"

She threw her hands into the air and exploded, "I was kidnapped!"

He leapt to his feet. "What are you talking about?"

Bushes nearby rustled.

Bert put a finger to his mouth. "Sh-sh-sh."

They stared at the bushes. Suddenly, a rabbit dashed out, crossed the lawn, and disappeared into the night.

Katrina leaned close to Bert and whispered, "I was kidnapped and sold to terrorists." She took a quick step back. *My secret came out so easy,* she thought. *It's floated beneath every-thing, every moment of my existence...hey...Dad's voice is gone! How come I feel so sad?*

"Give me a break," said Bert, jamming one hand into his hip.

"I spill my guts and you don't believe me?" She shoved a wayward blond strand out of her face and glared at him. "Well, it's true! There used to be a camp in Mississippi where kids were trained to be terrorists!"

He crossed his arms over his chest. His head tilted as he squinted at her.

"Don't believe me!" she spouted, arms rigid at her side, fists clenching. "I don't care!"

His chin hitched to one side. His words came slow. "It is a bit far-fetched."

She rubbed her palms together. "Okay, I'll start at the beginning. Regina—my birth mother—hated my Dad and me. I don't know why. Anyways, Regina hooked up with a guy named Jake—he said he was my uncle but he wasn't…"

"He wasn't," echoed Bert.

Again that skeptical expression, fumed Katrina. She shoved back a spiral and continued, "My grandparents on both sides got out of East Germany when the Berlin Wall got put up in the 60s and had to pay back the favor by doing whatever was asked of them."

His brows fused. His voice held an odd edge. "Who was doing the asking?"

Upright palms jounced at shoulder level as she said, "Who knows? But whoever it was took Regina away, too, when she was a kid—every summer for a couple of months. Jake came along much later. He rigged a plane Regina was on. It crashed in the Everglades."

The breeze picked up the wayward blond spiral. Bushes rustled. Clamping onto the spiral, Katrina squinted at the bushes. She cleared her throat. "To make a long story short," she said, "my father remembered stuff then the FBI came and got me and other kids. That place is toast!"

Bert took her arms in his arms and held her close. "No wonder your father freaks out. I would, too!"

Chapter 6

"O ur Miss Waters is already halfway through the conditioning process," twittered Jonathan while clicking a button on
the remote he held in his hand.

As a section of bookcase opened like a door into their office
in the Administration Building, Meredith raved, "Knocked me
right off my feet when the little weasel told me!" Her right hand
flailed with each word while her left hand clutched paperwork
against her breast. She was dressed all in white like he, polo
shirt, cargo pants, socks, and deck shoes. Ruby-eyed spider pins
larger than those given to spiderlings bejeweled their collars.
The torsos of the pins were vials containing lethal venom.

"I thought I detected a hint of southern accent in her voice,"
he said, taking long strides into the dimly lit secret passage. He
paid no attention to his wife's safety when it came to operating
the bookcase doors—and for that matter, anything else.

"Never picked up on the accent," she said, sticking close to
him. "Should've known something was amiss when Blondie
didn't jump for joy when offered counselor status. I figured it
was a hormone thing, you know, that time of the month."

Jonathan cringed. *Woman talk repulses me,* he thought while
clicking another button. As the bookcase slid back into place, he
clicked another button, and the bookcase in the office on the
third level of the warren opened. Few were privy to this
passageway. Most accessed the warren by numbered code
punched into the keypad mounted on the wall to the right of
doors marked Maintenance, Authorized Personnel Only.

"Good thing I had the presence of mind to have that little weasel shadow our Miss Waters," said Meredith, stepping to the filing cabinet and opening the lowest drawer.

"Size is more external perception than internal reality," he said, scanning the monitors that picked up activity inside Granite Mountain and outside to a radius of over ten miles. His voyeuristic eyes saw nothing of interest.

"He's got the combined soul of a kamikaze fighter, gymnast, and political dictator," said Meredith, squatting in front of the file cabinet, "without the body." Her fingers scurried across file markers. "Waters. Come to Mama, Katrina Waters."

Oh, for those fingers to be doing that to me, thought Jonathan. He sucked in a breath, skirted the desk, and got a pair of thick rubber gloves out of the middle drawer. Pulling on the left glove, his left hand shot into the air. He let go. Rubber snapped against his wrist. He pulled on other glove in the same manner. Another snap.

"Yup," she puffed while standing up and placing the file on top of the cabinet. "Hand the little charmer an emotional scene and he'll produce tears on cue."

Jonathan checked the levels of serum in vials on the shelf next to the vivariums. *More than enough to ward off the agony of a widow bite. Recovery takes weeks without serum. No time for such nonsense.* He slid the lids off two vivariums and reached into one. "Come, little man," he cooed while slipping a gloved hand under a male black widow spider. As he transferred the male into the other vivarium, the female retreated into a corner of her web. "Judgment, Mississippi," he muttered, replacing the lid over the widows. "It was a shining star in the *jihad.*"

"Never heard of the place," said Meredith, penciling notations into Katrina's file.

Aware of the prickling effect his words would have upon her, he said, "The fewer having knowledge of the network, the better."

She slammed the file shut and exploded, "Again! I am left out of the loop, again!"

A twisted grin wrinkled his lips, one that he was careful not to let her see. *Oh, how I wallow in reminding her that she is a mere woman, not as privileged as I, the pre-eminent male.* As he watched the tiny male spider inch across the web toward the much larger female, Meredith's reflection appeared in the vivarium glass. *She approaches me. Ah, she pauses and hooks her hands on her hips.*

"Tell me about Judgment!" she demanded.

His right eye twitched. *The shrew makes too many demands of me.*

"Well?" she snapped.

He spun around and snapped back, "Feds got wind of the place. Raided it four or five years ago. This blasted tic is more pronounced, isn't it?"

Her bottom lip went slack. She ogled his eye.

"Isn't it?" he barked.

Her head tilted. "No," she stammered, squinty-eyed. "I don't think so."

"It is," he insisted with sharp disgust and then spun back to the vivarium. The female black widow was taking a hairy step toward the male. The male froze in place.

"Clonidine blocks Tourette's Syndrome spasms," said Meredith. "Might work for you."

"Get me some," he barked. Her reflection stiffened and then the back of her hand scraped her lips. *So my wife detests demands made of her, too.*

"Who ratted out Mississippi?" she asked in a more civil tone.

"Who knows," he grumbled and then thought, *mating of these widows takes too long. The male's final disposition is my interest, for the female is not content with seminal fluid. No, only blood completes her. Too often in nature, females have the upper hand. Ah, 'tis fortuitous to be born human and not spider.*

"The kids scattered to the wind," she said.

"Without a trace," he said while keeping an eye on her reflection. *She sits down at the desk. Her back is to me. I am free to act as I please. The woman intimidates me, no matter how I fight it. And justly so. I have seen her in action, as lethal as a female widow. Ending up like a male widow is not in my plans.*

"Tremendous loss to the movement," she said. She heaved a sigh. "And no records."

"That rule paid off for the network many times over," he said. "We'd all be rotting in the infidel's dungeons if a paper trail had come to light. Imagine when the movement hears we've recovered the Waters kid?"

"And Moro's got her under his spell," she said, rotating in the chair. "Hate to mention this—again—but have you broken into the Feds' computer system yet?"

His head wavered side to side.

She turned her back to him. "Blondie's old man is a computer wiz. She is, too. She could hack into anything."

He rolled his hands together. "We've got to get that kid into our ranks!"

"Her kid brother, too," she added.

"All must go smoothly," he said, "so when the time is right, he is easily lured into our ranks as she was."

"Hey, hon'?" she said. "Take a look at this."

No way will I take my eyes off these widows, he seethed. *The woman's reflection is distraction enough. Look at that, the male's palps are transferring sperm to the female. The last supper's right around the corner.*

"Go get her, Joe," hissed Meredith.

Jonathan glanced over his shoulder. One of the monitors was picking up Joe Ault's cubicle. Camille Jennes was pestering Joe like a gnat. Her ginger hair, bunched up in a clip, swished like a cow's tail swatting flies. She got in his face. His left arm fended her off. Jonathan rolled his eyes. "Praise Allah, the sound is down," he said. "I cannot tolerate that borderline schizophrenic and her infernal whining."

"Those two went four-wheeling last weekend," said Meredith. "She ended up in a ditch, trying to keep up with him."

"And he kept going," snickered Jonathan, engrossed in the action on the monitor. The black widows were the furthest thing from his mind.

Meredith nodded. "Joe saw it all in the rearview mirror, I'm sure. Too bad Gus Tanner came along and helped her back to…"

"Tanner's nosing around?" cut in Jonathan.

"Nah," she said, getting to her feet. "It happened not a mile from his place, and you know, she's got the voice of a banshee and it carries for miles."

Joe's right fist arced like a sledgehammer. Down it came on Camille's sniveling puss. Blood and a hairclip flew.

Jonathan turned away, his face twisting and his gut souring. *I can watch just about anything,* he thought, *but that was vile.* He gripped the back of the chair and took a wary, sidelong glimpse at the monitor. Camille had escaped for the door and Joe was lunging. "Get the slut," gurgled Jonathan, feeling his eye twitching and his groin tightening.

"He's got her blouse," yelped Meredith, stepping up to the monitor. "Look at the buttons popping!"

Joe flung Camille on the bed and tried to kick her, but missed. His foot smacked into the bed frame. He grabbed his toes and hopped about on one foot. Camille did a half-roll. Joe let go of his foot and straddled her. His knees kept her pinned as he pummeled her.

"That Ault's one nasty son-of-a-bitch," said Meredith. "Remember the day he broke the bone around her eye with a lamp? And as if that wasn't enough, the putz cut her with the broken light bulb and then burned her with a cigarette."

"A born torturer," boasted Jonathan, stepping around the desk and sitting astride the front corner. "The spring doesn't rise higher than its source."

"Tell me about the Thibault divorce," said Meredith, stepping behind Jonathan.

"Rich old bastard," he spat, watching Joe remove Camille's jeans amidst a barrage of hands and feet. "Vilified his stay-at-home, uneducated wife. Time and the best L.A. lawyer money could buy got him custody of Joe."

"Josh at the time," she murmured, massaging his shoulders.

"After the decree," he said, closing his eyes and taking great pleasure in his wife's talented fingers, "the old man drove off the old lady. Having nothing and nowhere to go, she resorted to picking up Johns." He looked at Meredith and gave an evil wink. "Ended up dead—so I hear."

She gave him a perceptive smirk.

"Old man Thibault cared nothing about Joe, Josh, whatever," he said. "Just a possession to be stuffed on the back shelf. He shipped the kid here the day after the decree. Took me less than a month to take control of that young desolate mind. But that snoop came along, what's his name? He lived over there in the Notch."

"Osborne?" she asked, sitting on the desk.

"Yeah," he said. "He got wise to our nightly activity. No matter what excuse I came up with, the thought nagged me that Osborne might squeal to the Feds like a stuck pig. Then a relative of his croaked out in San Diego, and I got wind of it. Joe was programmed, set to go, so I arranged a visitation with old man Thibault."

"Joe did okay, I assume," she said.

"Like a well oiled machine," he boasted. "Faked drunkenness, stole his old man's sport utility vehicle, and went joyriding into an intersection just as Osborne came along."

"What a coincidence," she quipped.

"Osborne's car hurtled sideways into oncoming traffic and exploded, killing him and several others. Lots of collateral damage and major television and radio network coverage. Man, did I fill that pinheaded judge with fluff at the hearing. What glorious achievements Joe, er, Josh had accomplished at Granite Mountain Academy." Jonathan slid off the corner of the desk, cleared his throat, and orated as though in court. "Your Honor. The chaos that is Los Angeles plus a preoccupied, negligent father drove this poor child to the bar—in the home, mind you—and subsequently, the garage where keys left in the ignitions of his father's many vehicles tantalized the boy. I submit to Your Honor, documentation of the Thibault's spiteful divorce. This child was a mere pawn, used by acrimonious parents to inflict emotional and financial pain upon one another! Your Honor. Consider the bitter divorce. Consider the accessibility of alcohol, the irresponsible father leaving keys in vehicles. Above all, consider this child!"

Meredith clapped her hands with great zeal.

Jonathan grinned. "Oh, the respect I got from that judge." In a mocking tone, he continued, "'This court thanks you for your insight, Mr. Aranea. To come all this way indicates that you see a potential in Josh that this court is not privy to. Therefore, this court hereby declares that all charges be dropped against Josh. Further, Mr. Thibault is liable for all injury and damage resulting from this horrendous event, which never should have happened in the first place! Parental rights are hereby revoked until such time either parent shows fortitude to step forward and advocate for their son in the manner in which Mr. Aranea has shown here today. Child support is hereby doubled, to be overseen by Jonathan Aranea, whom this court awards custody of Josh Thibault.'" Jonathan struggled to contain mirth. "The gavel came down so hard on the bench that the entire courtroom quivered, and the judge left the courtroom in a huff, black robes flying!"

"Of course, neither parent ever came forward," said Meredith.

"A year after the hearing, Mr. Thibault disappeared," said Jonathan, giving another evil wink. "Then citing abandonment and Mrs. Thibault's street-walking activities—plus lack of contact and monetary support—I was able to adopt Josh."

"Don't forget that added bonus," she said, batting her eyelids.

Jonathan drifted over to her. "Mr. Thibault neglected to change his will before disappearing," he said. "Josh Aranea, AKA Joe Ault, stands to inherit quite a bit, the day the court declares old man Thibault dead." Jonathan lifted her chin and gazed into her eyes. "That day approaches swiftly."

"Kids without families, fathers," she murmured. "Tsk, tsk, tsk. Makes our quest for spiderlings a piece of cake."

Jonathan wormed his tongue into her mouth, thinking, *Ah, the methods I use to rope in my spiderlings. Sweet-talking parents then priming immature minds with guilt, terror, tension, and stress. You are so bad your parents don't want you. They're getting or got divorced because of you. A terrible accident—your parents are dead. I come up with the most gruesome details. Along the way, a suicide or two—to be expected when ones so young are devoid of all hope. Although most fall into line! Brains open wide, and programmed spiderlings emerge, ready to submit to my every whim!*

Meredith came up for air. "Think the Feds are keeping an eye on Blondie?"

"Only ones keeping tabs is her family," said Jonathan, squinting at the monitor. Joe and Camille were on the floor, out of the camera's eye on the other side of the bed.

"Blondie's parents are no different from anybody else living in this dreamland called America," said Meredith.

Sarcasm winkled his face as Jonathan added, "Things like that don't happen in our neighborhood, least of all, in New Hampshire." He glanced at Meredith, a glint in his eye.

She flashed a perceptive leer and fingered his bottom lip.

"Granite Mountain exists due to American agencies disavowal of the efficacy of brainwashing," he said and then sucked her fingers into his mouth.

"Conversion is a nicer word," she murmured while tilting her head and watching him drag on her fingers.

He let go with a slurp and gave a stunted bow. "I stand corrected."

"Young minds are so easily wiped clean," she whispered while cuddling against him. Her hand drifted down to his crotch. "This being the last night of Ecology Camp, wouldn't you say the window of opportunity has closed?"

"A scholarship attached to her award of merit is only natural, is it not?" he lathered. "I know I never turn down a free ride."

Chapter 7

*T*he weeks following Spring Camp dragged for Katrina. She kept the picture of Bert and her atop Mount Jackson hidden in her bra, close to her heart by day, and under her pillow by night. His voice seemed to whisper in the trees outside her window. He haunted her dreams. His fingertips stroked her cheek. She smelled him as his arms wrapped around her. His lips sought hers.

Stolen glances at the picture were hardly fulfilling. *But I have to keep infatuation reigned in,* she reasoned. *Chitchat runs rampant around Toffee Castle. If Dad catches wind of Bert, he'll put his foot down in a heartbeat. I'll never see Bert again. Doesn't matter that during closing ceremonies Jonathan Aranea, president of the college, personally awarded me, Katrina Waters, a certificate of merit, plus a scholarship to summer camp. Mr. Aranea called me the most outstanding member of this spring's Ecology Camp. Did that stun Dad or what? But then that night when he thought I was out of earshot, he whined like a baby, "Can it be my baby girl's going away from me again?"*

"You've got to stop worrying about her so much" whispered Julie. *"She's not your baby girl anymore. It's difficult. I know. I worry, too. But Katrina can take down an elephant after all those self-defense classes you force her to take."*

"But this camp lasted only two weeks," he moaned, "and every second of it, I've been going nuts. Now I've got to look forward to an entire summer?"

Katrina did her best to shake off the conversation, though she couldn't help sympathizing. The love she and her father shared had only deepened during their years of separation and after her return—a miracle that happens for few children. *But like Miss Matthias says, "Sooner or later, my dear Katrina, you have to lead your own life."*

At last, the calendar page turned to June. Schools in Massachusetts let out for the summer and Katrina headed back to Granite Mountain. *Imagine. Me, an instructor. My own group. Sharing ecological issues with like-minded teens. Oh, I can't wait to see Bert!*

The morning of her arrival, she milled around, making idle conversation with Brita and other campers she had met at spring camp. Her parents and Adriano got bored and wandered off. An hour passed as she half-listened to Camille bellyache with a mouthful of jelly sandwich about having to man the folding table that doubled as sentry post. Then a shiny black Volkswagen convertible coasted their way. *Hey, Bert's at the wheel!* Her heart flip-flopped. *He's looking around for Dad and Mom.* She did the same. *Good, Dad and Mom are nowhere in sight!* Her eyes met his. The toothy grin that took over his face made her flush all over. She looked down at her white tee shirt that proclaimed in red, white, and blue script, Granite Mountain—Planning Our World. She smoothed out wrinkles that weren't there.

"You came back," he said while easing the car along side of her. His bronze features glowed against his khaki outfit.

"Yeah," she said and gave him a timid smile. *Oh, how I wish I could put my arms around him and plant a few thousand kisses all over him!*

He shifted the gear into park then hooked his left arm over the door. "I'm a guide, now," he said with pride.

"Wow," she breezed.

"I'm so glad I'm not your counselor anymore," he puffed.

Her jaw dropped. *He doesn't like me anymore?*

He slung his right hand over the steering wheel. Grinning like a Cheshire cat, he winked. "Now you and I can go out!"

Anguish melted like ice cubes on hot August pavement. Her cheeks dimpled as a smile broke on her face. She clasped her hands and glanced at the heavens. *There is a God!*

"That's only if you want to," he teased, a coy look about him.

"Oh, I do…" she stammered, "…but…" She pursed her lips and double-checked the area for her family.

"But?"

"My Dad," she muttered. She peered at her right shoe raking the ground. "He won't let me date."

Bert chuckled. His fist nudged her jaw. "What Dad don't know won't hurt him."

Her hands covered her mouth to hide a giggle. Her eyes squeezed shut.

"Kat!" cried Adriano.

Her eyes shot open as she gasped, "Addie!"

He galloped like a horse toward her. Right behind him, her parents, arm in arm, enjoying the comfortable warmth of their own familiarity. The instant Katrina returned from Mississippi, she had sensed the electricity that flowed between her father and Julie. There was an ethereal rightness, a cosmic correctness to having a mate, a partner. As they stroked each other's arms, pangs of jealousy wracked Katrina. *They can't keep their hands or eyes off each other. Why can't they let me have the same thing?*

"Gotta go," said Bert, chucking the car into gear. "See you in a while."

Katrina shriveled as the Volkswagen headed off toward the cluster of cabins. Kicking the ground, she groused, "Darn it all."

"Kat?" said Adriano, yanking on her tee shirt.

She heaved a sigh. "Hey, Addie." She bent and picked him up.

"Who was that?" demanded her father.

"Counselor from spring camp," she said, withholding Bert's name and the fact that he was no longer a counselor.

It seemed forever until her family took off for Brighton. Immediately thereafter, Bert showed up and picked up where he had left off in the spring. Making up for lost time, he took Katrina on long walks, eating meals with her, and teaching her how to pack a canoe and kayak, how to accomplish open-water rescues, and other outdoor stuff. Now that he had wheels, they took spins with the top down to a Jackson ice cream shop that was located in a basement cooled by thick granite walls. Long after ice cream sundaes melted into frappes, they continued to discover common denominators. She told him many things about herself. He didn't give much back, only that he was born in New Mexico. He said he wanted to hear her voice all the time. A month into summer, his team won the weekly baseball game and right in front of everybody, he grabbed her hand and didn't let go for the longest time. She was ecstatic.

One night, they were sitting by the campfire, letting the smoke smudge them to keep away the mosquitoes. Everybody else had given up the battle and had gone inside. She went to leave with them, but his hand held her back. Then he kissed her. Her toes tingled, and it seemed as if only the two of them existed at that moment—no crickets, no breeze, no bugs.

Five days before the end of summer camp, Katrina and Meredith were heading for lunch when they ran into Jonathan. He was dressed all in white: tennis shoes, socks that reached his knees, shorts, and polo shirt with embossed red letters, Granite Mountain College, above the left breast. The spider pin that clung to his lapel was like Meredith's, larger than others Katrina had seen. A round-brimmed hat protected his face from the noonday sun. His legs were long and spindly, not very hairy.

"Where are you off to, my husband?" asked Meredith.

"Checking in on Mr. O'Mara, our new Academy professor," he said in a low, rolling style. "Headmaster Timothy tells me Mr. O'Mara is setting up his classroom for the fall term."

"Already?" asked Meredith.

"An eager beaver," said Jonathan. "A quality I admire."

Meredith pulled Katrina in front of her and held her by the biceps. "This young lady's an eager beaver, too," she spouted. "She picks up everything the very first time."

"Is that so?"

Katrina noticed his right eye twitching. Then she noticed he caught her noticing. Embarrassment washed over her. She broke from his gaze and turned. Leaning against a nearby tree was Chas. Something percolated his zombie-like eyes.

"Miss Waters is not one of those fluffy chicks who's afraid to get dirt under their fingernails," spouted Meredith. "Not at all!

She is the fastest ever to climb the gym rope hand over hand—boys included! She even beat Bert up a cliff!"

Jonathan leaned around Katrina and trapped her in his gaze. "A young lady such as yourself is perfect for the challenges available at Granite Mountain Academy."

Katrina looked down, wringing her hands. "I don't think so," she muttered.

"And why not?"

"Dad won't allow me to be away from home that long." She looked up. Jonathan was straightening. His right eye was twitching like crazy.

Meredith cleared her throat. Getting his attention, she discreetly pointed to her right eye, nonverbally relaying the message to control his eye tic. They thought Katrina didn't see, but she did, and uneasiness strangled her. "Mary's Song" surfaced in her head.

"Might I suggest," sputtered Meredith, "that Katrina and I accompany you to see Mr. O'Mara? Have a look around the Academy—know what I mean?"

Jonathan cleared his throat. "Excellent idea." His hand clamped Katrina's head and held it a long moment. With a jolt, he let go. She felt a release of psychic energy, a purging of repressed emotions, fear, guilt. Tears of relief budded as excitement and expectation filled her. Her knees buckled.

Gripping her arm, Jonathan said, "Let us proceed."

Katrina gave a weak nod, thankful to hear "Mary's Song" drifting in her head.

"Excellent," cooed Jonathan. His eyelid twitched, as if winking at Meredith.

⤶

The next day, unaware of Katrina and Brita being in earshot, Meredith called, "Vic. I need a word with you."

The girls shrunk back into the hemlock where they had been taking advantage of its shade to organize their backpacks for an excursion along the Maine Island Trail.

"I added another guide," said Meredith.

"I trekked these waters plenty of times," protested Vic, marching up to Meredith. "I'll handle it this time."

Brita leaned over to Katrina and whispered, "Nobody challenges Meredith's authority. She's like a mama bear protecting her cubs if anybody tries."

Katrina nodded. "I've seen the hatchet fall on a few who dared."

Meredith braced her hands on her hips. "You will be second in command."

Katrina and Brita wide-eyed one another.

"This is a blatant incursion into my turf!" roared Vic. His stance resembled an incensed male grisly bear.

Meredith clenched her teeth and returned the threat, "Perhaps we should discuss this with Jonathan?"

Jonathan? Katrina wondered. *Not Mr. Aranea? Vic and the Araneas are on a first name basis?*

An ugly stare-down ensued. Meredith remained stiff as a board. Vic clenched his fists. Then Meredith spat, "Bert's in charge!"

"Bert?" yelped Vic. "I thought you assigned him something else today."

"You heard me!"

"We don't have enough kayaks!"

"That's been taken care of!"

Another stare-down. Then Meredith marched off to her car.

Vic spun around and stomped past the girls cowering against the hemlock. "That sleaze is always getting in my way," he growled. "Well, not this time!"

Meredith got in her car and slammed the door so violently that the entire car shook. Tires spun as the car fishtailed out of the parking lot, dust devils trailing.

Brita wormed her arms into the straps of her backpack and stood up. "Bert messed this up," she spouted. "I just know he did. He's a pet of all the staff. He controls the show around here, more than anybody knows."

"Come on," said Katrina, slinging her backpack over her shoulder. "Our groups must be wondering where we are."

Brita grunted. A pink bubble hid half her face.

"Sure is peaceful without Alice and Joe," said Katrina. The bubble exploded. "Wonder who Meredith bumped to make room for Bert?"

"It's not fair," groused Brita, plucking pink gum fragments. She wadded them into a ball and popped it in her mouth. "Bet Vic won't even show up at the dock now."

"Meredith will really rag on him then," said Katrina.

"I won't get to see Vic until we get back tomorrow night," Brita whined.

"I'd hate that to happen to me and Bert," said Katrina.

"You and Bert are moving way too fast," chastised Brita. "Didn't I tell you he can't be trusted?"

Katrina stopped in her tracks, jammed her hands into her hips, and glared at Brita. "What do you know about fast or slow? You and Vic haven't even kissed yet!"

Brita pulled up. She stood there for a moment, a dreadful look hanging on her face. In a barely audible voice, she said, "That's cold."

Katrina shriveled. "Gosh, I shouldn't've spouted off like that. You and I are best friends. We tell each other everything. Oh, I hate myself. It's not fair to use things told in confidence in hurtful ways. I-I'm sorry. I-I didn't mean…"

"Yeah, right," snorted Brita, plodding past Katrina.

Now I've gone and done it, thought Katrina, hurrying to catch up. They walked in silence. The dock came into view. "Everybody's dressed like us," Katrina ventured. She looked down at her red khaki cargo shorts and white tee shirt with red, white, and blue block letters, Granite Mountain College—Planning Our World. "Pretty soon, you and I will have spider pins. We'll be different then."

"True-blue counselors," grumbled Brita.

"Into your kayaks, folks," called Bert, seated in one of seven double kayaks bobbing at the end of the dock. "Time's a wasting. Trina, you're with me."

"I'm supposed to stick with my group," hollered Katrina.

"You are a leader, aren't you?" yelled Bert.

"Well, yeah, but…"

"Then get in and let's lead!" he hollered.

She glanced at Brita whose eyes warned against it. She squinted at Bert diddling with supplies. *If anything goes wrong,* she thought, *I've got those self-defense classes on my side.* She looked at Brita whose impression of people was right on—most of the time. *Best friends trust each other's advice, but…* Her eyes gravitated to Bert. Errant bronze strands played upon his forehead. *He doesn't know about those self-defense classes. Nobody knows. Dad says someday, it may be the surprise element needed to get me out of trouble. Yet Dad also warned about keeping the kidnapping a secret, and it hasn't made any difference telling Bert.* She pursed her lips. *Bert may be a pet around here like Brita says, but he's always been real nice to me.* "Oh, what's the stinking harm?" she belched and plowed past Brita. Tossing her backpack into the kayak, she stepped in behind Bert and glanced over her shoulder. Brita shook her head.

Spotting Chas standing at the tree line, Katrina waved. *Why doesn't he wave back? He looks so weird. Gosh, he's the one Meredith bumped to make room for Bert. He's got every right to be upset. Strange, he looks more worried than upset.*

Bert shoved the kayak away from the dock, leading the seven kayaks, silent and low, through sheltered waters. "Paddling's easier than it was at spring camp," she said.

"That's because muscle man's sharing the load," he said.

Her heart fluttered. Glancing over her shoulder, she said, "We're outpacing the others."

"How about that," he said, hitching his chin. He didn't look back. "Let's race them to the campsite!"

"Gee, I don't know about that," she said, again glancing over her shoulder. "My group's way behind."

He turned his head and hollered, "Hey, you guys!"

Frightened terns and other waterfowl took wing and clouded the sky as Brita's voice came back, "Yeah?"

"Race you to the campsite," hollered Bert.

"Row!" squawked Brita. Squeals and oars splashing joined the cacophony of waterfowl; and it all resonated across the water.

"Let's get cracking," yelped Bert.

Katrina oared with all her might, though Bert made it look easy, one powerful stroke after another. An osprey aloft eyed them zigzagging through the marshes, into a pristine estuary, and out a tide-scoured inlet. As headwinds dusted up whitecaps in the open water, Bert dropped his oar and grabbed his right bicep. His oar fell overboard. "What's wrong?" cried Katrina, holding her hair out of her face.

"Muscle cramp," he groaned. His fingers worked at the knot as the kayak circled, adrift in the rising swell, bobbing up and down and side to side.

Queasy, Katrina scoured the horizon. "We're all alone."

Clutching his arm, he reconnoitered the situation and then pointed. "Can you get us into that sheltered cove?"

"We'll be crossing the wind," she said, "but the current's taking us that way."

"That's right," said Bert. "Now apply what I taught you about using current and wind to your advantage."

She drew in a breath. *If Bert says I can do it, I can.* She dug her oar into the roiling waves and maneuvered the kayak alongside his oar. She hauled the oar into the kayak and then pointed the bow at the cove. A short while later, as she guided the kayak into the cove, a harbor seal slipped off a rock and into the water. As the kayak skidded onto the miniature beach, she boasted, "That went easier than expected."

"You're the best," he said.

She slung herself out of the kayak and rubbed her hands up and down her arms to deflect the stiff breeze that sliced through her. She gawked at the swift current running seaward.

"Tide like that shouldn't be tackled alone," said Bert, rotating his injured arm.

"We have to get out of this wind," she said.

He paused from flexing his bicep to scrutinize the rocks. "We can wait out the tide in that cutout. Come on."

She dragged the kayak up beyond the tide line and stowed the oars. Picking up the backpacks, she said, "It's getting dark. Won't the others come looking for us?"

"I'd wager against it," said Bert as his fingers dug into the muscle knot.

"Why not?" she asked.

"Vic knows I can take care of things," he said. His voice had a sharp edge she had never heard before.

"Vic never showed up," she said. "Remember?"

"Vic's not that easy to elbow," grumbled Bert, entering the cavern.

Gosh, she fretted, *spending the night here with Bert—with any man—doesn't look good at all. But what else can I do? It's too dangerous to fight the tide all by myself.*

"Spread a blanket over here," he said.

Out of the blue, she began to hum "Mary's Song." *If Dad ever finds out about this,* she thought, *I'm toast. I'll never see Granite Mountain again…or Bert.*

"Trina?"

"Huh?"

Bert's brow arched. "The blanket?"

She set down the backpacks and took an army-green blanket out of one. Spreading it out, she ruminated over self-defense techniques she had learned. *If Bert tries one little thing…*

"Lucky there's sand in here," he said, dropping onto the blanket. "Better than lying on rocks, that's for sure." He rubbed his bicep. "Hungry?"

She stood there, scraping her hands together. Her mind was a mass of clouds.

"Trina?"

Her eyes drifted to his. Her shoulder twitched.

"You okay?" he asked.

Embarrassment flushed through her all the way to her toes. *He's looking like he can see straight through my clothes!*

"Relax," he said. "We'll be out of here at first light. Get the trail mix and water."

Hands on hips, she stretched out her back. She hesitated. Then she sunk down onto the blanket as far away from him as possible. She towed the backpack up to her and fished out a package of trail mix. She handed it to him and watched him rip open the package, look up at the ceiling of the cavern, and dump some into his mouth. She swallowed hard. Her mouth was desert dry. She took a plastic bottle half-full of water out of the side pocket of the backpack. She twisted off the cap and took a huge slug. The taste was so disgusting that she swallowed immediately. "Want some?" she asked, offering him the bottle.

He shook his head, continuing to chew.

She ran her tongue along the inside of her mouth. *Perhaps the bad taste is just my imagination.* She took another sip. *Nope.* She gawked at the label and sputtered, "I'm going to recommend a different brand of water when I get back to camp."

He swallowed then asked, "How come?"

"It's gross," she spat.

He zeroed in on the bottle. "That bad?"

She nodded.

He seemed about to speak, but then decided not to. He swiped the back of his hand across his lips and dropped back on the blanket. He winced in pain and clutched his right bicep.

"Gosh," she said. "Wish I could make the pain go away. Wait. Maybe I can." She spun the cap onto the water bottle and drilled the base into the sand. As she unbuckled the first aid kit from the backpack, wooziness streaked over her. She searched the contents of the kit. Finally, she held up a tube of muscle cream.

Bert rolled onto his side and managed to sit up. He wriggled his shirt over his head.

Her eyes gobbled up his broad chest, bronze, smooth, and shadowed by a puff of hair and washboard abs. Her mouth filled with saliva. Sensations ripped through her that she hadn't felt before. Rooted in the sand on which she knelt, she swallowed hard. Touching a male other than a family member in such a manner scared her half to death.

"You okay?" he asked.

"Guess all that rowing's got me dehydrated," she said, plucking the bottle of water out of the sand. She gulped down all the water without a second thought. One side of her face scrunched as she squeezed the bottle so tight that it collapsed.

"Give me that," he said, snagging the bottle. He waved the spout under his nose and instantly pulled it away, his face twisting up. He examined the label. His upper lip twitched. Squinting at her, he said, "It's gross, all right." He tossed the bottle out of the cavern. "I like that song."

"Song?" she asked in a voice that sounded foreign and rippling. She tried to concentrate, but just couldn't clear the fog out of her brain.

Bert's voice undulated, "That song you've been humming."

"'Mary's Song?'" she mumbled, unsure if the words had actually come out. As she twisted the cap off the tube of muscle cream, her hands didn't seem a part of her. She set the cap on the backpack then squeezed the tube. Cream overflowed her palm, but she couldn't stop squeezing as the world revolved like a madcap merry-go-round.

೧

Katrina opened bleary eyes. Sunlight streaked into the cavern. An army blanket kept her contained like a cocoon, like Bert's arms did on Mount Jackson. Only difference: this time, she felt unprotected, vulnerable. She freed an arm and got up on one elbow. Her head throbbed as her eyes focused on her clothes scattered in the sand. The night crept back in a blurry haze. Shadows jostled. Distorted shouts. Flashes of light. A hand slithering across her body in places she had never been touched. "You have fantastic skin," he said.

Her voice was slushy, not her own, "I don't think we..."

"Mature people show how much they mean to each other this way," he said as her tee shirt slid up over her face. He kissed her. She was powerless to resist.

Self-defense classes didn't prepare me for this, she thought, trying to shake off the horror of it all. She spotted a deflated, tan balloon in the sand. Shivers skittered up and down her body like tiny spiders. *That's not a balloon! That's a condom!* She squinted out of the cavern. The plastic bottle minus its cap was lying in the sand. *Bert tossed it there last night.* As her tongue moistened her lips with bitter residue, she felt filthy, disgraced, and worse, responsible. *Coming here was a mistake—my mistake. Dad's right. These camps are not a good idea. I should've listened to him. I should've kept my big fat mouth shut about the past. A big mistake telling Bert—my big mistake!* She held the blanket against her nakedness as if that might protect her from the responsibility that was all hers, from violation that couldn't be taken back.

Movement was brittle and graceless as she groped for her clothes and got to her feet. She shook sand off each article of clothing then slipped it on over places she had never been sore. Shaking out the army blanket, hard, she attempted to release her torment. She stuffed the blanket under one arm and her sneakers under the other arm and started out of the cavern. When a butterfly barrette lodged between her toes, she bent to pluck it out and almost keeled over. She fingered the barrette, her eyes hunting for its mate that was nowhere to be found.

Outside the cavern, the sky was blue and bright and the ocean glassy as her feet sunk into the warm sand. A fresh breeze fanned her face as she eyed Bert standing beside the kayak at water's edge, his left foot propped upon the bow. Wretchedness rose inside her. She looked up to stop tears from overflowing. A gull riding a morning thermal looked down with a reproachful eye and squawked. Recalling the bald eagle she and Brita had seen, Katrina brooded, *Oh, to be an eagle and fly away from my rotten life. Why didn't I listen to Brita?* Katrina swiped away the moisture trickling down her cheek, drew a shuddering breath, and picked up the plastic water bottle. *Leave nothing behind to spoil Mother Nature. I told Chas that.* His image drifted in her head—so did the concern that riddled his face back at the dock. *Chas… Chas knew about this?* Feeling like throwing up, she headed to the kayak and tossed in the bottle. Bert half turned.

She padded the seat with the army blanket. No sooner did she lower herself onto the seat than he shoved the kayak into the water and jumped into the front seat. He snatched up an oar and gored it into the sea. His biceps flexed with each stroke. "Your shoulder is much better today," she said, her voice small and whimpery, and she hated it. She hated his silence that stuck to her like a burr.

He paused from rowing and again half-turned. A bruise was ripening on the side of his chin.

"What happened to your face?" she asked.

A troubled expression came over him as waves slapped the outside walls of the kayak. He turned and gutted the sea with the oar.

She pursed her lips. *I hit him?*

As the kayak shot out the narrow inlet and into open water, she stared at his back. *If only I could remember.* She glanced back at the cove. She shoved blond spirals out of her face as a maternal need to protect him wracked her entire being. *How can I possibly feel that way after what he did to me? How about protecting myself?* She pressed the heels of her hands into her throbbing temples and wailed, "My mind's all screwed up!"

And it seemed as if Bert didn't hear her at all.

Angry, confused, and hurting all over, Katrina tramped to the Administration Office. *He's not getting away with this! Only I need more time to figure out what to do. And I'm definitely not going to run home, tail tucked between my legs like a bad puppy! I'll never be able to face life. I'll never be able to face Dad!*

"Katrina?"

"Meredith," puffed Katrina, spinning around. "I-I want to go to the Academy, but Dad…he's totally against it. But I have to go and…"

"Not another word," cut in Meredith. Her hands clasped in delight. "I'm on it! I'm *positive* that Jonathan, er, Mr. Aranea, will make sure your father sees all the wondrous opportunities that Granite Mountain Academy has to offer." She clapped wildly. "Wait until Jonathan hears about this!"

Chapter 8

Steadfast in his ability to gain control of the vagaries of the subordinate personality and manipulate them as he saw fit, Jonathan Aranea shook hands with Ken Waters in a manner that appeared to be genuine. He was pleased. *Waters shows up alone for the tour of Granite Mountain Academy,* he mused. *No distractions like that brat son of his or his squaw. Though she does seem to support Kitty's every whim. Look at that Patriots warm-up jacket Waters wears. It curdles my gut.* Jonathan stifled his scorn. *Cursed tic persists in exposing my intentions.* He drew his hands together and flexed fingers and knuckles. *Patriots. We shall see about these American Patriots.* In an engaging voice, he said, "I must apologize that Headmaster Timothy Aranea will not be joining us today. Previously-scheduled student interviews in Vermont have called him away."

In truth Timothy had withdrawn into the bowels of Granite Mountain, acknowledging the fact that he was often too ingratiating, so much so that he ingratiated himself right into invisibility at times thereby failing to win over a target. "Nothing must undermine us sucking in that curly-haired blond," Jonathan had insisted.

"I am in total agreement," Timothy had said.

"Just wait until the movement hears that we recovered the Waters girl," Jonathan had crowed.

Timothy had bowed his head, declaring, "Your name will live until the end of time."

Even now, those words made Jonathan heady. He lifted his

ashen profile into the sun and inhaled a lungful of mountain air. "Clouds have lifted," he exhaled. "Morning chill is nearly gone. The sun works wonders on the human spirit, do you not agree, Mr. Waters?"

Waters grunted.

Jonathan misread Ken's sour puss as adversity of an over-protective parent to allow a precious offspring to spread its wings. While that was at the crux of the matter, another factor entered into the equation: This morning, Ken and Julie had another row over Katrina. "You have no right to deny her from attending prestigious Granite Mountain Academy," Julie had scolded, her finger wagging at Ken. "And I am not going to be a party to you making a fool out of yourself in front of that high-falutin' college president!" Poor little Adriano squalled something awful when forced to stay home. "You'll see Katrina when she gets home," thundered Julie without any sympathy at all, which was not like her—at all. Ken hated any family member being upset—especially at him. This day, two were furious at him. If he didn't approve of this place, his baby girl was also going to be mad; and that would make it three. The whole day was shot as far as he was concerned. He ran his hand through his hair.

"Mr. Waters?" prodded Jonathan. "Mr. Waters?"

"I see you got windmills," said Waters.

Jonathan squinted, slack-jawed, at Waters, now taking off that idiotic jacket. The thump-like whir of blades that had grown to be as inconsequential to the ears as crickets struck Jonathan. "Y-yes," he stammered, his eye twitching. "We do have windmills."

"Big bucks," said Waters, voice bland. He slung his jacket over his shoulder and held it in one hand while stuffing his other hand into a pocket of his jeans.

Waters is too intent on finding fault with Granite Mountain to pick up a measly eye tic, assumed Jonathan. Pulling himself together, he said in a florid manner, "Windmills pay for them-selves within five years. Outlay drops with every technological advance, which I might add, occurs every day on this campus.

In our classes the latest generation turbines are engineered. Prototypes rapidly put the downside of wind power in the past." He eyed Waters. *That num-nut isn't listening to one blasted word!* Jonathan took Ken by the arm and gestured with an upraised palm. "This way to the Academy."

Waters gawked at the hand clamped to his arm and then at Jonathan.

Quickly letting go of the arm, Jonathan started for the Academy. A chipmunk dashed out from beneath a hunk of granite embedded with a brass plaque proclaiming, Administration Building. Startled to see the men, the animal chipped, did an immediate about face, and disappeared under the hunk of granite. *Blasted rodents!*

"Turbines don't bog down building supports?" asked Waters.

"I assure you, Mr. Waters," said Jonathan, fighting to control his tone, "these granite structures can withstand more than the five hundred pounds of stress that have been placed upon them."

"Take long to install?" asked Waters.

"A few hours," breezed Jonathan. "The one over there on the roof of Technology Hall generates about five thousand kilowatt-hours of energy per year, a cost of nine hundred dollars if taken from the fossil-fuel-powered grid. More than enough for the average household that consumes roughly thirty-five hundred kilowatt hours per year."

"The average *American* home uses ten thousand," commented Waters.

Jonathan clenched his jaw. *This buffoon is not going to make a fool of Jonathan Aranea!* He cleared his throat and said, "Most windmills are designed for public or commercial buildings rather than private homes. New turbines spin with less than five miles per hour wind speed. Having fewer moving parts, turbines require less maintenance. Less electricity dissipates because it is not transmitted long distances over power lines."

Waters displayed little more than a hitch of the chin.

So I know what I'm talking about, streaked through Jonathan's psyche. *I now can get on with the business of cutting the cord.* He climbed the steps of Granite Mountain Academy and opened the front door. The musty smell of academia bowled him over. Squelching a cough, he led the way into the building. "Granite Mountain Academy's roots run deep with strong bonds to the community," he said. "We serve residential students as well as day students from local towns. All enjoy sports and other outdoor activities regardless of the season." He awaited a response, but got none. "Granite Mountain Academy is self-sustaining," he continued, "and teaches students that concept. That plus the latest technology in virtually every field is the main focus of parents and students who enroll here. Cooking, sewing, mechanics, and other basic skills are part of the curriculum, provided at different venues that surround Granite Mountain."

"How about safety concerns?" asked Waters, glancing over his shoulder when the front door clanked shut and the noise echoed throughout the Academy.

"Safety is of topmost importance," said Jonathan, stiffening. "Observe the fire alarms and sprinklers. We also have…"

"No, no," cut in Waters, "I mean safety relating to runaway blades."

Jonathan's jaw dropped. "Runaway blades?"

"Windmill blades," said Waters.

Jonathan dug his fingernails into the palms of his hands. His blood boiled. His ability to gain control of the vagaries of the subordinate personality and manipulate them was sorely being tested. "Grates confine turbines," he spat.

"Ah," said Waters, eyeing the white suit Aranea was wearing as if noticing for the first time. He took a second look at the pewter spider pin with the glowing red eyes attached to the lapel and then focused on Aranea's clenched fists.

Rats, thought Jonathan, relaxing his fists. *Waters picks up my agitation. Although it seems he has not spotted this beastly eye tic of mine!*

"Vibration?" asked Waters.

The capitalist pig toys with me, fumed Jonathan. "The effect of vibrations on buildings and inhabitants," he charged, "though unknown as yet, is of little concern."

Waters suppressed a yawn.

Livid, Jonathan fumed, *Oh, to kick this fool and his kid off Granite Mountain forever!* In a tone that had lost depth and control, he said, "Projects such as mini mills for lifeboats, streetlights, and portable generators are underway on this campus. Lightweight fiberglass turbines consisting of helical, cylindrical rotors eliminate all possibility of runaway blades. Our windmills can be used right in your backyard, if you wish to do so."

"I don't think so," scoffed Waters.

"Another nuclear power plant instead?" taunted Jonathan.

"Good point," said Waters, brows elevating.

Why is this Waters not like other overindulgent American parents, stewed Jonathan, *who find honor in having their precious brats recommended to a much sought after academy, especially by me, president of this prestigious campus? I am at a loss…*

A classroom door burst open. As the racket echoed throughout the building, a black hairy pate poked out. "Mr. Aranea! I knew I heard voices!"

Jonathan, thankful for the distraction he had spurned earlier, called, "Mr. O'Mara! Please come and meet Mr. Waters!"

The short pudgy type with dark features waddled out of the classroom. O'Mara's brown dress shoes were grimy and misshapen from an incorrect stride. Prolonged sitting had caused wrinkles to snake across the lap of O'Mara's brown pants. The top three buttons of O'Mara's yellowed white shirt were undone and a mass of black hair slopped out.

Containing revulsion, Jonathan said, "Mr. O'Mara is our new Assistant Director of the Math Department. He was looking for a change of pace from professorship at Boston Metropolitan College. His two sons will attend Granite Mountain Academy in the fall."

"Luck was truly on my side when I ran onto Granite Mountain College while vacationing in this glorious backcountry," said O'Mara, grabbing Waters' hand and shaking effusively. His grasp was clammy, and his breath stunk of reheated coffee.

"A step down on the career ladder, isn't it?" asked Waters, easing away his hand then swiping it up and down his pant leg.

O'Mara squinted kind of funny at Waters and then at Jonathan who thought, *idiot!* The telltale tic reflected displeasure and second thoughts. *Perhaps Arum O'Mara is too soon out of training.* Voice rolling, Jonathan explained, "What Mr. Waters means, Mr. O'Mara, is that a college professor is not as important as Assistant Director. Isn't that right, Mr. Waters?"

Waters nodded with a look that conveyed, holy mackerel, people sure get riled in a hurry around here.

"On the contrary," gushed O'Mara, appearing as if the light had just turned on in his brain. "It is truly a step up!"

"Next year, our current Director of the Math Department is planning a sabbatical," said Jonathan. His voice held a brittle edge. "I have thoughts of appointing Mr. O'Mara Interim Director, depending, of course…" His dark eyes bore into O'Mara's. "…on how this year goes."

O'Mara clasped Jonathan's hand and shook it wildly. "Why, that is the highest of honors, Mr. Aranea! Truly the highest of honors!"

"Good Irish name—O'Mara," said Waters, head tilted, studying the pudgy man. "You don't look Irish."

"The mixing of bloodlines is great, these days," said Jonathan, brushing his palms together to be rid of O'Mara's slime. "Heritage is often difficult to discern."

Waters hitched his chin without taking his eyes off O'Mara. "Think you'll like living so far from Beantown?" he asked.

"Oh, my, yes," bubbled O'Mara. "Hands-down, this is truly the most beautiful country the missus and I have ever seen! Why, I see beauty even when taking out the trash! Even in the rearview mirror when driving about! Now, I know the remoteness doesn't appeal to everybody, but that's just fine with me and the family. As far as I'm concerned, things can stay just as they are!"

Well, well, mused Jonathan. *Waters looks positively agreeable! O'Mara's actually softened up the capitalist pig. Simplicity just might pull this off. Perhaps sequestering Timothy was unnecessary.*

"I interviewed in the spring," O'Mara rambled on. "You should've seen the crabapple blossoms. Colored the entire campus!"

"Wait until winter," injected Jonathan. "Withered crabapples galore cling to the trees and glow like fire through new fallen snow."

Waters glanced at Jonathan and asked, "You live near here?"

"Mrs. Aranea and I maintain quarters in the Administration Building," replied Jonathan. "It's more than adequate owing to our lack of progeny."

The front door opened then closed. Its echo was joined by footsteps that grew louder and louder. A tall young man, sturdily built and wearing a khaki cargo short outfit, came into view. "Mr. Sag," called Jonathan. "Do you have a moment to spare?"

Hand on the doorknob to O'Mara's classroom, Sag paused and looked at the three men. His hand dropped. Turning, he said, "Yes, sir, Mr. Aranea."

"Mr. Sag is one of our brightest students," said Jonathan. His right eye twitched as he considered Sag and his self-assured stride. *Indeed, an upcoming spiderling.* Once known as David Gringas, Sag had the duty of using offspring or wives of targets to secure cooperation of targets. *Showed his mettle by stabbing two brothers during a brawl, which, of course, he instigated during a wild party at the two brothers' home. The target was not at home at the time. One died from chest wounds. The other lives, carrying scars. Needless to say, the target cooperates.* "Mr. Waters," said Jonathan. "Meet Vic Sag."

Sag put out his hand. "A pleasure, sir."

The two shook hands, but then Waters' brows fused. *He has noticed Sag's confident grip,* fretted Jonathan, *odd for one so young. He studies my clean-cut spiderling and the red-eyed spider pin attached to his lapel. I must deter him from seeing the legs of O'Mara's pin, sticking out beneath that crumpled collar.* "Mr. Waters," spouted Jonathan, "is considering enrolling his daughter in Granite Mountain Academy."

Waters shot a look at Jonathan.

"Katrina Waters?" asked Sag.

Waters shot a hairy eyeball at the young man.

"I'm one of your daughter's counselors," boasted Sag. "I have to say, she is one special young lady."

"You drive a black Volkswagen convertible?" asked Waters. Sag uttered a tentative, "No."

Jonathan quickly interceded. "This is your second year at the Academy, am I correct, Mr. Sag?"

"Yes, sir," said Sag, tugging his eyes off Waters and shifting them to Jonathan.

"Like it here?" Waters asked.

"I do, sir," replied Sag, sidling up to Jonathan.

"There are plenty of mentors who help new students over any unexpected rough spots," said Jonathan, "and their families."

"Newbies are not just tossed into the deep end," added Sag, "hoping they swim. No, sir. Not only was I taught to swim, but I'm also being coached to swim better."

"Is that so," said Waters, glancing at O'Mara who had quieted down. "Salaries tend to be low up here."

O'Mara jumped to attention as though somebody had flipped a switch. "No problem for me!"

"Some of the highest test scores in New Hampshire come out of the North Country," said Jonathan, "and Granite Mountain Academy is leading the charge."

"A rosy picture," said Waters dubiously.

Jonathan took a handkerchief out of his pocket and wiped his brow. *I've got better things to do than play cat and mouse with this moron. One more minute of this and I'll outright make off with his precious daughter! Drat. Waters sees this accursed eye tic of mine, which most assuredly will persist long after my demise. Blast fate. All is lost.*

Waters sucked in a chest full of air, ran a hand through his hair, and exhaled, "If only for the sake of peace on the home front…"

Chapter 9

*B*e *wary,* cautioned instinct, raspy and muffled after its prolonged dormancy. *Survive. S-u-r-v-i-v-e...*

Katrina jolted awake, eyes wide, heart thumping. Chaos of other girls preparing for the first day of classes engulfed the barracks-like dorm. Yet something else was in the air. She cocked her head and listened. *Music?* She snagged a blond spiral and held it behind her ear. Her breath came to a standstill. *It is music! It wasn't here yesterday!*

Doctor Edie's voice swelled in Katrina's mind, "Background music is a common mind control technique, subliminal messaging..."

Katrina squinted at the fluorescent lighting and then the sparse, utilitarian grayness of the dorm. *A camera's mounted in the far corner! There's also a camera in that fire alarm in the middle of the ceiling—I bet my life on it!* Like a ghost, the past seeped into her soul, but this time, instead of her being kidnapped, her willing parents had been given more than enough time to clear out before the real program began. Dread chilled her being worse than trekking to Brighton Junior High School on a sub-zero morning. *The warning signs were staring me in the face all along. Meredith tried to make me forget about home. Jonathan grabbed my head like that. And then "Mother Mary" came back to me. Why is this the first time I'm picking up on any of it?* She swallowed hard. *Come on now, this is ridiculous. Nobody's holding me here against my will—not like in Judgment...* Visions of cruelty and indoctrination wrapped around Katrina, making her feel like prey ensnared in spider silk. Resistance was futile. The only thing left was a para-lyzing sting. Her hand flexed as if gripping cold, unforgiving metal. The recollection was all too clear: her index finger pulling the trigger, the gun shoving her back, and the dummies slump-ing inside that school bus. *Those dummies… Were they just card-board faces peering through the school bus windows? Or were they the faces of real live kids? Kids who never came back at the end of hot, sticky days? Did I kill…? Oh, God, I'm relapsing! Doctor Edie says it's post traumatic stress. She says the struggle to purge the past may very well continue the rest of my life. She says the techniques she taught me to deal with the terror might not work. But wait until she hears about this! No, she's never going to believe me. Oh, I detest Regina for being so mean to Dad and me! So mean to everybody!*

"*Ach so,*" drifted Gammy Getchen's voice. "Is right you forgive you Mama. She victim, same you." The replica of Mrs. Claus knitting took hold of Katrina's hand. "Me and Gampy blame. We see happen. We no stop. We much blame. We fear bad people, they come take my little Regina—you Mama. I worry much, what will happen? Terrible, terrible happen you Mama. *Arm, arm kind von mein.* Evil people make her bad. Make think no good no more. Forgive you Mama. No to blame."

"I suppose Jake wasn't to blame either," Katrina had pouted.

Gammy Getchen spat on the ground. "Aurch!" she snapped. "That Jake! He devil! Make think he you Daddy brother!" She jabbed a knitting needle into the ball of yarn. For a moment she pondered what she had done then her head wavered side to side. She heaved an all-consuming sigh. "Is right forgive," she muttered, "so forgive Jake we must."

"But it's so hard," Katrina had whined. "I don't think I ever can."

"*Arm, arm kind von mein,*" Gammy Getchen had whispered while pulling Katrina to her full bosom. Her wrinkled old hand stroked Katrina's curly blond pate.

Katrina crawled onto Gammy Getchen's lap, and they rocked and rocked.

"Earth to Katrina. Come in, please."

Spiraling back to the dorm, Katrina sucked in breath as if for the first time. Her eyes scanned Brita chewing a wad of bubble gum and dressed in school uniform, navy blue vest and skirt, white button-down blouse and socks, and black soft leather oxfords. A pewter spider pin held fast to her lapel. Red eyes skewered Katrina.

"You see a boogieman or something?"

Katrina stared at Brita as instinct counseled, *Do not let the evil in. Fill your mind with positive things. Perform like expected. Buy precious time. Survive. S-u-r-v-i-v-e...*

Brita yanked on Katrina's wrist, shrieking, "Quit the frigging humming and get out of bed! We're going to be late for class, and it's only our first day!"

Katrina pursed her lips, but tears burned beneath the surface. *"If the bad people caught me crying,"* I told Doctor Edie, *"they got real mad and punished me."*

The front door of the dorm slammed, but Katrina was too lost inside herself to notice. Now, only she and Brita were left in the dorm.

"What's the matter with you?" spat Brita, pitching away Katrina's wrist. "I never seen you so spooked!"

Tell Brita about the terrorist camp in Judgment, Mississippi, cried an inner voice. *Tell her about the background music that drones on and on no matter where or what the time of day. Tell her about the spying cameras. Tell her it's happening here! But what if Brita can't be trusted? What if she isn't friend enough to keep her mouth shut?*

"I think I should go get somebody," said Brita, chucking her hands into her waist.

"I'm okay," snapped Katrina, shoving aside blankets. She got to her feet, grabbed her toilet supply case, and brushed past Brita, heading for the bathroom. *I fooled those awful people in Judgment, Mississippi, even though every so often I have to fight them off in my head again. Here I am again in the same situation, but this time I count myself lucky. Memory, instinct, whatever it was, zeroed in on the music and cameras and warned me to watch out.* Katrina paused, one hand on the bathroom door. *I have to concentrate, stay emotionally unattached to everything and everybody. Like the way I blocked out Regina and Jake and the brainwashing in Judgment, Mississippi. Though I have a basic understanding of the brainwashing process, I'm not stupid enough to think I'm above it. Fighting it in the wrong way assures conversion. I've always been able to control my emotions and do what I have to in order to survive. I blocked out back-ground music, spying cameras, all the bad stuff, and kept my head filled with Dad, Ralph, and "Mary's Song." Those idiots in Judgment, Mississippi never had the faintest idea that every time they called me Kitty Star, my Ralph scampered into my mind and we would play all the time. I could feel his silky gray fur and his arching spine. He purred along with me every time I hummed "Mary's Song." His paws kept beat, kneading the blanket over my belly.* Katrina shoved open the bathroom door and marched to the sink. She rotated the tap full blast, cupped her hands beneath the spout, and splashed water onto her face. *I took for granted the life given back to me. I didn't give a second thought about how Dad, Gammy Getchen, and everybody else had suffered while believing I died in that plane crash with Regina.* Katrina stamped her foot. *Well, they're not going through it again! I'm not either! I won't allow myself to be vulnerable! I won't be cowed into submission!* She shut off the water and yanked a towel out of her toilette case. Blotting moisture off her face, she programmed herself: *Keep good things in mind. Don't let the music and wickedness in. Don't make a single move without thinking. Think. Then think again. Make the best possible decisions. Minimize pain. Maximize odds for success. Live to tell the tale.* Background music intruded on her preparation, making her cringe. *Messages are hidden in it—just like in Judgment! I'm not fooled for one minute. But why is this happening to me again? All I want to do is go where I want to, do what I want to, be what I want to! Is that too much to ask?* She squinted into the eyes in the mirror. *Miss Matthias said I was cut out for this place. Did she single me out? Sure as birds fly and babies cry!* Katrina ran the towel across her lips. *Those self-defense classes Dad made me take didn't prepare me for this.* She swallowed hard. *Or for that night on that island.*

"You forgot your clothes," squawked Brita.

Katrina turned to stone.

Brita plunked down underwear and pieces of uniform on the counter. "For crying out loud!" she shrieked, shoving on Katrina's arm. "Hurry up!"

As Brita left the bathroom, Katrina grabbed the clothes and toilette case, ran into a stall, and latched the door. Cognizant of the camera, she squirreled a cotton swab out of the toilette case by hiding it behind a container of deodorant. While getting dressed, she manipulated the cotton off the ends of the swab and stuffed it into her ears to drown out subliminal programming. *When I get home at Thanksgiving, I have to buy some earplugs. But I'd better watch out. Some things I need to hear. Keep out the bad, that's all.* She smoothed out her uniform then adjusted the collar. Her finger snagged the pewter spider that made her special among students. She pursed her lips. *Special, huh? Well, there's no way to control a kid who won't be controlled, and I'm one of those kids!*

"Hurry up," squalled Brita, pounding on the stall door.

"Just a sec'!" shot back Katrina, unlatching the door and charging out.

"I got our backpacks!" shrieked Brita while barreling out of the bathroom.

At the mirror, Katrina ran a pick through her hair and arranged a style that covered up her ears. She hooked the butterfly barrette around that foolish spiral that always fell in her face. She met her eyes in the mirror. Her brows came together. *The other barrette's still on that island. Sure was convenient about that island being there. And Bert hurting his arm—yeah right! That was a put on. All of it was a put on! He planned to take advantage of me!* Katrina spun around. *Ever since we got back from that island, he's been avoiding me. What, I'm not good enough for his carnal pleasures? Maybe he's just not man enough to face me.* She crumpled against the sink cabinet. Her fingernails clicked together. *Too bad nobody came looking for us. He would've been in deep poo for sure.* Her eyes narrowed. *Nobody came, because the Araneas and others were in on it! How many others were in on it, too? Well, I'll show them! I know something about how the game is played. I'm not going be the fool anymore. They're going to get a taste of their own medicine!* Katrina moistened her lips, tasting once again the water's bitterness eternally lodged in her memory. Her hand came down hard on the sink. "I drank every bit of that water!" she cried. "Bert never so much as touched one lousy drop!" She clamped her hands over her mouth as her eyes shot to the camera. *Did anybody hear that? No. Today's the first day of classes. Who's got time to spy on bathrooms?* Her hands fell away from her mouth. *That night is one big blur. I rubbed lotion on his shoulders, got dizzy. Shadows. Shouts. Light flashes. It's so fuzzy! I couldn't say no. I couldn't push him away. My muscles were limp as that rag doll Dad gave me when I was three. What good are self-defense classes against drugs?* "Mature people show how much they mean to each other this way," he said. *Was he real or just my drugged mind playing games? But that condom...* She bent over the sink, moaning, "Oh, I feel like throwing up." She straightened and glared at herself in the mirror. *I have to do whatever Bert says or he'll tell Dad! Doctor Edie says blackmail is an effective brainwashing technique. What a stinking fool I am! I'm such an easy target!*

Bert came alive in the mirror, goring an oar into the sea, the bruise on his chin ripening. "I hit him?" she whispered. "I couldn't have. My muscles were useless. So who did?" The maternal need to protect Bert stalked her. She fished around her toilette supply case and took out the picture of her and Bert taken on Mount Jackson. *Look at that son-of-a-gun smiling like that. Hooking up with me was no accident, was it? Checked out that island beforehand, didn't you? Thought you shared my passion about the environment. Thought you and I... You blabbed about me being kidnapped, didn't you? Who'd you tell? Meredith, huh? She wanted to know real bad—I know she did. And Mr. Aranea—Jonathan—oh, I can still feel his hand on my head, the way he shoved me.* Katrina rubbed her temple. *And that feeling of exhilaration...* She hummed "Mary's Song."

Brita stuck her head into the bathroom and hollered, "Are you coming or what?"

Katrina double-checked her hairstyle to make sure the cotton couldn't be seen.

"Katrina," whined Brita.

"Call me Kitty," yelled Katrina while sprinting out of the bathroom. Outside the dorm, she noticed Brita's short hair jouncing. "Wait! I have to tell you..."

"Not now," bellowed Brita. She hucked a wad of bubble gum into the bushes. "We're mega late!"

At intervals throughout the day, Katrina fingered the cotton in her ears. Music was playing in every building, classroom, bathroom, cafeteria, even outside—a constant bombardment. Cameras were ever-present, too, some more obvious than others. *I've got to figure out a way to stop what's going on around here*, she thought. *If only I could wave a magic wand and fix things, make this stuff blow up in the faces of those doing it.*

That night in the bunk below Brita, Katrina yanked the army blanket over her head and pretended to be lulled asleep by the background music like everybody else. She peeked out at the timber door at the far end of the dorm. *Bet that keyhole is a peephole.* Something deep inside her anticipated the door opening. She could almost hear hinges grinding—and footsteps, thunk, thunk, crossing the plank floor. A scream! "Don't let them take me!"

Katrina bit on the blanket to squelch her fright. *Memories,* she told herself. *Only memories.* She stopped biting the blanket. *But what did happen to those kids taken in the middle of the night? Why did I survive while others cracked? What made me so special to be kidnapped in the first place? Dad insists nothing could have prevented it. Very bad adults did it, and I was just a helpless child. It's not my fault. If anybody's to blame, it's him—that's what he says. But he did try to stop Jake and Regina—we both tried—with all our might! I kicked and punched, even bit Regina. She slapped me every time I did. Then Dad was unconscious on the floor. Oh, I hate mean people! Doctor Edie says, "Hatred causes destruction; love causes construction. You don't have to love Regina, but don't allow yourself to hate her. It's so easy to hate, but hate is an ugly emotion that degrades the hater and causes bad thinking and physical illness. Better to see a wrong and use love to try to right it."*

The lights went off. The bathroom light cast eerie, elongated shadows similar to scenes in horror movies where audiences are allowed only glimpses of the dreaded monster. Katrina nudged aside the cotton in one ear. *Brita's snoring. Camille's babbling in her sleep.* Katrina heaved a sigh. *Maybe I'm where I'm supposed to be. Or maybe I'm hanging onto this terrorist thing like a life buoy and if I let it go, I'll have nothing.* She envisioned Adriano, his arms wrapped about her neck, planting a kiss on her then asking, "Know how much I love you?"

"Too much?"

A decisive hitch of the chin. "No such thing as too much."

Dad and I used to do that, thought Katrina, *but not anymore. Gosh, I miss it. No matter what, I can't let Addie become a target. He's never going to end up in a place like this. Well, Dad, you raised me with the strong concept of giving back to the community and that's what I'm going to do, give up everything that's my life and play along. Lead a shadowy double life. I have to or somebody I love might get hurt because of me. It's the only way to put an end to these places. Gosh, I don't know if I have the stuff to pull it off!* Katrina buried her face in her pillow so nobody could hear. "One little white lie," she whispered, "and I'm nailed—either by these people here or by Dad—everything I do will be scrutinized." She turned her head, thinking, *I should walk away from this, go home, report it to the authorities, let them deal with it. But if Judgment, Mississippi existed and this place still does, there must be other places. How many are there? Think of all those innocent kids. No, I have to keep my mouth shut until I find out about other places and then report them.* She pursed her lips and nodded firmly. *Picture Daddy's face, Addie's, Julie's, everybody I care about. Don't let the evil into my head. Keep the luck I've been blessed with on my side. Try not to get involved if anybody messes up. Help only when it's safe to.*

A couple of hours before dawn, Katrina fell asleep, "Mother Mary" moving in the background of her mind. She had learned in Judgment to squeeze in an hour of sleep here, two hours there. It had come in useful. It should prove useful on Granite Mountain.

Chapter 10

*M*assaging an old-fashion tumbler half full of Rob Roy between his palms, Curt leaned against the balcony railing and stared into the glow of comfortless Atlanta lights. A breeze out of the north fanned his face. Behind him inside the condo, Penny diddled with something or another. He felt remote, friendless, a tiny island on a humungous map, ocean all around. Worse, a tide of thoughts was rising and sailing upon it, Julie Waters. *Must have a slew of wee ones by now. And here I dither, childless, an only child, butt end of the Shirlington family tree.* He filled his mouth with his signature drink and held it. *Curious. Penny's in the same boat as I. Yet she has not once spoken of popping a babe-in-arms. Maternal instinct isn't her cup of tea, I must assume.* The inside of his mouth numbed. *The Waters family really got it together after the Cohasset fiasco. Lots of friends. Envy that.* He wallowed in the funk as Rob Roy eased down his throat. He waited for the booze to lighten his mood. It didn't happen. It never did.

⌒

That day had been one horror story after another, adding up to one big pile of crud. He had just sat down at his desk and was giving Emily, the Cat her first ear rub of the morning when Leander Holt sprinted into the office, clutching a fist full of eight-by-tens. "Satellite photos," panted the brown-haired analyst. "Vapor's seeping out of Granite Mountain!"

"New Hampshire?" asked Curt as that same old distant ache throbbed. He eyed Holt, a high-strung sort, a trait that tended to cast doubt upon Holt's expertise despite his six-foot athletic build. But a keen eye had gotten Holt the job; and he earned every penny of the salary it paid.

Amid a flurry of nods, Holt squawked, "Southern end of the Presidential Range, a mile north of Route 302!"

"I am aware of the orientation, my dear man," said Curt. "Stats, if you will."

Holt elbowed Emily, the Cat off the desk and spread the photographs over a never-ending mound of paperwork. "Taken zero hours six minutes," he gushed. "Point in question…fifty twigs west of peak, one point zero eight clicks above mean."

"Deduction?" asked Curt.

Holt straightened and rubbed his palms on his pants. He took a step back and then offered, "Terrorist cell?"

Curt cast a dubious eye at the analyst.

"It's a known fact," expounded Holt, right hand jouncing, "that terrorists are like certain breeds of spiders: they conduct the majority of activities under cover of darkness." A tremor wracked his body. "Spiders. Yecsh! And terrorists do so more these days due to constant satellite surveillance."

"Your repugnance of spiders," remarked Curt while leaning forward to study the photographs, "and correlation to terrorists are enough to give me the heebie-jeebies."

Ignoring the comment, Holt hovered over Curt's left shoulder, jabbing his finger on the photographs. "The wisp rising near the peak is clear enough. Carved out of the southern slope, here and here, is a dirt-and-crushed-rock landing strip and heliport."

"A campus complete with heliport," said Curt, scratching his head. "A bit unusual, I suppose, but these days, that does pop up."

"Structures encircling Granite Mountain are pretty solid," said Holt. "Granite, I suspect, like this archway and large building. Cluster of bungalows at the mountain's base to the west. A kilometer to the left, another."

"An excess of undeveloped terrain," rumbled Curt. "A person could live off the land there in blissful solitude." He leaned back in the chair and entwined his fingers on top of his head. "All things considered, Granite Mountain looks to be a stupendous locality to get away from it all."

"That's what they want you to think," yipped Holt, hooking his hands on his hips.

"They?" echoed Curt, squinting at Holt.

"Terrorists!" exclaimed Holt. "Take a look!" He pointed to each photograph. "First few shots, you see a cloudless dark landscape—only streetlights here, here, and here. In this next shot, steam wiggles out above the tree line like a night crawler after midnight. In subsequent shots, steam rears up like a cobra, heads east, and dissipates. Dawn is crystal clear. I tell you, there's a sleeper cell inside Granite Mountain!"

Curt contemplated the photographs. "Underground hot springs don't come and go like that." A storm gathered in his head. "Get enhancements of that vapor or whatever it is at the specific point in time it occurred plus the ones right before and after."

"Enhanced subterranean infrared images?" suggested Holt while collecting the photographs. "Just to be on the safe side?"

"Sure," said Curt.

A short time later, Holt scurried back and planked eight-by-tens onto the desk. "Newly-arrived thermal images of the Middle East," he said. "See these red spots?"

Curt squinted at the nearly invisible specks. "Desert animals?"

Emily, the Cat jumped off the monitor and smack on top of the thermal images. Holt worked around her, his finger moving west to east across one of the photographs. "Miles of them along these ridges."

Curt picked up the feline. "What kind of animal migrates this time of year?" he asked while rubbing his chin across silky fur.

"None that I know of," blubbered Holt. "Those things haven't moved in hours!"

Uneasiness crept over Curt like a tarantula on the hunt. Putting Emily, the Cat on the floor, he inspected the red spots. "Indiscriminately spaced. Dug into the sand. Looks like we underestimated poorly-trained and ill-equipped conscripts."

"So deep that heat scanners almost failed to detect them," added Holt.

Curt grabbed the phone, but the warning to coalition forces sweeping north came too late as conscripts slithered out of the sand like hordes of spiders, stinging with easy-to-carry mustard gas, anthrax, sarin gas, and other agents. Troops unequipped to deal with such weaponry dropped like flies. So did the conscripts, also unequipped, to whom life held no value.

The Centers for Disease Control was now required to work day and night to find remedies for new threats that were needed yesterday; in addition to previously needed remedies for the bites of disease-bearing insects, water and food contamination, and basic sanitation and hygiene difficulties. Air, water, and soil samples streamed in, all needing analysis and results forwarded for action.

Just after lunch, which had gone unobserved, Holt had rushed back, choking on his own spit. "Enhanced thermal imaging of Granite Mountain outlines a warren that expands with each descending level!"

"Well, I'll be damned," Curt had said.

"All of us be damned!" raved Holt. "Each level has four chambers, north, east, south, and west!" His finger traced a central stairway down into the fifth level.

"No elevators," said Curt.

Holt scratched the side of his chin and shivered. "Looks like a giant spider. Those chambers look like its legs drawn up. Yecsh!"

"Pull yourself together, mate," said Curt.

"A trunk line runs along the central stairway," said Holt, his finger striking the images in several places. "Connects to generators powered by windmills on the roofs of these buildings."

"Quite a few windmills," observed Curt, "wouldn't you say?"

"That I would," spewed Holt. "From the amount of heat loss on the third level, I believe every bit of electricity those windmills produce is needed. Communications, computers, telephone, teletype, intercom and visual circuits."

"No wonder windmills," reasoned Curt. "Tapping the power grid that much certainly attracts attention."

"Plumbing runs along here," said Holt, his finger tracing each level then out beside the parking garage. "Wells are here. Sewer ducts end up in a private sewer treatment facility, here."

"Jump on this," said Curt.

As Holt sprinted out of the office, Emily, the Cat arched into an all-encompassing stretch then sat back on her haunches and stared at Curt. He stared back. "Night vision goggles had to be worn," he muttered. "Lots of night vision goggles." An abbreviated meow lifted one side of the feline's face much like Elvis was known to do. "A complex process," continued Curt. "Many years of nights—many undetected nights—of workers wearing goggles." He picked up the phone and dialed. "All traceable to manufacturers."

Curt was calling it quits for the day. Emily, the Cat had settled in for the night on the mouse pad. Holt trudged into the office and flopped onto a chair near the door.

"What's up?" asked Curt, taking off his clinic jacket.

Holt heaved. "Been nosing around."

Curt tossed the jacket over the back of his chair. "Let's have a go at it."

Holt rolled his eyes and sucked in a lungful of air. He exhaled, "FBI's got a spook at Granite Mountain."

"Why weren't we informed?" Curt demanded. "Never mind! I know the answer! Lack of communication between FBI, CDC, CIA, and other agencies. Miscommunication. A hoarding of information. Rivalry. Distrust. Green-eyed jealousy of wanting to top each other. Jealousy that might someday cause ruination of these United States." He took several aimless paces and stopped. He squinted at Holt whose head bobbed side to side, whose face scrunched like a dehydrated pickle. Curt gripped the back of the chair. "Spook have a name?"

"Pomoroy," said Holt. "Robert Pomoroy."

⌁

"Cheers is on in five minutes," called Penny.

Curt glanced at his watch. 9:55. He heaved a sigh then turned away from the lights of Atlanta and trudged into the condo. *Without Penny to keep schedules, smooth the way, and remind this old fuddy-duddy of priorities, my world surely would collapse.*

Chapter 11

*T*his war goes on much too long," groused Jonathan while scanning the monitors. No significant activity in his homeland or in and out of Granite Mountain.

"There is comfort in knowing our leaders are still at the helm," reflected Meredith, seated cross-legged in the high back chair near the door into the warren. "Only insignificant ones are being lost."

He glared at her, his right eyelid twitching. "Still at the helm—there is the problem. It is long past due for old leaders to step down and make way for the next generation."

"Next generation being Jonathan Aranea," she quipped.

Someday, I'll wipe that smirk off her face, he thought while tossing the remote on the desk. "I would have been *the* major power broker by now, if not for the conference to choose a unified leadership falling apart. I have accumulated sufficient support, but my aspirations have put me in bad odor with a few who now attempt to strip me of that support behind my back, criticizing, demeaning me and my work."

"Many are the bumps in the road created by this rivalry between old and new divisions," she said, "which only clouds preparations for a worldwide Judgment Day."

His fist came down hard on the desk. "The conference must be held in January!"

"And if it isn't?"

Again, he glared at her. Her head rested against the back of the chair. Her eyes were closed. His bravado didn't faze her in the least. He spun around to the vivariums and raged, "I don't count on anybody as linchpin for my success! Not only have I— on my own—accumulated a colossal weapons cache beneath the orchard, but I also have those two projects."

"Making progress on neither," she jabbed.

"It is not my fault that the environment hinders assault on the Mount Washington Observatory!"

"Ah, New Englanders love their weather," she sniggered. "Not getting their minute-to-minute meteorological fix will make them fret like cavemen during a nocturnal thunderstorm."

"The tree line is too far below the observatory to provide cover," he raved, "and that does not take into account the sparseness of trees that are less than eight feet tall and their skimpy branches that only spike out their trunk on the east side due to habitual winds out of the west. The inhospitable summit lies in the middle of three major storm tracks. In winter, only snow cats venture there. In summer, nights are downright hostile no matter the temperature or weather conditions at lower levels."

As if she hadn't heard a single word, Meredith got to her feet, crooked her elbows at shoulder level, and stretched, grunting like a troll. She smacked her lips then asked, "Have you secured the atomic self-destruct device?"

"Old leaders deem our warren too inconsequential."

"Inconsequential, my butt!" she blasted, jamming her hands into her hips.

That's more like it, he thought as a lecherous grin twisted his lips. In a controlled yet dangerous voice, he said, "Support of the outdated movement is inconsequential." He tapped on the glass of the vivarium labeled, Theraphosa Lebloni - Guyana. The Goliath Bird Eater Tarantula inside the vivarium took an aggressive stance and hissed. Jonathan leered at the tarantula. "It is only a matter of time before I find another source. Until then, I have wealth enough to make headway in my four-pronged strategy to bring an end to the capitalist infidels *and* the outdated movement. Ultimate will be the destruction. Only a matter of time."

"And the Aranea name shall live as long as time itself," she added.

He gazed at the ceiling as if praising a divine being and twisted a kink out of his back. "I still find it incredible how well the transfer of hardware went from the underground supply depot near Mount Cushman to the four missile silos." He reveled in the memory of straining diesel-powered engines cutting through the silence as he had waited outside phony mine entrances. The dew, always heavy and cold, had gotten in his bones, but it was well worth the misery.

Earlier, Bert, Joe, and Vic had waited behind a natural-looking blind off Route 302. Upon spotting the trucks, Joe signaled with a flashlight. High beams signaled back. Drivers switched off headlights. Donning night vision goggles, drivers and spiderlings double-checked the area. Nobody around. Spiderlings opened the blind as though it were a door. Trucks veered off the highway. Bert jumped onto a running board and showed the way while Joe and Vic reset the blind and then melted into the woods. "Easy as apple pie," boasted Jonathan.

"So goes the American idiom," yawned Meredith. "Are the missiles set to go?"

He stepped to his desk and sagged onto the chair. "Programming their control has hit a snag."

"Computer glitches," she slushed. "Don'cha love 'em?"

"Katrina Waters will soon fix that end of things," he said with an air of confidence.

"She wears training wheels and doesn't know it," said Meredith.

"That she does," he said, his tone building to the one he used during sex. "She ripens swiftly into a spiderling—definitely one of our most crowning achievements."

"She wants to be called Kitty," said Meredith.

"Excellent," he crowed. "She takes the name given to her in Mississippi."

"I wondered where she came up with that name," she said.

"Old man Waters trained his daughter well," he said. "With her knowledge of computers, the clock ticks for Boston, New

York, and the Seabrook and Three-mile Island Nuclear Power Stations. Her high level of hacking skills is a bonus that will enable us to poke around websites and e-mails all over the world. Who knows what else we can get our hands on?"

"It's a roll of the dice for any of those missiles to achieve target," she said.

"Ah, yes, but hitting just one? Especially if that one is a nuclear power station? One city in ruins brings about a powerful economic disruption. Time allowing, I intend to construct more silos."

"Civilization in chaos," she said.

"This device empowers me," he said while offering up a remote control as though it were the bread of the Last Supper. "Detonating explosives rigged beneath road bridges within a fifty mile radius will isolate Granite Mountain and allow the Day of Judgment to continue. Only the warren will survive." He stopped short of disclosing, *The future for the human race exists in my seed alone, which of course, does not include my barren wife.*

"There is no indication whatsoever that the Feds are on to us," she said.

"Odds of achieving sweet fruition are certain," he said, his thumbnail toying with the edge of a remote button.

"Have you selected the four spiderlings?" she asked.

"The ones to smash glass vials of sarin on concrete floors of American subways?" he asked.

She nodded. "To coincide with the firing of the four missiles."

"Armageddon in a cloud," he raved. "Hovers close to the ground. Everything dies without damaging structures, paperwork, machinery, anything non-biological. Short-lived contamination allows immediate control."

She grunted. "The sheer terror of it all will freak people out so bad that streets will overflow with chaos and rioting. A real nightmare for law enforcement. People flooding hospitals by the thousands, believing that they've been poisoned."

"Psychosomatic ailments," he said. "I have narrowed the selection to six. Final choice will come before the end of the year."

She hinted at her three choices. "Joe, Vic, and Bert excel beyond my wildest dreams."

"I too cannot be more pleased," he agreed. "With little guidance they procured bomb-making materials then assembled and rigged the devices."

"And it took them less than two years to acquire the anti-aircraft missiles," she reminded him.

"And over fifteen hundred pounds of plastic explosives," he added, "half a dozen rocket propelled grenade launchers, ninety rockets, two mortars, seventy-five mortar rounds, two thousand blasting caps, and six hundred fifty-eight hand grenades. They even got their grubby hands on refrigerated trucks with tires reinforced with titanium steel to transport weapons-grade plutonium."

"Ah yes," she said, "plutonium can't be exposed to more than a temperature of forty-seven degrees."

"Those three spiderlings played an integral part," he said, "in accumulating construction materials to build the warren, sneaking it in through a network of trails, abandoned railroad corridors, and what look to be old logging roads. They stole lawn tractors, snow blowers, and other equipment throughout New England for my dummy corporation, Granite Mountain Home Maintenance Company. Taking care of our own venues keeps money cycling in our pockets. Those three hijacked so many trucks of food and other basic necessities that my warren will survive for a minimum of ten years after the Day of Judgment."

"Problem is," she said, "when is that day? Yeah?"

Jonathan gawked at her. The telephone was against her ear. *When did the telephone ring?*

"Camille Jennes wants to see you," said Meredith. Covering the mouthpiece with her hand, she grumbled, "Something's got to be done about this slut."

"I don't have time for her nonsense!" he barked.

Meredith snickered and took her hand off the receiver. "Enter." She set the receiver on the cradle. "That Joe Ault will fuck a catcher's mitt."

His eye twitched worse than ever as Jonathan recalled seeing Meredith and Joe Ault going at it hot and heavy. *Of all people— Joe Ault. Ault was supposed to be in class.* Jonathan picked up the remote and defiantly switched off the monitors as Meredith opened the door with fanfare and palmed the way into the office. Camille buzzed in, sniveling, "Joey threatened to kill me! Himself, too!"

Barefoot as usual, thought Jonathan. *Look at that slinky, black leather miniskirt. And that chartreuse top shows more flesh than it covers.*

Meredith wiggled spindly fingers. Eyes twinkling, she mouthed a toothy, "Bye." Taking a bow, she backed out the door and pulled it closed.

Flopping on his desk, Jonathan grumbled, "What pissed-off deity curses me so?"

"Excuse me?" asked Camille, tossing her ginger hair over her shoulder.

He straightened and squinted sidelong at her. *Stinking makeup's a mess from all her bawling. Gobs of makeup can't hide those bruises and scars Ault heaps on the whore.* He cleared his throat then inhaled, filling the deepest reaches of his lungs. Slowly, he let out air. "And why would Joe do an asinine thing like killing himself?"

"He's gonna lose his job here," sneered Camille.

"Lose his job," seethed Jonathan while picking up a pen. *Losing Ault because of this featherhead is out of the question!* He squeezed the pen, tighter and tighter. *Ault always comes through. Voracious, efficient, a despicable predator.*

"Betcha wanna know why," she said, jamming her hands into her hips.

"Absolutely," he said dryly, despite his insides festering like a volcano.

"Well!" she puffed, then in an emphatic beat, "*I* told *him* that *I* am going to report *him* to the *cops*, and that will make *you* mad and *you* will fire *him*!"

"Did you," said Jonathan, setting the pen onto the desk ever so delicately. *If this slut goes anywhere near the cops, I'll kill her with my own bare hands!*

"*Joey* says nobody's gonna believe me."

Jonathan clasped his hands in front of his face. The tips of his index fingers tapped his bottom lip as he watched her examine her artificial nails that extended well beyond her fingertips. *Chartreuse—matches that skimpy blouse.* "I assume you haven't gone to the cops yet," he said.

She shook her head. "Joey says he'll call my allegations phony—a story I concocted to ruin his future potential. He says he's gonna be president of the United States someday. Phshyeah right. He's gonna say that he was in class when I say he hit me, and you'll back him up and tell the cops that I'm a borderline schizophrenic."

"True," said Jonathan, rolling his chair around and scanning the vivariums.

"What?" she squealed, running up next to him and staring him down.

His insides boiled. *Even my collection of spiders does not faze this featherhead.* He unclasped his hands. *Featherhead?* His eye twitched. *Ah, yes-s-s, my featherheads...* He gripped the armrests of his chair and pried himself up. As he stepped toward her, she backed up. "Have you ever seen one cop on this campus?" he asked.

"Well..." she said, backing into the bookcase.

"Everything gets handled here," he said in a quiet tone. "No outsiders. No cops."

"But Joey threw hot coffee in my face!" she wailed and it struck Jonathan worse than a slap in the face. As he recoiled, she darted to the other side of the room. "He shoved me down the stairs. I got a wicked bad urinary infection from him screwing everything in sight, and I got the crabs from him, too! A couple of times, he came at me with a baseball bat!"

"Baseball bat," echoed Jonathan. *Wish the brute had whaled this featherhead good, pounded her into putty right then and there. Entirely forgivable.*

"Uh-huh," she whined, peering down at her toe scraping the floor side to side.

"You fear for your safety."

"Well, yeah."

"Joe's some sick prick."

"Uh-huh."

"You should get out of his room."

"Nah-uh," she postured. "He'll get somebody else in two seconds flat. He has his eye on that blond hussy, you know, Kitty."

His eyelid convulsed. *Ault knows full well that blond hussy is off limits! I am to have my way with her first.* He braced himself upon his knuckles on the desk. *The trap is set. Only thing left is the waiting. Ault had better lay off Kitty or…*

"Mr. Aranea?" asked Camille, worming into his line of sight.

His brows came together. He straightened and said, "Fair enough. I'll put an end to all this, right now, once and for all."

Stepping out of his path, she asked with childish eagerness, "I'll go with you!"

"Not a good idea," he said, opening the door for her like a true gentleman. "Better for you to wait in the conference room." He gestured for her to go first.

"Well," she said, shoulders drooping. Then hope bubbled in her face and she straightened. "You're right!" She hurried past him and paused at the conference room door. "Good luck, Mr. Aranea!"

"Same to you," he sang out, his hand waving high in the air as he took elongated strides down the hall. When the metallic click of the conference room door closing reached his ears, he stopped dead and fished a remote control from his pocket. He pressed a button. Another metallic click. The conference room door had locked. He turned and started back. He heard Camille tap on the door. Her voice was small, *that whiney garbage.* "Hello? Mr. Aranea? Are you there? Hello? Anybody?"

He slowed a notch, leering at the conference room door. A smirk grew on his face.

Her voice elevated. "Somebody? Please? Let me out."

"Truly a shame that I will not do as Miss Featherhead desires," he crooned upon entering his office. He depressed several buttons on the remote, and the monitors glowed to life.

One picked up the conference room adjacent to the office. "There you are, my complaining slut." He changed channels. Now all the monitors picked up the conference room. Spasms seized his right eyelid as he pressed another button.

Camille stopped pounding on the door. Hands hanging in midair, she looked up at the soundproofing shields descending, surrounding the interior of the conference room. She took a step back. Then another. And another. She rammed into the table and scoured the room for an escape route. Her eyes kept returning to the door through which she had entered, now a solid wall.

Jonathan cackled with anticipation. His thumb hovered over another button. Unable to stand it any longer, he jammed on the button and kept it down. "Complain about this, slut," he seethed.

A cover resembling a cable connection point lifted on the conference room wall like a sleepy eye. As a feathery appendage the size of a toothpick fondled the outside perimeter, Camille turned to stone. Fright widened her eyes. A second feathery appendage did the same. More appendages and then the torso of a feather leg baboon spiderling appeared. It acted like a sentry. Then another spiderling jostled the first spiderling out of the hole and scooted up the wall as the first spiderling plummeted to the floor. A silk filament stopped the freefall, allowing the first spiderling to drift down to the floor. Meanwhile, spiderlings spilled out the hole as if bursting from a cocoon. Dozens. Hundreds. Thousands. The hole vomited spiderlings. The lack of a web was no handicap for the feather leg baboons that fanned across ivory walls.

Camille was howling. Jonathan didn't have to turn up the volume to know that. Saliva lathered out the corner of his mouth as he sniggered, "Scream your guts out, my complaining Camille."

She scrambled onto a chair and tried to balance, but the chair overturned, and she splattered on the floor. Rolling to her feet, she clambered for a corner. She glanced over her shoulder. A rogue wave of spiderlings was rolling toward her. She looked up. Another wave on the ceiling. She clawed along the wall to the next corner and then to the next. The rising tide of spider-lings changed direction and closed in on her. She turned and flattened into the last corner. Her fingers dug at her face.

"This makes shelling out big bucks for that conference room worth every last red cent," oozed Jonathan, indulging himself.

The feather leg baboon spiderlings, bred for killing, were straight out mean as chelicerae flipped out of their mouths like switchblades and jabbed Camille with venomous tips. Intensely painful, one jab wasn't necessarily deadly—yet so many, many jabs? The spiderlings preferred their prey alive but not squirm-ing while partaking in the juice of life; however, in this case the competition was so great that not one spiderling was about to stop to wrap up Camille. All too soon, it was all over, and Jonathan was lying on the floor of his office. Having no clue as to how he ended up there, he zipped up. "Fewer spiders next time," he mused. "Prolong the pleasure. What happened to the remote? " He looked for the remote. It was on the floor a short distance away. "How did it end up there?" He rolled onto his belly and slithered to the remote. Fingering the buttons, he glanced up at the monitors. He heaved a sigh and jabbed a button. Sitting up, he watched insecticide cloud the conference room and the ensuing deluge of feather leg baboon spiderlings. "If Camille isn't dead from spider venom," he grunted, "she is now." He studied the carnage. "Pathetic. Truly a waste of elegant creatures." He picked up the remote and got to his feet. A press of another button retracted the conference room floor. Death plummeted two levels where devices sensed the added weight in a cart and activated the tracks. The cart moved into a crematorium at the center of that level.

"I must remember to fire up the furnace at midnight," muttered Jonathan. His mouth gaped into a yawn. "No, I shall do it now before fatigue causes inattention. Camille Jennes must not stink up Granite Mountain another moment. This late in the day, telltale smoke is hardly observable after traveling through three thousand feet of frigid granite-lined pipe. Less smoke than the smallest campfire." He pressed a button. Flames erupted inside the crematorium. Turning to the monitors, he pressed another button and watched the soundproofing shield in the conference room roll up out of sight while the sides of the floor coupled. The conference room was back to normal—except for furniture. He pulled out the keyboard attached to his desk and typed an e-mail:

Alice. I have grown tired of the furniture in the conference room and

disposed of it. Assign Bert to acquire additional furnishings. Make

it Middle Eastern design. - J. A.

The next morning, Jonathan made a point of being on campus as students headed for classes. Running into Joe Ault was no accident. The sweetest smile plastered his puss as his hand clamped Joe's arm. "A moment, Mr. Ault?"

Joe gawked at the fingers goring his arm. His mouth flopped open. Confusion riddled his face as he shot a look at Jonathan.

"That Camille Jennes," said Jonathan lightly. "She has a flair for dramatics."

"Ain't that a fact," blustered Joe, tugging on his arm. "She's come up missing, you know."

Towing Joe along, Jonathan said in low, ominous voice, "You demonstrate to me, spiderling Ault, and to peers and fellow radicals, that you are a model for urban terror."

A grin plastered his face as Joe loosened up and fell into stride with Jonathan. "Sweet," tooted the young thug.

Jonathan yanked Joe around to face him. Spasms seized his right eyelid. "But, spiderling Ault, you serve nobody's interest but your own. You are competitive to the extreme, self-centered to a fault, morals of a snake in the grass. You wouldn't know loyalty if it smacked you in the face. You downed Camille too much, too often. You know it. I know it. You deserve to take the heat."

"Heat?" blustered Joe, sticking out his chin in defiance. "For what?"

Jonathan's manicured nails penetrated Ault's arm.

"Ow!"

"Your sex toy came to me."

"I'm gonna kill that..."

"Do not waste another moment on the thought," cut in Jonathan. "The problem has been eradicated."

"Eradicated?"

Jonathan pulled Ault close then whispered a syrupy warning, "Another irritation like that and your sorry ass will also be eradicated."

Chapter 12

*A*utumn smeared scarlet, acid-yellow, and rust upon the face of Granite Mountain. "I've never seen so many leaves!" exclaimed Katrina, raising her hands to the sky and spinning around. "It's raining leaves!" She waded through a huge pile then turned and jumped into the middle.

"Hey!" shouted a perturbed landscaper. "What do you think you're doing?"

Burning leaves and woodstoves sweetened the chill like no other place or time of year. Smoke pirouetted out chimneys and sashayed across the countryside as starlings, crows, sparrows, and wedges of geese spackled an ever-earlier dusk. Forsaking ice-laced habitats, they steered by the sun, moon, and stars, by church spires, covered bridges, and courthouses. The promise of a distant summer beckoned. Bears fed on apples, acorns, berries, beechnuts, and honey, until accumulating ample fat to sustain them through winter dormancy. The circle of life, so full of wonder, awed Katrina, which led her to question the existence of evil on Granite Mountain. Nevertheless, she had put two and two together—Meredith and Jonathan were the ringleaders of a web of deceit. Their modus operandi was similar to that Katrina had experienced in Judgment, Mississippi: ensnare kids who exhibited such traits as shyness, aggressiveness, moodiness, or cheerfulness and use them to catch the eyes and hearts of strangers—or better yet, targets. If cornered, kids used such traits to get out of suspicious circumstances. All had above aver-age I.Q. levels, but for some, indoctrination caused a sort of living on the edge, needing a command before putting one foot in front of the other. *If only I could inspire these kids to bloom as they were born to be,* Katrina mused. *But how to do that without raising suspicion? How to do that and protect me? I learned a hard lesson on that island: I'm not invincible. Gosh, it would be so easy to go home for Thanksgiving and not come back. But then what would happen to the kids? Brita? And Bert? No, I have to come back.*

So Katrina reinvented herself, becoming a trusted member of the Araneas' entourage. All the while, her photographic eye and keen sense of hearing recorded places and conversations for further analysis. She spent sleepless nights, fretting, *Why can't I come up with a plan to tear down this place? It boggles my mind that I'm caught up in terrorism again. Dad was right to freak. I can't trust anybody. I have to be wary of my surroundings, be ready to strike out at anybody who intends to do me either physical or mental harm.* Without family, friends, Doctor Edie, the burden weighed heavy. Katrina had no break from the tension and isolation, no way to get concerns off her chest. Dull headaches nagged her at times. Exercise relieved them. The latest round of pushups and sit-ups topped out at eighty each. She knew full well that a quick exit required both physical and mental acuity. *The last thing I need is to get lost in the woods.* So she volunteered for trail projects and expeditions, which gave a good cover to study the lay of the land and refine outdoor skills. As insurance for hiding the cotton in her ears while on campus, she added a madras bandana to her uniform. *If it works, I'll turn Brita onto the idea. She has a right to know about the background music and protect herself. Her hair is so short, only a bandana or headband will hide cotton in her ears. But the guys won't wear bandanas—headbands maybe.* All the conniving turned out for naught, because the instant Katrina stepped into Mr. O'Mara's class, he snapped, "Take off that bandana! Personal touches to uniforms are strictly forbidden!" So the bandana remained in her pocket— except in the dorm.

One day, Alice, in her usual inebriated state, burst in, blasting, "Impromptu meeting in the caf'! Hey, freak! What's that on your head?"

"Nana 'Lizbeth gave this bandana to me for good luck," said Katrina.

"Sh-yeah right," slushed Alice, grappling for the bandana. "No such thing as good luck around this place."

Katrina quelled her first instinct to deflect Alice. *I have to befriend everybody—even Alice. Brainwashing made her the way she is. It's not her fault.*

"This thing's older than the hills," muttered Alice, fingering the bandana.

"Nana 'Lizbeth wore it in the 60s," said Katrina, taking off the bandana and handing it to Alice.

"Nana 'Lizbeth," murmured Alice, holding the bandana as if it were a newborn baby.

"I adore the colors, don't you?" prodded Katrina.

Deep thought consumed Alice.

"I'll make one for you," offered Katrina.

Alice's left eye narrowed on Katrina.

"What kind of material do you like? I'll get some when I go home for Tha…"

"Stuff from home ain't allowed, punk!" spat Alice, hurling the bandana then stomping away.

Katrina caught the bandana. *Great, now Alice is going to squeal.*

Nothing ever came of the incident. And nobody objected to her wearing the butterfly barrette. *If they only knew how this barrette reminds me of Dad and all the good things in my life: Ralph, Addie, Mom, Toffee Castle; yet it also reminds me of the one I lost on that island. I have to get that out of my system. I have to clear my head of Bert in order to focus on destroying this place and others like it. Why didn't I listen to Brita when she warned me about him? Bet she won't listen to me either when I tell her that Granite Mountain is a terrorist recruiting and conversion cell. Wish I knew for sure if I can trust her. She and Vic are quite an item lately. And Vic's tight with Bert. If word gets out about my suspicions, who knows what will happen. I've been playing hard to get, but I really don't have to. Bert pays no attention to me. Although I have a sneaky suspicion that someday, he'll try to take advantage of me again. Well, I'll be ready for him, and whatever the price, it's worth it. I'll get him to open up about what he knows about Granite Mountain. What do I have to lose? My virginity?*

At lunch the next day, Katrina noticed Joe and Vic turn wary when Bert showed up. *They're afraid of him. Like Brita says, he's a pet around here. He controls the show more than anybody knows. He can't be trusted. Just like kids in Judgment. Nobody's friends. They come together for projects and activities with outstanding results, but friendship never enters the picture. Bet Brita isn't my friend either. I better keep my mouth shut for the time being. I'll talk it over with Doctor Edie when I go home. She'll know what to do, but problem is people in her position are required by law to report illegal activity. I can't let her to do that. I need to get more information about what's going on around here and to track down other places. Think I'll work on Brita from the brainpower angle, since that is highly regarded around here.* The perfect opportunity presented itself the next morning. Leaving Mr. O'Mara's class, Brita razzed, "Smarty pants. The way you're going, you'll be Student of the Month for September. How do you do it?"

"I sing," breezed Katrina. "It's a great way to boost intelligence."

Brita gave Katrina a sidelong squint. "I hear you sometimes, but not in class."

"I sing in my head," said Katrina. "Things I need to know I put in the song. I do better on tests that way. Plus it keeps out bad stuff. You should try it."

"You think?" asked Brita.

"If I get Student of the Month," said Katrina, "you can, too. What's your favorite song?"

Brita blew a bubble. The bubble popped. "Delilah."

Katrina raised her hands like a conductor and sang, "My, my, my Delilah…"

Brita gave a hearty laugh and then joined in.

From then on Katrina goaded Brita into singing. Other kids joined in. Mr. O'Mara also joined in, none the wiser.

Everybody fell for Katrina's schemes, especially the one using ear cleaner sticks to build a replica of Granite Mountain. Meredith and Jonathan were so impressed they ordered more ear cleaners. Concerns about janitors discovering scads sticks devoid of cotton in the trash vanished.

The first weekend in October, Bert, Joe, and Vic left for an encampment out west. Leadership, self-confidence, and physical training were on the agenda, but as far as Katrina was concerned, *Those guys are already too full of themselves.*

Named Outstanding Student for the Month of September, Katrina was ecstatic when Jonathan awarded her a two-year-old Siberian husky. The blue eyed spay, which Katrina named Mickey Blue Eyes, had black eyebrows that shaded to gray out to the tips of the ears. A gray and black v draped the husky's shoulders and a smaller v splashed the base of her tail. All-encompassing shakes created blizzards of white fur tinged with gray. However, the excited yapping known to the breed had been silenced by a laryngectomy. Food treats, which were like candy to the husky, made training easy and a great deal of fun. Yet leaving Mickey Blue Eyes alone in the dorm was out of the question. If Katrina did, upon returning, she would find toilet paper billowing out of the bathroom, drifting across beds, and cascading like waterfalls. *Some difference from sleepy old Ralph. I'll have to cage Mickey Blue Eyes in the kennel near the woods when we can't be together. Too bad…*

One other behavioral tic bothered Katrina to no end— Mickey Blue Eyes went berserk whenever the Araneas arrived on the scene. The first time it happened, Katrina and the husky were stretched out on the grass beneath the hundred year oak near the Administration Building. It was so quiet. All of a sudden, Mickey Blue Eyes jumped up like a crazed wolf! From then on, Katrina kept a lookout for the Araneas.

Students of the Month were equipped with short wave radios and given free reign; so with a four-legged friend adding to self-preservation, Katrina scoped out escape routes during free times and weekends. The only option was Route 302 west then Route 93 south. She eliminated going east, since she had never been further than Jackson—and that was with Bert for ice cream. Those times, she saw nothing but him.

With eye to compass and map, Katrina mentally recorded

the lay of the land, man-made and natural forms, bridges, roads, streams, mountains, and insignificant landmarks. She came to know the land inside and out; and the mountains got into her blood. The solitude cleared her head, energized her, and erased problematic humanity for a time, which helped her to face mounting uncertainties.

Snow wasn't remotely in the forecast, so Katrina modified a dogsled into a wagon. While honing skills as a sled driver, she built stamina for long distance running, crossing streams and logs, climbing and descending steep grades, and practicing sled repairs. Not wanting her location known at all times, she fabricated complaints about the short wave radio being full of static, which garbled and broke transmissions. The day she spotted the first transfer tower disguised as a white pine atop Granite Mountain, she stared at it, hands on hips. *Disabling that tower might help me escape, but how in the world do I do that?*

Mickey Blue Eyes panted.

"So you agree the situation looks bleak," said Katrina, scanning the landscape. "Hey, look! Over there! An overgrown logging road! Let's see where it goes. Mush."

The packed dirt road snaked through the woods and ended at a natural-looking blind. "This is man-made," she whispered while stepping along the blind. She tugged on a branch. Nothing happened. Going to another branch, she walked into a spider web. Brushing it off her face, she carped, "Creepy, ugly spiders!"

At the end of the blind, she tugged on a thick, jagged bow. The entire blind jiggled. She scrutinized the construction then took hold of the bow again and pulled with all her might. The blind pivoted like a door and knocked her down. She gawked at the other side of the blind. "That's Route 302—the road Dad uses to bring me to Granite Mountain!"

Mickey Blue Eyes licked her face.

"We just found our first escape route, girl." She got to her feet and while brushing woodsy debris off her clothes, heard the whir of tires on pavement. She yanked the husky and the wagon off to the side, shoved the blind back into place, and ducked.

With an arm slung over the husky, Katrina waited. The whir of tires passed. All got quiet.

Standing up, Katrina studied the connection between the blind and the indistinct logging road that disappeared into the woods. "Somebody built this blind to conceal this road."

A rustling noise spun her around. "Who's there?" Unable to pin down the origin, she imagined one of Alice's monsters stalking her. She glanced at Mickey Blue Eyes. "Not terribly bothered, are you?" She shook out her wrists. "Must be a squirrel." She glanced at her watch and then at the sky. "Getting dark. And we're way out here in the middle of nowhere. The logging road will have to wait. Let's get back to campus."

Days later, Katrina and a group of other students were hiking the Webster Cliff Trail on the way to a two-night campout on Twin Mountain. *I've never been this far west on foot,* she thought while breathing in the frosty morning. Still, the temperature was unseasonably high. Daylight had shrunk to less than twelve hours, so sunrise hadn't come yet to the west side of Granite Mountain and wouldn't until after 10 A.M. She pulled her knitted cap down over her ears, thinking, *How utterly ironic: having to cover up my ears, even though cotton's not in them.* She glanced at Brita who was peering into the dark hollow beneath an overhanging boulder, a part of Bugle Cliff that blocked the right half of the Webster Cliff Trail. *Now's the time to tell her the truth about Granite Mountain. Let chips fall where they may.* She sucked in a deep breath and exhaled, "Brita, I..."

"Bears eat leaves and pine needles," cut in Brita. "Even their own fur. It all passes through their digestive tracts and forms anal plugs, so they don't poop until spring."

"Eew, groshe," sloshed Alice, stumbling up the trail.

"It's true," claimed Brita, her chin tipping up. "Vic told me so."

"Vic told me so," sneered Alice, weaving back and forth.

Katrina latched onto Alice's arm. "Watch out!"

"Wha'?" slushed Alice, inches from Katrina's face.

Waving off the stink of stale alcohol, Katrina said, "You really should lay off the J.D. You might fall and hurt yourself."

"Join AA or some'in?" snorted Alice.

"AA helps lots of people," said Katrina.

Alice made a sloppy effort at freeing her arm, spluttering, "Fat chance! Been fuelin' on 'skey sinsh I'sh tirteen." She shoved Katrina into Brita then fished a nip out of her jacket pocket.

"Look," said Katrina, regaining equilibrium. "I just want you to know it's never too late to find you."

"Yak, yak," scoffed Alice while twisting the cap off the nip. She swilled down the contents and belched. "Find yersef, mish bishy-bwody. Ish none-ah yah freakin' beeshwaxsh!"

Katrina jammed her hands into her hips. "Saying stuff like that is hurtful, you know!"

Alice made a face and wagged her tongue.

"You are by far the nastiest person in the whole wide world," exploded Brita.

Alice waved her off.

Katrina shook her index finger at Alice. "This isn't any way to make friends."

"Friends in thish godforshaken plash?" slushed Alice.

"Brita and I are friends," said Katrina. "Aren't we, Brita?" Getting no response, she glanced at Brita who seemed to be avoiding eye contact while blowing a pink bubble that instantly solidified in the frigid air. Katrina felt as though she had been kicked in the stomach. She dropped her hands from her hips. "Brita?"

Brita rolled her eyes and puffed, "Sure."

Alice snorted. "Where'sha cheeshy bandana?"

Katrina lifted her jacket and dug her hand into a pocket of her cargo pants. "Here," she said, yanking out the bandana like a magician does a string of handkerchiefs. "This is yours if you promise to be nice and not drink."

Surprise blanketed Alice. She thought over the offer. Then she spat, "Up yours!"

"That drunk's not about to change her ways," scowled Brita, shaking her head.

Alice got in Brita's face. "I can quit whenever I want to!"

Brita pushed back with sadistic pleasure. "You're too stupid to quit. Face it. You ain't never gonna amount to nothing!"

Alice took a quick step back. Her face turned ashen as her mouth dropped open.

"Brita," chastised Katrina. "That's a terrible thing to say!"

Alice sent Katrina an odd look. Her right hand shot into the air as though taking an oath. "Swear I'll quit when the time is right!"

Call it instinct; call it a hunch, but Katrina sensed a deeper meaning to that oath and Alice's decisive nod. *A hint of alliance? Friendship?* She watched Alice wobble up the trail, her head echoed with "friends in thish godforshaken plash?"

"A black bear must be hibernating in here," said Brita, once again peering into the dark hollow beneath the overhanging boulder. "The dirt's disturbed here and that's bear dung over there on the ground."

"If a bear's in there," said Katrina, rubbing her arms, "I hope it's hibernating."

Brita shifted back to a safe distance. "Cubs are born in January or February," she said. "They suckle on their warm mammas and by spring they're fuzz-balls. That's when you really have to watch out. Mama bears get mean, even when you're not close."

Katrina drew a shuddering breath. "Something I've been meaning to tell you…"

"Mama bears are mean in the caves, too," said Brita. "They only half sleep after their cubs are born." Then she sighed. "Gosh, I really miss Vic."

"Listen to me," said Katrina, grabbing Brita's arm. "This is important!"

"I have something important to tell you!" exclaimed Brita.

"What?" Katrina snapped, clutching her hat with both hands.

"Vic's really pissed off at Joe," said Brita.

"I noticed," huffed Katrina, pulling her hat down over her eyes.

Brita glanced around then in a low voice, said, "Joe came on to me."

Katrina lifted her hat and peered at Brita.

"He's so strong," groaned Brita, waving her head. "No matter what I did, I couldn't stop him. He even ripped my blouse!"

"When?" asked Katrina, her hands sagging to her sides.

"The night before Vic, Bert, and Joe left," said Brita.

"Why didn't you tell me?" demanded Katrina, palms gesturing.

Brita shrugged. "He was about to…well, you know, but Vic showed up and punched out his lights."

Katrina crossed her arms over her chest. "Guys around here think girls are meat!"

"Don't worry," said Brita, her hand fluttering. "Vic's gonna get back at Joe."

"He is?" asked Katrina.

Brita nodded. A smug look plastered her face. "You know, it's Joe's fault Camille ran off."

"I feel sorry for Camille," said Katrina. "Always daydreaming over those foolish decorating magazines."

"Those two have the most awful knock down, dirty fights," said Brita, starting up the trail.

Katrina plucked a handful of pine needles off a tree. Traipsing after Brita, she said, "Camille says she's going to wear white gloves someday and use lace doilies on her table."

"But she never sits down to eat," said Brita. "All she eats is jelly sandwiches."

Casting off one pine needle after another, Katrina wondered, *Should I reveal how I double check everything I put into my mouth? Even food is suspect on Granite Mountain.*

"Camille's not one for the wilderness," said Brita. "That's a fact."

"She says that's true of all fine ladies," said Katrina, tossing away the remaining pine needles.

"Well, I'm sure fine ladies don't ever complain as much as she does," said Brita.

"Can't argue that," muttered Katrina, trying to rub pine pitch off her hands. "But I have a hunch that Camille's a lot more intelligent than she lets on."

"You think she wants us to misjudge her?" Brita asked.

Katrina shrugged. "Maybe she's not worried one way or the other what we think. Maybe to her grace is more important than smarts."

"Grace is it?" puffed Brita. "Well, at least she finally got up the guts to stand up to that scumbag, Joe Ault."

Katrina stopped in her tracks. "She stood up to Joe?"

Brita nodded.

"But he can take Camille with his pinkie finger," cried Katrina, scurrying after Brita, "and his other hand tied behind his back!"

"Nobody knows that better than Camille," said Brita. "She did it in a round about sort of way. She went to Jonathan."

"Jonathan?" echoed Katrina, catching on that Brita called Jonathan by his first name.

"She told me she was going to get Jonathan on Joe's case," said Brita. "Don't know if she did or not. Never saw her after that. Maybe Joe and her made up and went to that same island you and Bert faked getting stranded on. After they did it, they had it out just like you and Bert, and she said that's it and ran off."

"Bert and I didn't…" stammered Katrina.

Brita butted in, "Vic punched out a tree 'cause of that trip. He's still pissed off about it. I swear, sometimes his temper is as bad as Joe's."

Katrina coughed. *Wish I could tell her how Vic blows his top whenever I brush him off, but I'm not about to upset her like that day on the dock. It took forever to smooth things out after that.*

"Vic's hand was all swelled up when he showed up at the campsite that night," said Brita. "When I told him you and Bert got lost, boy, did he get pissed! He punched out a tree with his other hand. Know what? Remember how you said we haven't kissed yet?"

"Gosh, Brita," said Katrina. "I was such a rat to say that. I'm so sor…"

Brita broke in, "Vic and I went all the way that night—have been ever since."

Katrina gasped.

Brita nodded. "He says mature people show how much they mean to each other that way."

Katrina covered her mouth as those same words sprang from the blurry memory of that night on that island. *Both Vic and Bert took advantage of me? Then Vic took advantage of Brita the same night? Are they planning to use it against us? Wait a minute. Vic and Bert and the Araneas are in cahoots. Gosh, now more than ever, I have to warn Brita.* Wringing her hands, Katrina ventured, "Know how I wear my hair all the time?"

Brita kicked the ground. "It'll be years before mine's long enough to fix like yours."

"I fix it this way," said Katrina, "because the background music…"

"Ish," Brita winced. "Isn't that music the worst?"

"It's more than that," said Katrina. "That music is a way to…"

"Help!"

"That sounds like Chas!" cried Katrina. She sprinted toward the clamor. Bulldozing through campers, she found Chas plopped in a dry streambed and holding his foot below a blood-ied ankle. Mickey Blue Eyes was buzzing around him, panting like crazy.

"I dropped my candy bar in the water," Chas sniveled. He had the dumbest look on his face. "And when I tried to get it, that moose over there came at me, and I tried to run, and I…"

Katrina squinted at two female moose chewing their cuds. *Humph,* she thought. *They don't look at all bothered.*

Brita snickered. "I'll report in." Planting the radio handset against her ear, she meandered away as other campers headed west.

Katrina swung her backpack off her shoulder and squatted down to get the first aid kit out of one of the pockets.

"Don't trust anybody with your secrets," whispered Chas. "Not even Brita!"

Meeting his soulful eyes, she said, "You're not jealous of Brita…"

He smiled thinly. "You're the only one who treats me like a person."

"You can't have me all to yourself," she said while taking antibacterial lotion and a package of gauze out of the first aid kit.

His finger wormed into his ear and wiggled. "I know, but I heard you about to tell Brita something, and I know what it is."

Sloughing him off, she said, "You're imagination's running away with you."

He leaned toward her and whispered, "You was about to spill your guts about being kidnapped."

She fell back on her ankles. "H-how…"

"I heard you tell Bert," he said.

She swallowed hard. "It's not polite to eavesdrop."

He bowed his head.

"You've got to stop this habit of hanging back a safe distance and spying on everybody," she said.

"But I have to protect you," he said.

She bent to patch up his ankle. *If what he says is true,* she thought, *I should be thankful I've earned his trust.* "So you've been following me?"

"They're sending somebody to take the village idiot back to the infirmary," hollered Brita.

Chas grabbed Katrina's wrists. "Don't let them take me, Katrina!"

She narrowed an eye on him. "You called me Katrina, not Kitty."

His grip tightened as he whined, "Please, Katrina!"

"You need to have that ankle looked at," she said.

"No, no," he slobbered. "I did this to myself! I had to stop you from telling Brita your secrets! I can walk! Please, Katrina! Don't let the hounds take me back!"

She squinted at Brita chatting on the radio and then back at Chas. *Is it inherent curiosity that makes him follow me,* she wondered, *or is it something else?*

"Please," he pleaded.

"Hey, Brita," yelled Katrina.

"Yeah?" hollered Brita.

"Chas is okay. Tell them not to send anybody."

"Oh, for crying out loud," roared Brita.

As Katrina packed up the first aid kit, Chas took a candy bar out of his pocket. She eyeballed it, and he offered it to her. She shook her head, saying, "That much sugar isn't good for the body or the mind."

"Plus high sugar diets attract mosquitoes," he said, glancing around. "No skeeters in this cold."

"Stop kidding around," she said, weaving her arms into her backpack.

"Only if you promise not to tell anybody around here about your past and what you know about Granite Mountain," he said.

"Only if from now on you only eat stuff that's good for you," she countered.

He nodded and held out the candy bar.

She looked down at his hand and then at him. "Okay," she said, taking the candy bar. She stuffed it into her pocket as his hand slid into his left pocket and came out with two more candy bars. He offered them to her. After she took them, he took a package of chocolate chip cookies out of his right pocket. An assortment of other sweets came out of other pockets. He handed over so many sweets that she was running out of places to put all of it. She couldn't help cracking a smile. "That it?" she asked.

He nodded.

"Now," she said, helping him to his feet, "I want you to break out of that cocoon you're in and show yourself. You act like you have a sign around you neck with big red letters, 'Beat me up and I'll let you get away with it.' Kids pick up on the way you act like animals smelling prey."

A petrified look enveloped him.

"Look," she said, tugging him along. "There's always going to be people out to hurt you or take advantage of you, stuff like that. What you have to do is be careful who you trust. But you have to know yourself first."

"But I-I don't know how," he whimpered, faking a limp.

"The key is to block out everything else," she said. "Focus."

"On what?" he asked.

"On what's good for Chas Riley," she said.

"But," he stammered, "I don't know what that is."

"Well," she said. "Do you like to build stuff, run like an Olympic athlete, write stories?"

In a voice not more than a hoarse whisper, he said, "I make up songs."

"You write songs?" she asked.

"Well," he mumbled, looking around to see if anybody was in hearing range. "I don't write them down."

"Gee," she said, "I never hear you sing."

"I'm afraid," he said.

"Afraid?" she asked.

His entire body convulsed. "I'm afraid to write down words, too. They might catch me and they'd…"

Supporting his small frame, she said, "It's okay. I know how that feels. Tell you what, write down your songs and give them to me. I'll bring them home and keep them safe and sound until you want them back. Just let the creative juices flow. It's a great emotional outlet, a way of getting stuff off your chest. I'm a firm believer that certain music brings about violence; other kinds dismantle violence. Do it for yourself. Make yourself feel happy, just like you let yourself feel sad or afraid. Sing me one of your songs."

"I can't," he said.

"There's nothing you can't do," she said.

⌣

The long shadows of dusk stared them in the face as they passed the Mount Washington Hotel. *Wonder if Dad's really going to take us there for vacation next year,* Katrina mused.

By this time, Chas had no problem, keeping pace. They caught up to other students at a gas and convenience station. After purchasing refreshments, which preserved packed supplies, Katrina followed him to the grass on the left side of the store. Spying a telephone on the outside wall, she calculated, *The distance from Granite Mountain to that phone is about ten miles. Sure would be nice to call home right now.* She tossed her backpack and followed it to the ground.

A short while later, Brita slithered up next to Katrina and toyed with a wayward blond spiral. "Wish I could do stuff to my hair like you do to yours," said Brita. "Mine's too short."

"I'll help you do something different when we get back to the dorm," said Katrina.

"So," said Brita, "you wanted to tell me something?"

Every nerve in her body went numb as Katrina glanced at Chas. *He's more interested in the taste of that apple he just bought than anything else.* But then Chas stuck his finger in his ear and wiggled it, sending Katrina a glance that suggested she fudge the truth.

"You gave in to Bert on that island, huh?" whispered Brita, her eyebrows jiggling.

Katrina pursed her lips and sat up. She tightened shoelaces that didn't need tightening.

"Your secret's safe with me," said Brita.

Katrina rubbed her palms together as if unable to get off grime. "I-I, uhm... Hey! How about a round of Delilah?" She raised her hands and signaled for others to sing along. "My, my, my Delilah...." She glanced with Chas. A thin smile wrinkled his lips. Then he began to sing.

Chapter 13

*C*urt's to do list was immense, but the holidays were right around the corner and Penny requested his participation. He tried to keep his head on traditional matters, but a closed-door meeting with higher-ups that related to the aerial reconnaissance of Granite Mountain hadn't gone well. "A plume of steam coming out the peak," General Colin Thornton had echoed. *Rather blandly,* thought Curt, recalling the General's powerful, patriarchal personality that had dominated the room.

Circling the conference table and placing copies of the intelligence summary in front of participants, Curt had noted the tension and strain etched into faces. He had noted the heavy silence. *No jokes. No bantering. No small talk. No thermal urns of coffee, bowls of sweetener, or creamer packets.* The situation pressed on him like a giant hand, so he spoke up. "Sensors picked up heat loss at lower points surrounding the mountain. In all probability, the heat comes from ventilation ducts."

Subordinates, heads bowed, stole glances amongst themselves. Thornton ignored the summary. Leaning back in his chair, he asked, "Any dwellings or individuals of interest observed at the sources?"

"Negative," replied Curt, though he was of a mind to add, *Somebody very special to me is in the area.*

Thornton picked lint off the hilly belly of his uniform. He brushed off his medals. "Geological or meteorological conditions may have generated it."

"Negative," replied Curt, "but…" Raising a copy of the intelligence summary to eyelevel, he tapped his right index finger on it. "…the major concern here is the possession of deadly chemical, biological, and nuclear weapons."

"The minor concern?" asked Thornton.

"A subterranean sleeper cell similar to Judgment, Mississippi," said Curt while rolling out a diagram of Granite Mountain, "if that can be deemed minor."

Thornton braced his palms on the arms of his chair. His fingertips drummed. He heaved then leaned over the table and stared at the innards of the mountain. "Nothing indicates Judgment is, er, was part of any larger scheme."

"But Gen…" started Curt.

"Tell me this," cut in Thornton, sarcasm riddling his tone. "How on earth can anybody chop up and move that much granite without one set of eyes taking notice?"

Feeling as if cold water had been thrown in his face, Curt glanced around the room. Subordinates avoided his eyes. The summaries remained unopened. Baffled, he swallowed quite laboriously then resorted to the more emotional aspects to make his case. "The U.S. government cannot afford to wait for any enemy capable of world mass destruction to throw the first punch! Especially in these United States!"

Thornton fell against the back of his chair and guffawed. "Yeah. Especially in Cow Hampshire!" His hand slapped the arm of his chair. He had a jolly good time of it, but not so much as a peep from subordinates.

"The spook…what's the bloke's name…" stammered Curt. "Pomoroy…what's Pomoroy got to say?"

Thornton's gray-blue eyes hardened, giving Curt the long, hard stare characteristic to many generals: cold, steely, tight-lipped, a stare that seemed to bore through flesh of any who angered or disappointed.

Ah, I hit a nerve, Curt mused.

Thornton's fingertips drummed on the arms of his chair.

"We must stand this activity on its head," Curt spouted. "Eliminate it altogether. There is no choice in the matter. The money trail loops all the way back to Aranea's father, Mohammad Achmed al Hadi, whose assassination prompted the smuggling of his only survivor, a son, AKA Jonathan Aranea, into the U.S. The average observer may surmise that erudite writers, philosophers, and engineers produced by Granite Mountain College in the late 70s added the notoriety that fueled the expansion now pimpling the slopes of that inconsequential rise. Truthfully, Jonathan Aranea took the college to the next level. No history lecture divulges that fact. Surely the General recognizes that the stainless steel turbines perched atop roofs of those granite structures are peculiar indeed!" *Good God*, thought Curt at the time, *I spout off akin to Holt!*

Thornton heaved then rose to his feet. "I will take the matter under advisement."

"But General…" protested Curt.

"Gentlemen," said Thornton, "I have more pressing flap to attend to."

"Flap?" fumed Curt, his eyes stalking Thornton exiting the room with a briskness that belied sixty-two years. "This is outrageous!"

Subordinates scooped up intelligence summaries and crowded out the door. Several slid sidelong glimpses at Curt. *Something of which I am not privy goes on behind the scenes,* mused Curt. *Something bad—man-urinating-in-public bad. Why am I left out of the loop?* Depleted as used up tissue culture in a Petrie dish, he had picked up the remaining summaries. *A total waste of time and energy pulling these together.*

An hour later, the phone rang, and the voice on the other end said, "Don MacPhallon, FBI, D.C. Bureau."

Curt shoved back his chair, having all he could to stop himself from jumping up and snapping to attention.

"Until Robert Pomoroy gets word out, stand down," said MacPhallon, not one to stand on ceremony—no fluff, just straight to the point. "Stale communiqué indicates Pomoroy's run onto a New Mexican terrorist training camp, heretofore, unknown. Incommunicado since."

Curt was not about to make waves. *No, MacPhallon is a friend of Peter Blair, M'lady's father. Both Vietnam vets. MacPhallon, a tunnel specialist, was the last to see Pete before Pete came up MIA. MacPhallon was the one who located Pete years later. Both received the country's highest decorations for gallantry, heroism, and wounds inflicted. MacPhallon has held several high-level posts since, making him no stranger to Washington. He helped Pete to fill in pieces about Jake going to his death over a candy-colored clown. The consequences of MacPhallon getting back to Peter that I'm in Atlanta make me shudder. Old friendships rekindled? Lovely chats? Dinner at Mr. and Mrs. Ken Waters? No. Knock on the door, rattle the window, howl like a dog, but M'lady? You'll not be waltzing back into this chump's life. Penny is not deserving of it.*

So with his hands tied on the Granite Mountain matter, Curt tried to rid himself of the lugubrious mood he was in and do as Penny requested, focus on the holidays and the shindig she was hosting. Clad in a black three piece suit, white shirt, red tie splashed with holly, and black hose and shoes, he stood at the kitchen bar, mixing a Rob Roy in an old fashion glass. *The fake Christmas tree all a-twinkle and the red and green holiday decorations in every room are a bit much, considering that it isn't Thanksgiving yet, but Penny is known for enthusiastic holiday spirit—and it's not so bad seeing staff all dolled up. Feels a bit New Englandy amidst southern fare, drawl, and showers—instead of drifting snowflakes.* He slugged down some Rob Roy. The alcohol's thick heat spread down through his esophagus all the way to his stomach. He eavesdropped on a nearby conversation. Getting only a word here and there, he stepped closer.

"Numerous experiments claim subliminal persuasion is effective," said Nate who was dressed in a double-breasted, pinstriped, black suit, white shirt, and solid green tie. Curt couldn't recall Nate's last name, but his wife worked with Penny.

"The only real threat from subliminal messaging is the implications," said Penny, her left hand and the Cosmopolitan in it emphasized every word.

The wench looks smashing in that emerald silk frock, thought Curt. *Sweeps her slenderness like dawn across Camelot. Brings out her eyes. I must find a moment to speak to her about that.* He eyed her legs and green one-inch heels. *I say, quite lovely.*

She smiled at him.

Her eyes sparkle like the Queen's crystal.

She winked.

Flushing head to toe, he took a slug of Rob Roy.

She chuckled in that special way of hers then said, "Today's highly advanced technological research has uncovered much about human brain functioning, thus control comes easier. Many children immersed in today's culture of violence and decadence lack the moral base to resist."

Quite the intelligent wench, thought Curt, scratching behind his ear. *Always knew she was. Rather amazing, what. Never know what to expect. Strong. Not the least bit fragile. Her puckish nature keeps me moving. Yet that emerald ring on her finger burdens me with guilt. Known her too long not to have replaced it with a gold band.*

"What scares me the most," said Penny, "is that the medium for takeover is already in place—the television set—doing more than just entertaining in living rooms and bedrooms."

What good is knowledge of any sort if it is ignored, Curt felt like saying. Still put off about Thornton, the pompous cad, shelving Granite Mountain, Curt swilled down the rest of the Rob Roy on the way to the bar to mix another. About to swill down the next one, he stopped himself. *Slow it down a bit, Curt, ol' boy.* He took a sip then headed toward the balcony, intending to watch the rainy night pass over Atlanta. Halfway there, however, a different conversation caught his ear. "…he's a former top scientist in the Soviet biological weapons program," said Danielle Franks, biological expert for the CDC.

Curt stopped dead, ears pricked.

"He's warned us about the Soviets covert development of smallpox as a weapon in the 80s," said Danielle. Her red spikes made her a lot taller than her five-foot-five height dressed in an ankle length red gown.

"I expressed a similar concern last week," spoke up Curt, shoehorning into the edge of the conversational circle that instantly enlarged to include him. "Iraq, North Korea, Russia, and France have hidden supplies of it in violation of international rules." He checked himself from revealing his suspicions pertaining to Granite Mountain. Getting shot down again did not appeal to him.

"Reports indicate that Libya, Syria, and Iran also possess samples," added Leander Holt, who was wearing a white sport coat and shirt, red tie, and black pants and loafers.

"With major holes in the defense against biological attack," said Curt, "I urged vaccination of U.S. citizens and emergency preparations should an outbreak be detected."

Danielle put all her weight on one heel and commented, "Better safe than sorry."

"Not going to happen," said Curt. Taking a slug of Rob Roy, he noticed eyebrows lifting as if demanding substantiation. He eyed his glass that seemed to be habitually empty and said, "Army's top biological defense expert and director of USAM-RIID went off on me. Few vaccines or treatments are readily available to defend against germ weaponry."

"USAMRIID?" asked a familiar face that Curt just couldn't put a name to.

"Army's Medical Research Institute of Infectious Diseases in Fort Detrick, Maryland," explained Holt.

"The military's efforts," continued Curt, "to develop defenses against biological weapons are hampered by lack of money from Congress and lack of interest on the part of drug companies in the twenty or so medical products just waiting to go."

"Leaves serious holes in defending against the nerve poison botulinum toxin, plague bacteria, and viruses that cause brain infections," said Danielle.

"I am told USAMRIID is trying to fill those holes as best they can," said Curt, sarcasm tracing his voice.

"The lab has developed vaccine-like preventative treatments for the seven forms of deadly botulinum poison," said Danielle, "but there's no money to pull off full-scale production."

"Iraq acknowledged the production of thousands of gallons of toxin," said Holt. "Isn't anybody paying attention?"

"The very question I ask," said Curt. "All I get are shrugs and 'We're kind of helpless on that point.'"

"World Health Organization resolutions specify that small-pox virus stocks are supposed to be restricted to either the CDC in Atlanta or in the Russian city of Vector," said Danielle.

"That's what they'd like everybody to believe," said Holt.

"So life-saving break-throughs just languish in the lab," spat Danielle. "Even if drug companies offer help, getting the Food and Drug Administration to approve the production of large quantities of the vaccines will take years."

"Too much group-think," said Curt, scowling. "Much too much bloody group-think."

"Ignoring you, are they?" twittered Danielle.

"I'm afraid I've become a renegade, a troublemaker," ranted Curt. "Why, drug-resistant germs are on the rise in these United States! Forty percent of streptococcus pneumoniae strains are resistant to penicillin and erythromycin, causing meningitis, sinusitis, ear infections, and pneumonia."

"Supports the argument against unnecessary antibiotic use," said Danielle.

"Time and time again, we in public health have warned that," said Curt, "but is anyone out there listening? N-o-o-o! Doctors continue to prescribe antibiotics for bacterial infections that resemble viruses. Half of the hundred million antibiotic 'scripts each year—unnecessary. Vaccination is the only way to reduce illness and accordingly, the need for antibiotics. Something has to be done, but how to do that when nobody listens?"

Danielle lifted her glass. "To our resident doomsday prophet."

Uneasy laughter broke out as glasses clinked.

Curt saluted with his empty glass, his mind rumbling, *To the evil web ensnaring Granite Mountain, endangering New England and M'lady—so far away—and yet so bloody near.*

Chapter 14

*I*t's so hot!" Katrina carped while harnessing Mickey Blue Eyes to the converted wagon in front of the kennel. She swiped a bead of sweat off her upper lip then peeled off her down jacket and tossed it into the wagon.

The husky panted with anticipation and did the jig.

"Okay, girl. Hike."

The wagon shot westward into the woods where decomposing leaves and pinesap tainted the moisture-laden air. In the distance evergreens and white birch speckled the rock-crowned mountains, a scene resembling a black and white photograph with a touch of sepia. Twenty feet or so before the first fork in the trail, Katrina commanded, "Whoa."

Mickey Blue Eyes braked and glanced back at Katrina.

"Look at that stream," said Katrina, pointing to the right. "Following the streambed is a way to avoid detection." She dropped the reins and untied the hatchet from the side of the wagon. "Mickey sit, stay."

Fourteen paces into the woods, Katrina chopped a bow off a hemlock and let it lay where it fell. She chopped several others in the same manner here and there so as to not call attention to her work. *There, that's enough to build a blind if I need one. Wish I could come up with a plan to tear down the Araneas' evil empire.*

Back at the wagon, she stowed the hatchet then commanded, "Hike." Arriving at the first fork in the trail, she commanded, "Gee," and Mickey Blue Eyes veered right. They crossed the log bridge that Chas had helped Katrina to build over Webster Brook, and a short distance later, Katrina noticed mountain laurel bushes on the left. "There's a great place to hide supplies," she said. "Whoa." She squinted at her down jacket and two backpacks stowed in the basket of the converted wagon. "Think I'll leave off some stuff right now."

After consolidating supplies needed for the day into one backpack, she tossed it into the wagon. Extra supplies went into the other backpack. She rolled up the down jacket then tied it with string and slung it and the extra backpack over her shoulder. "Sit, stay," she commanded, stepping off the trail. At the base of the mountain laurel bushes, she squatted and dug through years of accumulated leaves and debris. With the backpack buried, she brushed her hands together and stood up. "Well, it's a start, but I'll need all kinds of stuff. A couple more backpacks, too." She glanced at Mickey Blue Eyes so attentive to her every move. "What do you say, girl?"

The husky wagged her tail, panting and pitching her head this way and that.

Just then, a branch snapped.

"Who's there?" she cried. The breeze whispered in the pines. "Is that you, Chas?" She glanced at Mickey Blue Eyes. The husky was unruffled. Katrina tucked her hands in her armpits and listened. A train thumped along the tracks that clung to the mountainside across Route 302. Its mournful whistle reminded her of Chas the day she patched up his bloody ankle. She could almost see his soulful eyes and hear his plea, "You're the only one who ever treated me like a person. I heard you tell Bert you got kidnapped when you was four. Don't trust anybody else with your secret. Don't tell you know what's going on." She stared at her wrists as if his hands were gripping them at that moment. "Don't let the hounds take me!" he had cried. "I did this to myself to stop you from telling Brita!"

Is his eavesdropping more than a habit, wondered Katrina. *Is he taking everything he sees and hears back to the Araneas? Is friendship, better food, and teaching him to block out evil going to bring him back to himself? Will he survive if I leave? Maybe I should take him with me. But what about Brita? Is friendship with her possible? Or is Chas right? And what am I going to do about Bert—the kingpin in the Araneas' web of deceit?* She grabbed the reigns and yelped, "Mush!"

Mickey Blue Eyes lurched forward. The front of the wagon jerked off the ground. The harness tore, freeing the husky as the wagon upended into the ditch. "Great. Just great," griped Katrina.

Mickey Blue Eyes shook from head to tail, hard. Her feet skipped off the ground.

Katrina peered skyward at the thin cloud layer dimming the sun. "I'm not going to waste this day." Snagging the leash in one hand, she swung the backpack over her shoulder with the other hand. "I'll come back for the wagon later." She signaled with the leash. "Hike."

Mickey Blue Eyes trotted ahead as Katrina settled into a pace that she knew built endurance. Just before the junction of the Webster Cliff Trail, the husky put nose to the ground and then darted off into low level hardwoods on the right. "If only to have a nose like that," muttered Katrina, stopping to check her compass. "Mickey knows exactly what animals have been here. Hmm, if the Araneas figure out that I'm trying to escape, they might try to cut me off at Webster Trail. It won't be wise to stop at the Ranger Station either. This might be the perfect place to scope out an alternate route." She charged after the husky. "That scent must be good enough to eat!"

They passed an out-of-the-way, weatherworn shelter and then the south side of a ridge. "Hey, look at that," yelped Katrina. "We found a moose yard! These trees are big enough to catch the snow and keep it from getting too deep for moose and deer to get stuck in yet spaced so there's running room from predators. The lack of snow makes it hard to tell if any have been here. Probably not. Deer and moose don't group until it snows a lot."

Mickey Blue Eyes got up on hind legs, front legs braced against a tree, and sniffed at a raw spot. "A deer ate the bark," said Katrina, fingering the spot. "Funny how animals survive." Her eyes traversed the trunk. "The top's been broken off in a storm."

Three branches spiked out, forming a sort of cradle. "Imagine a snow owl up there on a wintry day? Sitting on top of a dead mouse and keeping it warm until deciding it's time to eat?"

Mickey Blue Eyes dropped to the ground and was instantly hot on another scent.

"Did you know that deer and moose often travel miles to reach a traditional yard like this?" asked Katrina, walking the boundary of the yard. "Moose get bored after being in one place and after a while, leave. Deer are smarter. They stay put." She came to a steep embankment. To the right was what appeared to be an old logging road that disappeared up the mountain. "Wonder if that's the same road that ends at the blind beside Route 302? Nah, too far north. Let's see where it goes." Starting up the road, she glanced over her shoulder at the husky cowering at the furthest edge of the moose yard. Blue eyes pleaded to be excluded from the junket. Katrina slapped her thigh. "Come, Mickey Blue Eyes." Coaxing proved ineffective, so Katrina backtracked then clipped on the leash. With the first tug, paws dug into the earth, fangs glistened, and blue eyes iced. A second tug and the husky reared up, turning downright nasty—snarling, leaping about like a crazed kangaroo, head snapping side to side, and teeth chomping on the leash.

"What is the matter with you?" cried Katrina, shielding herself behind a tree. "Stop it!"

The husky was hearing nothing of it.

Katrina squinted at the road that seemed to be calling her. Glancing back at the husky, she said, "I have to find out where this road goes."

The dog raised her muzzle high in the air and howled an eerie protest.

"Okay, okay, I get the point," said Katrina. "You're turned off about going with me. Well, I'm not about to pretend I understand, not when slamming doors, car engines backfiring, or kids screeching don't bug you. Only the Araneas rile you up, and I don't blame you for that." She puffed herself up. "Okay. I'll go alone." Standing with authority, she pointed a finger and commanded, "Stop."

Mickey Blue Eyes pulled into herself. Worried blue eyes ping-ponged from Katrina to the road and then in the direction of the Academy.

"Lay down."

The husky flattened on the ground and whimpered.

Katrina squirmed out of the backpack then took out a reversible jacket and put it on, camouflage side out, red side in. She crammed the backpack beneath a hemlock then inched up to the husky and grabbed the leash. After securing the leash to the nearest tree, she stared at the husky. She offered her hand, and Mickey Blue Eyes licked it, tail thumping the ground and stirring up leaves. "Oh, gosh," moaned Katrina, dropping to one knee and hugging the husky. "I hate leaving you." She let go and roughed up the thick mane. "Be back before you know it." Heading up the road, she glanced back. *Poor dog. She looks worried sick.*

A quarter mile later, the road ended at a pile of brush. *This looks like that blind at Route 302. Those evergreen vines growing on it look like somebody planted them.*

Experience told Katrina which branch to pull. As she did, the pile opened toward her. On the other side was an entrance to a mineshaft cut out of a cliff. Her eyes followed the contours and crevasses up to where birch and pine saplings had taken root. She gawked at a fat squirrel complaining from a perch in a nearby oak and then the purple-tinged sky. *Rain. Soon.* She squinted into the dark mine entrance. *Stay away. I'm getting in way over my head.* She shook out her wrists and insecurity. *A window of opportunity stands before me. It needs to be opened.*

Motivated by the experience of being kidnapped and brainwashed not once, but twice, Katrina entered the mine. Several yards in, she spotted scanty tracks left in ground more rock than dirt. *Only a real heavy vehicle can dig into ground this hard.* The tracks ended at a granite wall. She fingered it, first to the left then to the right. She applied pressure to a natural-looking blemish. The ground vibrated as the wall retracted to the left. Before her stood a giant tube that resembled an ogre's throat. She took a quick step back, a mishmash of emotions tearing through her:

surprise, excitement, anxiety, fear, anger. She noticed a stairway to the right, narrow, almost inadequate, granite encased. *If I go down those stairs, there's no quick escape.* She peered over her shoulder. *It would be so easy to run.* She clenched her fists and eyed the stairway. *I have to do this!* Her heart raced. She took the first step down then the next and the next. Light faded into darkness. Feeling her way along, she heard the sound of footsteps—her own. She sat down and removed her hiking shoes, knotted the laces together, then slung the shoes over her left shoulder and continued. The darkness grew less dense. A pinpoint of light appeared and then a camera. She flattened against the wall and squinted at a door below the light. *How do I get past that camera and into that door? I could cover my head and run real fast.* She rubbed her hands up and down her arms against dankness and doubt. *Hope nobody's monitoring the camera. Worth a try.* She pulled the hood of her jacket over her head and face, careful not to impair her vision, and took a deep breath. *Okay. Here goes.* Making herself as small as possible, she charged down the stairs, yanked open the door, and ran inside. She took refuge behind a row of black metal cabinets and held her breath. Her lungs nearly burst as she listened. *Turbine fans. A bird's chirping! Background music.* She hummed "Mary's Song." *Subliminal messages are not going to put me into the Araneas' preferred state of mind.* She sucked in a breath. *E-e-w, smells like a rotten carcass!* Her nose twisted up as gooseflesh spiked up and down her arms. Peeking from beneath her hood, her eyes grew accustomed to the florescent lights. She was in a huge granite room confined by a low ceiling. Consoles lined the left wall. Tiny lights blinked red, yellow, green, blue, white. *This is a communication center.* The bird chirped. *What's a bird doing way down here?* She inched along the black metal cabinets to the end. The bird was in a cage hanging on the opposite wall near a huge steel door painted with huge red symbols. *Some sort of foreign language.*

Mounted over the door, a camera focused down. Another camera on the wall to the right above an archway focused on the door. Cables coursed along the wall and out the archway.

Telephone, fax, intercom, and camera lines. I've seen them before the times I tagged along with Dad on installations and servicing computers. The yellow ones are video. The red and white twists are audio. Not quite sure about the other ones. Where's all the information going? And to whom or what?

A grinding sound pulled her eyes to the steel door. *It's opening!* She ducked behind the cabinets. A technician in a white lab coat, staring at a clipboard, hurried out toward the archway. When he was gone she tiptoed to the closing door and squirreled a peek inside. Cold-looking technicians, also dressed in lab coats, were hustling about beneath florescent lights. *Who are all these people? What's that guy staring at behind that tinted window?* The hair on the back of her neck bristled. *There's Mr. O'Mara!* She covered her mouth. *And Meredith!*

The metal door clanked shut and latched. Katrina stared at it. Silence closed in on her. Pulling down her hood, she tiptoed to the archway and out onto a landing. She squinted up the narrow stairway then down. *The cables link into that main trunk line. From the size of it, there are hundreds of substations. I saw stations at camp and the Academy and dorm, but where are the rest? At the college? The police station? Hospital? Library? Gosh, this whole thing's a lot bigger than I thought.*

Voices pierced the silence. Her eyes widened. Slamming against granite, she shot a look down the stairs. *Jonathan's coming! Somebody else is with him!* The voices faded. She discovered she was barely breathing. Her heart thumped against her ribcage. She swallowed hard and pulled away from the wall. She crept down the stairs to the next landing. She stopped to listen. Fans hummed.

She entered another granite-lined room. Steel beams reinforced the low ceiling that had a crack running the length of it. Her thumb and index finger pinched her nose against the stink as she breathed through her mouth and scanned computer equipment and medical paraphernalia: microscopes, Petri dishes, glass tubes in racks, shelves stacked with boxes labeled gloves, hypodermic needles, masks. Rows of cages contained rats, monkeys, dogs, and other animals, sick, lathering at the mouth, flopped on their sides on the floors of their cages, panting final breaths. An apricot-colored miniature poodle convulsed and then was still. A rhesus monkey clinging to its baby spotted Katrina. Black eyes bulged as it emitted a perverted squeak and shrunk back.

Alarm raced through Katrina. *Don't screech mama monkey!*

The monkey pulled her baby close and hid her face against its head. Baby's arm swayed to and fro.

Katrina choked back vomit. *The baby is dead! The stink in the air is death!*

"Feed in technical and military data," boasted Jonathan, "and my latest plan and blam!"

Katrina crouched down.

"Cool!" hooted Joe Ault. "Total meltdown!"

Katrina inched along the row of wire mesh cages, peering through them as curious black Norway rats stretched up on hind legs and checked her out. *Norway rats aren't black*, she reminded herself, a ploy to defuse trepidation. *Their forefathers were, but years of breeding have produced smaller and more docile white rats.*

"Not only that," said Alice, "but biological or chemical agents will…"

Hey, there's Bert, thought Katrina. *And Vic, too! Those guys are supposed to be out west!*

The group passed and their voices got out of range. Katrina scanned the room. Seeing nobody, she scooted after them to an exit and another landing. She looked down a stairway. *Shoot, I lost them.* She crept down a level and into a long hallway with doors lining both sides. *What's behind these doors? Those tacky lapel stickers that everybody wears on campus are stuck to the doors.* "Hello! My name is ___" Alice Milton was hand-scrawled on the first sticker. Joe Ault was on the next. Then Timothy Aranea. *I thought he lived in Gorham!* The next two names were unfamiliar. Bert Moro was next. She fingered the scrawl, her mind filling with that mountain sunset with his arms wrapped about her. *Does he ever think about that? Think of me?* Then she thought of that island. She pursed her lips and stepped to the next door. *Vic*

Sag. She looked back at the doors. *Are any of these people worth the trouble of saving?* The sticker on the next door had been peeled off, but bits of it remained with the smudged letters C, A, M. Katrina stepped back, mouthing, *C-a-m...* Her eyes knifed the door. *Camille's in there? No, the tag's been ripped off! Camille isn't coming back!*

Katrina glanced over her right shoulder then her left. Her hand went toward the door handle. A door slammed. She gasped. *Voices! Footsteps! Coming down the same stairway I did! I gotta get out of here!* Racing down the hall, she heard Meredith and Mr. O'Mara laugh.

At the end of the hall, Katrina looked to the left. *More steel doors.* Central Storage was painted on the closest one. She bolted for it, but then Jonathan's voice came toward her. She spun around and raced to the steel door at the other end. As she flattened against it, cold transferred into her body. Pushing away, she spotted light seeping around the edges. "Yes," Mr. O'Mara gushed, "I agree wholeheartedly with the entire plan!"

Katrina shot a look over her shoulder. *They're closing in!* She squinted at the door handle.

"That you, O'Mara?" shouted Jonathan.

With nowhere to run, nowhere to hide, Katrina shoved down the handle and shouldered open the door.

"And me," hollered Meredith.

Daylight blinded Katrina as she stumbled out the door. She bashed her toe against an obstacle and flopped onto concrete. As the door handle clicked shut, she eyed the concrete wheel chock over which she had stumbled and then at the door she had exited. "Authorized Personnel Only" was painted on the door. *I'm in the parking garage near the Administration Building!* The door handle clicked. *They're coming!*

Rolling under the closest car, she scraped her elbow on the frame. She clenched her teeth against the pain as Meredith coughed. Two pairs of shoes passed. Footsteps faded. *Jonathan must've stayed inside.* Wary, Katrina inched out from beneath the car. Keeping low, she hustled between the cement wall and parked cars to the exit where an ice-cold cloudburst, which should have been snow this time of year, splattered her searing face. She looked up and parted her thirst-cracked lips. Her tongue spooned in moisture as lightning illuminated the near darkness. *A thunderstorm this time of year? Ridiculous.* She rubbed her elbow. *Oh, no! Mickey Blue Eyes!*

She stumbled into the woods and climbed against the storm's runoff, slipping and sliding. A misstep landed her in a rocky gully on all fours. She filled her lungs with air then dunked her face into the frigid white water and drank. She came up, lungs bursting for air. Shoving soggy blond spirals out of her face, she staggered to her feet. Her shoes, still wrapped around her neck, rammed her chest. She sat on a log and dragged her shoes off her neck. "I'm so tired," she groaned. Hopelessness loomed as she massaged her calf muscles. "I can do this!" she hollered. Collecting her wits, she put on her shoes, stretched out her legs, and stood up. She bent at the knees a couple times, listening to thunder rumbling to the east. *Rain's letting up.* As she set off, her water-logged shoes griped. *Oh for dry clothes and a warm bed.*

By the time Katrina got to Mickey Blue Eyes, it was misting. The dog leapt about, rasping—more frenzied than Fred Flintstone's Dino. "Settle down," hacked Katrina, her tortured lungs struggling for air.

Released from the tree, the dog tore the leash out of Katrina's hands and bounded downhill, eager for dryer quarters and supper. Katrina tried to keep up, but footing was tricky on the slick leaves and mud. Her feet slid out in front of her. She tumbled head over teakettle then slid on her butt into a boulder. She heaved like a locomotive. Her entire body seemed to be on fire. Bones and muscles cried out for mercy. Then Mickey Blue Eyes licked her face. "I'd appreciate it," said Katrina, "if you'd slow down!"

A pair of untied tan boots stepped into her vision. Thinking she was hallucinating, she looked up.

"You forgot this," said Chas, holding the backpack she had stashed under the hemlock.

"If I could feel my arms," she said, trying to find footing, "I'd hug you."

"Give me your radio," he said.

She fell back. "Radio?"

His hand jounced. "Hurry up! They're down at the kennel. They're waiting!"

She shook off pain and fatigue and took the short wave radio out of her jacket pocket. He grabbed it, smashed it on the ground, and stomped on it. "It got wrecked when you fell," he said, handing the remains to her.

"How lucky is that?" she said.

He snickered. "Let's get outta here."

"I can hardly lift my feet," she moaned.

He pulled her arm over his shoulder then hooked his arms under hers and set her on her feet.

"You're a lot stronger than you look," she said.

"Next time you go poking into Aranea's lair," he said, "close up the mine entrance so nobody knows you was there."

She winced. "Forgot about that."

"I took care of it," he said, "and your wagon's at the first fork in the trail near the kennel. It broke down there, remember?" He winked.

"Every time I turn around," she said, "you come to my rescue."

"Helps clear the conscience," he said.

"What did you say?" she asked.

"I...I..." he stammered, "...I was a real slime ball, uh... We're at the main trail. Here, lean against this tree." A stiff wind whistled through the trees as he retraced their steps about fifteen feet, stopped, and broke off a pine bow. After obliterating their footprints, he tossed the bow and a few others over their entrance to the trail.

"Why did you call yourself a slime ball?" she asked.

"No time now," he said in a near whisper.

Shoving hair out of her face, she leered at him. "We really have to talk."

"Later," he said.

"Promise?"

He nodded.

They rounded the thick, spruce-lined trail. The clearing was ahead, roiling in mist. Spotting Meredith, Bert, Joe, Vic, and Alice milling around the kennel, Katrina stopped in her tracks. Chas lost his grip on her.

Mickey Blue Eyes growled and sidled up to Katrina. Her eyes changed to red in the filtered darkness. Fangs glistened.

"Be cool," whispered Chas. Taking Katrina by the hand, he towed her at a slow, deliberate slog. "Those guys smell weakness like wolves after wounded deer."

"There they are!" hollered Alice, her index finger nailing the trio like a laser.

"Where in hell have you been?" screeched Meredith, all puffed up and looking like a riled grizzly on hind legs.

"Meredith's really mad," whispered Katrina.

"That surprises you after the discovery you just made? Surely you've put two and two together. Our Mrs. Aranea plays a vital part in recruiting and training future terrorists. You are an integral part of Jonathan's plan."

Katrina gawked at him.

"Here comes Bert," warned Chas.

"Look at you!" raved Bert, swinging Katrina up into his arms. "You're a mess! And your beautiful hair—it's a sloppy mass of pine needles and leaves!"

He's really worried, thought Katrina. *If not, he's a good actor.* She glanced at Chas for his take, but his head was bowed, and he remained silent.

"I want an explanation," demanded Meredith, "this instant!"

Mickey Blue Eyes lunged at Meredith.

Grabbing Joe's arm, Meredith put him between her and the husky.

Chas grabbed the leash and dug his heels into the ground, appearing to lack enough weight to control Mickey Blue Eyes. He circled a nearby tree and used it for leverage.

Meredith kept a wary eye on the husky while storming, "I'm waiting for that explanation!"

Chas hung his head. "We was hiking," he mumbled. "It rained real, real hard, so we ducked in a cave, and there was a wicked rumble." His hand wormed into his pocket and pulled out a granola bar. "Rocks and boulders caved in, so we had to dig our way out." His teeth tore off the wrapper and let it fall on the ground. "I can show you the place if you want me to. We should fix it up. It's a great refuge."

"Refuge, my butt," snorted Alice. "Kitty's knees are all messed up."

Katrina gawked at her muddied, blood-caked knees. The memory of tripping over the concrete chock in the parking garage accosted her. She looked into a sea of probing eyes. "Tripped over a rock," she said, "getting out of that cave."

"I don't know why this stunted pigmy's allowed to roam about," blasted Alice.

"*Pigmy* is a short person due to a racial trait," shot back Katrina. "Chas is physically well-proportion and is therefore a dwarf. Dwarfs are quite adept in the woods."

"Trina's fortunate Chas went with her today," added Bert.

"You should've radioed for help!" charged Meredith.

Katrina took the radio out of her jacket pocket. "I fell on it."

Meredith gawked at the remains of the radio, completely flustered. Katrina found that comical, but withheld reaction. She shot a look at Chas who kept his head down. *A real cool pretender all right.*

"You two are never to take off on your own again!" spewed Meredith. Her eyes knifed Bert. "You should've gone with Kitty! She is your charge!"

Katrina's eyes went wide and made contact with Bert's. *Charge?*

Horror sheeted over Bert. Alice and Joe sent each other side-long glances. Chas merely stared at the ground and mowed granola like a cow chews its cud. Meredith gagged on the realization she had let the cat out of the bag. The color drained from her face. Flailing her hands, she howled, "Back to the dorms! All of you! Out of my sight!"

Chapter 15

*I*t is getting to the point where seeing my wife turns the belly, Jonathan mused while observing Meredith on a monitor, inspecting the Boy's Dorm. *She has become stringy, not at all as firm and muscular as in younger days. She continues to be physically fit, true; however, that skin on her upper arms... ugh, how it flaps. And those small wrinkles in the bends of her elbows—dry, powdery, disgusting elbows. Her face is withering like a crabapple hanging from a tree in winter. Plastic surgery can correct such flaws, but that will not make her a teenager. I dare not even mention the idea. She would hit the ceiling. Meredith thinks she is perfection. Humph. At least she could shave her armpits and legs once in a while. Face and bikini waxing would also go a long way, too. What is this? Ault is in his cubicle? He should be in class. Well, well, well...*

Jonathan spent the next fifteen minutes staring at the monitor as Meredith and Joe Ault went at it hot and heavy. His turn-off of her was now complete. "The quest for the perfect person is a legend," he muttered. "Nonexistent outside the imagination."

〰

That night, Meredith crawled into bed and yanked up the covers. "Why is it so cold in here?"

Content that her nakedness was out of sight, Jonathan smiled. *Turning down the thermostat has worked.*

"But you and your eternal sterno can warm me up," she gurgled, flopping her cold arm across his chest. Her clammy body from which time had stolen suppleness made him cringe. Her mouth clamped onto his. Her spindly fingers slithered down to prop him up. Fending off a rush revulsion, he squeezed his eyes shut and fantasized about Katrina Waters. *Supple. Firm.* Meredith rolled on top of him. *This routine is well rehearsed: aging nakedness looming over me, her hand bringing herself to climax the same instant as I. As always, she rolls off to lay unabashedly naked to babble about Granite Mountain matters. After-play and cuddling never enters the picture. Ah, well, satisfaction. No ecstasy. Just satisfaction.* He opened his eyes to her pasty backside. As she reached for a bottle of Madeira wine on her end table, he looked away and stuffed a pillow against the headboard. Wedging himself up, he rested his head in the crook of his right arm. He heaved a collective sigh.

"Alice spotted our Miss Kitty picking the lock on the shed at the firing range," said Meredith, uncorking the bottle.

Listening to the wine spilling into two glasses, he visualized the contents of the shed: automatic weapons, shoulder-held missile launchers, domestic stagings, and shot-up mannequins— the quintessential American family splattered with fake *and not so fake* blood.

"Kitty did not cut and run," said Meredith, handing a brimming glass to him. She leaned against the cold headboard without pillow or blanket. After each gulp she smacked her lips. "Real gutsy now that she's got that mutt."

Jonathan took a sip of wine. "It is not by happenstance that grades have earned her that mutt," he gloated while staring at his reflection in the glass.

"She fell for the ruse, hook, line, and sinker," said Meredith, rolling her empty glass between her palms. "You had pegged her, all right."

He swallowed hard. *Oh, to peg that luscious blond.*

"Quite the inquisitive mind," said Meredith while reaching for the wine bottle.

"Minds like that are the easiest to convert," he said.

She offered the wine bottle to him.

He shook his head.

She shrugged one shoulder, filled her glass, and put the bottle back on her end table. "You have no concerns about her going home for Thanksgiving and not returning?"

"Everything she says and does indicates she belongs to us," he said. "Why risk sending up red flags by not allowing a home visit?"

Making a face that indicated agreement, Meredith raised her glass. "To another success story."

With an ingenuous upturn of the lip, he clinked her glass and said, "The day comes swiftly when my Miss Waters achieves spiderling status. I will then give her that special command that will turn mutt into predator."

"Fear never enters the picture when Kitty is presented with new situations," said Meredith.

"True," he said. "Security tapes reveal she has discovered the west entry to the warren."

"So that's why she returned so late the other day," said Meredith, rolling her eyes. "I should've known."

"Let her make all the discoveries she wishes," he said. "The music and other passive techniques are working. When she's completely under our control, I will send her and the mutt out, secure in the knowledge that if things get hot, one command will activate the mutt and thus insure fruition of the goal."

"Oh, to be there the first time she gives the command," said Meredith.

"I have studied the two from the office in the Administration Building," he said, picturing the husky trotting trimly at Katrina's heel, responding sweetly to strangers, always gentle. Their close relationship gave him goose bumps. "Both take training quite seriously."

"Quick learners," added Meredith. "Exceptionally bright."

Jonathan snorted. "Perhaps too bright." He took the last sip of wine then placed his empty glass on his end table. "I must put a tail on her when she goes home."

Meredith polished off the rest of her wine and set the glass on her end table. Lying on her side, she faced him. Her fingers scooted across his chest.

He got out of bed. "Training has failed to eradicate the mutt's hatred of me."

"Hates me, too," she puffed. "Went berserk yesterday when it spotted me. Snarling. Bristling. Like a wolf intent on ripping out my throat."

"Yet they perform as if whelped from the same womb," he said, heading into the bathroom.

"What do you have in mind for those two?" asked Meredith, rolling over to pour another glass of wine.

"An international company headquartered in the southern part of the state," said Jonathan, stepping up to the toilet. "Generates a billion dollars into the economy."

"Awesome target," she said. "Lots of people. Staggering losses."

"Four hundred million dollars in payroll," he said, studying urine streaming into the water and making bubbles. "Think of the economic impact."

"Don't forget about the fear factor," she added.

"Won't take much C 4 and nails strapped to the midget to do a lot of damage," he said. "Hmm, he has not reported Kitty's exploit into the warren. I must look into that."

"Don't you think the Georgia mission should go off first?" she asked.

He stepped away from the toilet and flushed it. "I am processing alternative plans that may enhance Georgia," he said while washing his hands. "Something during Laconia Motorcycle Week or the NASCAR races at NH International Speedway."

"Those happen too far into the future," she said.

He grunted. "One way or the other, it is time to bring my Kitty into the ranks."

"You're not alone when it comes to new ideas," said Meredith.

He grabbed a hand towel and stepped back. Wiping his hands, he considered his manliness in the mirror. *Getting gaunt. Can't recall the last time I ate. Humph. Meals have become so unimportant. Not healthy. Ah, well, health means nothing to a martyr.*

"What better way to put an entire nation—and entire world—into abject grief than to assassinate Pudge McCarthey?" she asked.

He squinted into the mirror. "The singer?"

"You got it," she crooned. "I put Leanne in touch with her father. A reunion is in the works. I suggest Kitty and that mutt accompany Leanne—correction, Annie—to insure the mission's success."

Jonathan pondered pretty little Leanne Thomas, AKA Annie Mast, daughter of Matt Thomas, stagehand for McCarthey. *It has long been suspected, though never proven, that Matt Thomas had something to do with the drug and alcohol overdose death of Leanne's mother, backup singer for McCarthey. Immediately after the funeral, Matt dropped Leanne off at Granite Mountain Academy like a hot potato and forgot about her. Always thinking ahead, I, Jonathan Aranea, brainwashed the sweet young thing and then took her. Graduated the Academy two years ago. Progressing quite nicely at Granite Mountain College. Hmm. My wife is not a lost cause after all. At least her brain remains in top form. I believe the trial assignment is at hand for my Student for the Month of September.*

Chapter 16

*M*orning, Emily, the Cat," said Curt upon entering his office the day before Thanksgiving. "Half a day then a four day break. Gonna miss me?"

The feline, lounging on a red folder that topped a mound of other paperwork, opened one sleepy eye in Curt's direction and issued an abbreviated meow. The eye closed and the cat curled into a ball, purring.

"My dear Miss Emily," said Curt, nudging aside the cat, "don't think for one minute you'll be lolling away the day. Get real like the rest of us have to." He set his first Styrofoam cup of coffee for the day on the desk and sat down. "Foolish paperwork never ends. Sick and tired of it."

Sick and tired of nights, too, raced through his mind. *Sick and tired of sleeping in fits and starts. Sick and tired of waking up to dreary days with Penny gone off to work and no M'Lady.*

Curt opened the red folder and scanned the summary: *The following documents were produced from a microchip attached to a jackknife belonging to Robert Pomoroy, Special Agent, FBI. Pomoroy "misplaced" the jackknife at a gas pump outside a New Hampshire convenience store located on Route 302 near the Mount Washington Hotel.*

Curt felt his throat close. He flipped through the documents and stopped at one entitled, Granite Mountain, New Hampshire. "What the bloody..." he sputtered. His jaw dropped. Blinking in disbelief, he sank back in his chair. "Aranea's got V-MADS?"

The acronym was not new to Curt. It stood for Vehicle-Mounted Active Denial System, nicknamed, the People Zapper, which harnessed high-powered electromagnetic microwaves into pulses of energy and when fired at the speed of light, vibrated water molecules under the skin causing the temperature to soar to one hundred thirty degrees within seconds. The target cooked like food in a microwave oven.

Curt gawked at Emily, the Cat, now sitting up. Her jaw gaped into a yawn so wide it was a wonder her jaw hinges didn't dislocate. Her mouth closed with a snap. She stood up, stretched, then climbed on top of the printer and proceeded to wash.

Curt picked up his coffee cup and took a sip. His thumbnail scored lines in the Styrofoam while he scanned the next document. "Aranea's stockpiled tunable laser guns," he muttered. "Bloody shame the like of Jonathan Aranea has gotten his grubby hands on them for nefarious exploitation. Lasers should benefit mankind—restore vision and such." He chugged down some more coffee, set the cup aside, and read the next document: *Jonathan Aranea is masking audible ELFs (extra-low frequency waves) in background music. Audible ELFs produce vibrato at a cycle-per-second range, which causes subjects to enter altered states of consciousness. The transfer from left to right brain releases body opiates, encephalin and beta-endorphins.* "It feels good, like opium," mumbled Curt. "Subjects lust after more—like watching the tube. Right-brain activity outnumbers left-brain activity by a ratio of two to one, hence, an altered state or trance. A beta-endorphin fix. Most sixteen-year-olds have spent more time in front of the tube than in school. The medium for takeover has arrived. An alpha-level, 1984 Orwellian world of glassy-eyed inhabitants who obey commercials. Buy, buy, buy."

He flipped to the next document. A snapshot was paper-clipped to the top right corner. He held it up for a better look at the naked teenager strapped to a chair in a stark white room. She was wired to an EEG machine.

Curt read the text: *Jonathan Aranea uses inaudible ELFs that are electromagnetic in nature and used in submarine communication.*

Aranea exposed subject in attached photograph, Brita Fry, alias Roberta Jeffrey, to ELFs. In less than ten seconds, he controlled her mental and physical functions. "Wonder who got close enough to get a picture like that," muttered Curt. "Pomoroy?"

He scanned the next page. "Just as I suspected, Aranea's gotten hold of smallpox virus, anthrax, and other biological weapons. He's even got the antidotes. Potassium iodide. Look at all this."

Curt leaned back in his chair, musing, *More people have died from smallpox than all wars and epidemics combined. Death typically occurs with massive hemorrhaging. Unlike anthrax and other biological weapons, smallpox is transmitted from person to person and kills a third of its victims. Quite the clever bloke that Aranea.*

Curt glanced at the snoring Emily, the Cat, draped across the printer. *Too bad Aranea's not on our side.* He got to his feet, intending to go to the Conference Room for a caffeine fix, but Leander Holt tramped into the office, bellyaching, "Got the FBI's assessment report on Granite Mountain."

"I take it you're not in agreement," said Curt.

Holt tossed the report on the desk. "See for yourself."

Curt scanned the cover page. His brows came together. Snapping up the report, he snorted, "This came out of a meeting that took place months ago! What's to be gleaned from it?"

"Background info, fingerprints," snorted Holt. "That's about all."

Curt flipped through the report, reading aloud in places and commenting. "*Self-sufficient environ exists within the stomach of Granite Mountain*—we already know that. *Aranea's official office is located above the main entrance of the Administration Building*—okay. *Private office located in underground. Access through key padded doors in campus buildings and a door in the parking garage marked Maintenance, Authorized Personnel Only.* Know all that. *Granite removed through main stairwell that connects to...*" He choked and took a step back as if a right hook had just caught his chin. "Why that pompous..."

"Huh?" belched Holt.

"Thornton," snapped Curt, his index finger jabbing the

report. "That scoundrel knew all along about this and baited me with it in hopes to brush me off."

Holt leaned close and read aloud, "*Granite removed through main stairwell that connects to missile silos that resemble mine entrances. Construction accomplished at night and blasting during thunderstorms.* How 'bout that?"

Curt continued to read. "*Jonathan Aranea, American name for the only surviving offspring of assassinated Mohammad Achmed al Hadi and family, smuggled as a teen into the United States via Canada by Timothy Aranea, aka Rashid al Sadun, protector—presently Headmaster of Granite Mountain Academy. Aranea graduated from a little known private school on the west side of Granite Mountain. Out-of-business for many years. No trace of owners. Building replaced by cottages used for Ecology Camp. Graduated valedictorian at Granite Mountain College. Self-proclaimed prophet. Inheritance and strong-arm gained Aranea control. Structures girdling mountain built from granite offloaded at night through structures that resemble overgrown mine shafts accessible by lanes resembling abandoned logging roads. Structures house businesses controlled by Aranea and provide concealed entry into subterranean complex. Aranea connected to foreign radical factions. Locals tuned out on Aranea's activities and therefore are suspected to be under his thumb.*"

"Holy mackerel," said Holt in barely a whisper. His hands scraped up and down his pant legs.

Curt read on. "*Aranea hand-picked well-rounded professors sympathetic to radical beliefs while others who were needed to advance his goals but didn't follow his vision were brainwashed into submission. Classrooms of both Academy and College consist of topmost achievers from schools all over the world. Most are suspected to be brainwash and infantile predation victims of the Araneas and carry mental activation buttons assuring loyalty and assistance.*"

"Everybody blends in," said Holt. "No smelly bums with straggly hair to attract attention. Totally visible. Hiding in plain sight."

"Potential political and economic implications are staggering," said Curt then read on. "*Meredith Blevins Aranea: Born and raised in Maine. Maine alumni, graduated third in her class. Director of ecology and engineering camps. Aids in the recruitment of elementary and junior high school students for terrorist activities."*

"Can you beat that?" said Holt.

"Aranea's an avid collector of spiders and other predatory insects," read Curt.

"Sick," hissed Holt. "And just like the spider, Aranea continually evolves. Lives almost anywhere it pleases. Can't stand spiders!"

"A bit edgy there, mate," said Curt.

Holt audibly shivered.

Curt read on. *"Security is lax. Dogs in dorms. Chosen students able to activate harmless-looking dogs into predators. Clandestine activity exploits technology, develops biological and chemical agents, and conditions youth for future terrorist activities. Conclusion: nonlethal activity. No response recommended."* Staring at that last line, highlighted in red, he reiterated, *"No response recommended."*

"Can you believe that?" yelped Holt.

Curt shook his head. An eerie feeling came over him as he reached for his coffee. "Something's missing from this picture." He took a sip and immediately bristled. He set down the cup, opened the desk drawer on his right, and yanked out a tissue in which he spat cold, acrid coffee. He balled up the tissue. "Coffee is stale as yesterday's news." He tossed the tissue into the trash as though playing basketball. "Time for fresh Joe." Heading out of the office, he held his hand over the trash can and let the cup drop.

"So?" asked Holt, trailing like a puppy dog.

Curt stopped, and Holt plowed into him. Curt eyeballed Holt, but wasn't seeing him. "Something's missing from this picture."

"Like what?" asked Holt.

"Think about it," said Curt. "Every time we open our mouths, we get blown off."

"Won't argue that," puffed Holt with a decisive nod. He pursed his lips.

"This time around," said Curt, "we keep suspicions under our hats."

"Good idea," said Holt, starting for the conference room.

Curt followed. "Thanks for that red folder. Aranea's more dangerous than we thought. How'd you manage to get your hands on it?"

"Red folder?" asked Holt.

"The one you left on my desk," said Curt.

"Wasn't me," said Holt, entering the conference room.

Curt stopped dead. "You didn't leave that red folder on my desk?"

"Nope," said Holt, turning back to Curt.

Curt eyeballed Holt. He cleared his throat. "I should've known better. You're not the sort to just drop off critical information."

"Critical information?" echoed Holt.

Curt scanned the conference room. It was empty. The television was off. In a low voice, he said, "Aranea got his grubby paws on V-MADS, ELFs, lasers, and biological weapons. Even has antidotes, potassium iodide, and such."

"Holy mackerel," whispered Holt. "The radiation-blocking pill!"

In the open kitchen area, Curt pulled a Styrofoam cup out of the wall dispenser and offered it to Holt.

Raising his palms, Holt shook his head. "None for me."

"So how did that folder get on my desk?" said Curt, holding the cup underneath the coffee spigot.

"Administrative booboo?" suggested Holt.

"I don't think so," said Curt, watching the stream of coffee fill his cup. He shut off the spigot and backed away. He took a sip and savored the freshness, pensive. He smacked his lips. "It wasn't any accident that folder showing up on my desk."

"Somebody has a lot more access to information than you and I," said Holt.

"And that somebody knows we're sniffing around," said Curt.

"*And* is way ahead of us!" spouted Holt, yanking a cup out of the dispenser and filling it with coffee.

"On the opposite spectrum, so to speak," said Curt. "However, I suspect that whoever left it has his hands tied—just like us."

"Probably figures the more people sniffing around from different angles will get the plug pulled on Granite Mountain," said Holt, pouring an inordinate amount of cream into his coffee.

"And that would be the end of the world for Thornton," grumbled Curt. "Thornton's into this for the glory." As he watched Holt shovel spoonful after spoonful of sugar into his coffee, *end of the world* echoed in his head. "Potassium iodide," he said. "The radiation-blocking pill. Aranea is up to a whole lot worse than Thornton thinks."

Holt nodded. "That's a go on that one."

"How about getting a layout of Granite Mountain—the entire area—fifty, no, a hundred mile radius?" asked Curt. "And photos of Aranea and his cohorts."

Between chugs of coffee, Holt asked, "Pictures of the kids?"

"Those, too," said Curt. "And see if you can get background on Brita Fry, alias Roberta Jeffrey."

"I'm on it," said Holt, tossing his empty cup into the trash and heading for the door.

"Holt!"

"Yeah," belched Holt, spinning around.

"Brochures of Granite Mountain Academy," added Curt. "College and summer camps, too."

"Gotcha," said Holt, holding up a hand as if firing a gun.

The red folder took over Curt's mind. Slowly it transformed into a red leaf clinging to a maple in autumn. His knuckles appeared, gripping a steering wheel. Ahead, through a windshield, a highway gently rose and fell curving through the most colorful and thickest forest on earth. *Oh, New Hampshire. Snow-capped mountains in winter. Whitest clouds on earth soaring against the most crystal blue sky. Snow sprinkling evergreens. How is it possible that Granite Mountain exists in M'Lady's neck of the woods?*

Chapter 17

*T*hanksgiving break couldn't come soon enough as far as Katrina was concerned. When it finally did, she hugged those she loved every chance she got and told them how much she had missed them.

In honor of her return, Ken, Julie, and Addie had decorated Toffee Castle inside and out. Imitation candles glowed in the windows, and turkey, spices, and apple and pumpkin pies perfumed the air inside and out.

As Ken set a fire crackling in the hearth, Katrina raced to her room and feasted on the lavender walls peppered with family portraits and snapshots of summer trips to the Cape, Maine, and Rhode Island, and skiing in Vermont. She took down her group picture taken at Spring Ecology Camp and chucked it facedown in the bottom drawer of her bureau. She bunched up her hair in a clip then soaked away Granite Mountain in a steamy, strawberry-scented bubble bath, listening to background sounds she used to take for granted. Her soul breathed anew. Donning her purple tee shirt with florescent yellow block letters rising like the sun on the front, Brighton Junior High School, Brighton, Massachusetts, she vowed, "I'm wearing this every moment, even when I go to bed—in my own bed!

With Ralph nestled against her, Katrina slept deeply, not for just a couple hours but the entire night. Upon awakening, it took a moment or two to realize she was safe and sound at home with family. She felt like joining the dust particles frolicking in the sunlight that slanted through transparent Priscilla curtains.

Katrina caught up on life's events that had passed her by, plus anything else that wasn't Granite Mountain or had the last name Aranea. A comedy show on TV made her laugh until Dad, Mom, and Addie thought she had gone bonkers. Televisions weren't abundant on Granite Mountain and those that were there were for show, switched on during the rare family weekend, sometimes for assignment groundwork. *What a contrast between Brighton and the hell I left behind on Granite Mountain. I'm so lucky. So blessed. Still I just can't leave the evil behind, let go, and truly enjoy being home. I have to do something to stop places like Granite Mountain from existing. It's not like I'm a first-timer. That gives me some ability to putting an end to the brainwashing and training of kids to do the despicable. Everybody has the natural right to live free of harmful conditioning, exploitation, and domination. Health, happiness, and realization of spiritual potential are the very basis of freedom. My entire being detests the notion of returning to Granite Mountain, away from family, friends. But I'm prepared for it. I'll picture what it will be like to be there again, the things that scare me, and those terrible people.* She breathed slowly, in through her nose and out her mouth. *I have to dispel fear so I can function at my best.*

Doctor Edie called first thing Friday morning. Katrina reeled with guilt about not exposing Granite Mountain. *I can't tell her. She'll run to the authorities. Even worse, she'll tell Dad. I'm positive that Granite Mountain is far more reaching than just New Hampshire. It's connected to Judgment—I just know it. Just like I know Camille didn't run away like everybody says. Otherwise, she would've turned up by now—somewhere. The world will know about Granite Mountain and the Araneas in due time. And if Bert thinks he's going to take advantage of me again, he's sadly mistaken. Gosh, when what happened on that island comes out, it's going to be way embarrassing!* Her heart flip-flopped, harboring so much resentment toward Bert—so much attraction. While trying to come up with a plan to bring down Granite Mountain, Katrina made it a point to attend self-defense classes, that in addition to her daily workout routine.

Noontime on Friday, half the state of Massachusetts gathered at Emma LaRosa's home for traditional Italian fare. Even though yesterday was Thanksgiving and all the gorging that went along with it, Katrina couldn't resist indulging on Emma's spaghetti.

"Spaghetti isn't served on your precious Granite Mountain?" razzed her father. He stuffed a fork full of salad into his mouth and chomped. A smug look plastered his face.

"I know your game," said Katrina, using the edge of the napkin tucked into the collar of her purple tee shirt to dab sauce off her mouth. "You know full well that spaghetti's one of my favorite dishes and if I miss it enough and other stuff, too, I'll put Granite Mountain behind me. Well, you're way off base." She twirled spaghetti strands around her fork, thinking, *Wish I could tell Dad—tell everybody else here—everything. Tell them freedom's at stake. Just wait till I find out about other places like Granite Mountain. I know there's more. I feel it in my bones. I'll put an end to all of them. That's my goal in life—my career path!*

"*Mangia*," shrieked Emma in that ancient voice of hers. Her wrinkled and spotted hands gestured Italian style. "My goodness, *cara mia principessa*! You have turned into a feather!"

At sunset, Ken pulled the car into the garage and shut off the motor. Katrina got out of the back seat. Instead of heading for the back door, she walked down the driveway. Out of the corner of her eye, she saw her father and Mom exchange curious glances.

"Kat!" squealed Adriano, grabbing hold of her hand. "Where ya goin'?"

"To look at Toffee Castle," she puffed, lifting her face to the winter sky. She sucked in the fifty degree air. *This time of year usually calls for a lot heavier attire than this purple sweat suit I'm wearing.*

"I like when you and me go for walks," said Adriano, who had rarely left her side since her return. His hand skipped along the picket fence. "Wish you don't go 'way again." His lips puckered the same way hers did at times. "How come you call our house Toffee Castle?"

Katrina gazed at the hours that possessed the ageless beauty of a bygone era. "It's the color of toffee candy. Don't you think the trim looks like chocolate kisses?"

Cocking his head, Adriano squinted at the house. "Toffee's our favorite candy, huh, Kat?"

"Yeah," she said, squeezing his hand. "First time I saw this place, I was eight, and those rhododendrons were a mass of pink and white." She recalled running to the front gate and calling over her shoulder, *'Daddy, I love this place!' He was sitting in a wheelchair. Nobody ever explained to me how he broke his leg and arm.* "Still love this place," she murmured.

"You don't have to leave it," said her father, standing beside her, hand in hand with Julie.

Katrina cringed.

As Christmas lights clicked on, setting Toffee Castle aglow, Adriano shrieked, "Our house looks like a fairyland! Listen to the tinkling music!"

Only subliminal message in this music is love, mused Katrina.

"Has it snowed at Nahampsha?" asked Adriano.

Katrina lifted the gate latch. "An inch or two. But it melts right away. By now snow's supposed to be so deep that you need snowshoes." She swung open the gate then pulled Adriano through ahead of her. For some far off reason, she wondered how Chas was doing. *Wish he would've come home with me. Can't imagine what he can be doing.*

"Mommy says snow is angels pillow fightin'," said Adriano, letting go of her hand and barreling up to the front portico. "They fight so bad that their pillows rip and feathers fall out all over the place and turn to snow!"

"If Mom says that's snow," said Katrina, winking over her shoulder at Julie, "then that's what snow is!"

"Snow smow," blustered her father, dropping Julie's hand and tramping up the front steps. "Schools around here are just as good as that foolish Academy."

Katrina frowned at Julie who frowned back. They bit the insides of their lips and shrugged.

"And," exhorted her father while unlocking the door, "I have no problem paying for any school you choose!" He shoved open the door and stepped aside. "None whatsoever!"

"Me, too!" interjected Adriano, racing into the foyer.

"Oh," driveled Katrina, "Addie's going to pay, too?"

Adriano gave a robust nod. His lips puckered. Hope over-flowed his eyes.

Julie wagged her index finger. "My two little boys should stop moping about Katrina and let her do her thing. She's doing awesome and is having the time of her life!"

Katrina's insides knotted. *Time of my life,* she thought. She shook her arms out of her jacket and hooked it on the coat rack.

"Your hair needs a good trim," said Julie, pushing blond spirals out of Katrina's face. "Where's your other barrette?"

Katrina brushed away Julie's hand. "I'll get a trim when I come back at Christmas." While kicking off her sneakers, she adjusted the remaining butterfly barrette.

"With your grades you can get into any school in Boston," insisted Ken.

"They won't let me keep Mickey Blue Eyes," said Katrina. "They won't even let me bring her home for a couple of days."

"I'll buy you another dog," countered Ken.

Katrina bunched her fists and spat, "No!"

"Whatever dog you like," he said. "You pick it out."

"No," she wailed, jerking her head side to side. "No!" Tears welled. Unable to stop the flow, she fled up the stairs. "You don't even try to understand!"

"What'd I say?" slobbered her father.

Late Saturday morning, Katrina peeked around the door casing into the mahogany-paneled office. Her father was hunched over his desk, engrossed in his latest computer project. The eraser end of the pencil in his hand was flipping through computer printouts. Hi-tech manuals, folders, and papers littered the floor around him.

"On my way to Phyllis Royal's," she said.

He grunted.

"Phyllis and I might take in a movie or do some shopping," she said while drifting over to the floor-to-ceiling bookshelves that spanned the length of two walls. "So count me out for the day. I'll grab eats at the mall." Her fingers ran along the bind-ings of ancient reference books and collections of literature that she and her father had found while rummaging through old bookstores. The artwork and blue covers on several signified they were original. *Too bad the Tom Swift series burned in the manse,* she mused. *Dad says he had pipe dreams when he was a kid about becoming a dashing Tom Swift, inventing amazing machines and driving roadsters, wearing a duster coat and flat cap, and solving dilemmas. I should tell him I think he is a dashing Tom Swift. Bet he can help me solve this Granite Mountain dilemma.* She pressed a hidden button that few people knew about. A section of bookcase opened toward her. She stepped around it and peered at the other side. *Addie and I used to have a blast playing here, running up and down that staircase.*

The phone rang. "Yeah?" said her father.

Katrina straightened, took a deep breath, and put on a happy face. Turning, she said, "See you later."

He put a hand over the receiver and squawked, "Call if you're going to be late." Without waiting for a response, he took his hand off the receiver and focused on the call.

Three doors down from Toffee Castle, Katrina paused in front of the library and scanned her surroundings. *Good. Nobody's keeping an eye on me.* She paused again in front of the drugstore. *Still nobody.* She ducked into the drugstore and purchased three sets of earplugs, one to wear on campus, one to hide outside in the statue of Jonathan Aranea, and one to hide in her mattress.

Exiting the drugstore, she scanned her surroundings then scooted off to the train station. As she took a seat on the train, the conductor hollered "All aboard."

Forehead leaning against the window, she stared out at buildings and bustling streets streaking by. *How many times did Dad and I do this very same thing? Long as I remember. After I got back from Judgment and the casts were taken off his arm and leg, we traveled this route, lots of times. He lost so much when that horrible manse in Cohasset burned down. Well, that fire doesn't make me the least bit unhappy. Still don't understand how a candy-colored clown figured into getting me back. Wonder what it looked like? And where it is? People just whisper about it. Wish I could ask what it had to do with Regina and Jake, but when I do, everybody freaks—especially Dad.* Katrina heaved a sigh. *Feel so guilty sneaking off like this…using Phyllis. But I had no choice. Research is out of the question at Granite Mountain. Cameras monitor every move. And there's no such thing as privacy at the Brighton Library—any place else in Brighton, for that matter. People are always coming up to me: Ka-tri-na! You're ho-me! How do you like New Hampshire? How's your parents? How's Addie? Blah, blah, blah. Hiding electronic trails from Dad, computer-wiz extraordinaire, is impossible, too. Mom told me electronic trails helped him recall events that led up to my kidnapping and then my rescue from Judgment. How he walked in on Jake and how Jake pressed the exit key on the computer. But later, Dad traced Jake's trail to secured sites of government agencies like the FBI, CIA, and War Department and sites of small towns all over the world: Russia, Israel, Iran, and Iraq. Strangest of all was the out-of-the way town, Judgment, Mississippi. Jake forgot to take printouts that listed sources for biological agents, chemical warehouses, and airline, subway, and train systems across the United States and the world. Dad got spooked, so he backed up all the data and installed stronger security software. He was never quite sure that Jake didn't find a way around it. Dad stowed the backup disc in the fireproof safe that Pop Pop Peter dug out of the ashes of the manse. When Dad found the disc, it spurred him into believing that I didn't die in a plane crash. He told the FBI about Judgment, Mississippi, and they rescued me and the other kids.*

"Boylston Street," said a male voice over the loudspeaker. The train lurched to a stop. Katrina got off and rode the escalator up to the kiosk. Outside, everything that was Boston smacked her senses. Bumper-to-bumper traffic: cars, buses, taxis, trucks. Knockwurst grilling inside a nearby pub. Pollution. Urine. Horns. Sirens. Cursing. Laughter. Pigeons pecking at the sidewalk. Sparrows chirping and flitting about. Whistles. Cops. Nameless pedestrians lost in thought, passing and crossing streets, heading to destinations known only to themselves. Shoppers gazing into store windows. A child pointing to a toy in a window. His mother pulling him away. The child dropping to the sidewalk and screaming bloody murder—screams that sent chills racing up and down Katrina's spine as memories of screaming children being dragged off in the middle of Mississippi nights ripped through her mind. A time or two at Granite Mountain, she had awoken to screams and was never sure if she had been dreaming or not.

"A quarter, missy?" asked a bag lady, palm extended. Her other hand gripped the bar of a shopping cart that contained all her worldly possessions.

Katrina backed away.

The bag lady squinted, shrugged, and started on her way. She stopped, stooped down, and picked up something, examined it, and tossed it away.

Just then, two teenagers on skateboards hopped the curb and came down with a clunk. They nearly mowed down Katrina and the bag lady. Offering no apologies, they sped off.

"Hooligans!" shrieked the bag lady.

Other skateboarders and in-line skaters were hurdling cement obstacles in front of a church while folks on nearby benches soaked up the November sunshine. The breeze toyed with fountain water, turning it into mist that Mother Nature swallowed.

An entirely different world than Granite Mountain, thought Katrina, turning toward the library. *How does so much diversity exist in one world? One country? New England? It feels so good to be here, in downtown Boston, but the feeling I get roaming the White Mountains with Mickey Blue Eyes is like none other. Too bad the likes of the Araneas taint those mountains. And Bert Moro. But I can't think about him now. I have only a few hours before the library closes.*

Inside, her steps echoed off the marble vastness as she sprinted down the turning stairs to the restroom and then sped up to the second floor and into the computer room. All the computer stations were empty, so she took the most isolated one. She pulled up the Internet and typed "brainwashing."

"Whatever I learn," she whispered, "has to help me to stop the Araneas and others like them. I don't know what else to do." A shiver raced through her. "I just can't know about that place and do nothing about it."

Information flashed on the monitor. *To attain new converts, a brain-phase must be created within a short period of time—a day or a weekend.* "That's exactly what happens at ecology camp!" she exclaimed. Her hands covered her mouth as she skimmed her surroundings. *Nobody's around.* Her hand fell away from her mouth. She peered at the monitor. *Meetings or training takes place in areas where participants are cut off from the outside world, remote or rural settings.* "Got that right," she whispered. *Long hours of work or intense physical activity and unique experiences cause physical and mental fatigue. No relaxation, reflection, or adequate sleep. Alertness is reduced. Resistance wears down.* "That's me," muttered Katrina, "sucking up everything new under the sun with only a couple hours of sleep. If I'm to get anywhere with this, I have to get better rest. I have to encourage other kids to do the same. But how to sleep away from the music?"

Limited bathroom use. "Humph. Never thought about that, but there was a time or two I couldn't wait to hit the head. Something to watch for."

Eating is overlooked. Meals are short and inadequate, which creates tension. "Chowing down on the run happens a lot," she whispered as the clamor of knives and forks filled her head. "Everybody swills down food during the short time between activities, almost in self-defense, knowing they'll be hungry again—and real soon. No meaningful conversation in Granite Mountain cafeterias, that's for sure. Thirst is just as bad. There's never enough water. Terrible how Mr. O'Mara keeps that big pitcher of ice water on his desk and won't let anybody have a drink. It's like he's torturing us with it. Brita asked for a drink one time and O'Mara told her, 'Haul your butt back to your seat, if you know what's good for you. Stop your sniveling, brat!' Sniveling brat," repeated Katrina as revulsion grew inside her. Readjusting herself in her chair, she continued to read. *Controllers subvert positive human values, telling targets that their life won't work if they don't keep agreements. Anxiety over doing so alters internal chemistry causing the nervous system to malfunction. Conversion potential increases.* "We had to vow to defend Granite Mountain," muttered Katrina, "no matter what. Hmm. No matter what?"

Agreement to complete training assures a high percentage of converts. "I fell in love with the adventure and the mountains. And Bert. I would have agreed to anything."

If intimidation doesn't work, targets are forced to leave. Witnessing such disgrace causes others to be more determined to see it though, and that aids in conversion. "Had me on that point," she whispered. "I would've hated to leave. Failure just isn't in my vocabulary."

Guilt is played upon to get participants to relate innermost secrets. Activities emphasize openness. Katrina winced. "I confided in Bert about being kidnapped and then he took advantage of me on that island. Emotional blackmail. What if he took pictures?"

Abnormal levels of anger, fear, excitement, or nervous tension result in impaired judgment and suggestibility. Maintained or intensified, mental takeover is that much easier. Existing mental programming is then replaced with new patterns of thinking and behavior. The number one most fearful situation is speaking in front of people, so trainers put participants on the spot or verbally attack them in front of peers, which causes many participants to mentally go away and enter an alpha state that makes them suggestible. "Wow," whispered Katrina. "Fear's a biggy."

Radical or high sugar diets cause the nervous system to malfunction, making it difficult to distinguish between fantasy and reality. Sugar contained in brownies and soft drinks throw off the nervous system. Many cults use the spiritual diet of vegetables and fruits, no grains, nuts, seeds, dairy products, fish, or meat. Targets become spacey. "Now that Chas pitched junk food, he's not so messed up."

Other weapons used to modify brain function are regulation of breathing, mantra chanting in meditation, the disclosure of overwhelming mysteries, special lighting and sound effects, programmed response to incense, intoxicants, electric shock treatments, and lowering blood sugar levels with insulin injections. A repetitive beat like that of the human heart causes altered states of consciousness, hypnotism, an alpha state, where eyes open wide and people are more suggestible than in full beta consciousness. Mental assault is accomplished by a deluge of new information, lectures, discussion groups, encounters, or one-to-one processing where the controller bombards the individual with questions. "Academy teachers are real good at that," muttered Katrina.

Continued use brings on a feeling of elation and eventually hallucination. Reality merges with illusion. The cessation of thought brings about withdrawal from everyone and everything. "That's why Brita won't let her parents visit and refuses to go home for school breaks. She's around Vic and the Araneas all the time, totally under their control. That's how come she never notices Vic ogling me. Bert's a puppet, too. Teachers keep saying thought-stopping techniques make better Academy soldiers. We march every day, thump, thump, thump, generating a kind of self-hypnoses, which adds to susceptibility and suggestion. A lot of kids think it's fun. If they only knew."

An hour and a half of daily meditation for weeks on end keeps the mind in a fixed state of alpha away from full consciousness. "Nirvana? Garbage! If that's true, why is everybody so insecure and incomplete like Chas? When he's himself, he cares so much about stuff."

Obsessed people appear cool and collected. Some call themselves true believers, labeling others who don't accept their ideas or haven't taken their training as devils. They talk about the devil, going to hell, Armageddon. They believe that new life and order can only be achieved by eliminating old ways. "What old ways are the Araneas trying to eliminate? Doctor Edie says that people who love and are loved don't need to look for allies. Those who hate are mentally unbalanced or insecure people, without hope or friends. Sometimes that leads them to become obsessed with a cause. That's part of the reason Regina and Jake were like they were."

When a speaker gestures upon key words, they are giving embedded commands. A left hand gesture accesses the right brain. Specialists train media-oriented politicians and spellbinders to manipulate voters this way. "Slimy," muttered Katrina.

Sound and lighting are primary tools used to induce an altered state of consciousness. Monotonous music hooks many people right away. Extra-low frequency waves (ELFs) effect people within seconds. Waves below six cycles per second cause emotional instability and disrupt body functions. At eight cycles, a person feels high. Eleven cycles induces agitation that leads to riotous behavior. "Sick," muttered Katrina, leaning back in her chair and lacing her fingers behind her head. "The Araneas know this stuff. Well, now I know, too!" She leered at the monitor. *The subconscious recalls a previous state of mind and responds to post-hypnotic programming, which may be permanent for some while for others lasts four days up to a week—a similar length of time hypnotic suggestion lasts on somnambulistic subjects. Programming is forgotten unless the subject is instructed to remember while in the trance. Weekly exposure reinforces programming, which can be detrimental. External signs of trance: relaxed body, dilated eyes, swaying back and forth. Rolling voices like those of hypnotists can induce trance thus entrenching commands in the mind.*

Subliminals hide in audio input and visual media like television. The subconscious perceives a picture or suggestion that flashes on the screen too fast to be consciously seen. Viewer in turn performs as asked. Often, designs and advertisements contain subliminals. Stores use subliminals in music and pictures, instructing customers not to steal, and it is said to work. Katrina scratched her head. "There's simply no way of knowing."

Merry-making and humor are used to show others the joy of being a member. "Camille was real happy that day I arrived for Spring Ecology Camp," said Katrina. "I was jealous. But the next day, Camille was grumpy and used words I didn't understand. Others used vicious language—I don't like that." Katrina pursed her lips, thinking, the Araneas think I'm converted. That's why they let me come home. They're not afraid I won't go back. Well, I'm going back, but not under their control like they think.

Arrowing down, Katrina read aloud, "Ivan Pavlov, a Russian scientist, trained a hungry dog to salivate at the sound of a bell. Up until then, salivation had always been associated with the sight of food." Leaning back in her chair, Katrina envisioned Mickey Blue Eyes freaking out at the old logging road and the times the Araneas come around. "Too bad Mickey Blue Eyes can't tell me...wait a minute...that mother monkey holding her dead baby...those labs...the sick and dying animals. None of them sounded the alarm that I was there. They couldn't, because just like Mickey Blue Eyes, their vocal cords had been cut. Bet Mickey Blue Eyes came from inside Granite Mountain, not an animal shelter."

Katrina squinted at the monitor. *Pavlov opened the door to experimenting with people and studies relating human behavior to the nervous system, known as conditioned learning. He supported the neural concepts, induction and irradiation, as valid for higher mental activity and tried to apply his laws to explain human psychoses. He assumed that the excessive inhibition of a psychotic person was a protective mechanism—a shutting out of the external world and injurious stimuli that caused anxiety. The concept became the basis for treating psychiatric patients in Russia, providing them peaceful environs. He was not responsible for brainwashing techniques often ascribed to him. A bold, vehement nonconformist in science and personal life, he fiercely took up the cudgel for what he believed regardless of the force of his opposition.*

Katrina typed the word, cudgel. *A short heavy stick shorter than a quarterstaff used as an instrument of punishment or weapon.* "Is that what I'm doing? Taking up a cudgel for what I believe regardless of the force of my opposition?"

Chapter 18

A couple of days after bringing Katrina back to Granite Mountain, Ken and Julie left Adriano off at the preschool and went to the grocery store. Pulling a carriage out of the stack, Ken heard the automatic doors open behind him.

"Jeanette!" exclaimed Julie. "How was your Thanksgiving?"

Ken turned. Jeanette Royal was patting her stomach, saying, "Ate too much."

"Sorry I didn't get to see Katrina, again," said Phyllis, right behind her mother, pushing a packed carriage.

Ken gave Phyllis a sidelong once over. "You two didn't take in a movie the Saturday after Thanksgiving?"

"Movie?" asked Phyllis, moving aside so a woman entering the store could get by.

"You two didn't go to the mall?" asked Ken as insecurity pestered him like a dull headache, there, but not painful enough for medication.

Phyllis squinted at him and said a drawn out "N-o-o."

"She told me you two were getting together," insisted Ken. "Saturday."

"Phyl, her father, and I were visiting family in Lowell," said Jeannette, "the entire Thanksgiving weekend."

Ken and Julie exchanged frowns. "You must've heard Katrina wrong," said Julie, grabbing his arm. His eyes narrowed on her hand and then on Phyllis who merely shrugged. "We have to go," said Julie, smiling at the Royals and towing Ken into the store. "Nice to see you two. Drop by and see us."

Adrenaline surging, Ken asked, "My baby girl lied to me?"

"Don't go having a hissy fit," whispered Julie, letting go of his arm. She grabbed an abandoned shopping cart and headed to the fresh vegetables.

"But why did she feel the need to lie to me?" he whined.

"Something doesn't jell," she said, stopping to pick out a head of lettuce.

"Doesn't jell, all right," he said, trailing her to the cucumbers. "All she took back to Granite Mountain was a couple of backpacks and they were just about empty. No personal touches. Not even that picture of her and that…that guy!"

Julie gave him a one-eyed leer. "You've been in her room."

"As a matter of fact," he spewed, "I have. Did you know that she brought home some of the stuff she took with her in September?"

"Uh-huh," said Julie, tearing several plastic bags off a roll.

"Admit it," he said. "She doesn't intend to stay there. I told you Granite Mountain isn't the chummy place that chest-thumping hypocrite Aranea tried to push on me."

Julie stuffed two cucumbers into one of the bags. "You're making too much of this," she said, putting the plastic bag of cucumbers into the carriage.

"I am not," shot back Ken.

"You are," she said calmly.

"Don't speak to me like I'm Addie!" he spat.

"Then don't act like him," she said, picking out tomatoes and putting them into one of the two remaining plastic bags.

"Listen," he said, running a hand through his hair. "Every day while she was home, she went to those self-defense classes. Right?"

Julie nodded while knotting the plastic bag of tomatoes. She placed it into the carriage and pushed on to the bananas.

He trotted after her, spouting, "You know as well as I do how she resented those classes. Now they're okay? Every time I turned around, she was working out. You saw her."

"Why on earth are you so crabby?" asked Julie, putting a bunch of bananas into a plastic bag then into the carriage.

Ken flailed his hands. "My baby girl's changed!"

"Change is inevitable," said Julie, going to the deli. "Everybody goes through lots of change, getting to adulthood, and even then we still continue to change."

"Changed enough to start lying to me?" asked Ken.

Julie rubbed his arm while squinting at the cold meats. "She's away from home for the first time since coming back to us. That alone is a growing experience in anybody's book."

"May I help you?" asked the deli clerk.

"I'm not buying it," said Ken.

The deli clerk eyed Ken kind of strange and then Julie.

"Half a pound each of hot ham, salami, and provolone, please," said Julie. "Oh, and bologna! Addie loves bologna."

"I wish you'd stop for just one blessed second," said Ken, "and listen to me. I just can't slough this off as easy as you."

"There's nothing either of us can do," she said.

"Uh-huh," he said with a decisive nod. "When I get home, I'm calling Katrina. I'll get to the bottom of this!"

"You'll do nothing of the sort," scolded Julie, taking packages of cold cuts from the clerk.

"Will that be all?" asked the clerk who seemed to want to distance herself from the querulous couple.

"Thank you," said Julie, smiling to calm down the clerk. She pushed the carriage to the seafood section. "Ask Katrina about it at Christmastime. For all we know, she was out buying Christmas gifts. You wouldn't want to spoil the surprise for her, would you?"

Slack-jawed, Ken thought, *Christmas gifts? The logic is undeniable.* "B-b-but…"

"No buts about it," said Julie, waving a hand in the air. "Come on. Let's finish grocery shopping. We've got our own Christmas shopping to do."

His hand raked across his scalp. *Something's amiss,* he fumed. *I just know it, but arguing is getting me nowhere.* He took in a slow, deep breath and rotated his shoulders. "I'm not…" he started to say but then noticed Julie was out of hearing range. He grunted and scampered after her. Catching up, he said, "I'm not going to put up with my baby girl lying to me. It's my fault she ended up in Judgment. I can't let that happen to her again."

"You're making too much of this," said Julie, putting a gallon of milk into the carriage.

"You always say that," he yelped.

"That's because it's true," she said.

"You couldn't possibly know how I feel," he said, hands on hips, chin jutting out.

Julie cringed. Turning to him, she said, "I'm just as sick about this as you are. Look, I was saving this for a more appropriate time and place…" Her left hand hooked on her hip as her right palm gestured. "But here's the deal. We are pregnant again—finally! There's no way on God's green earth that I'm going through what I did for Adriano! Get that into your head!"

Chapter 19

*T*he next time Katrina set off on an excursion Bert tagged along, though she got the feeling that he had bigger things on his plate. She made a point to bore him, making a big deal out of catching the occasional snowflake on her tongue, listening to babbling brooks, any silly thing to ensure their return to campus occurred after curfew. Aggravated, he talked Meredith into letting Katrina go off on her own again. Continuing to return late, Katrina figured, *Eventually, nobody's going to notice. If I have to take off for good, a search for me won't start for hours. By then it'll be too late.* On several occasions, she detected shadows but when she confronted Chas, he didn't admit to being the shadow. He didn't exactly deny it either. "Bert and I ain't the only ones assigned to keep an eye on you, you know."

"Let me hazard a guess," she said. "Brita is, too."

He hung his head and nodded. "Sorry."

Katrina avoided looking for other mineshafts for a while, instead circling Granite Mountain at lower elevations. One day, she discovered a nearly undetectable convergence of logging roads. *Bet this ends at the blind off Route 302,* she mused. *One of these roads comes from the east and one from the north.* She got down on one knee and roughed up the dog's thick mane. "Won't be too much longer," she said, "before I can trace these roads. It's gotten to the point that when you and I show up late, all we get is a huffy, 'Where've you been this time, Kitty?'"

At last convinced that nobody was paying her mind, she left the dorm at first light one Sunday morning. Nobody else was up. Even the guard wasn't around. Since she hadn't signed up for any extra curricular events, her presence wouldn't be missed. Being tracked wasn't a major concern, because the one inch snowfall two days ago had melted. Temperatures were averaging seven degrees warmer than normal, the twelfth warmest season in one hundred and one years. Five years ago, temperatures had averaged seven degrees colder than normal. *That's New England for you,* she mused. *Wish winter would just get started. Mickey Blue Eyes and I want to go skijoring.* Yes, the mountains coursed through her blood like the sun across an August sky. And as much as she didn't want to admit it, so did Bert.

Halfway to the convergence of roads, Katrina tied Mickey Blue Eyes to an oak that was well off the trail. If the day got hot, the withered leaves that clung to the oak would shade the husky. A nearby stream provided drinking water. Retrieval distance was manageable no matter where Katrina exited the mountain. Bending at the knees, she hugged Mickey Blue Eyes. "Wish I didn't have to leave you here." The husky licked Katrina's cheek. Her tail thumped the ground. Katrina stood up. "No time to goof off." She pointed a finger at the dog. "Stay. No noise."

Mickey Blue Eyes flattened on the ground, worried eyes glued to Katrina who stepped back and pursed her lips. Both hated to part. Both feared parting.

At the convergence of trails, Katrina checked her watch. *I'll follow the road coming in from the north first.* It ended at a pile of birch, pine, and other brush fashioned similar to the blind in front of the first mineshaft, orderly with propagated evergreen vines. *Danger,* warned the inner voice. *You're way over your head! Do not enter the forbidden world again.* She ignored the voice, determined to find a way to bring down Granite Mountain. She knew exactly which branch to pull. The pile of brush opened like a door to another mineshaft chiseled out of granite. *Stay away! Stay away!* cried the inner voice.

"I have to do this," she whispered, clenching her fists. "I just have to!"

Inside the tunnel, scanty tracks marked the rock-hard ground and ended at a granite barrier. She applied pressure to a blemish in the granite. The ground trembled as a huge section of the barrier retracted to the left. Gawking at another giant tube, she scratched her head. *What in the world are these things?*

To the right, another narrow stairway descended into darkness. Her heart raced. Experience had taught her that there's no quick escape route from Granite Mountain. Nevertheless she stole down the stairway. Light faded just like in the first stairway. Feeling her way along, she heard her footsteps. She stopped, removed her hiking shoes, tied the laces together, and slung the shoes over her shoulder. Cold seeped through her socks, chilling her feet, chilling her insides as she continued.

Seeing a pinpoint of light, she whispered, "Déjà vu." The pinpoint grew, brightened the way. A door came into view, above it, a camera. *Didn't get caught running into that first door,* she thought while pulling the hood of her jacket over her head. She took a deep breath. *Stick with me, lady luck.* She charged down the stairs and through the door and found refuge behind the same type of black metal cabinets as in the first cave, in the same type of dank, granite communication center. Fluorescent lighting. Ventilation turbines humming. Background music. Tiny colored lights blinking on consoles. *And the same stink,* she thought while pinching her nose.

"Mary's Song" sealed her mind as Katrina stole along the cabinets, muscles primed for a fight to the death. At the far end, she eyed a huge steel door on the opposite wall. *Another canary and more cameras. More cables, too. What is going on?* She reached into her pocket and pulled out the language translator that she had designed with a little help from her father during Thanksgiving break. She had told him that she wanted to translate Italian into English and vise versa. It wasn't a lie, only a half-truth. Upon returning to Granite Mountain, she had added Arabic, Kurdish, and Farsi. She drew the symbols that were painted on the door and the translation came back: DANGER! BIOLOGICAL, CHEMICAL, AND NUCLEAR RESEARCH IN

PROGRESS! APPROPRIATE ATTIRE AND CLEARANCE REQUIRED! "Gosh," she whispered.

She stuffed the translator into her pocket then scurried to the archway and out onto the landing of a narrow stairway. She went down to the next landing and entered a long hallway that had one door on the left and one on the right. She cracked open the left door to a sort of anteroom. *What's behind all those curtains?* She slipped into the room and studied the control panel next to the first set of curtains. She peeked through the curtains. Hooks dangled from ceiling track and a primitive electric chair was kitty-corner on the right. Horror bubbled inside. Dropping the curtain, she took a step back. She eyed the other curtains. *I'm not sure I really want to look behind those.*

But curiosity overcame trepidation. Behind the second curtain, spigots jutted out of the ceiling and wall. Behind the third curtain was a shallow tub and shackles. She covered her mouth as her mind raced. *These are torture chambers! Hell on earth! In New Hampshire! Right under the nose of the United States government!* She began to sing, softly, quivering, " 'Mother Mary speaks to me, "Let it be." ' "

But letting it be just was out of the question as Katrina shoved aside the curtain of the fourth chamber. Her entire being quaked. *That's a total-immersion tub! I saw a picture of one just like it at the Boston Public Library.* Her eyes explored the shackles and then the chains that hung from hooks in the ceiling and held up the cover. She glanced around: a steel rod, a butcher knife, handcuffs, leg shackles, waist chains, rolls of electrical tape. *Hey, what are all those cards tacked to the wall?* She stepped over to them. *Who are all these kids?* The sheer volume of cards overwhelmed her as the spirits of the children seemed to float all around her. Tears filled her eyes. *I should've been able to save these kids.* She pushed away tears streaming down her cheeks. *These cards are the Araneas' trophies! Well, the world's going to know about these kids, and what happened to them in this room! And no matter what, my picture—and Addie's!—won't ever end up here!*

She charged at the last curtain and yanked it aside. Inside was a wooden stock that looked like the ones pilgrims used to publicly disgrace wrongdoers. Lengths of ropes hung from ceiling hooks. Her fist jammed against her mouth. *I can't take anymore!* She ran to the door at the far end of the anteroom, down a stairway, and into another hallway. Three doors were on each side, spaced about twelve feet apart. She glanced over her shoulder then up at the camera attached to the ceiling. *Nobody's watching me. I wouldn't've gotten this far if somebody was.* She hurried to the first door on the right and cracked it open. *Wow, look at this bedroom!* She tiptoed into the richly appointed room. *That bed looks like somebody left in one big hurry.* She glanced at her watch. *Too early for brunch.* She eyed the monitors and television imbedded in the wall opposite the bed. *Somebody gets his jollies, spying on everybody. Sick.*

She opened a door. *A closet. Jonathan's clothes!*

Behind another door was a bathroom. A third door opened into another bedroom. The bed looked unslept in. Inside the closet were Meredith's clothes. *The Araneas must fight a lot to have separate bedrooms.*

Another door opened back into the hallway. She tiptoed to the last door on the same side of the hall. Inside was a hotel-like suite: dining room, living room, bathroom, and bedroom with two king-size beds. *No personal stuff. No clothes in the closet. A guest room? Who in their right mind would ever want to stay here?*

She left the suite and crossed the hallway to a door that opened into a conference room furnished with a long mahogany table, cushioned high-back chairs, and an easel. Several electric outlets were on the walls; nothing was connected to them. *There's only one door in and out.* She shivered. *This room gives me the willies!* She hurried out.

Behind the next door was an office with dozens of monitors embedded in the left wall. *Nobody's safe from Jonathan's probing eyes. Piecing together what I know so far, I think this office must be near the Administration Building.* A noise drew her attention to the bookcase. *There it is again! Hey, a secret passage is on the other side of this bookcase—just like in Dad's office!* She felt around the shelves. *Where's the secret button?* She heard a squawk and looked up. *It's a clock shaped like a black widow spider. Gosh, look at the time! I better get going!* She turned. Her eyes popped. *Terrariums!* She stepped over to the desk and supported her weight on it while reading the labels stuck to the terrariums. "Cobalt Blue Spider. Orange Starburst Baboon Spider. Trap Door Spider. Baboon Spider. Cameroon Bird Spider." She squinted into the one of the terrariums. "That's one huge spider! Look at all those baby spiders! Her blood ran cold. I'm getting out of here!" She fled out of the room. In the hallway, one glimpse of the stairs reminded her of the torture chambers up one level. "Not going back up there!" She sped off the opposite way, not caring if she got caught, down the hallway and into another hallway. "Hey, there's the door that got me out of here the first time!" She charged for it, shoved down the handle, and bolted into the parking garage. She jumped over the concrete wheel chock and raced out the side entrance. Fresh air choked her. The glare of the sun blinded her. She flinched, but didn't hesitate, and made it to Mickey Blue Eyes in record time.

"Where's your shoes?" asked Chas, lying on the ground with the dog's snout on his chest. He broke off a piece of beef jerky, which Katrina had brought from home after Thanksgiving, and fed it to the dog. She had also brought flavored milk, nuts, and granola from home. Julie was going to send more. The bread and bologna made everyone feel the fullest. Katrina took pride in seeing fellow students snubbing the usual sugar-laced diet that threw off the nervous system. The difference it made was remarkable. Alertness improved by leaps and bounds. Chas had even lost most of that zombie look.

"You going to baby sit my dog every time I go inside Granite Mountain?" asked Katrina, gasping for air. She bent over, hands braced on thighs, and spotted her mucked-up socks. She grappled for her shoes that were supposed to be hanging around her neck. "Where's my shoes?"

Chas put a finger in his ear and wiggled it. "Good job closing up the mine entrance."

She nodded. "Thanks for reminding me of that. You're a lifesaver."

He shook his head and got to his feet. "Uh-uh. I'm a real slime ball."

"How come?" she asked, straightening her spine.

"Bert didn't do it."

"Do what?"

"Report you got kidnapped."

"You told about me being kidnapped?" shrieked Katrina.

Mickey Blue Eyes bristled. Chas dropped his head onto his chest. His hands covered his face.

"Why, Chas?" demanded Katrina.

Mickey Blue Eyes whined. Chas shrugged.

Katrina wrung her hands. Anger and disappointment bubbled inside her. She grabbed him by the shoulders and shook the daylights out of him. "Why did you do that? Why?"

Mickey put her muzzle to the heavens and bayed as much as severed vocal cords allowed. Chas also looked to the heavens and bayed, "I'm sorry! I'm sorry! I have to!"

Echoes filled the mountains as Katrina shoved Chas, crying, "You have to?"

His hands banged his head as he howled, "If only to remove myself from this disaster that's my life! Go to some calmer place! I wanna wake up and not be on Granite Mountain anymore!"

Chapter 20

*E*mily, the Cat, snoozing in front of the computer monitor, didn't bat an eye when Curt pushed his chair away from the desk and swiveled toward the window. He clasped his hands behind his head and gazed out at a leafless peach tree that his mind was too troubled to acknowledge. "Another leak to the ill-mannered, prying media," he carped. "Always demanding answers. Can't one day go by without a leak? Hmph, leak—insufficient interpretation of the torrent of war strategy that fills the front pages of newspapers. 'Undisclosed sources report...' What a crock. That phrase is more of a ploy to give credibility than avoidance of putting sources at risk."

The need for victories in the Middle East was becoming crucial as protestors swarmed the Washington Mall; their numbers grew with each passing day. Senate Foreign Relations Committee hearings on the war were forcing the discussion into the open. The Administration declined participation, which cast a pall on the actual intentions for the war and gave the impression of being undemocratic and untouchable. Poll numbers plummeted as Americans lost faith. Few, however, disputed that the world would be a better place if democracy got a toehold in the Middle East. On the other hand, the war was costing thousands of American lives to say nothing of billions of dollars. The historic opportunity to remake the politics of the entire Middle East was failing. In addition, the message that the U.S. wanted to send—the U.S. will not tolerate terrorism or threats of mass destruction—was being blatantly disregarded. Iraq made a preemptive strike on Iran, using deadly chemical and biological weapons. Threats to neighboring countries now a reality, a new one just came through: "Back off America! The Middle East belongs to the True Believers! Weapons of mass destruction are in place around the world. True Believers are not afraid of Judgment Day."

"WMDs," muttered Curt. "Even in New Hampshire, I presume. It gets under my skin that months have gone by, giving Jonathan Aranea time to catch wind of Thornton scraping together troops and equipment for an invasion of Granite Mountain. Plenty of time for Aranea to maneuver and avoid attack. Undercover agents are in place, acting like tourists, employees of various businesses, or artsy folks seeking peaceful surroundings to let their creative juices flow. Meanwhile, military and government agencies dither. What in bloody Hades are they waiting for?"

"Waiting for?" asked Leander Holt.

Brows fusing into a frown, Curt swiveled his chair. "How long have you been standing there?"

Holt shifted an armload of folders and paperwork and coughed. "I-uhm…" he stammered. He plopped the armload onto the desk. "Just got here. Here's some info you requested."

Curt pulled his chair up to the desk and picked up a brochure that had slid off the pile. His face scrunched. On the cover was a metal turbine on a roof of a building jutting out the base of Granite Mountain. "Out of place, wouldn't you say, considering the Greek-style architecture?"

"The latest generation of turbines," explained Holt, hanging off Curt's left shoulder. "Prototypes are engineered and manufactured there—right under our noses."

Curt grunted. "Hard to fathom how it slipped by us."

Holt tapped his index finger on the brochure. "That's the Administration Building. Ex GIs, WWII, did the work. Says so inside."

Curt unfolded the brochure and scanned the information. "Used to be veteran housing. Now student dorms. Students matriculate from across the globe. Ecological, humanitarian, and technical curriculum. Some of the highest test scores not only in New Hampshire but nationwide are coming out of both college and Academy. Produced well-known writers, philosophers, and engineers."

"Jonathan Aranea included," added Holt, sitting on the edge of the desk. "Then he took over—even before graduating. Kept pretty low to the ground then all of a sudden, shows up as college president. He's the one who added the Academy."

Curt tossed aside the brochure then pulled the map of New Hampshire from the stack and spread it open. His finger traced Route 93 north, Salem to Concord, passing Plymouth and Lincoln, taking Exit 35 onto Route 3, drifting east at Route 302, going through Crawford Notch, and turning north on a nondescript road. He picked up a red permanent marker and circled Granite Mountain.

"Levels of the warren hallowed out of the mountain came out fuzzy," said Holt, opening a slash folder labeled Infrared Enhancements. "So I got enhancements made." He spread out the enhancements. "I highlighted the levels—circular in nature and wider the lower they go, corresponding to the mountain's contours. First thing comes to mind is a spider's orbed web."

Curt leaned over, studied the enhancements, and read a notation: Spiderlings (label given to conditioned students) enter warren through a door marked Maintenance, Authorized Personnel Only, located in the parking garage. "Took quite some time to build such an extensive network," he said. "Never mind materials."

"Tunnels radiate from the center, here," said Holt while pointing. "Tube-like structures, here, here, and here, might be quick hideouts similar to the raised funnel that the common house spider constructs in the corner in its web. Hapless victim comes along, spider rushes out, grabs victim, and delivers poisonous bite. Kind of what we suspect Aranea's doing to those he wants in his clandestine world."

"Notify General Thornton about the tubes," said Curt. "He'll slough it off, more than likely, but overlooking just one means dire consequences for our troops."

"If you ask me," said Holt, "Thornton already knows. He's got his own agenda."

"He can't say we didn't warn him," said Curt. "While you're at it, inform him that Aranea's private office here on the third level of the warren and his office in the Administration Building here are connected by this secret passage with entry on both sides through door-like sections of back-to-back, wall-to-wall bookshelves. If he's not careful, Aranea will slip through his fingers just like that." He snapped his fingers. He read another notation aloud: "Caution advised: Spiders and similar predatory species encased in numerous vivariums in Jonathan Aranea's office."

Curt and Holt exchanged agitated stares. Holt swallowed hard. His face was stark as death as he sniveled, "I hate insects."

"Spiders aren't insects," said Curt. "Body structure differs. Two parts, a fused head and thorax plus an abdomen. Eight legged. Eight eyed. No antennae or wings."

Holt stepped over to the guest chair and gripped the back of it. "Hate all of 'em!"

"You got one mean case of arachnophobia," jabbed Curt.

"I'm the first to admit it," yelped Holt.

"Spiders suffer an unsavory reputation," said Curt. "It's due to their appearance and tendency to lurk in dark places or dangle from threads. Plus gross exaggeration of their ability to poison humans. They rarely attack humans, unless threatened. Dying from a spider bite is one in fifty-six million chances."

"Individual risk varies," countered Holt. "I got bit once. Didn't see the thing, but Doc says it was a spider bite. Talk about a welt!"

"According to an old English adage," said Curt, "'If you wish to live and thrive, let the spider run alive.' To some extent I agree with the notion, but in the case of Aranea..." He shoved Emily, the Cat away from the monitor. Ignoring feline protest, he woke up the computer.

Holt stepped over and peered at the monitor. The dictionary came up, and Curt typed in Aranea. *A genus of orb-weaving spiders including the common garden spiders.*

Holt took a quick step back and shrieked, "Aranea's named after spiders?"

"Al Hadi was a genius," said Curt. "Middle East combatants hide in spider holes. He intended New Hampshire to be a spider hole for his survivors."

"But only Jonathan survived," said Holt.

"And he takes it to a new level," said Curt, "seeking retribution by manipulating young minds and sending them out into the world to be push buttons for terrorism. Let's get our own assessment team up there to have a go at what's percolating."

"Doubling as hikers?" suggested Holt. "No snow in the area."

Curt nodded, saying, "Ski areas must be sweating. No snow, no skiers. No skiers, no money. No money, no bills paid and no food on the table."

"I'll have the team get a thorough survey," said Holt. "Ventilation outlets, central chimney, identify every insignificant-looking thing. Vehicles coming and going."

"The General won't be putting us on the shelf this time," said Curt.

"And it'll be my pleasure to stop up this *spider* hole," blubbered Holt, leaving the room.

Curt braced his elbows on the desk and held his head between his palms. "Let Thornton give me even a hint of flack," he mumbled. "There'll be another one of those convenient *leaks* to the press. He'll abhor the media getting a hold of this. What a field day the press will have with innocent children being handpicked to carry forward terrorist goals. Yes, sir, I'll do like those blimey radicals who lack base for popular support—get the message out to millions via rabid media coverage and create a national nightmare."

Emily, the Cat arched against his arm. Pulling her to his chest, he straightened and rubbed his chin on her back. He stared at the remaining information that Holt had brought. "What's in that envelope?" He dumped the cat on the floor and opened the envelope. "Pictures." At the bottom of the first picture, handwritten scrawl identified the image as Jonathan Aranea. "Quite the lanky bloke. Dark brown eyes. Hair color is a bit off; looks like a dye job. Teflon quality about him, cool yet dark." The carrot-colored hair on Curt's arms spiked. "Deadly intentions streak through his eyes." Curt turned over the picture and squinted at Jonathan's Arabic name. He didn't even try to pronounce it. He scanned height and weight statistics and then plunked the picture face down on the desk.

The next picture identified Meredith Blevins Aranea. *On the bony side of athletic,* mused Curt. *Brown hair rapidly graying. Could use a dye job. Cut's a bit mannish.* He flipped over the picture. *No alias. Born and raised in Maine. Same height as husband.*

Curt went on to the next picture. "Timothy Aranea, Headmaster of Granite Mountain Academy. Dark brown eyes and hair. Heavy-set. Average height. Unmarried. Former protector of Mohammad Achmed al Hadi. How about that?"

Going on to the next picture, Curt mused, *Aram O'Mara, Assistant Director of the Math Department. O'Mara. Hair and eyes a trifle dark for an Irishman.* Curt turned the picture over. *Former professor at Boston Metropolitan College. Married. Father of two boys—both enrolled in Granite Mountain Academy.* As Holt trekked into the office, Curt said, "This bloke isn't Irish."

"His first name is anything but Irish," said Holt, plunking his armload onto the desk. "Say. Why don't you look up Aram in the dictionary?"

Curt glanced at Holt, eyebrow arching. Holt's head bobbed like a bobble doll. Curt pursed his lips then flicked aside the picture and typed Aram. Both men squinted at the screen. *Aram: ancient name for Syria.*

"Well, I'll be," said Holt.

Curt looked up at Holt and asked, "You brought me something?"

Holt snapped to as if just awakening. Yanking a book out of the armload, he said, "I managed to get my hands on last year's yearbook."

Curt took the book and opened it on the desk. "Granite Mountain Academy," he read aloud, "hand in hand with Granite Mountain College, displays academic excellence and expansion of youthful minds."

"Yeah," snorted Holt. "Meanwhile, underneath it all is a clandestine culture, Aranea at the helm, personally selecting kids with the sole purpose of molding them into the most lethal angelic-looking terrorists ever known to mankind. Bet they claim they do it at the will of a greater power, too."

"Indubitably," said Curt, flipping pages. He stopped at the junior class picture. "Alice Milton. Bert Moro. Vic Sag." He glanced at Holt. "Background checks?"

"Not yet," said Holt, "but I seriously doubt that those kids come out of ghetto back alleys."

"I suspect they come from all walks of life," said Curt. "Aranea's spiderlings have to blend in to avoid suspicion. Take this Chas Riley. Marked by dwarfism."

"Good cover," said Holt. "Keeps authorities off-guard. Here's some campus shots that came in with a bunch of other stuff from the Bureau."

Flipping through the snapshots of youthful faces milling around granite edifices, emerald lawns, or shadowed woodlands, Curt oozed with bitterness. "Pomoroy must've taken these."

"The plant?" asked Holt.

"Yeah," huffed Curt. "The settings are anything but tense. Redheads, brunettes, blonds. Innocents learning to play Aranea's deadly game. Several types of uniforms. Depends on activity, I suppose. One would expect practical jokes from any one of them—firecrackers, water balloons, things of that nature." In the midst of swallowing phlegm, he focused on the next picture. He choked.

"You okay?" asked Holt, slapping Curt between the shoulder blades.

Red faced and watery eyed, Curt struggled to recover as his finger pointed at the snapshot. "Ka-tri-na Wa-ters!"

"Uh-huh," said Holt, flipping the snapshot. "Says here her name's Kitty Star."

Eyes bugging out, Curt spluttered, "That was the wee one's name in Judgment!"

Chapter 21

You're not going in there with me," said Katrina, tossing her head side to side. "It's hard enough for me to get out."

"Please," Chas pleaded. "I can show you the way."

"You already have," she said, recalling the crude map he had drawn in the sand behind the kennel. Two more entries into Granite Mountain awaited her, one to the south above the parking garage and one to the east. The map also outlined five levels to what Chas called the warren. She had seen only three, but exploring all five was pushing the envelope. "I want you to go back and wait with Mickey Blue Eyes."

"At least let me go with you to the mineshaft," he bargained.

She stopped and put her hand on her hip. "If I agree, promise you won't beg to go inside?"

His head tilted slightly. Holding up three fingers, he said, "Scouts honor."

"Let's go," she said, waving him on.

As they tramped along the logging road that snaked through the woods to the east entrance into Granite Mountain, the sky was gray, threatening snow. The woods looked ugly and shadowy, as if stalked by death, martyrs taunting a truth too hard to accept. Katrina knew they needed heavier clothing, but Chas wasn't one to wear more and she would have to give heavy clothing to him before going into the mountain. She couldn't risk getting overheated and having to peel off layers. Carrying clothing would slow her down and leaving behind traces of her presence was out of the question. She was still

189

stressed about the shoes she had lost the second time into the mountain. *Those shoes have to be inside the mountain, because we retraced my trail outside the mountain and didn't find them. Gosh, I hope they're out of sight.*

"Jonathan will kill me if I don't tell what you're doing," said Chas, "but telling kills me, too."

Katrina stopped in her tracks and gawked at him.

He stopped. His eyes avoided hers. "Jonathan told me my mother was a high-powered professional—well-educated and successful—but she gave up her job and moved with my father from L.A. to a quiet little town fifty miles away, because they thought it was the perfect place to raise kids. Then I came along and didn't meet their expectations—you know, small and stuff, no hope to be athletic or star of the baseball team. Jonathan says I disobeyed them a lot, and they threw stuff at me and yelled about spawning a freak. They even threatened to get rid of my dog, but I don't remember my dog at all. I tried to kill myself—that's what Jonathan says. Child protective service got involved..."

Moments passed. The wind picked up, howling, and with it, traces of snow.

Katrina shivered. "So what happened?"

"Can't talk about it," he muttered.

"It's the only way to get it off your back," she said.

He gave a one shoulder shrug. She started to walk. Not hearing his footsteps behind her, she was about to turn around when she heard him running to catch up.

"Just because someone's well educated and successful," he said, "don't mean they'll be a good mom or dad."

Don't turn him off again, she thought.

"My father divorced my mother because of me," he said.

Katrina stopped and jammed her hands into her hips. "Says who?"

"Jonathan," said Chas, trudging ahead.

"Figures," she spat, dropping her hands to her sides and starting after him.

"Jonathan says my mother drank like a fish," said Chas.

"One day, she got so blind drunk that she burned me with a cigarette. You ever smell flesh burning?"

Katrina gritted her teeth, holding temper in check.

"My mother crossed the divider line and crashed into an oncoming truck," he said.

"Jonathan told you that," said Katrina.

Chas nodded.

"You have to know by now that the Araneas are manipulating your emotions," she said.

He nodded.

"So everything they tell you—or tell any of us—is bogus," she said.

He nodded.

The road ended like the others at a brush blind. She opened it as before. On the other side was the same kind of mineshaft that ended at a granite barrier. She pressed the familiar blemish. The ground shook as the barrier slid left exposing another dark tube. "Do you have any idea what that is?" she asked.

Trying to look innocent, Chas looked up. *Rehearsed innocence,* she thought. "You know what that is," she said.

He kept silent.

"Why can't you tell me?"

He lowered his head and stared at the ground.

"Have I ever done anything to hurt you?" she asked.

In a voice that Adriano might use, he said, "N-o-o."

"You can share anything with me," she said, "if you're willing to. You know that, don't you?"

He shuddered.

"Chas?" She touched his shoulder.

He peered at her, tears pooling his eyes.

Are those crocodile tears or are they for real, she wondered. Then memories of Judgment accosted her. *No, Chas isn't just a precocious child actor miming. He's been through the Araneas' chambers of horrors. His mind is blocking it out.* She put her arm around his shoulders. "When you're ready," she said, "I'll be here to listen."

"But what's going to happen?" he whined.

This time she shuddered. "Wish I knew, but I can't predict the future. I can say whatever happens will happen for a reason and we'll see it through—together. Right?"

He smiled a thin smile.

She squeezed his shoulders and then let go. Stepping to the top of the dark stairway, she looked over her shoulder. He had a sad, lost-puppy-dog look about him—an unhappy, empty look that pined for her not to leave him behind. "Don't even go there," she sputtered. "You promised."

Hanging his head, he mumbled, "I'll close up the mine entrance so nobody knows you was here."

She descended the stairway the same way she did the other two. Taking off her shoes, she worried about those she had lost. Inside another communication center, she hid behind black metal cabinets. Everything was the same: consoles, turbines, music, canaries, cables, cameras, huge steel door, icy-faced technicians, and that disgusting stink.

"Mary's Song" protected her mind as with muscles primed for a fight, Katrina headed to the archway and onto the landing of a stairway. She looked up, musing, *I have to go up there one of these times.* A noise sent her scooting down to the next landing and into a long hallway that had a door on each side. She cracked open the door on the left. A state trooper was asleep on a chair tilted back against the wall. His legs hooked the rungs. His cap was pulled down over his eyes. She quietly closed the door and tiptoed across the hall. The instant she cracked open the door, half a dozen dogs leapt against wire cages, clawing, fangs snapping, and making the most grotesque sounds. *Laryngectomies—just like Mickey Blue Eyes. That racket's going to wake that statie.* She stepped inside, pulled the door closed, and flattened against it. She frowned. *These dogs are intent on tearing me apart. They'd devour me even before I'm dead, if they could get to me.* She spotted heavy leather clothing and gloves hooked to the cages and chains and ropes wrapped around tires on the floor to the left. Cattle prods, pry bars, bite sticks, and burlap bags hung on the wall. *This is why Mickey Blue Eyes freaks. It's not the logging roads. It's the scent of the inside of this mountain and the memory of what happened in here. She didn't come from any shelter. She came from here. I don't blame her one bit for hating the Araneas. I do, too, no matter what Doctor Edie says about hating. Not only do they oversee everything that goes on around Granite Mountain, they're training dogs to kill. But Siberians are a non-aggressive breed. How are they doing it?*

Sliding along the wall to the right, she came to a clinic-like area. She glanced at the dogs that were beginning to settle down. Still their eyes never left her. *Gosh, wish I could make them better. Looks like they need a square meal and warm blankets to lie on, not ice-cold granite.* She took a step. *There they go again, on the attack. That's what they are! Attack dogs!*

Rage filled her—and then grief. She spun around and flattened her hands on the wall. "Oh, my poor Mickey," she moaned, thumping her head against the wall. "Wait a minute…" She turned and fell against the wall. "Attack dogs are trained to attack on command." She pressed her fingertips into her throbbing temples. "What's the command? Will Mickey Blue Eyes respond to it, too?"

Chapter 22

I *don't know what or why or anything else,* fumed Ken, a couple days prior to picking up Katrina for Christmas break, *but something's going on with my baby girl and the Royals are at the bottom of it!*

Since that day in the market, he had been keeping tabs on every little thing the Royals did. Today, he was scheming to run into Jeanette who had a set routine of marketing Monday and Friday mornings at 8:50. As fate had it though, a flat tire on Julie's white minivan got in the way. "If you don't change the tire right now," whined Julie, "I can't finish my Christmas shopping—that is, unless you take me…"

"No, no," he sputtered, wanting nothing to do with that. "Take my car." After she left, he discovered the tire was not only flat but threadbare, totally beyond repair. The others were marginal. "Why can't women just break down and buy tires once in a while?" he grumbled. "Now I have to add the tire store to everything else I have to do." He hauled the undersized spare out of the trunk, mounted it, tossed the flat into the trunk, and sped off to the market. Jeanette was halfway down the frozen food aisle. "Another half hour," he grumbled, "and I'd've missed her." He strolled along the freezer, pretending to be searching vegetable choices. Failing to get her attention, he feigned a coughing fit.

"My goodness, Ken," she cried, rushing to him. "You all right?" She whacked him on the back.

Bingo, he thought, faking more coughs. Watery eyes, a red

face, and a snotty nose completed his performance. *Could've won an Academy Award for this!* He popped a cough drop into his mouth, which just so happened to be in his pocket. He cleared his throat rather loudly. "So," he blustered. "Where's the Royal family spending the holidays?"

"Florida," she said, opening a freezer door and taking out a package of breakfast sausages. "My parents winter in Lakeland."

"Oh, what a shame," he said, sarcasm spiking his voice.

She eyeballed him.

"Uhm...not really a shame," he stammered. "For you...but I...uhm...and Julie...we had it in mind to invite you...and the family...for supper...you know...while Katrina's home for the holidays."

Jeanette seemed to find him comical, and of course, Ken took umbrage. "That's so nice of you," she said. "But we're leaving tomorrow and won't be back until the week after school starts. My children have assignments to complete. I won't have them falling behind. They promised to make up whatever they miss."

Ken scratched his head, thinking, *The Royals can't cover for Katrina if they're not around. Well, I don't care! They're all in cahoots! I just know they are!*

"Ken?" asked Jeanette, jabbing his arm.

He looked down at his arm and then at her. He cleared his throat again and said, "Maybe spring break?"

"Sounds like a deal," she said and then gave him a sidelong look of levity. "Happy holidays." As she hurried off, he squinted at her. *That woman's one hell of a good actress,* he mused. *Don't tell me she's on the up and up.*

The next day, he sat in his car down the street from the Royal home. When they came out to pack up their car, he ducked behind the steering wheel. Then they drove off. He tailed them—all the way to the Rhode Island border.

Early the next morning, Ken, Julie, and Adriano started out for Granite Mountain. Katrina had insisted that they come early. "Promise me you're not going to spoil the holidays with your craziness," said Julie, clasping Ken's hand resting on the floor shift.

He glanced at her hand then at her. "I've been on the losing end of several go-rounds with you," he said, "since that day in the market. I'm acutely aware that I'm facing an uphill battle in which you refuse to participate."

"Please?" she whined. "I want this Christmas to be ultra special."

He looked into the side view mirror and mumbled, "I'll keep my big yap shut."

"What's a yap?" asked Adriano.

Julie gave the boy a fleeting smile and then squinted at Ken. "You're not the least bit convincing."

He kept his eyes glued to the road ahead while thinking, *She reads me like a book!*

"You've been simmering on this much too long to go soft this quick," she said.

His eyes narrowed. "What are you making such a big deal about?"

"I'm telling you," she said, "if you're not careful, you're going to scare Katrina off. If she's struggling with something like you think she is, going nuts won't gain you any ground. The only thing you can do is just be there. When she's ready to open up, shut up and open your ears. I truly believe that the only thing she's facing is the fear of how to accomplish her hopes and dreams. But if indeed you're right, find out what she's mixed up in and don't minimize it. Don't burden her with your own hang-ups."

He shot a look at her. "Hang-ups?"

"You always do that," she said.

"No, I don't," he stormed.

"Yes, you do," she insisted, "and it's time you stopped. Life gives Katrina her own set of worries. She doesn't need your imaginary ones."

"I have an imaginary friend," spouted Adriano.

"Yes, dear," said Julie, smiling into the backseat. She glanced at Ken. "It takes a lot of energy to deal with adolescent concerns. Best thing is build some quiet time for you and her. Reassure her—if she needs it. And for heaven's sake, don't push for information or clarification. Maybe all she needs is a little attention from you—like when you helped build that translator at Thanksgiving. If you ask me, she's made peace with the past and is facing new choices. It's time you did the same, my love." She squeezed his hand.

He looked over at her.

"Besides," she said, eyes sparkling, lips holding back laughter, "when Adrienne is born, Katrina will be her special guardian angel, wait and see."

He rolled his eyes as amusement sheeted his face. "Here we go again."

"Mama," whined Adriano. "You forgot! My name is Adri-*a-no*!

On Granite Mountain, clouds were a blinding white against the cobalt blue sky and Katrina was waiting, suitcase and all, perched on the front step of the dorm. The palms of her hands cradled her chin. The instant she spotted the car, she jumped to her feet, waving and smiling like crazy. Ken and Julie sent each other astonished glances.

"Pop the trunk, Dad!" hollered Katrina, running up to the car. She tossed the suitcase and other paraphernalia into the trunk and hopped into the car. "I'm going to sleep for a week!" She hugged Adriano, and instead of kissing Ken and Julie, tapped them on their heads. "Let's go! Did you make spaghetti, Mom?"

"Per your instructions," said Julie.

Ken glanced in the rearview mirror at Katrina buckling up. He struggled to contain the question festering inside him since Jeanette and Phyllis had let the cat out of the bag about Thanksgiving. Noticing how thin and baggy-eyed Katrina looked, he asked, "You been sick?"

"Uh-uh," puffed Katrina, winking at Adriano.

Julie gave Katrina the once over. Her brows came together. The look she gave Ken was like an iron band tightening around his chest, crushing his heart, and robbing him of breath. Imagining the worst, he thought, *I should be here to help my baby girl, to comfort when she's sick. Protect her. I've got to get her back in her own bed every night.* He envisioned the night that Katrina returned from Mississippi and the way she had trotted off to bed as if she had never been abducted. Ralph was in her arms. The third time he peeked in on her, a whisper came through the darkness, "Don't worry, Daddy. I'll be here in the morning." The past didn't cloud her life, but for him the healing had never begun. Like an infection, it festered. *It's all my fault Regina and Jake took my baby girl. It's all my fault she languished in Judgment, Mississippi all those years.* He just couldn't pat himself on the back for finally piecing the clues together that led to her safe return and freedom for many other youngsters. He just couldn't stop himself from wondering: *Why did she lie about the Royals?*

"We should stop for a sandwich and potty break," said Julie.

"I'm okay," said Katrina, clasping her hands behind her head and dropping back on the back seat.

"Not me," said Adriano.

"There's a convenience store near the Mount Washington Hotel," said Katrina. "Use the bathrooms there and grab some sandwiches to eat on the way home."

"My goodness, you're in a big hurry," said Julie.

"Spaghetti and my own bed," said Katrina. "Can't wait. Hey, listen to that great music!"

Suddenly aware of the Four Tops belting out a song on the radio, Ken glanced at Julie. Her eyebrows jiggled up and down. The Turtles came on next and then the news. "At this hour, authorities are investigating an explosion outside a two-story, glass-fronted McDonald's restaurant in southwest Washington, DC. The incident occurred during the crowded lunch hour. Eleven people were injured, one seriously. Officials disagree on whether the explosion was a terrorist act or just criminal in nature. Eye witnesses report a male looking to be in his late teens had leapt from the vehicle he was driving and ran from the scene seconds before the car exploded. The identity and whereabouts of the male suspect are unknown, but a radical Moslem group is claiming responsibility."

"It makes me furious," said Ken, "that someone can claim divine motivation as an excuse to kill and maim others. Very self-serving."

"No God commands such cruelty," said Julie.

Ken glanced in the rearview mirror. His stomach knotted. *My baby girl's pulled into herself like a turtle. She's fallen into a funk.* By the time he pulled into the convenience store parking lot, she appeared to be asleep. *Something's up. I just know it.*

The next morning, Katrina walked into his office and announced, "I'm going to check out the neighborhood."

"When will you be back?" he asked, taking pains not to look away from the computer screen. Even so, a light had come on in his head. *Here's my chance. I'll see what she's up to.*

"I won't be long," she said, kissing him on the head. "An hour or so." Her footsteps faded down the turned staircase.

He leapt to his feet. At the office door he picked up the sound of the front door opening. He raced to the staircase. The front door closed. He ran down the stairs, grabbed his jacket off the rack, and cracked open the front door. A slit of sunshine hit him in the eyes. He blinked hard. *She's at the end of the walk! She's opening the gate!*

The gate closed itself as Katrina headed down the sidewalk and Ken slipped out the front door. He speed-walked to a rhododendron bush then parted branches to see her glance over her shoulder and then cross the street. She turned the corner of the block. Glancing up at the sun, he filled his lungs with air. *Tailing's going to be a big problem.* He barreled out the gate and down the street to the corner, unnoticed all the way to Brighton City Hall where Katrina jogged up the marble steps. "I can't go in there," he grumbled, running his hand through his hair. "Half the place knows me. I installed all the city's computer systems, for crying out loud. What in God's name is she up to?

Well, standing here like Phillip Marlowe isn't going to make it."

Crossing the street to the park where trees provided cover, he feigned a contemplative state while keeping an eye on City Hall.

"Well, if it isn't Mr. Waters!"

He spun around and up and downed a petite, agile-looking woman. Her black eyes and short bouncy hair shimmered like mined coal.

"You don't recognize me." Laughter interlaced her speech as she put out her hand. "I'm Miss Matthias, Katrina's Ecology Club advisor…well, ex advisor."

This Miss Matthias laughs too much for my comfort, ruminated Ken. *Yet I can understand Katrina's attraction for her. But as I keep telling my baby girl, demons charm with a smile.* He glanced past the woman to the door of City Hall. *But does my baby girl listen to her dear ol' Dad? No-o-o.*

"Are you waiting for somebody?" asked Miss Matthias.

"Uh…no," he breezed then palmed the air. "Just enjoying this unusually warm weather." Clasping his hands behind him, he looked like a monk walking down the path away from City Hall. *Don't need Katrina catching me talking to Miss Matthias,* he mused.

"How is Katrina doing at Granite Mountain?" asked Miss Matthias, tagging along.

"Fine," he said. Realizing that Miss Matthias had been heading in that direction in the first place, he stopped and looked at the sky. If he had been wearing an aba, it would have been swaying as he shifted from one foot to the other.

"Well, I won't disturb your meditation any longer," said Miss Matthias, continuing on. "Tell Katrina I was asking for her."

"Most certainly," he said and then under his breath, "When hell freezes over." He glanced at City Hall. *The door's opening!* He slithered behind an evergreen bush. *Katrina's grinning ear to ear. What's she so tickled about?*

⬿

Christmas Eve tradition called for each member of the Waters family to open one present before hitting the hay. The youngest went first. Choosing the biggest gift he could find, Adriano tore into the silvery blue wrapping adorned with Santa Clauses, sleighs, and reindeer. "It's the sled I asked Santa at the mall for!" he squealed.

"All you need is snow," said Katrina while searching for a present tagged with her name. When Julie coughed, Katrina glanced at her. Julie's eyes were steering Katrina to one particular gift wrapped in pink glittery paper. Katrina picked up the gift, saying, "I take it, you want me to open this one." Julie looked like she was about to burst, so Katrina unwrapped the gift. "A Rocky video?"

Julie wriggled up to Ken. Their eyes ogled one another.

"Baby!" squealed Katrina. "We're having a baby!"

When the commotion died down, Katrina handed Julie a giant box wrapped in red and white stripes and blue stars. "It's not much," she said, "but..."

Julie unwrapped the present. Another box was inside. Another box was inside that one. The last box contained a packet that she carefully opened. She peeked inside then pulled out forms stapled together. Her head tilted as she read the computer-generated card paper-clipped on top of the forms. Her eyes widened and rolled toward Katrina.

"What is it?" asked Ken, taking the forms.

Adriano squinched his face and asked, "Mama's present is papers?"

Ken read aloud the card clipped to the forms: "It is time for Mrs. Julie Waters, my Mommy J, to be my honest-to-goodness mother. A few hours in court the day after tomorrow and we will be a complete and legal family. Please adopt me, Mommy J." Slack-jawed, Ken glanced at Katrina.

"I know I only paid ten dollars for that packet at Family Court Services," said Katrina, "but I thought you'd like it. It's what *I* really wanted for Christmas. I knew I had to be the one to go to City Hall and ask for it, so I..."

I'm such a schmuck, thought Ken.

"This is the most beautiful present I've ever gotten," said Julie, putting her arms around Katrina. "A gesture straight from the heart. Driven by love."

There wasn't a dry eye in the room, which, of course, included Ken's. *If Regina had survived that plane crash,* he thought, *she never would've allowed Katrina to be adopted—even if I had managed to keep the harpy out of our lives. Regina couldn't deal with happiness, especially as genuine as this.*

The day after Christmas, Katrina came into his office and announced, "I'm off to the Royals."

Ken kept his eyes glued to the computer screen. *Good heavens, how long is this Royal business going to continue?* The light that was coming on in his head didn't glow as bright this time. The Royals were definitely out of town. "So," he asked in a singsong voice, "what are you and Phyllis up to today?"

"Mall," puffed Katrina. "Stuff like that."

"When will you be home?" he asked.

"Nine-ish."

"Long day," he said.

"I'll try for earlier," she said then kissed him on the head.

Listening to her footsteps thumping down the stairs, he asked himself, *Do I really want to feel like a schmuck again?* The front door opened. The front door closed. He ran his hand through his hair. He jumped up and scrambled out of the office. He slid down the banister, grabbed his jacket off the rack, and paused. *Schmuck!*

Cracking open the front door, he saw Katrina pull the hood of her pink slicker over her head as the gate closed behind her. *It's beginning to rain.* When she disappeared down the street, he slipped out the front door. At the rhododendron bush, he parted branches. Katrina glanced over her shoulder. She turned the corner of the block.

Rain dampened his jacket but not his determination as he hurried to the corner and ventured a peek. *She's crossing the street.* On the other side, she glanced over her shoulder. *If it wasn't for this rain and fog, she would've seen me.* He followed her into the subway station and stood off to the side at the top of the escalator. *She's buying tokens. She keeps checking her watch.*

Katrina grabbed the tokens and hurried through the turnstile.

Ken sprinted down the escalator and tossed a ten-dollar bill at the ticket agent. "Hurry it up, bub," he squawked.

"Hold your horses," said the unintimidated agent, counting out change as if it were the first time he had ever done that.

Ken grabbed the bills and stuffed them into his jacket pocket. "I better not miss that train," he snarled. While scraping coins and tokens off the edge of the counter into his hand, a coin fell on the floor. He didn't take time to pick it up, instead racing to the turnstyle, stuffing tokens into the slot and shoving himself through. At the second set of escalators, he stopped and looked to the left. *Did she take the outbound?* He looked to the right. *Or the inbound?* His eyes ping-ponged between the two. "Shoot," he blasted.

Taking two steps at a time down the outbound escalator, he was halfway down when he spied Katrina making her way through the crowd on the inbound side. He spun around and bumped into riders all the way up the escalator. At the top of the inbound escalator, he spotted the train coming to a stop. He slid down the sidewall. She stepped into the third coach from the end. He ran for the second coach from the end. Passing her coach, he turned his head away and kept low. *She can't see me anyway. The windows are all steamed up on the inside and rain-slicked on the outside.* He made his way down the aisle and chose a seat where he could see through the door windows to the back of her blond head that bobbed above a seat in the third car. *Schmuck.*

She stood up as the train approached the Boylston Street Station. He slid into the seat way out of sight as the train lurched to a stop. The doors slid open. *She's leaving!* He bolted for the door then trailed her up the grinding escalator to the exit. Outside the kiosk, he got too close. When she stopped and glanced around, only a dark curtain of rain kept her from seeing him. *She seems to be taking in the smells and sounds of the city. She's not dressed warm enough to be hanging around like that. I know I'm not. She's going into the library. Can't blame her for wanting to get warm.* He crouched over, shielding himself from the downpour, and waited. He danced the jig to keep warm. He ran his hand through his hair. *Where in the world is she?*

The walk sign at the corner lit up. A crowd of people crossed the street and came his way. As they passed, Ken fell in among them. Passing the library's glass-enclosed lobby, he saw no sign of her. At the far end of the windows, he swung out of the crowd. *Only way to find my little girl is to go in.*

Inside the massive lobby, Ken felt small, insignificant, in plain sight. *It's going to take all day to find her. I'll ask that guard at the checkout.* "Excuse me, sir. I'm supposed to meet my daughter, but I'm late."

"What's she look like?" snorted the guard as if accustomed to the refrain.

"Blond, spirally," said Ken, his index finger corkscrewing down the side of his head. His hand leveled to where the top of her head came to him. "This tall."

The guard pointed a thick index finger and said, "Young-un fitting that description headed off that way, five, maybe ten minutes ago."

"Thanks," said Ken, hurrying off.

A search of book aisles and reading tables turned up nothing. About to give up, he spotted Katrina skipping up the stairs from the basement. *She made a pit stop,* he thought while hanging back behind an aisle of books. *Could use one myself but…* He followed her up to the second floor to the computer room. On the opposite side of a bookshelf, he pretended to be searching the books while peering through them. *She's logging onto the Internet. Could do that at home or at the Brighton Library three doors down from Toffee Castle. Schmuck. She's researching a school project, that's all. But she usually tells me about them. Sometimes, we even work on them together—like that computerized language translator we worked on during Thanksgiving. But coming all the way to the Boston when she can do the same thing on her own computer in her bedroom? Humph. She's afraid of Addie bugging her. He's always busting into rooms without knocking—like when he busts in on Julie and I when we're getting familiar.*

Time dragged. Ken heard Katrina mumble a few times, but couldn't make out the words. After a time, she got up, stretched, and gathered up her belongings. He shadowed her down the stairs to the lobby. *She's heading toward that guard! He might ask her if I found her?* He ran his hand through his hair.

An alarm went off, and the guard hot-footed it down the hall toward the atrium. As Katrina left the building, Ken heaved a sigh of relief. But then a recorded message came over the loud-speaker, "The library will close in thirty minutes."

"Not much time," mumbled Ken, racing up the stairs to the computer that Katrina had used. He logged on and waited. His mouth was parched. His fingers tapped on the edge of the keyboard. "Foolish computer's too slow! I better forward the addresses of the sites she visited to my computer. I'll go over them later." Upon finishing, he picked up his jacket and shook out the moisture and wrinkles.

"The library will close in five minutes," warned another recorded message as Ken stepped out of the library into wind-driven rain. Down the street he ducked into a micro brewery, ordered a dark beer, and made a mad dash to the men's room. He came out feeling like a wrung-out mop. Not caring who might see, he flopped down on a stool, leaned his weight on the bar, and shivered. He chugged beer, wiped his runny nose on the sleeve of his jacket that clung to him like spider silk to a bug, and grunted, "Schmuck."

Chapter 23

"*D*id you hear that?" asked Penny, glancing into the condo from the balcony.

"Hear what?" asked Curt.

She hugged her pale yellow satin robe around her. "Somebody's at the front door."

"This late?" he asked, half-glancing at his wristwatch, which he'd already taken off for the day. During past Christmas-New Year shut downs, he never bothered to put on a watch, but this year, the escalating war in the Middle East had eliminated the shut down thus requiring the wearing of his watch. *Isn't it interesting,* he mused, *that the United States suspends actions during Middle Eastern religious holidays, but it doesn't work the other way around?*

The knock came again, and this time, Curt heard it. Doing an about face, he spouted, "This is one heck of a time to come calling."

Penny dashed into the condo; and the jasmine that had sweetened the air went with her. The scent didn't rise from the garden below where the change of season had taken its toll. The scent had come from Penny—and Curt noticed.

A brisk, male voice filtered out to the balcony as a fifty-ish-looking man shambled into the living room. Though he was dressed in a faded blue jogging outfit, his straight–clipped features disclosed a military background. The manner in which he scanned his surroundings suggested more. As Penny gestured to the sofa for the stranger to sit, Curt scraped his fingers across a five-o'clock shadow that should have been dealt with earlier. Barefoot and clad in a white tee shirt and light-weight gray sweatpants, he shuffled into the living room. The stranger who hadn't taken the invitation to be seated extended his hand and asked, "Doctor Curt Shirlington?"

"And you are…" asked Curt, taking the man's hand.

"MacPhallon," said the stranger, flashing FBI badge and ID. "Don MacPhallon."

Curt nearly dropped in his tracks. "I must say. You are a chap full of surprises. Working undercover?"

MacPhallon gave himself a quick once-over. "Oh, the clothes," he breezed. "Got dropped off half a mile away and jogged in. Better that way."

"Please," said Penny, again gesturing to a chair. "Coffee?"

MacPhallon gave her an exploratory glance. His hands scraped together.

"Or perhaps something stronger?" she ventured.

"Bourbon—straight—if you got it," said MacPhallon. His eyes followed her until she disappeared into the kitchen.

"What can I do for you?" said Curt, sitting on the sofa.

MacPhallon dropped onto the chair and clasped his hands. Making eye contact with Curt, he said in a cold, dry tone, "You dispatched a crew to Granite Mountain."

Curt wanted to belt out, *What in Hades do you expect?* Instead, he spoke in a matter-of-fact tone. "Irregular situation up there, wouldn't you say?"

"Jonathan Aranea is not an individual to fool with," said MacPhallon.

"Katrina Waters attends Granite Mountain Academy," countered Curt.

"FBI's aware of that," said MacPhallon, "and her history."

Efficient, observed Curt. *Orderly. Time to test a theory.* "Ken Waters and Peter Blair," he said, "are not aware of the wee lass being involved in another sleeper cell."

"Not at this point in time," hedged MacPhallon. His right eye squinted toward the kitchen. His palms grated together.

Bourbon is high on this chap's list of priorities, mused Curt.

SPIDERLING

"As unpalatable as Katrina Waters' presence is on Granite Mountain," said MacPhallon, "to extract her would be a big mistake."

"For the United States," added Curt. "Not for the wee lass."

"When do you plan on telling them?" asked Penny, returning with a tray laden with three old fashion glasses containing mixed drinks and clinking ice cubes. She extended the tray toward MacPhallon and pointed with her nose. "The Bourbon's closest to you."

"Thank you, ma'am," said MacPhallon, picking up the glass. One gulp did away with a large portion.

Curt exchanged looks with Penny. She extended the tray to him. He took the glass of Rob Roy and filled his mouth. He didn't swallow. It worked faster that way—more often than not.

"The fewer involved the better," said MacPhallon, staring into his glass.

Penny took her Cosmopolitan off the tray. Sitting next to Curt, she propped the tray against the coffee table. She sipped the drink, looking like an actress prepping for a role—knees together, ankles crossed.

"On a short leash that Pomoroy," said MacPhallon. "No following inside. One of these days, he's going to take the midnight train."

Curt swallowed. The inside of his mouth tingled. He wanted to conceal what little he knew, what he speculated, but speculation is one thing, facts another. Appearing knowledgeable, he said, "The Granite Mountain cell is linked to the Middle East."

MacPhallon raised an eyebrow and studied Curt. He leaned back, crossed his legs, and said, "I'm going to take flack for this."

"Goes with the territory," said Curt.

MacPhallon swilled down the rest of the Bourbon. "CIA, State Department, and military leaders assume they have the Middle East hemmed in. I—rather the FBI is not convinced. Nukes both in country and out. Failure in either case means disaster, no matter how we look at it."

Curt's brow fused. Pieces of the puzzle fell into place. His stomach flip-flopped. What was the completed puzzle going to look like? "A nuke is set to go off in the Middle East concurrently with one in the continental United States?"

"Inside Granite Mountain," said MacPhallon. "Additionally, Aranea and his cohorts are planning an attack similar to the way Jake Waters, or whatever his name was, intended before Regina Waters hid the vials of sarin in the candy-colored clown."

"I can't believe the threat's that real," spewed Penny, taking the empty glass from MacPhallon.

"I've never seen anything like the info Pomoroy's feeding us," said MacPhallon as his eyes followed her to the kitchen, "and I was a tunnel specialist in Nam. Four silos are inside what look to be deserted mines. The missiles are nuclear equipped."

Curt shook his head. Sloshing Rob Roy around in his glass, he wondered, *What's eating at MacPhallon?*

"Seems to me," said Penny, returning with the bottle of Bourbon, "Mr. MacPhallon has deeper concerns."

The wench thinks like me, Curt mused while watching her refill MacPhallon's glass and then set the bottle smack in front of MacPhallon.

"Thank you, ma'am," said MacPhallon. He took a swig. "Pomoroy's the sort to go down with the ship; and I can't figure out a way of getting a life boat to him when Granite Mountain goes down."

"You two must've worked together a long time to be this attached," said Penny.

"You might say that," said MacPhallon.

"Aranea's the classic primordial tyrant," baited Curt. "He uses violence to maintain his grip on power."

"Like the spider that continually evolves," said Penny, "so does the terrorist."

Both men squinted at her. Curt took several gulps of Rob Roy. "Leander Holt and I surmise that Aranea has the magic bullet," he said, "capable of bringing down the United States in a single stroke—and single-handed."

MacPhallon nodded. "Pomoroy's gleaned information that there's uncertainty about the cohesion between Middle Eastern factions and Aranea. He's ready to dump them, a full-fledged mutiny, and wage his own assault on us infidels. He's got the assets. He's got the brainpower."

"What's the time frame of addressing the situation?" asked Curt.

MacPhallon dragged his hand down the side of his face and neck. His eyes rolled. "Six months to a year."

"No bloody way," blasted Curt, setting the glass down hard on the coffee table. "Six months is utterly out of line, never mind longer!"

MacPhallon swilled down his Bourbon, grabbed the bottle by the neck, and filled his glass. "Battlefield advisers, scouts, and interpreters with ground forces inform us that an invasion force of a minimum two thousand basic combat as well as a thousand specialized skilled troops will not be adequately trained and coordinated before then. Building up equipment stocks nearby must be accomplished before deploying troops. An Army task force of Apache helicopters is needed, but getting them into the area without attracting attention? Focus is supposed to be on the Middle East, not New Hampshire."

Curt sucked in a chest full of air and got to his feet. "I see your point," he said. "I've been onto it only months, but six more? A year? And Aranea not get wind of it? It's a bloody miracle he hasn't already." Anxiety built in the pit of his stomach.

"The FBI is an organization full of fine people who love America," said MacPhallon, "but it is not meeting the times or this challenge."

"Where is Emily, the Cat when we need her," said Penny.

Curt shot a look at her. "Great minds think alike."

She sent him a perplexed look.

"Forward spotters recommend we take out the ammo dump that Pomoroy told us about," slushed MacPhallon.

The Bourbon is having its affects on the chap, thought Curt.

"Cache includes anti-aircraft missiles," rambled MacPhallon, "plastic explosives, homemade bombs, at least six RPGs, ninety rockets, two mortars, and seventy-five mortar rounds."

"A significant threat to helicopters," said Curt, pondering the scenario. His thumb and forefinger squeezed his bottom lip.

"Plus," MacPhallon emphasized, "thousands of blasting caps, hundreds of grenades, untold machine guns and ammo rounds. Aranea's having Pomoroy rig all roads and bridges within fifty miles to explode via remotes when Aranea gives the word. Granite Mountain will be isolated with enough food and supplies to keep going dozens of years. But Pomoroy's jerry-rigging the bridges to our specks. He's not done yet."

"Can't make a move without consulting Pomoroy," said Penny, dropping onto the sofa, not as prim and proper as before.

MacPhallon gawked at her. He seemed surprised by her presence.

Curt swallowed hard then asked, "Other choices?"

MacPhallon shook his head. "Negative." He heaved a sigh. "Battle used to be a simple thing. Generals studied maps strewn on their desk. Got up and barked, 'Follow me, men!' Everybody ran off after him, yapping, 'Yes, sir! Yes, sir!' Not that way anymore. We got contract officers, lawyers, and worse—the media. Where, when, why, and how? Everything laid on the table for the world to see before we get a chance to get it done."

"Terrorists follow no rules," said Curt. "No military codes of conduct."

"They target civilians," said Penny, "and perceive us weak, because we value life. That thought pattern emboldens Jonathan Aranea. He is fully aware of world reaction and slyly uses it."

"He's got the finances without Middle East backing," said MacPhallon. "It's a fact he also gets illicit aid from misguided nations. Contrasting that, the war has had a huge drain on resources, which includes allies, for the United States."

"Every person who comes into this country should be known," said Curt, "and why they are coming."

"People worry too much about civil liberties," said Penny, "but checks and balances in this country make that worry such a waste of time. In the meantime the real bad guys slither around unchecked."

"What about a Stryker Brigade Combat team?" Curt asked. "Thirty-five hundred men deployable to global hotspots within ninety-six hours? The Stryker troop vehicle can be dropped on

Granite Mountain, ready to fight upon landing. It's a tank, so Aranea can't take it out that easily. State-of-the-art equipment will take him out first. Meanwhile, another of the same vehicle full of infantry cruises in at sixty miles-per-hour."

MacPhallon filled his mouth with Bourbon, clearly a ploy to remain mum.

"What happens to the kids while all this is going on?" asked Penny.

MacPhallon swallowed quickly. "My point exactly. If we swarm in there like angry hornets to snatch them…kaboom!" His hand slapped against his glass and ricocheted off it as if exploding.

"What about valium?" suggested Penny. "A massive spraying in and out the mountain? It's been used to calm riots."

"Critics contend that violates international treaties," said MacPhallon, "and Federal law. The military wants no part of it."

"Military being General Colin Thornton," spat Curt with a haughty air.

"He's no lightweight," warned MacPhallon. "Even the Administration is bowing to him on this occasion."

"I'm prepared to lock horns with the General," said Curt as the cuckoo clock chirped midnight.

MacPhallon winced. "Thornton's really pissed off about being yanked from his Middle East command and put in charge of the Granite Mountain operation, which he deems is degrading. He's going to get himself some glory one way or the other."

"One way or the other," said Penny, "substances like valium make people unconscious and unconscious people fall down, causing injury—sometimes serious."

"Don't matter," said MacPhallon, waving her off. "Proper strength of the spray presents a hassle. How much to use inside the mountain and in the different chambers? How much to use outdoors? Air currents, valleys, etc. etc." He chugged his Bourbon and didn't go back for more. "Serious consideration for arresting Aranea months ago was snaffued when Pomoroy got the inside scoop that Aranea has pre-programmed kids to achieve his goals even if he's put out of commission. Military and political analysts are mining the Araneas and their spider-lings for possible moves. Will the kids be rudderless without Aranea? Give up WMDs in exchange for survival? Do his dirty work and unleash those weapons to wreak maximum devastation? What if they strike out on their own? Roaming the countryside, looking for targets? His graduates are doing that already."

"The Araneas are substitutes for the faith those kids have lost," said Curt. "Kids see hope in the Araneas, so admit it or not, they pose a real danger."

"That's affirmative," said MacPhallon, looking as if he was about to salute.

"You haven't weeded out the programmed kids," said Curt.

"Spider-shaped pewter pins set Aranea's spiderlings apart," said MacPhallon. "Only a few are programmed to follow through."

"And they remain a mystery," added Penny.

"We have to throw the first punch," said MacPhallon. "Pomoroy's procuring intelligence maps and charting out invasion routes."

"How about pinpointing a Hellfire missile carried by a remote-controlled Predator drone?" asked Curt.

MacPhallon scrunched his face and mumbled, "Have to evac' the kids before the brown stuff hits the fan."

"And also find a safe house for the kids to go," added Penny.

"No other choice but to wait until everything's in place," said Curt. "Makes for quite a delay."

"Can't afford that much delay," insisted Penny.

"Can't afford anything less," countered MacPhallon in a low, slushy voice.

The chap's completely lost decorum, mused Curt. *He's going to stagger out of here like Uncle Charlie going home on a Friday night.*

"Another consideration has to be taken into account," slopped MacPhallon. "Deadly chemical powder with particles small enough to penetrate protective gear."

"Aranea's got dusty weapons?" asked Curt.

"Confirmed," said MacPhallon. "The dust form of the blister agent mustard that Iraq used during the eight year war with Iran. He's also been developing deadly nerve agents that can penetrate the latest protective gear."

Penny drew up her legs and wrapped her arms around her knees. "Nightmare scenario," she puffed while resting her chin on her knees.

"So plans remain in flux," said Curt.

"By necessity," said MacPhallon. "At present the invasion force contains only one fully deployed heavy armored division."

"And stockpiles of vaccines are inadequate," said Curt. "The crew I sent to New Hampshire…"

"Cut off," said MacPhallon.

"Robert Pomoroy," said Curt.

"Indirectly," said MacPhallon. "Your crew will be checking in soon."

"Pomoroy still incommunicado?" asked Curt.

"He's back," said MacPhallon.

"That cell in New Mexico is another wake up call," said Curt, looking to confirm another assumption.

"Not the slightest inkling it was there," said MacPhallon. Shaking his head, he yawned. "Gives pause to wonder how many more cells are there—or reconstituted cells—on our hallowed ground."

"A question that should've been asked," said Curt, "before everybody went off half-cocked to rescue Katrina Waters in Judgment, Mississippi."

Chapter 24

*A*fternoon sun streaked through the trees, striping the
kennel clearing in light and shade as Katrina drilled
Mickey Blue Eyes. The scant inch of snow that had fallen on the
Presidential Range during the holidays was gone by the second
week of January. Only traces remained in places the sun didn't
go. The seasonal deficit was such that not one ski area had
opened. The discovery of the vicious dogs inside Granite
Mountain spurred Katrina into retraining the husky. *I'll start
from scratch,* she thought. *Try to deprogram bad behavior. Wish I
knew that word. I can't let Mickey Blue Eyes turn into a killer.*

"How come you keep making your dog do easy stuff?"
asked Chas.

"She acts weird sometimes," replied Katrina. "Mickey Blue
Eyes, heel."

"Got any trail mix?" he asked.

"Front pocket of my backpack," she said, pacing back and
forth with the dog walking smartly at her side. "Help yourself."

Chas fished out a package and while opening it, said,
"Weird—like up at the logging roads."

"Strange, don't you think?" she asked. "Mickey Blue Eyes,
sit. Stay."

Chas dumped trail mix into his mouth and crunched away,
his eyes on Katrina backing up a short distance and then stopping. As her hands fell to her side, he swallowed. "Jonathan's
hard-wired all the dogs around here," he said. "Just like he done
to me. Like he done to everybody."

"Think so?" she asked and then pointed at the dog. "Mickey Blue Eyes, drop."

As the dog flattened on the ground, Chas said, "'Fess up. You poured over dog training books at the library. You searched the Internet. Can't tell me you didn't."

Her heart skipped a beat. *Should I tell him that isn't the only research I did? Tell him about brainwashing? That the only way to resist it is to be a Buddha, allow no emotions, positive or negative, to surface? I was a Buddha because of Regina, long before Mississippi. But the Araneas are managing to mold other kids into puppets that will work and die for them and their cause. Oh, I hope Chas is okay. I think he's on my side, but... I know Bert, Joe, and Alice are totally hooked. I saw how they manipulate others—as if they have a common enemy. Until I figure out who that is, I'm not telling anybody about what I know. It might blow up in my face. But it's so hard to watch the strong-arming and do nothing. I have to do everything in my power to disrupt what's going on. I'll get kids to flub up, really mess things up. There's already distrust in the ranks. I'll build on that.*

"Did you read about dogs that are bred for certain traits?" asked Chas, stuffing the half-empty bag of trail mix into his pocket.

"At ease, Mickey Blue Eyes," commanded Katrina. Getting down on one knee, she opened her arms to the gleeful husky. "Understanding hardwired characteristics helps break habits. Some habits can never be broken." She and the dog tumbled on the ground. "That's why I think I can break what that man hard-wired into Mickey Blue Eyes."

"Man?" asked Chas. He laughed, which he rarely did, but it was a terrible laugh. "You don't mean Jonathan?" His levity vanished as he dropped on the ground next to her. "If anybody can deprogram a dog, you can, but after, can you do me?"

"If only I..." she began.

He clasped her arm. "I care about you," he said. "And I think you care about me. But...but I know you don't...you don't look at me like I was...well...you know...normal. Like I was someone you..."

"Chas, I..."

He put his index finger against her lips and whispered, "It's okay. Just remember this. No matter what, I'll always do my best to get you through stuff."

"Stuff?" she asked.

He let go of her arm. "You're so lucky," he sulked. "You got a family that cares about you. I see how you and them are. You can go home to them any old time you want to. I can't. I don't have a family."

Noticing his eyes narrow, she followed his line of sight. *Bert's coming. I don't like the look on his puss.*

"You got options," continued Chas, his eyes glued to Bert, "when you decide you need them. But stop hiding stuff from your family—and from me. We can help you find your way…"

"I helped you find your way," interrupted Katrina. "I got you to stay away from junk food, to sleep more, and…"

"That don't get me a family! Or out of here!"

"You just can't give away your power to control your destiny," she pleaded. "People do that too willingly. Don't let yourself be one of those people."

"You need to come with me, Trina," said Bert.

"Don't go!" cried Chas, grabbing her wrist. "Call your father!

She squinted at Chas. "Dad?"

"Trina," said Bert.

She leered at Bert's beckoning hand and then his face. His eyes avoided hers. *He's uneasy,* she thought. *Something's up. Something dangerous! I'll have to face it if I'm ever to find out what the Araneas are up to and uncover other places like this.* She shoved his hand aside and got to her feet. As she swiped dirt and grass off her pants, Mickey Blue Eyes clung to her leg and Chas scrambled to his feet, wailing, "Don't go with him!"

"Take the dog back to the dorm, Chas," said Bert, turning and heading toward the Administration Building. "Let's go, Trina."

Katrina followed, Mickey Blue Eyes still clinging to her leg.

Bert spun around. "Do as you're told, Chas!"

Katrina stopped. Her closed fist nudged the dog's muzzle. "Mickey Blue Eyes, stay."

Chas grabbed the dog's collar as Bert clamped onto Katrina's arm and tugged her away. She glanced over her shoulder. *Chas and Mickey Blue Eyes aren't moving. Chas looks like he's about to bawl. Mickey Blue Eyes is whining.*

Bert veered off into the parking garage and dropped her arm. Nearing the door marked Authorized Personnel Only, he said, "Don't let anybody see you use this door."

She slipped earplugs out of her pocket, careful, so Bert didn't see. She wormed them into her ears as he punched a series of numbers on the keypad mounted on the wall. The door unlatched. He grabbed the handle, paused, and then looked at her.

Something in his eyes, she mused. *Something…*

He yanked open the door and led the way along the same corridor she had roamed three other times. She passed the corridor on the left where name tags were stuck to doors. She passed the corridor on the right where the Araneas' office was located. She shivered. *Where those spiders are.* Pretending to scratch the side of her head, she nudged an earplug and listened. *Just as I expected—background music.*

Bert stopped and got down on one knee. Fiddling with a shoelace, he whispered, "Earplugs won't help." Standing, he spotted the mortified look plastering her face. His eyes shot a quick glance at the camera and then back to the shoelace he had just faked tying. "You and I," he whispered, "are beyond earplugs."

She clenched her fists, grumbling, "I'm sick and tired of beating around the bush with you. Tell me what's…"

His hands cupped her face, and he kissed her hard and then gentle, seductive. Pulling her away from the camera, he removed her left earplug and then pulled her around the other way and removed her right earplug. He stopped kissing her and looked deep into her eyes.

Confused and feeling vulnerable, Katrina hummed "Mary's Song."

He smiled and backed away. "The cafeteria's over here." His hand made a sweeping gesture to the right and ended up in his pocket. The earplugs were gone when his hand came out. "Cereals, sandwich materials, and cookies are in those cabinets. Drinks are in here." He opened the refrigerator and took out a bottle of pink lemonade and a can of root beer. "For more substantial eats, you have to go out to the main cafeteria on campus." Snapping the cap off the bottle of lemonade, he slid a glimpse at the camera in the corner and then at her. He hesitated and squinted at the bottle. He handed it to her.

One sip reminded her of the island and the bottle of water. She pretended to swallow. Turning so he couldn't see, she spat lemonade into the bottle. Turning back to him, she pretended to drink some more. An uncomfortable silence surrounded them as they studied each other. Though she knew the answer, she asked, "Where are we?"

He started out of the cafeteria. "It's called the warren."

She dashed to a trash container and dumped lemonade out of the bottle. When he turned to see if she was following him, she leaned against the door frame and pretended to drink. "You coming or what?" he called.

I have to act spacey at some point, she thought while plodding after him. *Pass out, too, I guess.*

They turned to the right past the doors with the labels. "Tacky, huh?" he said, barely looking. Six doors down on the left, the label stuck to the door read, *Hello! My name is Chas!* The thirteenth door on the right read: *Hello! My name is Bert!* He stopped in front of the fourteenth door on the right and on it the remnants of C A M. Handing her an unmarked tag, he said, "Write your name on this and stick it over the old one. Here's the key to your own special retreat."

She took the sticker and key, pretending to be spacey. She dropped both, also, the bottle. It didn't break, but pink lemonade slithered along valleys in the chiseled granite floor. Fumbling the key into the lock, she fumed inside. *I despise you, Bert Moro, for trying to drug me again. You're going to pay big time.*

He pushed down the handle and entered a ten-foot square cubicle. Neon lights glared. A fire alarm was centered in the middle of the ceiling. A camera spied in one corner. Wire shelves with nothing on them were attached to the wall above a computer perched on a desk. The desk chair was black. A full-size bed was pushed against one wall and a green army blanket was drawn back as though it were bedtime. Terror raced through Katrina. *I think I'm over my head.* She slumped a bit. Bert grabbed her arm, sat her on the bed, then hurried to the door and locked it. As he turned around, she plopped back onto the bed, but kept watching him through slitted eyes. He stepped over to the desk. *What's he doing? Preparing a syringe? More drugs? That lemonade didn't have enough? How can I fight him off if I'm drugged even worse than on that island? Wait a minute—I hit him back then! If the drug in the water made me do that, he'll think it's the drug in the lemonade making me hit him again. Just let him try to jab that needle into me. I'll flatten that pervert!*

Bert heaved a huge sigh, turned, and came over to the bed. He stood over her, quiet for a moment, and then said, "Hard times come to us all."

Somebody pounded on the door.

"Shoot," he spouted. He went to roll her onto her stomach. She squirmed. She almost got away, but he fell upon her.

"Get off me!" she screeched.

"Shut up!" he snarled, shoving her face into the pillow. The needle invaded the thickness of her right hip, stinging like a wasp releasing venom into her bloodstream. She choked for air. His mouth jammed against her ear. "For God's sake, shut up and I'll get rid of the pillow!"

She nodded. He lifted the pillow. She sucked in air. He fingered her hair, saying, "If you only knew what you mean to me."

Pounding on the door rattled the room.

"Hold your horses!" hollered Bert.

As her body shut down, "Mary's Song" drifted within the fog and her vision faded in and out of focus. She watched him unzip his pants and go to the door. He messed up his hair then unbuttoned his shirt. He tore off his shirt, balled it up, and flung it at the chair. It dropped on the floor as he glanced at her. He hurried back to her. His lips touched her cheek. His voice was liquid. "I'm not bad—just not as good as I want to be." He tossed the blanket over her. Distant pounding. Then "Got her again, 'ey dude?"

"Can't you ever butt out, Ault?" spat Bert. "I ain't no sixty-second man. I take time to enjoy my work."

"Quit your bitching!"

Vic, she thought as blackness sluiced over her like a tropical downpour. Visions of cruelty and indoctrination wrapped around her like serpents. *Brita…Alice…* A repetitive beat, thump, thump, thump, like a human heart, came from inside her, came from outside of her. *Jonathan… Meredith… O'Mara… Matthias…*

Katrina snapped out of a murky coma-like sleep, springing into a sitting stance, gasping for air. Several terrifying moments passed. *Who am I? Where am I?* Heartbeats pounded in her ears as her eyes shot to the left then to the right. *A cubicle—I'm in Camille's cubicle! All by myself.* She gathered the blanket to her neck. *My clothes are at the bottom of the bed! And the shoes I lost!* A tremor wracked her body. *Dad's right! Terrorists* will *stalk me all my life!* Shaking off the fog, she rubbed the soreness out of her arms. "Mary's Song" ebbed and flowed within her mind. *These aren't ghosts of the past, Doctor Edie. These ghosts are real!*

The door flew open, and Alice marched in. "Spiderling Kitty!" She tossed back her head. "Yeah, right!"

"Spiderling?" asked Katrina, dropping her legs over the edge of the bed. She stood up, woozy, then fell back on the bed.

"You're doing real good," snorted Alice, "considering. Lot better than me."

Katrina toggled to the foot of the bed. On top of the lost shoes was a spider pin. *This one's bigger than mine.* She picked it up. *Heavier.* She eyeballed Alice's pin.

"Get the big ones when Aranea figures he's gotcha under his spell," said Alice. "Now listen up. Here's how it works. The dorm keeps up appearances for outsiders, families, students who ain't completely indoctrinated. Keep a few clothes and other necessities on those shelves above the computer. The main closet's down the hall. Show it to you later. Special clothes and tools are in it for assignments."

"Assignments?" asked Katrina, putting on underwear.

"You'll find out soon enough." Alice made no secret of watching Katrina dress. She leaned close as if about to kiss Katrina. "Hell's a-brewing," she whispered

Strange, Katrina thought. *No smell of booze.*

Alice straightened, pulled a nip from her pocket, and downed half the contents. "Get a move on, Missy!" she barked while marching to the door.

Katrina slipped on the left lost shoe, but putting on the right, her toe rammed an obstacle. She tipped over the shoe. Earplugs plopped into her hand—all three pairs. She stuffed them in her pocket as Alice opened the door and scanned the hallway, back and forth, as if courting danger, as if expecting to get caught. Katrina sucked in a chest full of air then got to her feet and waddled to the door.

"This was on the floor," said Alice, pointing to a blank nametag on the door. She handed a pencil to Katrina. "Write your name on it or the Araneas will have your butt." Alice seemed antsy as Katrina wrote Kitty Star on the nametag. When the pencil bumped over edges of the previous sticker where the letters C A M lingered, Katrina almost puked. Without further conversation, Alice led Katrina to the door to the parking garage then turned and faded back into the warren.

At the exit ramp, Katrina felt off-balance, spacey. She drew in fresh air. Snow fell off a nearby hemlock and powdered her face as Chas stepped out with Mickey Blue Eyes. "Been waiting for you for days," he said as the husky jumped at Katrina, issuing warped greetings.

"Days?" asked Katrina, her eyes drilling into Chas.

"I got real worried," he whined, his head wavering side to side. "Some kids don't ever make it out."

Horror filled Katrina. Grabbing the leash, she bolted for the dorm. Chas hustled after her. She yanked open the door, but didn't look back. *He's there. He's always there!*

"Kitty!" shrieked Brita, jumping off the top bunk and landing like a cat. "You're back!"

"Not so fast," said Katrina, fending off Brita. "I saw you there."

"Oh, paleease," scoffed Brita.

"You were there and didn't stop them!" raged Katrina, furious and disappointed and wanting Brita to know. "You're supposed to be my friend!"

"Like Alice says," Brita sneered, raising her palms to shoulder level, "'Friendship is overrated.'" Arrogant, she blew a huge bubble. It popped. Her tongue slithered out of her mouth like a viper, curling around pink and pulling it in.

Katrina stormed off to the bathroom. "Stay away from me!"

"Listen here, girlie," spat Brita, grabbing Katrina's arm. "Jonathan's got assignments for you and me, so get used to calling me bestest friend!"

"You're despicable," said Katrina, shaking off Brita.

"I find you annoying, too, Miss Smarty Pants," hooted Brita. "Especially the way you look at Vic!"

"I don't look at Vic!" snapped Katrina, slamming the bathroom door. "He looks at me!"

"Liar!" shrieked Brita.

Katrina glared into the mirror. *Look at me! I let them get me! Look at those needle tracks!* She turned her right arm to the mirror then her left arm, recalling Internet information: *Insulin lowers blood sugar levels, puts people in alpha states, makes them suggestible for...* Her body stiffened. *...Electric shock treatments?* She searched her reflection. *External signs: Trance. Eyes wide open, dilated. I'm a spiderling?*

The front door of the dorm slammed.

Good riddance, Brita, fumed Katrina, going to the bathroom window. Outside, clouds darkened the day—and darkened her spirits already in the toilet. She wanted solitude, to go inside herself and never come out, but memories of being a frightened four-year-old arriving in Judgment, Mississippi, surfaced. Jake was hauling her out of the back seat of his sports car. A woman hurled money at him then snagged Katrina's hand and drawled, "No use in resistin', Blondie." The first night in that woman's decrepit shack, Katrina crawled into bed and tucked the covers under her chin the way her father always did. His voice echoed in her head, "Night-night, my sweet cherub." She remembered his face, the way he laughed, the way he walked, and all the good things that had once been hers. She never stopped remembering as days turned into months, months into years. One day, soldiers dressed in camouflage uniforms and helmets with plastic see-through visors kicked down the door of the dorm. Kids screeched so loud Katrina could barely make out a voice hollering, "Katrina Waters! Katrina, where are you? Katrina Waters!"

I had lived for that moment. I had prayed for that moment. The dream continued until at last, Dad wrapped his arms around me and Ralph rubbed against me, purring like crazy. The world I once knew, the one with Regina and Jake in it, no longer existed; and that nasty house in Cohasset had burned to the ground. Dad was married to Julie who's the best mother I could ever want. Then we all went to live in Toffee Castle and Adriano (not Adrienne as Julie had predicted) came along. Now Mom's pregnant again and says the baby is definitely a girl—Adrienne. What a joker. How would it look—Adriano and Adrienne? Katrina chuckled. *I've had incredible highs and terrible lows, but I'm alive. Still here. Still able to fight.*

Across the field, snow smoke rose off gnarly crabapple trees then the Canadian wind disbursed it. *Last spring I skipped beneath those trees. Pink petals sprinkled me as if I was a bride. I'll never see so innocently again.*

A blue jay perched on a branch and poked at freeze-dried fruit—prosperity to wild creatures in the winter. *What has that bird seen that he can't tell? Gosh, I feel older than the hills!*

Doctor Edie's voice echoed in Katrina's mind, "The first lesson of survival is that nothing changes the past."

Katrina heaved a sigh then plodded to the bathroom door and peeked out. The dorm was empty except for Mickey Blue Eyes asleep on the floor. The leash, still hooked to her collar, snaked about her head. The husky trembled and then yelped. "It's okay, girl," said Katrina, going to the bleary-eyed husky. A sloppy tongue licked Katrina's hand. "Let's stretch our legs. This place is making us nuts."

Mickey Blue Eyes did the jig while Katrina bundled up in ski pants and jacket then pulled on boots and gloves. At the front door, a blast of arctic air clubbed them as though they were naked. Katrina grunted. *Winter finally arrives on Granite Mountain.*

Snow swirled across evidence of wild things and other trespassing entities as Katrina trudged beneath the crabapple trees. *Wonder who planted these trees? Veterans who founded this place long before I was a twinkle in Dad's eye?* She touched the bark, rough, brittle, yet protective. "Emma LaRosa says, 'Time has a way of setting things right.'"

Snow fell off the trees and down her neck, cold, but not cold enough to drive Katrina inside. She pulled her hood up over her head and followed the trail into the woods. Her boots dipped into the snow and crunched fallen twigs and debris. *How many veterans used this trail? Oxen teams hauling skids of logs for the hearths, framing timber, and innards of buildings? If those veterans only knew that terrorists are using Granite Mountain to spread evil. They called themselves the greatest generation, yet the evil percolated under their watch. No, it's not their fault. Terrorism is as old as time. Nobody was paying attention, that's all. Wish I could meet up with one of them. He'd be wearing a World War Two army uniform, long woolen stockings outside his pant legs, hat cocked to one side. He'd tell me to never give away my power to control my destiny. And I won't!*

A chattering gray squirrel brought Katrina back just before she stepped into a brook. Icy fingers reached out from both banks and entwined in the middle. Beneath, trickles skimmed stones and gurgled like the brother she hadn't seen in much too long.

She swooshed snow off a boulder that looked so much like the one in the backyard of Toffee Castle. She climbed up on it then clapped the snow off her gloved hands and stuffed them into her jacket pockets. She gazed up the trail. A vision of oxen pulling a skid with a fully decorated Christmas spruce, lights twinkling, appeared. A child sat between a woman and the male driver who put a gentle switch to the oxen. The skid drew near. The driver smiled at Katrina.

"Daddy?"

The woman waved at Katrina.

"Mom?"

The skid passed. The child turned backward in the seat and cried, "Kat!"

Sobs roiled deep inside Katrina then burst like tidal waves across the countryside.

Chapter 25

*E*ntertaining and attending parties has bogged me down too much," fretted Ken, finally getting a chance to sit down at his computer to investigate the sites Katrina had visited. "It's been impossible to look over the information I e-mailed from the Boston Public Library. I didn't have a choice but to take my baby girl back to that wicked mountain. Then Julie wants me to help clean up the house. Then I get the flu! What's this? Stockholm Syndrome? A condition wherein captives or controlled individuals admire, fall in love, or sexually desire their captors. Give me a break. I'm going to check out one of these human-potential training meetings. It won't affect me!"

However, at one of those meetings, it wasn't long before Ken was swaying to the music. He felt alive, carefree, open-minded. He wanted to get up and dance, though he wasn't much of a dancer to begin with. Then he realized what was going on. Rage burst forth, but then, he recalled a warning on the site: anger or resistance accelerates conversion. "I'm a sitting duck!" he squawked, jumping to his feet and snagging his jacket. He gawked at the crowd, the hands and bodies swaying to the music. "I'm not about to wait around for some in-your-face charismatic doodah like that Aranea maniac to strut up to that podium and brainwash me into performing like the rest of these monkeys!" He charged to the exit where he put on his jacket then glanced over his shoulder. "Look at all those joiners," he fumed. "They *want* to give away their power!"

As he left the building, snow peppered his hatless pate. "Don't seem cold enough to snow," he muttered. "Temperature's eight degrees warmer than usual." He leaned against the hood of his car and ran his hand through his hair. "So many people looking for answers, meaning, enlightenment outside themselves. Is my baby girl's doing that? Good, Lord! She's fallen prey to Aranea! He's another Jim Jones. Charismatic. Slick as a hen's tooth. If Jones convinced nine hundred people to drink poison Kool-Aid, maybe Aranea can, too!. He's leading kids down the same path! Bet Sag is under that jackal's thumb. Come to think of it, that tree-hugger used the shock and confuse technique I read about on me when he awarded Katrina that scholarship! He finagled the bagel like those weird-looking Hare Krishnas at the airport who jump right in your face, loud voices at first then quiet, smoothly pitching books and begging for money. Yeah, the Hares got me—once. I couldn't give back that book they shoved in my hands. How would that look? Forked over twenty bucks! Boggles my mind I did that. Guilt sure is a powerful tool. Makes it hard to say no to my baby girl. Humph. She's smart as all get-out. Been around the block with all this stuff. Bet she figured out Aranea a long time ago. Yup. She's one up on him. But she's in harm's way without tools to deal with those jerks. They'll turn on her in a heartbeat!" He jumped into his car. "Better see what else my baby girl found on the Internet and give her a hand!"

That evening turned into the next day as Ken studied sites Katrina had visited. *Among reports of illegal and reprehensible acts members of diverse cults commit, child abuse is a common thread that often leads to death. Rarely do children receive formal education. They don't develop normally, physically, emotionally, or socially. Young adults recruited into cults tear apart parents, siblings, and friends— anyone who struggles to understand and help. The majority of cult members are recruited during high school or college years.* Chills ran up and down Ken's spine. "What on earth has my baby girl gotten herself into?" He ran his hand through his hair. "Those self defense classes I made her take won't get her through this. This is a mind thing!"

"Sh-sh-sh," said Julie, touching his shoulder.

His entire body went rigid as if petrified by spider venom.

"You're going to wake Addie," she said, nudging him.

He clutched his chest, belching, "Scare me out of my drawers, why don't you?"

"You been up all night?" she asked, sitting down on the edge of the desk.

"What time is it?" he asked, eyeing the flowery pink bathrobe and matching slippers she wore. She was warming her hands around a mug of coffee.

"After six." Taking a sip of coffee, she glanced out the window. "Sun's coming up."

Ken ran his hand up the front of his neck and around the back to a rock-hard muscle. When Julie began to massage his neck and shoulders, he dropped his head back and took in a slow, deep breath. "You're not going to believe what my baby girl is up to. You should see the information that she got at the library."

"She went to the library when she was home?" asked Julie.

He nodded. "That day I got home late drenched to the bone?"

Her eyes narrowed. "You didn't follow her."

He cringed.

She backed away from him, jammed her hands into her hips, and stamped her foot. "Oh, come on!"

"She lies to me," he moaned. "I lost my baby girl—again! What am I going to do?"

"You didn't lose her," insisted Julie, snagging her coffee mug and storming out of the office. "And she's not your baby girl anymore!"

Ken slapped his hands on the desk and pried himself up. In the kitchen, he tried to explain: "When Katrina came home from that Ecology Camp, she was so excited about going back. After summer camp she came back quiet, reserved."

"It's called maturity," argued Julie, taking a mug off the wooden rack Adriano had painted at preschool. "Being on your own does that to a person."

"It's not the same," he blustered. "My lit…er…we used to be so close. Talked about anything and everything! But when she came home for Thanksgiving, she was preoccupied, like she lost her spark, I tell you. Her sense of humor has gone the way of the dinosaurs!"

"I noticed," said Julie, filling the mug with coffee. "But everything's coming at her so fast. It's normal to take a step back after a major life event like moving away from home. I took a major step back when I did."

"And there's that adoption thing," he said.

"What about it?" she asked, handing him the mug.

"There's more to that than meets the eye," he said.

About to fill her mug, she stopped and put down the coffee pot. A hurt look sheeted her face. "How can you say that? Katrina wanted me to be her legal mother, simple as that!"

He waved his head to one side.

She wrapped her hair around her ears. "Well, isn't it?"

"I hate myself for undermining the glow you've carried since that day in Family Court," he said. "You're a mother for the second time, and you're cooking a third *wee one*—as Curt would say."

"Look," she said. "Give Katrina time to put it all in perspective. She's got spunk."

Ken groaned. "Nobody survives on spunk."

Chapter 26

So tell me, Mr. Riley," said Jonathan, collaring the dwarf who had been scrounging the refrigerator in the warren cafeteria. "How is it that you do not report Kitty's explorations?"

Like a spoiled two-year-old, Chas held up his hands, shielding his head, and bawled, "Timothy told me not to! I wanted to tell you! Honest! But Timothy… he says he'll hurt me if…"

"Liar!" spat Jonathan, his right eyelid twitching.

"It's true!" shrieked Chas. "He says he's gonna lock me in the Conference Room and sic spiders on me! He did Camille that way!"

Struck dumb, Jonathan let go of Chas' collar, thinking, *Timothy takes credit for my deed?* He shoved Chas away. "That's absurd."

"It ain't!" insisted Chas. "He says it made him feel good, too! He hated Camille."

As did I, thought Jonathan, clenching his teeth. He eyed the hyperventilating, undersized stoolie. Raising a finger at the tip of Chas' nose, Jonathan growled, "Get out there and keep track of Kitty. From now on you are to report directly to me."

Five minutes later, Jonathan paced the warren office. *Timothy? Disloyal?*

Alice stumbled in, slushing, "Was over Jackson way…"

"Don't you ever knock?" spat Jonathan.

She blathered on, "…picking up supplies you wanted me to get, and…"

"Drunk as usual," he snorted.

She tossed a wad of money on the desk. "…caught Timothy red-handed, forking over a manila folder to a Fed."

Jonathan squinted at the wad. His eyelid convulsed. "Timothy cozying up to the Feds?"

"Bribed me not to squeal," she said. "I tell ya, the size of that wad sure is tempting."

"Bribery is a useful tool," muttered Jonathan, picking up the money. "Rashid uses bribery as a means to an end."

Her face twisted up. "Who's Rashid?"

"You sure the guy was a Fed?"

"Whadda ya think?"

A knock on the door inflated his turmoil. "Enter," he blasted.

Bert swaggered in, spewing, "Two bridges left to rig with C4."

Jonathan leered sideways at Bert. "You ever see Timothy act out of the ordinary?"

Bert shot a glance at Alice. His brow crinkled. "Uhm…" His eyes jounced about. "No-o-o."

Jonathan tossed the wad on the desk. "Nothing at all?"

With a tentative air, Bert said, "Not lately."

Jonathan grabbed Bert's shirt and shook. "When then?"

"A month ago!" blubbered Bert, eyes big and round. "Going into your bedroom!"

Rage boiled within Jonathan, but then the vision of a brief-case etched with gold initials, T. A., iced his veins. "Only Timothy and I know the combination! And I haven't opened that briefcase in over a month!" He pushed Bert aside and bolted out of the office. Inside the master bedroom, he slammed the door and raced to the closet. He shoved aside clothes, hauled out the black leather briefcase, and opened it. "Files are missing," he hissed. "Camille Jennes' file. Trophies of elegant executions. The file I put together on the fall of Judgment, Mississippi. Timothy's been real interested in that. Damn it! I broke the cardinal rule—never leave a paper trail! Well, Timothy didn't get his hands on my Judgment Day plans. Those remain locked in my head. So, my fat pig, you conspire against me. Well, Jonathan

Aranea will not be rotting in the infidel's dungeon while Timothy lives."

Jonathan slammed down the cover then shoved the briefcase back into the closet and stomped to the bedroom door. He tore it open. Bert and Alice jumped back. "Meeting in the warren office in one hour," barked Jonathan. "Moro! Get locks and deadbolts changed on every door in this corridor, stat! No copies of keys! Clear?"

"Yes, Mr. Aranea!"

At the office door Jonathan stopped and glared at Bert and Alice. "Breathe one word of this," he snarled, "and I'll skin you both alive with my own bare hands!"

"Yes, Mr. Aranea!"

Jonathan shoved open the door. Inside the office, he rotated the lock then stomped to the only chair that still fit Timothy's bulk and slid it into the furthest corner away from the door. He checked the vials on the shelf. "Two missing," he grumbled. "A significant reduction in serum levels in the rest. Timothy has taken some. No matter, I still have sufficient antidote if my intention goes awry."

☙

They came directly from classes, Timothy, Meredith, Aram O'Mara, Chas, and Vic. All were dressed accordingly and attached to every collar, thick-bellied, ruby-eyed spider pins. Bert and Alice came in last, looking more sober than ever.

Jonathan contained his wrath, though spasms seized the muscles around his right eye as he watched Timothy suck food particles out of his top front teeth while his fingertips played upon a mountain of belly. Jonathan yanked out the middle drawer of his desk and grabbed a pair of rubber gloves. "The conference to choose a unified leadership has been postponed," he snapped.

"Any new date?" asked Timothy.

"Inconsequential," shot back Jonathan. "I take charge of destiny. Ultimate will be the destruction."

"And the Aranea name shall live as long as time," added Meredith, resting her head against the back of her chair and gazing at the ceiling as if giving thanks to a deity.

Jonathan slammed the desk drawer shut. "It's long past due for old leaders who demean my work to step aside!"

Timothy entwined his fingers. His thumbs tapped his lips as he asked, "Does that not put you in bad odor with major power brokers?"

Jonathan's eyelid convulsed as he put on the gloves and turned the vivariums. He rapped on the glass of one. Inside, a Goliath Bird Eater Tarantula, bred for such occasions, took an aggressive stance. "My most trusted protector joins those who attempt to thwart my efforts."

Timothy's brow pleated. "Surely my ward does not speak of me. Many are the bumps in the road created by this rivalry between old and new divisions, but I assure you that I am not one of those bumps."

"Ah, but you are," seethed Jonathan, sliding the glass lid off the vivarium.

"I have been in total agreement with your every step," said Timothy.

"My point exactly," said Jonathan, reaching into the vivarium and trapping the Goliath Bird Eater Tarantula in his hand. Leaving its face visible, he lifted it out of the vivarium and stepped around his desk, his eyes flashing with deadly intentions. He paused in front of Meredith.

"Get that thing out of my face!" she stormed as her face twisted and her hand came up and pushed his hand away.

He smirked. "My vindictive villainess still lurks beneath the surface as lethal as the female widow."

She leered at him. Then a lecherous grin twisted her lips. Her eyes slowly closed and opened as her head and eyes bowed. "You honor me."

Stepping over to Aram O'Mara, Jonathan extended his hand. "Judgment, Mississippi was a shining star for the *jihad*. A tremendous loss. Converts scattered to the wind." As O'Mara's eyes bugged out, Jonathan would have bet his wealth that the slime ball was peeing his pants.

Vic, Bert, and Alice pushed themselves against their seats as Jonathan passed. "The Feds got wind of Judgment. That's how Katrina Waters was sprung," he said, halting in front of Timothy and holding the Goliath Bird Eater Tarantula inches from his face. "The snitch is right under my nose. It was all a put on, was it not, my protector?"

"I am not the one," panted Timothy. His eyes bulged. "Never have you known me to be a snitch!"

"I know now," said Jonathan, opening his palm.

"No!" shrieked Timothy as the tarantula leapt upon him. He tried to brush it off as chelicerae flipped out of its mouth like switchblades. He fell backward wedged in the chair as tips dripping with venom speared his neck. Saliva driveled out his mouth as Timothy convulsed. Then he was still.

"Pathetic," said Jonathan with sharp disgust as the tarantula partook in the juice that had pulsed through Timothy.

O'Mara pulled a handkerchief out of his pants pocket and mopped perspiration off his brow. Chas whimpered and swiped away snot with the back of his hand. Alice took a swig of Jack. Vic and Bert tried to act cool, but blood had drained from their faces. Meredith studied her nails as if nothing had happened.

"A true waste of an elegant creature," grumbled Jonathan while spraying insecticide on the tarantula. It keeled over onto the floor. Jonathan stepped on it. "Get this fat pig out of here."

Self-assured strides were not the case as Vic and Bert left. Their desire to be out of that office was more than clear.

"I once promised to roast this pig," said Jonathan.

"So it shall be done," said Meredith.

"We should wait for nightfall to fire the furnace," said Alice, a quiver in her voice.

Jonathan waved his hand. "Just get it done. Now—to the matter of headmaster. Aram O'Mara. I hereby appoint you to the position."

"Oh! Oh!" slobbered O'Mara, leaping to his feet. "The great Jonathan Aranea honors this humble servant Aram O'Mara!"

His breath stunk of reheated coffee as he grabbed Jonathan's hand and kissed it as though it were the Pope's.

Jonathan pulled his hand away and ran it up and down on his pant legs to remove O'Mara's sweat. "Beware," he cautioned. "Ingratiating mannerisms imitate the departed Timothy."

O'Mara hunched over in a show of respect and obedience.

Jonathan's mouth gaped into a yawn. "We take our leave, wife," he said, putting out his hand.

"Yes, husband," said Meredith, taking his hand.

He opened the door, stepped aside, and bowed. She walked out before him, pompous, a blithe nod of the head. He straightened and glanced back at the rattled spiderlings. He smiled with hedonistic pleasure. "All of you back here tomorrow. Same time. Final preparations begin."

In the hallway, Meredith clapped wildly. "You were magnificent! Truly magnificent!"

"I was," agreed Jonathan. Leading the way to the master bedroom, he drew in deep breaths of satisfaction. He unlocked the door. This time, he went first. Picking up the remote from the end table, he depressed a button. He took off his tie, unbuttoned his shirt and scanned the monitors. *The midget lurks outside of Kitty's cubicle. Inside, she changes from school uniform to hiking clothes.* In a slow steady beat, Jonathan said, "The trap is set. All that is left is the waiting."

Meredith cuddled against him, purring, "Nothing can stop us."

Containing revulsion, Jonathan shifted away. "Truly a shame the movement will not survive to see my accomplishment." He opened the closet door and took a box wrapped in cellophane off the top shelf.

"The old guard deserves annihilation," she said.

He put the box on the bed and cut the cellophane with his pocket knife. He opened the box and gazed upon the ancestral robes that had been cast off when he and Timothy arrived in Liberia so many years before. "From this day forward, I cast aside western ways forced upon me by the assassination of the great Mohammad Achmed al Hadi. My hair and beard will grow. I will be pious to the Eyes of the Afterlife as I command my spiderlings to carry out the programs I have engrained into them. Children and women as human shields. Mass casualties from biological and chemical strikes. Hostages with explosives strapped to them."

"Americans are too squeamish to allow their countrymen to be blown up," said Meredith, her hand drifting down his chest and belly.

He turned his back on her. Still, he could feel her eyes boring into him.

"What's going on, Jonathan?" she demanded.

He raised his hand, asserting, "Jonathan Aranea is just a name, not born of my true self. Therefore, I cast it off. I am Mohammad Achmed al Hadi from this day forth." She came around him, but he avoided her eyes. "I hear the voice of my father who once sent me from his presence. He now boasts of me and commands that I take his name." Jonathan removed his wedding band and placed it in her hand.

Her fingers contracted around the ring. She looked as though she had just taken a slap across the face. "You cast aside your own wife?"

Without a shred of emotion, he said, "I make myself worthy to meet the virgins waiting in paradise." He did not tell her that the Great Deity still required him to bed the fair Katrina Waters before his martyrdom.

Meredith grabbed hold of his arm.

"Find yourself another stallion to romp with in the sack," he spat, his eyes spearing her.

Her hand dropped from his arm. She took a step back, scraping the back of her hand across her colorless lips. Pulling off her engagement and wedding rings, she seethed, "Don't think for one minute I won't find me another stallion. There are many to choose from around here—all more than willing." About to throw the rings, she stopped dead.

"Those rings are worth a great deal," sneered Jonathan. "Are they not?"

Meredith leered at him then stormed out the door that connected their bedrooms. "This is bogus!"

He stepped to the door and slid the new deadbolt into place and did the same to the hallway door. He sucked in a breath and exhaled, "So be it."

Clad in ancestral robes, Jonathan slipped the signet ring of his father onto the third finger of his right hand and the signet ring he had worn as a son of royalty onto the third finger of his left hand. He had recovered both rings after many years of searching.

Extending his palms, he gazed into the heavens beyond the granite ceiling and droned, "I now withdraw to the bowels of Granite Mountain to dwell as my desert ancestors, never to feel the sun upon my face until the Day of Judgment wipes the infidels from the earth. That day, I avenge the death of the Mohammad Achmed al Hadi. I will respond to the Great Eagle's message in kind, 'Submit to the only survivor, the middle son, whose brazenness and insolence spared him. Be that I alone survived through Great Decree, I, the son of Mohammad Achmed al Hadi, now Mohammad Achmed al Hadi incarnate, am omnipotent, invincible—a prophet and martyr possessing no fear of the dawning of the nineteenth day of the third month— the anniversary of the assassination. The Day of Judgment.'"

Chapter 27

*O*h, the stories Curt had heard about Robert Pomoroy. The Federal agent, spook, snitch, or mole if you will, in a teenager's body had established credentials early on as a rebel, a monster, and the most thoughtful human being alive. Brave if not foolhardy, Pomoroy snubbed hanging around a location when he deemed another more significant. Funny. Difficult. A perfectionist. A pain in the butt. A string of disgruntled bigwigs testified to all these traits. However, they knew from the start what they were getting—an insignificant essential nobody—and Pomoroy knew they knew. They would wait and wait for him to show up and then he would shuffle in, appearing like any other pinhead in faded jeans, not at all startled by their agitation. However, this time, at 3:23 A.M. at an undisclosed location in Delaware, Pomoroy was doing the waiting.

General Colin Thornton was the last to arrive, looking none too pleased about having his sleep disturbed. Pitching his rump onto a chair, he growled, "Out with it. I don't have all night."

Pomoroy fingered the buttons on the remote to the video projector. He heaved a sigh and tossed the remote on the table. "March 19th is Judgment Day."

"Specifics," barked Thornton, scratching an unshaven jowl.

Pomoroy braced his feet against the table and tilted his chair back on two legs. "All I know, you know," he said. "Speed bumps are your problem."

Good show, laddie, thought Curt, his eyebrows arching. *Heard about you going head to head with Thornton and Thornton losing.*

Thornton's backed by the Pentagon, true, but you're backed by Pentagon plus the Administration. To say that Thornton is put off is a right proper underestimation, which puts you, my laddie, in good standing with me.

"Look here, young man," blustered Thornton, his fist threatening. "Don't go throwing slang at me! I know your great ambition is to save mankind, and I could care less. I, unlike you, am not in any position to go off half-cocked."

"I," echoed Pomoroy with a cool air. "Humph. *I* don't think so. Half-cocked? I learned to thrash out details before an event and not be caught in the middle where it'll cost the success of the mission and/or lives. A person in your position never learns that the hard way—your kind is taught about that in cushy classrooms—at the Point, right?"

Thornton scowled. *About to blow,* thought Curt. *Comical. How's it feel to be put off, General?*

"Simmer down," said MacPhallon, raising his hands. "Now, look. Obstacles big and small muck up the soup bowl surrounding Granite Mountain—resistance, chemical attack, logistical headaches."

"To put it mildly," added Thornton. "How about the speed of armored units to cover the distance and accomplish ground assault? Why, in my estimation, it will take that size force some eighteen hours—that's if everything goes uncontested. For example, blown-up bridges will slow water crossings. Though my troops practice bridge-building to reduce delays, even the most rudimentary bridge requires some time to construct."

"I took care of curbside explosives," said Pomoroy. "They're the least of your worries."

Thornton grunted.

"What about extracting the kids?" asked Curt.

MacPhallon frowned. His head wavered side to side a tad.

"Shock and awe them," spewed Thornton. "They'll abandon Aranea. Being optimistic, they will also turn on him."

Pomoroy expelled a lungful of air and dropped his feet to the floor. "Won't work—not anymore than dropping leaflets urging them not to fight. Although, I have run onto a small band that's intent on annihilating the place."

"If that happens before we act," said Curt, "the loss of young lives will be staggering."

"Whatever we can take out of the enemy's hands," spat Thornton, "won't be used against us."

"Ooh-rah," muttered Pomoroy.

"What did you say, boy?" snapped Thornton.

Pomoroy chortled and shook his head. "General," he said, pulling his chair up to the table, "you underestimate the resistance."

"What about a safe house?" asked Curt.

"I've come up with one," said Pomoroy, "but getting kids to go there is problematical."

"I don't think they will," said Curt. "Not with their altered states of consciousness."

"Problematical?" asked Thornton. "Or too detailed for you, Pomoroy?"

"When it's right, I'll take action," said Pomoroy.

"That's your job," said Thornton.

"It is," conceded Pomoroy, tipping his head. "I created this project, employed the Feds early on, and lived with it for half my life, but…" He smiled a sad smile.

"But what?" demanded Thornton.

MacPhallon grimaced. "Katrina Waters entered the mix. Can't take chances with her, not only because her grandfather is ex POW Peter Blair, but also because of her background in Judgment, Mississippi. The press will have a field day if anything happens to her, not to mention her falling into the same situation a second time in her young life."

"The press poses a grave danger in saving those kids while pulling off an invasion," said Curt. "We must never forget that fact."

"Friggin' reporters," griped Thornton. "Always ramming microphones in my face and shouting. No decorum whatsoever. Cameras exploding, blinding me, leaving blue floaters and dull aches in my head. The spaciness debilitates thought. Foreign reporters are the worst. They taunt like cobras. They know damned well that in their countries the truth is never tolerated or given."

"The press can be manipulated," said MacPhallon. "If need be, I will give a brief statement and regret the lack of time for follow-up questions."

"That's it," snorted Thornton, "and give them handouts of bull pucky—enough to last while I make a quick incursion on Granite Mountain. I can drop a load of airborne troops so fast that Aranea and his consorts won't know what hit them and their missiles and WMDs won't be a factor."

"You won't get Aranea," said Pomoroy.

"Why not?" asked Thornton.

"He's isolated himself inside Granite Mountain," said Pomoroy, "nursing vulgar illusions of being a prophet and martyr via his worldwide Judgment Day. Nobody and nothing can rein him in. His bloated ego gets in the way. He's even taken the name of his father. That small band I told you about recently found itself needing a diversion. So they set up Timothy Aranea. Jonathan went bonkers and released a killer spider on Timothy right in front of a bunch of us. He made us carry off the whale— took four of us plus O'Mara and two American Flyer wagons minus wooden rails—half of him on one wagon and the rest on the other."

"Aranea's delusional," surmised Curt.

"Over the edge," said Pomoroy, nodding. "He wears ancestral robes all the time and doesn't shave. Eats dates and drinks zouhourat."

"What the hell is that?" asked Thornton.

"Yellow tea made from hibiscus flowers," said Curt. "Calms the nerves—debatably—and eases an upset stomach."

"Aranea's struck out on his own," said MacPhallon, "effectively cutting himself off from Mid East backing. He is in the financial situation to carry on, having cashed in about three-quarters of the assets left to him by his father—the assets we know about, that is.

"Don't put it past him to use Katrina as leverage," said Pomoroy.

Thornton waved them off. "The key is surprise," he carped. "Always surprise—tactical, operational, strategical. So let's wrap this up and get at it." He braced his palms on the armrests of his chair and went to get up.

"You failed to mention political surprise," said MacPhallon, "which means we can't get on with it."

Thornton slouched. His fingertips drummed the armrests. "Why not?"

"Intelligence chatter indicates an event is about to go down in the Middle East," said MacPhallon, "and its roots are in Fort Stewart."

"Come on," hissed Thornton, "Georgia?"

"Come on, General," snickered Curt, glaring at the General. "Cow Hampshire?"

Thornton's jaw dropped.

"Oh," said Curt, "so you remember taking that matter under advisement. Bang up job, General."

Pomoroy rolled his eyes. "Aranea's sending some spider-lings to Fort Stewart."

"Mission?" demanded Thornton.

"Aranea waits until the last moment to issue specifics," said Pomoroy. "Up till then, it's an intelligence collection operation."

"Great," rumbled Thornton, falling against the back of his chair. "Brainwashed kids involved in intelligence ops."

"I believe," said Pomoroy, "the real mission is prep for eliminating Middle Eastern rivals."

MacPhallon looked at Curt and said, "I want you and Penny at Fort Stewart. Your guise is to oversee immunizations of recruits coming in for training as reinforcements for the 3rd Infantry Division. Penny will bone up battlefield nurses on possible chemical, biological, and nuclear incidents both here and abroad."

Thornton snorted. "Gentlemen. We are staring down Armageddon here. We cannot keep dinking around."

"Progress has been made, General," said MacPhallon. "Security at generation plants, fuel and water supplies, and air and sea ports have been beefed up. If Aranea fires off one missile, field ops are prepared to stop it. Since he's infiltrated law enforcement not only in New Hampshire, but also throughout New England, the FBI will head temporary law enforcement and emergency workers trained to handle mass casualties and biological or any other hazardous materials. Doctor Shirlington, his wife, and their teams have put together a public health system that can handle large numbers of victims and detect disease outbreaks before they get out of hand. When this is over, there will be full-time anti-terrorism units within the State Police of every state in the union. Governors will have broader emergency powers. There'll be tougher penalties on terrorism hoaxes, a streamlined emergency management office, and a back-up plan for state agencies to access critical computer data during emergencies."

Thornton's fingertips drummed the arms of his chair. "You people continue your little chitchat without me," he said, getting to his feet. "I'm off to knock the hell out of Aranea and his spider web before March 19th gets here."

"You lack authority to engage," challenged MacPhallon.

Thornton rammed his fist on the desk, and those in attendance jumped. "Authority will be mine after I set my Commander in Chief straight about the FBI, its spook, and the CDC standing around with their fingers up their butts! How long have you been doing that? Years you say? Now, with Judgment Day staring us in the face, do you think for one moment that our illustrious President, who happens to be coming up for re-election, will allow this country to go up in smoke?"

Chapter 28

*K*en cradled Ralph in his arms and stared out the north-facing window of Katrina's bedroom. His fingernails raked through long, gray fur. Ralph purred as Ken grumbled, "My baby girl was supposed to come home for Presidents' Day weekend." Ralph clicked. "Then she informs me she won't be home for spring break… some mumbo jumbo excuse that includes that foolish dog." Ralph clicked again. "Yeah, cat, I can't accept it either. Here it is the second week in March and I haven't heard hide nor hair from her. What is up with her?" He eyed her desk and then the pile of neatly stacked papers on the far corner. He placed Ralph on the window sill then stepped to the desk. His left index finger spread the pile. "What's this?" He picked up a sheet of paper. "A song?" He perused the words scrawled below a musical score: *Feed me the food of your soul, as nothing else can ever satisfy me.* At the bottom was a signature. "Chas Riley," murmured Ken. "She introduced him to Julie and me. Strange little guy."

The next paper was also a song. *Devote yourself to me as I am and always will be devoted to you.* Ken grunted. "Chas Riley has a thing for my baby girl."

Other songs followed then a picture of Katrina and a young man standing at the edge of a cliff at sunset. "That's the guy in the black convertible," rumbled Ken. He ran his hand through his hair. "Got a bad feeling about the gaga look plastered to your face, baby girl."

Ken reset the pile of papers to its original form then scurried to his office and tapped a key to wake up his computer. Plopping on the chair, he said, "I'll get to the bottom of this." He pulled up the home sites for Granite Mountain: College, Academy, Camps. Then he went deeper, prowling computers that allowed each place to function—electricity, plumbing, course planning, etc. "The further I go the harder it gets to break through built-in security, mazes, and other barriers."

"Now what are you up to?" asked Julie, coming into the office with two cups of cappuccino made from the machine Emma LaRosa had given them for Christmas.

"Just a sec'," said Ken, feverishly typing. "Gotcha!" His hands flew victoriously into the air. He winked at her. As she smiled that silly grin that she had inherited from her father, Ken grabbed the cup and took a sip. "M-m-m, you're getting good at this."

Her eyelashes fluttered, picking up the golden hue filtering in the east window.

"Tapped into Granite Mountain computers," he said. "Found only bits of info—curriculum, how beautiful the area is; so I went deeper. Aranea graduated from a private high school on Granite Mountain then the College in the late 70s. No sign of where or when he was born."

"That's usually the first thing you find out about a person," said Julie, scraping froth from the edge of the cup with the demitasse spoon.

"Those digs are not on the up and up," said Ken. He polished off the cappuccino in one gulp. "I feel it in my bones."

Julie licked the demitasse spoon. Laying it on the saucer beside the cup, she said, "There's no safer place than New Hampshire."

"It's a terrorist camp," he spouted, setting his empty cup beside the keyboard.

She took a sip of cappuccino. "It's impossible for Katrina to be involved in something like that again."

He ran his hand through his hair. "I got an idea," he said. He pecked at the keyboard. "Enter."

"You've got to let the past be," she said. As pictures and information about missing kids popped onto the screen, she gasped. "Where in the world are all these kids?"

"Gone without a trace," added Ken, downloading the data.

Julie wound a strand of hair around her ear. "In this day and age, it's hard to hide anything, never mind human beings."

"Which makes me worry," said Ken, clicking on his email. "Katrina hasn't emailed me in weeks."

"You're such a worry wart," scolded Julie while stacking their dirty cups and saucers.

"Worry wart, huh?" he spewed. "Then explain this: Why did she use the Royals as an excuse to sneak off to the Boston Public Library during Christmas?"

Her eyes roamed the room as Julie pondered aloud, "At the market, the other day, Janette was telling me about her visit with her mother in Florida. That was during Christmas."

"Look at these messages," said Ken, pointing to the monitor. "She's gotten awful sloppy for somebody attending the prestigious Granite Mountain Academy."

Julie squinted at the screen. "See what you mean. Her diction is much more concise than that."

They made eye contact. "Messages," he said.

"Messages," she echoed.

"Sloppiness is her way of letting me know she's in trouble," he said.

"Come on," said Julie, tilting her head.

"Everything's okay until she started at the Academy," he said, scrolling through email all the way back to Ecology Camp. "Then she emails less often. See?"

"And she doesn't ask about Addie," remarked Julie.

"Last time she mentions him is here," said Ken, "just before Thanksgiving."

"Errors pop up in January," she said.

"She sent this one," he said, "just after calling to say the roads were a mess, so don't come for President's Day. Now, she's not coming home for spring break."

"Nothing wrong with going skijoring with Mickey Blue Eyes," said Julie.

"Baloney," huffed Ken. "There ain't any snow. I emailed her and told her to call."

"But she didn't," said Julie, picking up the dirty cups and saucers. "Did you check your personal email?"

"She always emails me at this address."

"Won't hurt to check," insisted Julie. "Only difference in addresses is your middle initial."

Clicking on his personal email, Ken raved, "Clearing spam from my business address is a pain in the butt. I don't have time to clear both addresses. Plus everybody knows I check my business address at regular intervals through..." His jaw dropped.

"Told you," said Julie. "Katrina mixed up the addresses, simple as that."

"My baby girl doesn't mix up anything," he spat.

Julie read the first message aloud, "Everything's good here. Did you and Julie decide what to get Seth and Emma for their twenty-fifth anniversary?" Julie and Ken gawked at one another. "Seth died years ago," she breathed. "And they were married over fifty years."

Ken read aloud the rest of the message, "I'm too busy to come, but I'm sure everybody else will be there—even Fleming. Tell him Kitty says, 'Hi.'"

"We haven't seen Detective Fleming," said Julie, "since six months after he brought Katrina home from Mississippi."

"And she has never once called you Julie," said Ken.

Julie read the next email. "Here she asks how Grandma Konstanze is. She always calls her Gammy Getchen."

"Her next email says there's a snow drought," said Ken, "and it hasn't snowed since the holidays."

"She lied about the storm on Presidents' Day," said Julie.

"She didn't want me up there," said Ken. "She says here, 'Can't wait for spring vacation. I want to build sandcastles with Adrienne on the beach in Cohasset like we always do.'" He exchanged anxious looks with Julie. "Adrienne?" he said. "Cohasset?"

Julie covered her mouth with both hands. Her eyes bugged out.

"If I bring this to Fleming," said Ken, toggling back to his business email, "he's going to think I've gone bonkers again. I need proof. Hey, look at this. Up till September, she signed off, Love, K. After that just Katrina. After the holidays she's sloppy—not like those before and after."

"Somebody else sent them," said Julie.

"That's my guess," he said.

"The ones before are definitely Katrina," she said.

"Then she starts sending to my personal address," he said, "and signs Kitty, the name she was given in Mississippi. I tell you, she's sending me messages. She's in trouble."

"You better get up to Granite Mountain," said Julie, "and get some proof for Detective Fleming."

⌒

"Where can I hire a guide?" asked Ken upon checking into the Village Bed and Breakfast in Jackson, New Hampshire.

"Gus Tanner's your man," said owner Eric Poppin. "Best the North Country has to offer. Born and brought up in Jackson. Knows these parts better than anybody. Roots go all the way back to the Revolutionary War. He's sharper and funnier than the image of a Vietnam vet or backwoodsman would have you think. His cabin's up off Old Jackson Road."

"I'll need directions."

"Not wise to go up there."

"Why not?"

Poppin shuddered. "Gus has got one mean hound dog."

A chill shot through Ken. He ran his hand through his hair.

"Tell you what," said Poppin, reaching for the telephone. "Let me put a call in to one of his hangouts. Gus is a creature of habit, stops by the VFW for a brew first thing when he comes to town." Poppin cupped a hand over the mouthpiece. "Might take a day or two for him to check in though."

"I don't have a lot of time," said Ken.

Poppin mulled it over then said, "Why don't you take a ride on over to the VFW. You'll be there when Gus shows up."

Mid afternoon, Ken walked into the musty VFW lit by a single light panel in the suspended ceiling. The outdated brocade that draped the windows reminded him of the back bedroom in the manse; and the same kind of gloom bathed the place when the door closed behind him. His eyes adjusted. A hulk was leaning against the bar, weight on one foot while the other foot hooked the brass footrest that ran the length of the bar. Great ham-like hands surrounded a half-empty beer glass. Nobody else was around. Ken hitched up his britches then walked up to the bar. "Looking for Gus Tanner."

"What's up?" asked the hulk with an unexpected soft-spoken voice.

Ken cast a sidelong glance at the hard-faced man dressed in a dark blue work shirt and black pants. Bushy, brown-streaked gray eyebrows covered more skin than the thin gray wisps sprouting out his pate. "You Tanner?" The answer was slow in coming. Ken wondered if it ever would. The hulk leaned his weight on his forearms. Oxen-like, dark brown eyes fixed on him. Skin sagged beneath the hulk's eyes like the bottom half of smiles. Age wrinkled his brow and weathered his nose. A well-trimmed gray beard and mustache outlined his heavy-jowled mug.

"Let me mull it over," said the hulk. Looking away, he chugged the last of his beer.

A frail old geezer with reading glasses perched low on his well-scrubbed nose scooted out of the shadows as if on cue. "More suds, Gus?"

"Nix that," said Gus, pushing the empty glass toward the old geezer. "Need a clear head." His imposing six-foot-three inch frame straightened then came about. Hands dug into his waist, which with his broad shoulders and spread-eagled stance made him look like a humongous hourglass. His bullish eyes fixed on Ken. "Me and this here gentleman's got business."

Ken took a quick step back, neck hair spiking. A face-off with Jonathan Aranea would've been a lot less intimidating.

"Give a holler," said the geezer, retreating to the shadows.

"What's shakin', man?" asked Gus.

Ken swallowed hard. "I, uh..." He cleared his throat. "...I'm writing a book."

"Book?" asked Gus. Amusement lifted his bearded jowls.

Ken nodded like a guilty child. "Evolution of Granite Mountain—haven and learning center for WWII vets to the place it is today."

Chapter 29

Within the two hours of sleep per night that Katrina could not avoid, she heard Mickey Blue Eyes snarl. She pushed away a cold nose that nudged her cheek. A whimper came next; then forty pounds of husky plopped upon Katrina. She opened her eyes. A hand covered her mouth. Sandwiched between her and the person to whom the hand belonged was Mickey Blue Eyes. Though prepared to take on anybody and anything, no matter the size, Katrina reigned in the instinct to fight. *This is not the time or place. Not if I want to know why Meredith is slinking around at this ungodly hour.*

"Stash the mutt in the bathroom and come with me," hissed Meredith.

Katrina nodded, telling herself: *Keep my mouth shut. Survive. Judgment taught me: the most menial comment can bring about devastating consequences. But someday, the guerilla tactics the Araneas are shoving down my throat will blow up in their faces. They haven't a clue how obsessed I am, how vigilant I am—except during the two hours of required sleep; and wouldn't you know that's just when Meredith invades my space.*

Meredith removed her hand and stepped back.

Katrina shoved the husky on the floor and got out of bed. "Come, Mickey Blue Eyes."

The husky cowered.

Hooking her hand around the dog collar, Katrina felt the weight of Meredith's eyes. She towed Mickey Blue Eyes into the bathroom. "Mickey Blue Eyes, sit. Stay. No noise." She closed the door, secure in the knowledge that the husky was safe, but then other concerns surfaced: *Is this about those e-mails I sent Dad at his personal address? Hope he picked up on that. He has to have picked up Chas' rag tag emails during the time I was being programmed. He should've figured out that I'm in trouble when I mentioned Seth LaRosa and Detective Fleming. But what if Dad goes off half-cocked? That'll give the Araneas the edge. Oh, if they hurt Dad, I'll... I need to get to a phone! I gotta warn him! But phones around here are tapped. That one at the convenience store near the Mount Washington Hotel probably isn't. But how do I get to it? And what if the Araneas have programmed me to resist a rescue attempt? Gosh. I'm way off base thinking that I can handle this all by myself. This needs a lot more muscle than both Dad and I have!*

"Move it," spat Meredith, opening the front door of the dorm.

Katrina grabbed her robe and marched after Meredith. *This is a march of doom,* she thought. *Stop it. I can't let anything get to me. If I can live through my own elaborate mock funeral the Araneas made me watch to prepare me for martyrdom, I can get through anything.*

Outside the dorm, Meredith barked, "Chas!"

He jumped out of the shadows, yelping, "Yes, ma'am!"

"Get that mutt out of the bathroom," snapped Meredith, heading toward Bert's black convertible, top up and motor running. "Cage it in the clearing."

"Yes, ma'am!"

"Jonathan wants you in his office in the warren at noon," she said. "Don't be late."

"I won't let you down," he said. Turning, he winked at Katrina who acknowledged him with a slight lowering of head and eyes. He passed her, deliberately brushing her arm.

As Katrina slid into the passenger seat, Meredith put the car in gear and said, "From now on, your base is the warren. Do not come out unless told to do so."

"What if my family visits?" asked Katrina.

Meredith snickered. "Don't waste your time dwelling on that."

Katrina gritted her teeth, resisting the urge to demand clarification.

Meredith drove into the parking garage and pulled into the sixth space from the door marked Authorized Personnel Only. She glanced around then handed a folded piece of paper to Katrina. "Memorize this code then burn the paper in a sink inside the warren. The code will never exit your mouth. Understand?"

Katrina nodded.

"You're coming along very nicely," said Meredith, getting out of the car.

Katrina hurried after Meredith.

"Punch in the code," said Meredith, stopping at the keypad.

Katrina unfolded the paper, read the code, and entered it. The lock released. She opened the door, held it for Meredith, and then followed. Their footsteps reverberated throughout the hallways as they rounded the corner to the left and headed past doors with tacky labels: Alice, Brita, Joe, Chas, Bert, and Kitty. They climbed the stairs along the main trunk line to the first landing where Jonathan waited, dressed in a long white robe and matching turban pinned with the ever-present, ruby-eyed spider. Rings on his fingers glittered as he rubbed his hands together and gurgled, "Welcome, spiderling Kitty."

Katrina gave the appropriate nod, but his drawn face and pallid skin surprised her. Fluorescent lighting muddied the hollows between the bone structures of his face. *He looks ten times as old as the last time I saw him. And his eye twitches worse than ever. The way he's looking at me gives me the creeps!*

Folding his arms beneath the aba, he said, "This way." White samite furled as he headed into the granite-walled communication center that she discovered the first time she penetrated the bowels of Granite Mountain. Dankness chilled her as turbine fans hummed, cameras spied, and canaries chirped. The black metal cabinets she had hidden behind loomed on the left. Ahead, tiny multicolored lights blinked on burnished metal consoles. Jonathan pressed an imperfection on the granite wall and stepped back. The huge steel door with red symbols rumbled open. He led the way into the room that Katrina had only gotten a peek at. The door closing behind her sounded like fingernails scraping across a blackboard. Gooseflesh spiked. Resisting the urge to rub her arms, she wondered: *How do I get out of here?* At black-tinted windows of the cubical in the center of the room, technicians spoke in monotone voices too low for her to discern. *Who are they? What are they doing? What are those tinny noises?*

A technician staring at a clipboard hurried past. Katrina almost squirreled a peek at how he opened the door, but stopped herself. *Getting caught at this stage of the game is not in my plans. I'm too close to finding out what's going on.*

"How's my star pupil doing?"

"Very well, Miss Matthias," said Katrina without looking. She would know that voice anywhere.

"Spiderling Kitty progresses beyond my wildest dreams," boasted Jonathan.

"Can I pick them or what?" spewed Matthias. "How about that added bonus of her being primed in Mississippi?"

Someday, Katrina fumed inside. *I'm going to spit in that woman's face!*

Matthias pointed to the center cubical and said, "That's a spider habitat. We present them with unexpected circumstances and environmental shifts to study their evolution. Their brains are highly developed, enabling incredible adaptation, learning, and recall. If prey is moved, spiders search the same spot in their web for hours. We teach them to expand that thought pattern, how to track down and do away with thieves. We have identified and isolated the silk gene, enabling the duplication of silk thread with the same strength and elasticity. Success has been limited. We're developing ways to mass-produce the fiber to use someday to our advantage."

"Thank Miss Matthias for explaining her project, Kitty," said Jonathan while heading to the first of a series of doors on the right.

Katrina bowed her head and in a soft, controlled voice, said, "Thank you, Miss Matthias."

"My pleasure."

"Over here is the processing lab for audio, video, photo-graphs, fake IDs, and the like," said Jonathan, holding open the door.

Katrina peeked in. *It's Brita!*

Brita didn't look. She was mesmerized by a video that went well beyond pornography. "Entertainment as you can see," said Jonathan, "captures the psyche. Videotapes of wives and daughters of turncoats in what I'll put mildly, compromising situations. Film and other temperature sensitive materials are stored in that refrigerator. Alcoholic beverages and drugs have also been known to make their way here. A warning: don't let alcohol, drugs, or sex interfere with your function."

Brita's in over her head, thought Katrina. *How do I get her to see the harm this evil is doing to her and everybody else? But if I try, she'll run straight to the Araneas or whisper it to Vic in the middle of the night.*

"In this room," said Jonathan, stepping to the second door, "hypnosis and subliminal tapes are produced for use around the campus, in seminars, and other venues. I have converted so many in the most miraculous ways. All surrender to me—as you did. In the entire history of mankind, not one individual has ever realized or believed that he has been brainwashed. Converts defend their manipulators passionately and claim they have been shown the light. Oh, I almost forgot to mention, the command for that dog of yours that will get you out of hot spots? Arachnophobia."

I should've guessed, thought Katrina. *Gosh, how do I de-program that word out of Mickey Blue Eyes?*

"This is the main lab," he said, opening the third door. He marched through the anteroom and into the glass-enclosed lab without stopping to don a white lab coat.

Meredith grabbed two lab coats and handed one to Katrina. They put them on then entered the lab where Alice was seated before a hermetically-sealed glass box. Her hands moved inside the gloves that were attached to the box. A rat raced around inside the box, banging its head into the glass to get away.

"See those bottles of bleach?" asked Jonathan. "Bleach kills quick-evolving microbes that become resistant to antibiotics. Why such microbes don't become resistant to bleach remains a mystery. However, don't be complacent. Some are beginning to tolerate bleach."

"That's one of my pet projects," spoke up Alice. "Finding out which microbes and then be able to use them as an advantage when the time is right."

"Antibiotics have a target effect that avoids harm to delicate human tissues," said Jonathan. "We are working on microbial adaptation and change that doesn't require the random inheritance of genetic advantage. Understand?"

"Some microbes mutate when stressed to promote survival despite harsh environments," replied Katrina.

"Bottom line?' he asked.

"Don't count on bleach to work if there's an accident," she said. "So no accidents."

The Araneas exchanged self-righteous glances. Then Jonathan breathed, "Excellent."

Alice snickered. "VX is one of the most toxic nerve agents ever developed," she said as the rat struggled in her gloved hand, biting and clawing. "The quality I produce here is remarkably good, I'm happy to say, and so is stability. Chas and I are working on weaponizing agents."

What's she injecting that rat with, wondered Katrina.

"Kitty's first assignment," Jonathan said, "is to help to put it into play."

Alice freed the rat and withdrew her hands. It raced around, became erratic, and keeled over. "The agent is biologically active," Alice announced.

"Autopsy the corpse," said Jonathan. "See if it can be a vector."

Katrina's insides reeled. *What did that rat die of?* She squinted at labels on containers. *Smallpox. VX. Sarin. Cholera. Typhoid. Botulism. Anthrax. Bubonic Plague.*

"We experiment with many things," said Jonathan, a glint in his eye. "We even have DNA extraction and amplification

equipment. Ultimate goal is to contaminate food with geneti-
cally modified ingredients. We are developing bacteria more
powerful than E. coli, bacillus globigi, and serratia. Here is a
virus that is related to the one that infects camels. We're about
to infect farm animals and contaminate food supplies, essen-
tially starving Americans—and the world." At the last door, he
inserted a key into the lock and twisted it. "Your computer geek
father taught you everything he knows. That knowledge is now
mine to use to eliminate old ways and achieve new life and
order."

He fits the mold of radical revolutionary, thought Katrina.
*Mentally unbalanced, insecure, without friends or hope for the world
as it exists—just like I read about at the Boston Public Library. He's
obsessed with creating an entire new world.*

"In this state-of-the-art computer lab," said Jonathan, opening the door, "you will design viruses and insert them into
American military computers. When I give the word, you will
disable air and defense systems; you will cripple the Internet;
you will disrupt corporate and government systems."

Don't count on it, thought Katrina. *My viruses are going to
backfire. They will screw up every computer on Granite Mountain!
And others they're connected to wherever they are! When I get on the
Internet, I'll figure out a way to get word to the FBI, CIA, and the
President. Just wait until I get my hands on these computers!*

"You will make emergency response centers and police and
fire departments ineffective," said Jonathan. "I want credit card
companies, automatic teller machines, banks, and residential
mortgage firms unable to do business. Complete chaos. Enough
collateral damage to stun even the experts who have warned all
along about the effects of mass-scale disruption. That's where I
got the idea in the first place."

"Interdependencies and cascading effects is what it's called,"
said Katrina, faking loyalty.

Jonathan was stunned. "My spiderling Kitty is my shining
star. You live up to your moniker."

The night passed as he familiarized Katrina with the warren.
Food enough to last selected inhabitants ten years was stock-

piled in the northern chamber. She learned that Bert was in charge of booby trapping the countryside and developing a chip to implant under the skin to allow the tracking of spiderlings far and wide. Jonathan bellyached about Bert having more than his share of trouble at getting either job done. The last stop was the lowest level of the warren. Jonathan looked Katrina straight in the eye, his eye twitching. *Seems like he's reassuring himself that I'm completely under his command,* she thought. At length, he said, "An automatic atomic self-destruct device and all its workings occupy this entire level, north, east, south, and west. You and a number of other spiderlings are programmed to arm the device from within the computer lab. The right word from me or upon my demise will set you to arming the device. In less than a half hour, the bomb goes off."

Shivers raced up and down Katrina's spine. *I have an uncanny knack of extracting myself out of situations when they heat up, but a half hour to get me and as many others as I can out of the innards of Granite Mountain before kaboom? What if some other spiderling arms the device? I have to find a way to stop the kaboom! What's the right word? He'll get suspicious if I ask about it. He might put me through more brainwashing.*

"Commit these instructions to memory," said Jonathan, handing a training manual to Katrina.

She flipped through it, commenting, "Attack sites with high human intensity. Skyscrapers, nuclear plants, football stadiums, airports, hospitals, targets of sentimental value like the Statue of Liberty, Big Ben, and the Eiffel Tower. Christmas celebrations, Fourth of July fireworks."

"My spiderlings have infiltrated communities and organizations in every country," boasted Jonathan. "Millions are breathing their last breaths, for Judgment Day is at hand."

"Let us adjourn for breakfast," Meredith suggested. "Other matters need to be laid to rest."

Katrina caught the evil glance Meredith gave to Jonathan.

In the cafeteria, Katrina was leery of food and drink, though her stomach growled in protest. Her own source of sustenance awaited in the supplies she had brought to her cubicle. Believing ice cubes and water from the refrigerator dispenser were safe, she filled a paper cup.

"Is that all you're having?" asked Meredith.

"I had a late night snack," said Katrina. "It's messing with my belly."

"Sit," said Jonathan, pulling out a chair. Katrina sat down. He took a seat opposite her. Meredith sat between them. A lecherous air hung about the Araneas.

Something's giving them great pleasure, thought Katrina, *but I'm prepared for the worst.*

"You are a true believer now," proclaimed Jonathan. "Friends and family no longer play roles in your life."

"Other than to advance the cause," added Meredith.

"Of course," he hissed. "A staged automobile accident has eliminated your family."

Katrina hadn't prepared herself for this. Battling emotion, she said, "Eliminated."

"On the way to your brother's preschool," boasted Meredith.

I'm not converted, thought Katrina, *not feeling like I do...but it's too late. I have nobody now.* Despair and turmoil overwhelmed Katrina. She recalled how she had clung to her father whenever the rejection that Regina had ingrained into her reared its ugly head. *Dad let me talk when I needed to. He didn't push. He spent so much time, making sure I returned to a happy routine as soon as possible after I came back from...Judgment?* She swallowed hard. *I'm going to make sure that the Araneas see their Judgment Day long before the one they're planning...whenever that is.*

Chapter 30

*T*he next morning, Tank, Gus Tanner's mixed breed dog, was sitting in the back seat of Gus's 4 X 4, which wasn't as old as its battered condition implied. Fangs and snarls waylaid Ken as he reached for the door handle.

"Quit-cha-bit chin'," snapped Gus, swatting the dog with his green army cap.

Tank cowered as though he had just committed a mortal sin. Flopped across the back seat, ears flat against his brindle head and a great jaw propped upon front paws, he looked like a grizzly hide.

"Tank's jus' grinnin' atcha," said Gus, leaning over and popping open the door. "He really likes ya."

"I can tell," muttered Ken, giving the dog a wary eye. Tank's soulful brown eyes lolled back and forth from Ken to Gus. Ken squinted at the front passenger seat. In front of the floor shift, a shotgun was bracketed upright to the dashboard. He ran a hand through his hair and took another look at the dog. He sucked in a lungful of brisk mountain air, zipped up his green windbreaker, and climbed onto the running board. One last check on Tank then Ken slid into the passenger seat.

"Buckle up," snorted Gus.

Ken gawked at the eccentric guide dressed in backwoods gear.

"No need to buckle every time, mind you," said Gus, "but seeing as we're off to the boonies, I ain't about to have either of us bucked off."

Ken reached over his shoulder and pulled the seatbelt down and across his torso. No sooner had the buckle snapped into place than the 4 X 4 lurched forward. In a heartbeat, Tank hung half his body out the driver's side window. His slobbering tongue whipped in the wind.

"Greatness of this area lies in the smallness," said Gus with a mixture of urbanity and world-weariness that came from seeing too much and resignation that the system was unchangeable. "People come here for the quiet, safe life. Artists, writers, and celebrities for the anonymity."

"How do a college, academy, and camps take over an entire mountain?" asked Ken while removing the rubber lens cap from the camera strung around his neck. *Nothing is inconsequential*, he thought while taking pictures. *Who knows what might support my suspicions that this place is not on the up and up.*

"Most was donated by a moneyed dowager," said Gus. "Ornery as all get-out. Froze to death, battlin' a bad case of flu. Strange though. That old widow, her dead husband, and family members that came before 'em always being staunch critics of development and then the dowager wills it all to that Aranea feller days before she kicks the bucket. Something stinks up the woods. Ain't no bear droppin', neither!"

"I thought everything around here is National Forest," said Ken, taking off his windbreaker.

"S'posed to be," said Gus, eyeing Ken's red, white, and blue Patriots sweatshirt. "When Aranea took over the college, he promised to leave the land as is and only allow students to camp in them there cabins and learn about ecology. Humdinger of a ruckus at the zoning board when he put forward the idea. 'Not for communal living,' as some old timers who got born 'round here chided. Come the next spring, half the old timers had croaked, so Aranea got the go ahead at the annual Town Hall Meeting."

"Humph," snorted Ken, leering at vapor rising here and there, undisturbed by air currents. "You like living way up here?"

"Way up here?" repeated Gus.

"Far away from things," said Ken.

"'*Things*' is all in how ya look at 'em," said Gus. "My *things* are a few good friends, the moon, the stars, my mansion on the hill…"

"Mansion on the hill?" asked Ken.

"Didn't put out much bread for it, but a real mansion, if ya know what I mean," said Gus. "Built it with my own hands, plain and simple—jus' like I like. As close to Heaven's I'll ever get."

Ken lined up a camera shot of the cluster of cabins where Katrina had camped. "This place sure blends into the surroundings."

"Folks drivin' down the road barely notice the place," said Gus. "Most of 'em end up at the trail that goes up the mountain and hafta turn back. Just like bananas, they are."

"Bananas?" asked Ken.

"Come in bunches," said Gus. "Uncrowded life draws tourist money and then they go home. That covered bridge you see over yonder generates more look-sees than Granite Mountain College attracts geeks."

"You're a Vietnam vet," said Ken.

Hardness sheeted Gus' face. "Ayeup."

"My father-in-law, too," said Ken.

"That a fact."

Ken nodded. "MIA six years."

Gus shot a look at Ken. "Window dressing?"

"Purple heart, bronze star, silver star, other stuff," said Ken.

"Got some myself," said Gus, sounding reflective.

"That *police action* was too costly and ill-conceived," said Ken.

"Had luck enough to be born in these United States," said Gus, "and that needs serious acknowledgin'. My folks raised me believin' certain things about this country. Nam comes along. River gunboatin' took me places never thought I'd go. These eyes got opened. Things I prefer never to see. Can't rightly figure if I'm a better person for it."

Ken sucked in a breath and exhaled, "New world order doesn't seem likely."

"Nah," said Gus, his face pinched in thought. "Old enemies lurk. New ones loom. Needs counter-balancing at times—like over there in the desert now. Dusty Nam."

"Line in the sand," said Ken. "Like those trespassing signs." He pointed to weather-beaten signs hanging off trees.

"Snuck in there once ta satisfy curiosity," said Gus.

"What'd you find?" asked Ken.

"Somebody got int'rested in minin'," said Gus. "Didn't take long for 'em to find out there ain't nuttin' but solid rock 'neath this here mountain."

The landscape shuffled into view, lacking leaves to disguise it. *Structures are traditional, untraditional, sometimes both,* mused Ken. *They seem to wear the personalities of those inside on the outside. No two the same. The better ones are made of granite. Others a mix of granite and wood, tumor-like additions—some real eyesores.* The occasional shack came complete with a functional wooden outhouse as rundown as the shack behind which it stood. Outhouses behind the better homes were ornate, nonfunctional, with crescent moons carved into the doors. Above the doors was painted lettering, privy. *Meant for contemporary looky-lous who might not know what they were looking at,* he ruminated. *How stupid do these people around here think we are?*

Hours passed. *This is one big wild goose-chase,* stewed Ken. *My foolish bones ache like crazy from jolting around this stinking 4 X 4.* As the sun slanted into the west, blinding Ken, he heard Gus bluster, "My gizzard's croaky as an unclogged drain. I'm in for callin' it a day and grub."

"Sounds like a deal," said Ken.

On the way to the main road, they passed a shack surrounded by junk cars, overturned snowmobiles, rusted barbecues, and broken wheelbarrows. Behind the shack was a muddy jumble of rundown outbuildings. Bordering the property was a towering berm. "How can anybody live like that?" asked Ken in the midst of snapping a picture.

"Miracle the place don't burn to the ground, what with kids messin' around and all," said Gus. "Firin' range out back."

A shiver zinged up and down Ken's spine. *Firing range?*

⌒

The Golden Eagle Inn and Tavern stood on one side of an oval green as if an arbitrator between the didactic Congregational Church on one end of the green and the eccentric granite town hall and courthouse on the opposite end. The white spire pricked the leaden heavens as if extracting holy substance while the courthouse boasted of steadfast and obstinate Yankee ethic. *The quintessential New England village green,* thought Ken while envisioning the century-old hardwoods and pines shading tourists in the summertime. *Makes it hard to wrap the mind around evil activity on Granite Mountain.*

On the porch railing of the Tavern, a black cat snoozed, front paws curled beneath its breast. A man sat on the stoop, smoking and keeping track of rug rats playing hopscotch on the sidewalk. He exchanged an acknowledgment with Gus that the average eye would have missed. A boy who seemed to be of no concern to the man balanced on the edge of the curb while dropping pebbles through the grate of the street drain. Gus tooted the horn and chuckled as the boy jumped back. "Tourists come for the hospitality known far and wide at the Golden Eagle—built around the time of the Revolutionary War. They shop for antiques, handmade crafts, jewelry, and candles and then swill down grub at the Eagle. Pancakes and orange pecan French toast slathered with butter and locally produced maple syrup are mighty good for the soul. Coffee's still percolated—rouses the senses if you're out and about real early. Excitement 'round here is the double feature on Saturday night."

"And no parking meters," observed Ken, stepping out of the 4 X 4 onto the brick sidewalk. Old-fashioned hitching post lamps that had been electrified flickered to life.

"Drop your film off at the pharmacy over there," said Gus, pointing. "Be ready after we chow down."

"Good suggestion," said Ken, hitching up his britches.

An hour later, Ken picked up the pictures and got back into the 4 X 4. At the Village Bed and Breakfast, he paid and thanked Gus.

"If I can be of any further service," said Gus, "jes' give me a holler at the VFW. I'm hittin' the place for another brew before headin' to the mansion."

In his room Ken spread the pictures on the bed and stepped back. He ran his hand through his hair as his eyes skipped across the pictures. "Every one of these buildings is made out of granite. Where did it all come from?" No trespassing signs flashed into his brain. Then the mine Gus mentioned. His tongue ran along his upper lip. "It came from mines?" He picked up the picture of the shack and eyed the junk cars, overturned snowmobiles, rusted barbecues, and broken wheelbarrows. "Gus says there's a firing range out back." He held the picture close to his eyes, but was unable to make out details. He reached for his camera bag and took out a small case that contained a magnifying glass. He held the glass over the picture. "The school bus looks all shot up… My baby girl talked about shot up school busses in Mississippi during sessions with Doc…"

Tossing the magnifying glass and picture on the bed, Ken bolted for the door. He left it ajar and scampered down the stairs. "Eric! I need to speak to Gus at the VFW!"

Eric Poppin dialed the number then handed the phone to Ken. After several rings, a soft-spoken male voice answered.

"Gus! This is Ken Waters! I need another look at that mine! And while we're at it, the firing range!"

Chapter 31

I nvigorated by a good night's sleep and the prospects of getting the goods on Aranea, Ken reached for the door handle of Gus' 4 X 4. Tank pulled in his head from the driver's side rear window, grinned at Ken, and then plopped his head out the window again. The weather was the same, cool, no wind, and vapor rising.

Gus put the pedal to the metal and shortly thereafter, swerved off the road onto a barely discernible track. Ignoring no trespassing signs, he threaded through trees for about a quarter of a mile until a pile of brush prompted him to stomp on the brakes. Tank tumbled into the well behind the driver's seat. The dog clawed his way back onto the seat as Gus gripped the steering wheel with both hands. "Somebody's covered up the entrance."

"This the only mine on Granite Mountain?" asked Ken, getting out of the 4 X 4.

"Ain't taken time to ponder it," said Gus, reaching for the door handle. Tank leapt out the driver's side window. "Come to think of it," said Gus, shouldering open the door, "seen no trespassing signs over on the east side. Leads me to think there's another mine."

"What's the bedrock like?" asked Ken.

"Nothing short of solid granite," replied Gus.

"Doesn't mean it can't be quarried," countered Ken while envisioning heavy machinery hauling blocks of granite out of the mountain, tunnels etched in bedrock, and rock-lined chambers of activity.

Gus tisked. "Heap o' work."

Ken jammed his hands into his hips. "Doesn't make sense." He sucked in a chest full of dewy mountain air and scanned the horizon. "Hey, Gus! Take a look at that!"

Gus followed Ken's line of sight. His brows came together. "Whall, I'll be. That ain't no cloud."

"Telltale signs of heat loss," said Ken, scanning for tapped maple trees. "Evaporators?"

"No sugar houses on this mountain," said Gus. He gave a whistle. Tank came running as the men hotfooted back to the 4 X 4. "Where'd you say you went to college?"

"College?" asked Ken while buckling up.

Gus chucked the 4 X 4 into gear. "Bedrock, heat loss, evaporators," he said as the vehicle lurched forward. "A bit technical for a writer piecin' a mountain."

"MIT," said Ken, gripping the door handle for dear life. The vehicle fishtailed and jounced through virgin terrain. "You suped up this thing."

Gus' right eye sparkled.

Trees closed in on the 4X4. Branches scraped the sides. Gus jammed on the brakes. "We'll hoof it from here." He reached for the door handle as Tank leapt out the window. "Day's heatin' up." He took off his jacket and tossed it into the backseat. "Trekking through these here woods this time of year's usually a lot rougher what with the snow and mud. This winter's sure been a dry one."

"Bugs know it," said Ken, swishing away insects.

"Those is mourning cloak butterflies you're swattin' at," said Gus, sprinting off. "Ain't natural seein' cloaks 'ntil late March or April. Corker of a winter, this one's been."

Ken ran his hand through his hair then ran after Gus. When he caught up, Gus was standing hands on hips over the source of the rising vapor, an airshaft sticking up less than an inch off the forest bed. A sheet of screening kept out debris. "Seen the likes of these in 'Nam," wheezed Gus. His nostrils flared like the feathered ruffs of a male grouse during the mating ritual. "My bones tell me there's a heap more than a colony of ants running 'neath this here rock pile."

"And my baby girl's in the middle of it," said Ken, bending over and gasping for air.

"So that's what you're up to," said Gus.

Ken squinted at Gus. "You knew I wasn't a writer?"

"Might look stupid," said Gus. "Even spout too much hill-billy. That don't mean I ain't sharp."

Tank growled and put his snout high in the air.

"Cool it," commanded Gus in a low tone. A snap of the fingers glued the dog to his ankle. "Let's split."

Ken hitched up his pants and took off after Gus and the dog.

Back in the 4 X 4, Gus yanked the wheel and headed back to the road. Another yank on the wheel put the 4 X 4 back onto the gravel road. Rounding a curve, he said, "Looky what we got here." Two teenagers were lolling at the side of the road, one with straight black hair that flowed at will and the other, bronze-toned and sitting on a boulder, left shoe off and rubbing his foot.

"Hey, Gus," hollered the black-haired teen leaping to the edge of the road and sticking out his thumb. "How 'bout a lift?"

Tank expressed a strong desire to devour the teen.

"Can it, Tank!" snapped Gus while pulling along side the black-haired teen. "Had it with hikin', Joe?"

Tank shriveled into the corner of the backseat, but his grin came and went, indicating continued displeasure.

"Got that right," said Joe, eying Ken.

Joe was a stranger to Ken, but not the pewter spider pin with red eyes clinging to Joe's lapel. The other teenager looked familiar. He wasn't wearing a spider pin.

Gus leaned in front of Ken and said, "Hop in. I'll drop ya."

"Sweet," belched Joe. "Come on, Bert."

Ken studied Bert slipping his foot into his shoe. *He's one of those counselors my baby girl had at the Ecology Camp. And the guy in that sunset picture with her!*

As Bert wriggled into the backseat, Tank showed his teeth. As Joe climbed onto the running board, Tank snarled. "No noise back there," spat Gus, glancing into the side view mirror. He shoved the 4 X 4 into gear. The vehicle pitched forward. He shifted into second. "Put on some miles, Joe?"

"Too many," snorted Joe. "You?"

"Been showin' this here gentleman the countryside," replied Gus. "He's writin' a book."

"Book," echoed Bert. "About what?"

Ken ran a hand through his hair and said, "Adult fiction."

"Porn," yipped Joe. "Sweet!"

"Adult fiction isn't necessarily pornography," said Ken. *Good heavens*, he thought. *How can my baby girl tolerate hanging around this kind of vermin?*

Gus pulled up at the four way stop sign at the entrance of Granite Mountain College. Joe leapt off the running board. "Thanks for the lift," said Bert while wriggling out of the back-seat.

"Sure 'nough, young feller," said Gus.

"Hey, dude," hollered Joe. "Good luck with the porn!"

Ken raked his hand through his hair. *Oh, to go back and lambaste that budding pervert.* He glanced in the side view mirror. The teenagers were standing there, watching the 4 X 4 leave. Moments passed. Bert picked up his backpack and limped toward the stone arch. Joe remained in place until the trees came together like opera curtains after the final act of *Madam Butterfly*.

"Those whippersnappers eyed you like back alley cats in heat," said Gus. "'Bout time you filled me in, wouldn't you say?"

"What do you mean?" asked Ken. Finding himself caught in the crosshairs of oxen-like eyes, he shot a glance out the passenger side window.

"That Joe Ault is a filthy cuss," said Gus. "Up to no good from the get-go—both of 'em. Struck me real fishy-like back there at the vents, them not showin' themselves."

Ken gawked at Gus. "They were there?"

Gus stared at the road ahead. "Ayeup."

"And you knew that how?"

"Footprints. Tank sniffing the breeze."

"They followed us the entire way?"

"Weren't hard to track, what with all our yakking and stomping the woods like greenhorns. I s'pect they hankered to knowd what we're up to. Tank gets wind of 'em, so they high-tails it down the mountain and wait us out 'side the road. Bet dollars to donuts, when we dropped 'em off, they tattled."

"To Jonathan Aranea?" asked Ken.

"Ayeup. Aranea ain't home-grown like he shoves down throats of us natives—same as you ain't no writer like you wants this native to believe."

Ken pursed his lips then tweaked them this way and that while squirreling a glimpse at Gus. Those oxen-like eyes caught him. "Okay! Okay! I came to get my baby girl! She's in the clutches of terrorists again!"

"Terrorists?" asked Gus. "Again?"

Ken swallowed hard and then rattled off Katrina's background: Regina, Jake, and Judgment, Mississippi.

"Sordid mess like that," said Gus, "puts fire in the belly, hotter than a smithy's forge. If your girl's the spitfire you say she is, I s'pect she's better at taking care of herself than you or I."

"Don't give me that," exploded Ken. "She needs me! And I'm going to come down on Aranea like a ton of bricks!"

"Cain't go huntin' in your skivvies," warned Gus.

"What?" shot back Ken.

"Goin' off half-cocked backfires every time," said Gus.

Ken ran his hand through his hair. "I don't have a choice."

"Don'cha mean we?" asked Gus.

"I can't let you get involved," said Ken.

"You hogtied me the first step you took at the VFW," said Gus.

"But…" began Ken.

"But nothin'," shot back Gus. "Spider holes like you hear about in the desert right here in New Hampshire? Don't set well with this country hick. Mind you, the window to get your girl out alive an' kickin' might be shuttin' down as we speak."

Ken winced.

"Won't be no small feat," said Gus, pulling up to the Village Bed and Breakfast.

Ken stared at nothing, feeling empty inside. The door handle was unreachable, a million miles away.

"Best give your woman a call an' let her know you're checkin' out," said Gus. "I don't have a phone, mind you, so you'll be callin' her when you can. Make clear that she's not to speak to locals, no matter what."

"Aranea's got the cops in his pocket?" asked Ken.

"Sure's pigs rut in muck. Seen any fences or machine-gun-totin' guards around Granite Mountain?"

Ken shook his head side to side. "Just weather-beaten no trespassing signs. I half-expected more."

"Most people around here figure security ain't needed."

"Sometimes the best security is none," said Ken.

"Don't rouse suspicion that way," agreed Gus.

"So every man, woman, and child within miles of here reports to Aranea?" asked Ken.

"Ain't healthy rulin' it out."

"I'll check out," said Ken. "That way everybody will think I went home, but then what?"

"We put our heads together," said Gus, "and get your girl out of that there mountain without gettin' ourselves kilt."

⌒

The front porch of Gus's honey-stained log cabin faced west, overlooking Jackson. "Got the basic stuff," as Gus put it. "Economical and durable. A place to lay the noggin, if you get my drift. Don't go for ritzy. Most high-end guest what set foot here is yourself. Set on down here on the front porch. I'll rustle us up some grub." Cold brew and beef jerky seemed fitting, considering the burly guide's persona and planning the rescue of a kidnap victim, so when Gus brought out a steaming pot of tea and peanut butter cookies, Ken's jaw dropped. "What more can a body want?" asked Gus while settling into a homemade Adirondack chair stained to match the cabin. "Wolfin' down grub an' overlookin' the valley. Bells ringin' on the half-hour out of yonder steeple."

Ken inhaled the early spring breeze perfumed with pine and hearths. A whippoorwill crooned triple time repetitions. An owl chimed in. *I haven't felt this peaceful in ages,* he mused. *Perhaps the last time was the day I asked Julie to marry me.* He pictured the way it was, walking along the Charles River and stopping near the Hatch Shell. *Julie looked so beautiful in the shade of that oak—still is. She loves me as I always dreamed she would. I hated to leave her in her condition, but she knows my baby girl needs me. Julie's so brave.*

"Mellow around here," said Gus. His foot stroked Tank. "Blows me away that evil is under our noses." The dog seemed to be asleep, but every so often a scent tweaked his nose and one eye slit open to check it out.

"How about pumping incapacitating gas down those vents?" suggested Ken.

"Got some of that incapacitatin' gas in your suitcase?" asked Gus.

Ken tisked. "Disable the windmills? You know, negate electrical power. Everything goes down: computers, refrigeration, air filtering. Everybody has to come out, including my baby girl."

Gus frowned and shook his head. "Ain't possible."

"Why not?"

"Backup generators?"

Ken ran a hand through his hair. "Forgot about those."

Gus smacked his lips and got to his feet, which put Tank on alert. In an instant the dog was off the porch, anticipating Gus to follow. "Now don' you go dancin' the jig, Tank." Gus pointed at the dog. Tank flattened on the ground. "Stay right here and keep an eye on this here city slicker."

"Where you going?" yelped Ken. Swept by insecurity, he started to get up.

"Stay put," said Gus. "I'm off to get supplies for the morrow's mission."

"I'll go with you," said Ken.

"Cool your britches," said Gus. "You're s'posed to be on the way home, remember? Be back in two shakes of a lamb's tail."

Ken withered in the chair. As the 4 X 4 disappeared, he felt as dejected as Tank slinking to the spot where it had been parked next to Ken's car. The dog plopped on the ground. Man and beast awaited the master's return—though not with a great deal of patience. The sky shaded the mountains from greens to blues to grays as the breeze played off last year's leaves on oak trees. Somehow, the scene reminded Ken of Adriano's fuzzy pate rising at the footboard in the middle of a Brighton night. The boy feared going to get a drink of water alone. "Imagine, a bogie man in Brighton," mumbled Ken, getting to his feet. "With hundreds of thousands of people around? Too many people. After I uproot Aranea, I should pack up the family and move to a place like this." He twisted this way and that, trying to unkink his back from pent up stress. High level ragged clouds picked up the last light. He braced a foot against the railing. Street and house lights began to twinkle beyond a dark smudge that swirled around skeletons of trees a mile down the hill. "Somebody lit a woodstove," muttered Ken. "One way or the other, I have to simplify our lives. Have to watch more sunrises and sunsets. I have to push myself away from the computer and go outside once in a while if for no other reason than to gulp down clean, crisp air, and allow my mind to wander away from stressors. It is going to be part of my routine! Like brushing and flossing my teeth. Morning, noon, and night!"

Tank sat up on his haunches, ears alert. He glanced over his shoulder at Ken.

"You know I can't give you permission to take off," said Ken. "Wonder if Gus made it down the mountain yet?" He eyed the expanding smoke. "Who needs a fire tonight?" He glanced down at his tee shirt. "Don't even need a sweater." He cocked his head to one side and once again, studied the smoke. His brows came together. His insides lurched. "Gus!" he yelped.

Tank hopped up, yipping as if to say, "It's about time you figured it out!"

Ken leapt off the porch as the dog sped down the dirt road, barking to beat the band and disappeared. Ken followed the barking until it ceased. Smoke led the way to Gus who was braced against a tree, watching the 4 X 4 burn. "You all right?" panted Ken.

"Cracked a rib or two," said Gus. "Be stiff in the mornin'. Luck has it, I wasn't belted in or I'd be upside down, neck broke, smoked like Canadian bacon."

"What happened?" asked Ken, squatting next to Gus.

"4 X 4 got doctored," said Gus. "Shur's thunder comes with lightnin'. Help me up."

"You need medical…" started Ken.

"I'm gettin' up," cut in Gus, "with or without your help!"

Ken wormed an arm under Gus's armpit and around his back then lifted. Gus grunted away the pain. His fingernails drilled into the bark of the tree as he steadied himself, sucking air and letting it out. "Wait here," said Ken. "I'll go for help."

"You'll do nothing of the sort," barked Gus. "Ain't about to show my hand."

Ken scanned the imposing woods. "We should've heard sirens by now."

"Tells us somethin', 'eh?" said Gus.

"We're sitting ducks," said Ken.

"Shotgun's gone in the 4 X 4," said Gus. "Better haul up to the cabin, quick like, 'fore somebody takes a pot shot."

Tank took the point, nosing the ground as Ken struggled under Gus' weight up the road. Where the 4 X 4 had been parked, Gus let go and studied the ground. "Yep," he said, "jus' what I s'pected." His eyes followed Tank hot on a trail leading into the woods. "Two of 'em came an' went that way. One stood lookout behind that there tree while the other did the dirty deed. Decommissioned your car while he was at it."

"They know I came here instead of going home," said Ken.

"Ayeup," said Gus, tracing footprints that only experienced guides could detect. "Lookout joined the doer here. Both size ten."

"Aranea sent them," deduced Ken.

"Sure's a frog's butt is waterproof," said Gus, rubbing his ribcage. "A-feared of you and me undoing his digs."

"What are we going to do?"

"Time for plan B," said Gus, heading back to the cabin.

"Plan B?"

"Sounds good, don't it?"

"There is no plan B."

"By the time you get my innards wrapped up, I'll come up with one."

Inside the cabin, Ken ripped apart a bed sheet. "Where does a guy like Aranea get money to run a college, academy, camps, *and* a terrorist cell?"

"Post says West Africa."

"You read the Washington Post?"

Gus ignored the question. "European and Latin American investigations turned up evidence of factions trading diamonds for missiles that can obliterate aircraft."

"Aranea has diamonds?" asked Ken while wrapping Gus' ribs.

"Gold and other such commodities, too, I s'pect," said Gus. "Rarely drop in value. Easy to hide. Easy to market for missiles. Diamond-buying operations got hatched in response to the U.S. freezing Middle East assets. But that Aranea feller's showed up long before all that, which puts the monkey wrench to my thinkin'."

"Why aren't the Feds keeping an eye on Aranea?" asked Ken.

Gus scratched the side of his face. "Gotta be a mole in play." Just then a cow bell tinkled. "Perimeter's breached!" He yanked the strip of the sheet away from Ken and jumped to his feet. He chucked the end into the wrapping around his ribs then grabbed the side of the log table. "Gimme a hand!"

Ken grabbed the other side of the table and strained to lift it off a large braided rug.

"Roll up the rug an' lift the trap door," said Gus. "Learnt about quick escapes in Nam." He climbed down the ladder and disappeared. Guns and ammunition rose out of the hole like cobras out of a charmer's basket.

"These AK-47 assault rifles?" asked Ken, astounded by the variety and amount of weaponry.

"Get your facts straight," said Gus, climbing back up. "Semiautomatic AK-47s ain't assault rifles. Assault rifles are selectable fire rifles capable of full automatic fire."

"Gun laws ought to be stricter," commented Ken, gawking at the weapon that looked like it could blow the torso off a terrorist with a single squeeze of the trigger.

"You're in the dark about firearms, man," said Gus, sticking rifles into bored out spots between cabin logs.

"I don't even own a gun," said Ken.

"States what liberalize concealed carry laws show decrease in crime rates," said Gus. "Bad guys fear armed citizenry more than fuzz. No plea bargains."

"Yeah, but…" started Ken.

"Yeah, but nothin'," spat Gus. "By the time the law decides there's a problem in these here New Hampshire hills and gets its act together, your young-un and her amigos are toast. It's up to you and me, man, ordinary bubs what's got a few firearms, that's gonna get 'em out of this. Now here." He jammed an AK-47 against Ken. "Put this in that there hole an' be on the ready."

"Not once in my life did I ever think I'd be doing this," muttered Ken, reluctantly obeying. He put his eye to the scope of the AK-47. The clock over the fireplace ticked.

"Got a bead on Joe and Vic," announced Gus. "Real skiddish they are."

"It's clear over here," said Ken.

"No backup," said Gus. "Give 'em a warnin'."

"But nobody's over here," argued Ken.

"Do it!" barked Gus.

The noise was deafening as the weapon knocked Ken on his butt.

"They hit the ground," yelped Gus, shoving open a window. "Next time, fellers," he hollered, "I shoot to kill!" A second later, he grunted with satisfaction. "They're off and runnin'."

The night seemed never-ending as Ken took shifts with Gus to guard the moonlit landscape. The next morning, Gus descended into the secret tunnel to reconnoiter the situation outside the cabin. Tank stared down into the tunnel as Ken paced from lookout hole to lookout hole. "What's taking Gus so long?" Finally, Tank stood up, tail wagging.

"Perimeter alarms were disabled," reported Gus as his wispy gray pate rose out of the tunnel. "Fixed up new ones. Won't nobody be findin' 'em soon. A rock pegged this note to the ground down the road a piece."

Ken unfolded the note and read it aloud, "'Get out of New Hampshire!! Both of you!!! Keep your mouth shut or you'll never see Katrina and Adriano alive!!!'" Crushing the note in his hand, Ken cried, "*Both* my children?"

"A bluff, I'd say," said Gus.

Ken's eyes bugged out. "What about Julie? I have to call her!" He raced for the door. "Addie has to be safe and sound with Julie!"

"Can it!" barked Gus, putting his formidable girth in Ken's path. "You're gonna get yourself kilt! Hear me?"

Ken pounded Gus on the chest. "If Aranea has my baby girl and boy, I know Julie—she'll come to find them and me!"

Gus grabbed Ken's wrists, shouting, "Telephone lines are tapped!"

"I need to hear her voice! I have to tell her I love her! Hear her say it back!"

Gus shook Ken. "Cool it, man! Good God! You're an egg dropped on hash with the yolk broke!"

Chapter 32

*T*wo days after Ken left for Granite Mountain, the front door of a preschool in Brighton, Massachusetts burst open with a bang and five preschool hellions raced past the director who was busy with paperwork at the front desk. The father of the hellions, a semi-toothless lummox, clomped up to the front desk and rifled through neatly stacked brochures and bulletins. His frumpy wife wandered over to a line of miniature easels and fingered one of the freshly painted scenes. She gawked at her fingertips and then glanced around for something to wipe them on. Finding nothing, she gave a shrug then smeared her fingers across the wall of enchanting designs painted in primary colors. The director was aghast, but kept her wits about her. Extending a hand to the lummox, who smelled as if he had been rutting with pigs, she said, "I'm Miss Lorrie."

"Pleasure's mine," he said, emptying a plastic container of business cards on the front desk. Stuffing a handful of cards into his pants pocket, he noticed Miss Lorrie's hand. He seemed surprised at first, but then pitched forward, latched onto her hand, and shook so hard that her head lurched back and forth.

When he finally released her hand, Miss Lorrie discreetly moved her hand up and down her skirt. She cleared her throat. "Please excuse the commotion," she said. "Our students are in the midst of morning exercise."

"Pshaw, think nuttin' of it, ma'am."

She blinked hard against his saliva that misted the air. "So. What can I do for you today?"

"Jes' got in the area. Me and the better half over there's been contemplatin' pennin' up the brood." He whipped a wad of money out of his pants pocket and held it at eyelevel. The bills were slimy and stunk as bad as he. "Willin' ta shell out big bucks fer the right corral."

The director's eyes bugged out at the sight of such a large wad. "Oh my..." she stammered. She glanced at the five hellions who were instigating mass misbehavior, chasing, hitting, and shoving. Children squealed, wailed, and moaned. The hellions then emptied boxes of crayons on the floor and set about crushing the crayons underfoot. Teachers were rapidly losing control. *Placement of such rowdy imps is hardly a good idea,* thought Miss Lorrie. *Still...* Her eyes wandered back to the wad of bills. *...The added income...*

Just then, the frumpy mother hooked a toe on a leg of an easel, setting off a domino effect. Easel bumped into easel, each crashing onto the floor in rapid succession. Paint containers attached to the easels spilled, and the colorful contents snaked across the floor. Rushing to stop the catastrophe, Miss Lorrie slid on the paint. Her feet went out from under her. Upon landing, she smacked into a miniature desk and her front teeth punctured her bottom lip. Blood spewed as she staggered to her feet, her hands gripping her head.

Meanwhile, a curly brown-haired girl pulled the long red pigtails of another girl and wouldn't let go. The red-haired girl howled as she ran in circles, trying to get away.

Shy tots scooted into cubbyholes and curled into balls. Others covered their heads with naptime blankets.

When it was all over, the semi-toothless lummox, his frumpy wife, and the five hellions had disappeared—and so had little Adriano Waters.

Chapter 33

*A*t Fort Stewart, Georgia, a familiar laugh drew Curt's attention to a teenager across the high bay area of the hangar. *Her hair is darker and straighter,* he thought. *No mistaking the shape of her face though—that belongs to the Ol' Chap. The wee one's inherited his mother's eyes. Nothing from Regina—thankfully. By the looks of those well-developed biceps sprouting out that blue tank top, the wee one can take on any transgressor she so chooses. Her adoration of that bronze-haired recruit she's chatting with is a tad put on. Oh, oh, she's leaving!* Chasing after her, he shoved aside recruits who got in his way. In the parking lot he caught up to her as she unlocked the door of a black Volkswagen convertible. Hacking for breath, he cried, "Katrina!"

She turned, standoffish as a stranger, cool and distant, though a hint of recognition zipped across her face. "Pardon me?" she asked in a voice thick with southern drawl.

"You know very well who I am, wee one," he spewed, "so lay down the armor."

Color drained from her face. She scanned the parking lot. Then her eyes locked onto his. In a low, urgent voice, devoid of southern accent, she said, "Hand me a form or something."

"Run that by me again?" he asked.

"Just do it, Uncle Curt!" she spat, again scanning the parking lot. "Hurry!"

Jaw gaping, he squinted at her. Her Mississippi background shot through his head and then Granite Mountain and the Day of Judgment—and all of it added up to disaster! He yanked an immunization form out of the folder he was carrying and handed it to her.

She pointed here and there on the form as if asking questions. "Call me Kitty," she whispered. "I attend Granite Mountain Academy in New Hampshire, but it's only a front for a terrorist cell inside the mountain, and I'm a part of it, but I think their brainwashing didn't work on me. The Araneas—they run the place—they don't know I'm working against them. They killed Dad and…"

Curt steadied himself on the trunk of the Volkswagen, his insides imploding. "J-Jul…"

Her face wrinkled as she nodded and pointed at the form. Her finger trembled as she choked on repressed pain. "And Addie. In a car wreck."

"They're all d-dead?" he bleated.

"Snap out of it, Uncle Curt," she whispered. "I don't know what happened—or if it happened at all, but listen…" She kept scanning the area and touching her cheek with her left hand. He noticed the wedding band on her third finger. "Everybody here thinks I'm Bert Moro's wife, but I'm not. Me and a bunch of other kids are posing as recruits and wives—fake IDs and all. Our mission is to infiltrate the military and when Jonathan Aranea gives the signal, we're programmed to carry out another mission. I don't know what it is, but I'm going to stop it."

Feeling like he was about to have a heart attack, Curt wondered, *Is it safe to tell her I know about Granite Mountain? That plans are in the works to crush it? That the clock is counting down to a Day of Judgment?*

"Somebody's coming," she whispered. "Where can we meet?" She stuffed the form into her backpack and opened the car door. She looked at him. "Uncle Curt?"

His brain was all mucked up, but he managed to clear his throat. In a voice filled with authority, he said, "Return that form to me at the medical facility first thing tomorrow morning." He strutted away, acting nonchalant, but his heart palpitated so bad that his inner ear throbbed. *M'lady's dead? The love of my life…dead? And the Ol' Chap? And Adriano? And never once has these eyes beheld the tyke?* His hand trembled as he took his mobile phone off his belt clip and dialed the number ingrained in his brain. *What if it's been changed?* An eternity of seconds slogged by. *One ring...two...three...four.*

"Can't take your call, right now," said Ken in a recorded message. "Leave your name and number. We'll get back to you."

Curt yanked the phone from his ear and gawked at it. "They're all dead and nobody's deleted the message? No, their parents wouldn't do that straight off. They'll want to hear the Ol' Chap's voice as long as they can—as do I." He put the phone to his ear, but the message had ended. He hung up and dialed the number again. He listened. When Ken stopped speaking, Curt muttered, "Feel like flying up there, but that's not possible, what with the wee here, needing assistance." Once again, a thought nagged him: *Perhaps Katrina isn't the Ol' Chap's lamb. Perhaps she's Jake's. The faction that backed Jake may want his daughter in their ranks. Time to run that blood test.*

"Doctor Shirlington? Sir?"

Curt gawked at a youthful medic, a Tom Cruise look-alike. "Er, yes, son?"

"The first phase of immunizations is complete."

Curt discovered he was standing outside the hangar where he had spotted Katrina.

"Sir?" said the medic.

Curt squinted at the young man.

"Next phase begins tomorrow?" asked the medic.

"Y-yes," stammered Curt. "Tomorrow. Fourteen hundred hours."

"Will that be all, sir?" asked the medic.

"Yes, son," replied Curt.

The medic stepped back, snapped to attention, and saluted. Curt returned a half-hearted salute. The medic executed the perfect about-face and while walking away, his frame relaxed. *Reminds me of Leander Holt,* mused Curt, *the day he discovered vapor rising out of Granite Mountain. Thornton dismissed it—and us. Why in God's name didn't I force the issue? Now the President's given Thornton the go-ahead to wipe out Granite Mountain regardless of innocent lives. Bloody shame MacPhallon didn't get on board sooner. Now, even his hands are tied. It's already too late for Ken, Julie, and Adriano. What if it's too late to stop the Day of Judgment from happening on March 19th? I'll dial up Pete.* Again a recorded message, this time Peter said, "Nobody is available to take your call, so please leave your name and number at the beep, and we'll get back to you as soon as we can." Beep.

"Curt Shirlington here. Ring me up, Pete." His voice was urgent, whiny, beyond his control. He hung up, his heart crying out, *M'lady can't be dead! How do I go on living, knowing she doesn't walk this earth somewhere?* Every hour on the hour, he made the same call, got the same recording, and gave the same response. Somehow, the sun went down and he was in his and Penny's private barracks. His mind acknowledged Penny being there, but she was a habit, automatically handled. He considered a Rob Roy. *Getting tartared up isn't wise. A clear head is needed. Sleep.* He tossed and turned; and when sleep finally came, he dreamt of driving a rain-slicked highway. Tires hissed. Headlights! Coming at him! Turning into a bomb! A fuse burned. A blinding white light! Darkness all around. He groped along a wall, descending a dank staircase, warping around the hard edge of a corner. Fire! In front of him! In back of him! Smoke stung his eyes. Blind, unable to breathe, he ran. He was running through a forest. A wolf heaved at his neck. "Curt!"

"M'lady!" he cried. "Where are you?"

Her hand touched his.

The telephone exploded. Curt snapped to life. Rain drummed on the tin roof. He glanced to the right. In dawn's half-light, Penny's imprint lingered on the sheets. The telephone blared. Kicking his way out of the blankets, he sat up and fumbled for the phone. He tried to speak, but his mouth was too sticky and acrid.

"There's been a training accident, sir," said a male voice on the other end of the line. "You are needed ASAP at base hospital."

Curt hung up and blinked at the clock radio. *6:08* A.M. He wiped perspiration off his brow. Like electricity, Julie, Ken,

Adriano, Katrina, Granite Mountain, and the Day of Judgment swept through him. He hurtled out of bed. "I'll fly to Brighton after resolving the hospital situation!"

Outside, winter rain bucketed as Curt held the hood of an army slicker tight to his face and charged through puddles that expanded and deepened here and there across the asphalt. Steam shrouded the base as a motley assortment of humanity huddled inside open hangar doors.

Inside the hospital, Katrina stepped out of nowhere and clutched his slicker. "Joe Ault's been killed in a training accident," she blubbered. Her hair dripped brown tint and her red tank top and black jeans clung to her frame like surgical gloves.

He grabbed her wrists and tore her hands off him. As he towed her to a nearby office, her wet bare feet squawked on the tile floor. "Everything's going to be all right," he said, seating her on a chair next to the desk. "Wait here." He darted out of the office to the ER. He yanked aside drapes of cubicles until finding Penny leaning over a gurney and tending to an injured recruit. Another recruit stood at the entrance of the cubicle, one eye bandaged. Curt knew him, but knew better than to acknowledge him. He stepped to the gurney. "Status?"

"Grenade detonated prematurely during a live-fire exercise," spoke up a training sergeant, sitting on a folding chair and filling out a form.

Curt and Penny eyed the sergeant.

"Don't, Joe!" shrieked the recruit lying on the gurney. "Don't do it! Grenade! Hit the deck!"

Curt gave the recruit a cursory examination. "Lost a pinky finger."

Penny nodded. "Nothing life-threatening. I got a line in. Awaiting orders to administer morphine and patch him up."

"Do it," said Curt, putting a hand on the recruit's chest. "What's your name, son?"

"Sag, sir. Vic...Sag..."

As the morphine took effect, Curt glanced at the recruit he recognized. "Your name?"

"Bert Moro, sir."

Curt pulled Penny aside. "Keep Sag under. I need time to get to the bottom of this."

Her eyes ping-ponged between Curt and Sag. "Yes, Doctor."

"Follow me, Moro," said Curt.

The fear that flooded into Katrina's swollen red eyes when Curt and Moro entered the office was undeniable. *He isn't too happy about seeing her either,* observed Curt. "I see you two know each other," he said while skirting the desk. "You're out of the bag, Pomoroy."

Katrina's eyes widened. "Pomoroy?"

"Robert Pomoroy." His hand wormed into his jockey shorts and pulled out a thin leather wallet. He flipped it open and flashed a badge. "FBI operative. AKA Bert Moro."

"Y-you're the p-plant?" she stammered.

His face displayed a forgive-me light. "Long before you arrived at Granite Mountain."

She jumped to her feet. Her eyes darted between Curt and Pomoroy. "You two let the Araneas mess with kids?"

"Nothing could be done before knowing what we're up against," said Pomoroy, stuffing the wallet into his shorts.

"In the meantime kids come up missing?" she cried. "Or dead? My Dad's dead! Mom, too! And Addie! Eliminated! How could you know and not stop it?"

"I'll put a call in to MacPhallon," said Pomoroy.

"MacPhallon?" stormed Katrina. "My grandfather's friend from Vietnam? My grandfather knows about Granite Mountain and me?"

"Not to my knowledge," said Curt.

Katrina put her back to them. "My family is dead, and it's all my fault! I should've gone home when I found out about Granite Mountain. I should've let somebody else take care of it."

"Until your family's status is confirmed," said Pomoroy, "let's assume the Araneas lied to you. They lie about everything." He touched her shoulder. She shook him off. "Look," he said, "the terrorist cells that exist in this country and across the world have got to be put out of action once and for all. This being your second time down this road, you of all people must understand that."

She spun to face him. "You knew about…"

He nodded. "Like you, I was kidnapped. I was six. Like you, I have the memory of an elephant. No matter what garbage the Araneas tried to brainwash me with, I remembered my identity. Like you, I learned to control the turmoil, grief, and rage. I can block out anything I choose. The day the Araneas loosened my tether, I headed straight to the FBI. Jonathan still isn't wise to me."

"I know," she said.

"How do you know?" asked Curt.

"I just know," she spouted. "I know lots more than people think."

"Tell me what you know," said Curt.

She shook out her wrists. "One day I was looking for something in Jonathan's office. Bert's file was with a bunch of others on his desk. The label on the top file said Camille Jennes." Katrina quaked, but as Pomoroy grappled for her, she shook him off and sat down. "Jonathan told us she ran away, because she and Joe broke up. What really happened was she threatened to go to the cops and report Joe for beating up on her, so Jonathan killed her. He did it himself and then disposed of her— he used that word, disposed, in her file. He disposed of her body in the crematorium. It's on the lowest level of the warren. He's gone completely nuts. He wears clothes that make him look like a sheik or something and never leaves the warren at all. He assigns me one thing and then another and then sends me down here to Georgia with Bert. I saw other files, too. He murdered a lot of kids, using spiders, nerve agents, torture, and sometimes an agent he invented that lacks a signature to hide the real cause of death. He dumps those bodies outside the compound, like in lakes or during snowstorms. He wants authorities to find them, because he knows he'll get away with it. He writes like he's bragging—that he's a prophet and soon to be a martyr."

Curt swallowed hard. "So who's this Vic Sag in the ER?"

"David Gringas," said Katrina.

"And his role at Granite Mountain?" asked Curt.

"Taking out the children or wives of special targets," said Pomoroy.

"Targets?" asked Curt.

"Targets who don't cooperate in whatever manner Jonathan wishes," said Pomoroy.

"You know of such a target?" asked Curt.

Pomoroy nodded. "Vic stabbed two brothers during a brawl he instigated at a wild party. The target, their father, wasn't home. Vic killed one son and stabbed the other. The father has cooperated since. If he doesn't, the surviving son meets the same fate."

Curt shook his head. "So all you kids are here, pretending to train, just waiting for the word to wreak havoc on our troops."

"That's part of the mission," said Pomoroy.

"Part?" asked Curt.

"We're to wreak havoc when an opportunity presents itself," said Pomoroy. "For example, who's going to suspect Army convoys, crisscrossing America and threading through crowded streets, are carrying biological weapons—anthrax, botulinum toxin, and aflatoxin? Hundreds of thousands dead, just like that." Bert snapped his fingers. "But Jonathan didn't count on Vic having it in for Joe."

"Vic set up the training accident?" asked Curt.

"Maybe not set it up," said Pomoroy, "but certainly buffed up on steroids just itching for the right opportunity."

"Motive?" asked Curt.

"Vic caught Joe nailing Brita to the ground behind the dorm," said Pomoroy.

"Joe did that to lots of girls," said Katrina, looking down at her fingernails. "Boys, too."

"Vic's no angel either," said Pomoroy. "I had all I could do to keep him off you."

"Like that night on the island, I suppose?" she said, glaring at Bert. "Tell me, what part of your investigation involves drugging and taking advantage of me?"

Curt jumped to his feet and circled the desk. "You shagged the wee one?"

Pomoroy raised his palms. "Absolutely not!"

Katrina crossed her arms. "I'll bet!"

Fist clenching, Curt stood eyeball to eyeball with Bert. "Explain yourself, young man!"

"Vic had his eye on Trina," said Pomoroy. "So I got Meredith to bump him off an outing. It's a good thing I did, because he planned on drugging Trina and taking indecent pictures—black-mail—and who knows what else."

"Vic was the one who laced the water?" she asked.

Pomoroy nodded. "I saw the way you acted after drinking it. I put two and two together and didn't drink any of it. I took the bottle cap to the FBI and had it analyzed. It and the unused bottle in the other backpack tested positive for several date rape drugs—not just one. I had planned on handling Vic myself."

"But he showed up," said Curt, backing away.

"Yeah," said Pomoroy, scratching the back of his head. "Knew he would, but not so soon. He sucker-punched me and…"

"I didn't hit you?" asked Katrina.

"You weren't about to hit anybody," said Pomoroy. "Those drugs made you limp as a rag doll."

"So Vic, he…" she stammered.

Pomoroy shook his head side to side. "I came to. He was putting on a condom. I jumped him, and he dropped the condom in the sand. Unfortunately, he had gotten you undressed and taken pictures."

"If he didn't, uhm…you know…" she stammered. "Then why was I so sore?"

"Racing?" guessed Pomoroy. "Working against the tide to get us to shore when I screwed up my arm?"

"Perhaps you had a reaction to the drugs in the water," added Curt while perching on a corner of the desk.

"What happened to the pictures?" she asked.

"Tossed them into the campfire, the next night," said Pomoroy. "Almost got caught. Can't take a dump without somebody knowing it." Guilt riddled his face. "I kept your barrette."

"You have the one I lost on that island?" she asked.

"I need it," said Pomoroy.

She gawked at him.

"It's a part of you I can keep with me," he said. "You're what makes this nasty business worthwhile. I almost went down for coming to your rescue on that island and again when Aranea planned to convert you. Remember that shot I gave you?"

She nodded.

"That drug set you down so deep that nothing got through," he said. "I'm teetering on the edge because of you. Going down for the third time. There won't be any coming back. So I figure, in my final moments if I can't see your face, that barrette's a piece of you to comfort me."

She looked down at the wedding ring on her finger. Twisting it, she slid a look at Pomoroy. His arms opened wide. She got to her feet and stepped into his arms. He drew in a chest full of air and closed his eyes.

Seen that connection only once in my pathetic life, Curt mused, *between Ol' Chap and M'lady.* He cleared his throat to let Katrina and Pomoroy know he was there.

They backed away from one another, but their eyes remained locked. "When Jonathan hears Joe is dead," she said, "and our mission has failed, he'll have our hides."

Curt rubbed his brow. "Can't see any way out of this."

"This is an awful thing to say…" said Katrina. Her head rolled as she pursed her lips.

"Spit it out, wee one."

"Too bad…too bad Vic…Vic didn't die, too."

Silence.

Without warning, Curt slid off the corner of the desk and shrieked, "Katrina!"

"I'm sorry, I'm sorry," she moaned.

Curt waved his palms. "No, no! It's all right, wee one! You're a genius! One fantastic genius! Vic is going to die!"

"You can't do that," she cried.

Laughing that deep English-Scottish laugh of his, Curt cradled Katrina in his arms. "Sag isn't going to die, but I have a way to make it look like he did. And Aranea is much too astute to show his face around here to claim cadavers, which, of course, requires proof of adoption."

"Terrorist dictum bans showing one's face to the camera," said Pomoroy. "The last thing Jonathan wants is nosey reporters asking questions and swarming Granite Mountain."

Katrina pulled away from Curt and looked into his eyes. "What about Brita?"

"Brita?" asked Curt.

"She's posing as Vic's wife," said Pomoroy.

"I didn't see her in the ER," said Curt.

"She's visiting relatives in Savannah," said Katrina.

"Actually," said Pomoroy, "Brita is scoping out nuclear reactors."

"When is she due back?" asked Curt.

"This afternoon, I think," said Katrina.

"That's when we tell her Vic died," said Curt. "What about Ault's wife?"

"Alice," said Katrina. "She didn't come. She was supposed to, but she got really drunk, so Jonathan wouldn't let her. Gosh, was he ever mad!"

"Anybody else we should be concerned about?" asked Curt.

"Not from Granite Mountain," said Pomoroy, "but I'd bet my soul others are here from cells we don't know about. When Judgment, Mississippi fell, terrorists and converts scattered."

"We'll get them," said Curt.

"But I'm the one who's supposed to keep Jonathan informed," cried Katrina as visions of his lecherous grin loomed in her mind. "He'll know I'm lying! He can tell when anybody lies!"

"I'll fix it so you won't have to lie," said Curt. "I'll work some of my own magic. When you go back to Granite Mountain, Aranea won't get a thing out of you, no matter what he tries."

Two hours later, Brita arrived on the base, sooner than expected, but the trap had been set. So it was sprung. "Joe's dead!" wailed Brita on the phone to Jonathan. "And Vic's on the operating table!"

"What the hell happened?" demanded Jonathan.

Brita kept wailing.

"Get a grip on yourself," hollered Jonathan.

Brita kept wailing.

"Put Kitty on the phone!"

"A grenade went off," said Katrina.

"How?"

Katrina controlled her cringing. "Don't know. Nobody's telling us a thing."

"Where's Bert?"

"Having shrapnel taken out of his eye."

"Nose around! See that you call back the second you know something!" The line went dead.

Brita spent the next several hours sedated in a private room on the other side of the hospital from Katrina who was spilling her guts to Don MacPhallon of the FBI. Pomoroy helped to clarify facts and outline locations of four missiles encapsulated in the silos on the fifth level of the warren. Targets were Seabrook and Three-mile Island Nuclear Power Stations, Boston, and New York. Access points into the warren were verified, not only through the parking garage, but also through innocent-looking businesses girdling Granite Mountain. The FBI now had specific leads to where the Araneas and their cohorts were hiding and also the location of the ammo dump.

"Jonathan's been on my case to finish designs for tracking chips," said Bert. "I used the excuse that I'm too bogged down with other assignments he gave me. In the meantime I flub tryouts of the prototypes."

"Isn't wise to let Jonathan know where you are all the time," said MacPhallon.

"I did come up with a tiny sensor that can be worn in underwear," said Bert. "It gives limited ability to track spiderlings on assignment. Aranea doesn't know about it."

"We could use it against him," said MacPhallon.

"Yeah," said Bert, "but he's smart enough to know that there are ways around sensors if a person really wants to deceive."

"Wish Chas was wearing a tracking device," said Katrina.

"How come?" asked Bert.

"Jonathan's going to send him to some big company in southern New Hampshire," she said, "with C 4 and nails strapped to him."

"When?" asked MacPhallon.

Katrina shrugged. "If I knew that, Chas wouldn't have to be tracked. Why don't you guys know?" An awkward silence filled the room. "Do you know that Jonathan's planning to send somebody into RFK Stadium during a game?"

"We heard rumors," said MacPhallon.

"I told Chas I found his file with his real name," she said. "Everything the Araneas told him about his parents was a lie. They're still alive. Gosh, was Chas mad. I made him promise not to do anything until we figured out a way of getting all the kids out of Granite Mountain. I promised him that after he'd be reunited with his parents."

"I'll make sure that happens," said MacPhallon, "after the invasion."

"Invasion?" she asked.

Pomoroy took her hand. "The military is planning to invade Granite Mountain just before Jonathan's Judgment Day."

"When is Judgment Day?" she asked.

His hand tightened on hers. "March 19th."

"I'm going back," she said.

"Let the military take care of it," said Pomoroy.

"No!" she cried, clenching her fists.

"Katrina is right," said MacPhallon. "She's the only one left who stands a snowball's chance in hell of getting any of the kids out of there."

⌒

The six o'clock news anchor led off with "A training operation turned disastrous at Fort Stewart, Georgia, today. Private Joe

Ault died instantly when a grenade went off prematurely. An hour later, Private Vic Sag, died on the operating table from complications associated with the accident."

At 6:25, Katrina called Jonathan and in a choking voice, said, "Vic died on the operating table."

"I watch the six o'clock news," snarled Jonathan.

After Katrina hung up, Curt and Penny exploded with laughter. "Yup," said Curt, "Sag died on the operating table while this surgeon, assisted by this nurse, attempted to reattach his pinky finger!"

Chapter 34

*T*he road ahead was heavy with an approaching thunderstorm that seemed to be a giant mauve-colored hand reaching out for the car, intent on deterring Katrina from returning to Granite Mountain. In the backseat, Brita stirred in a self-imposed drugged state, later enhanced by Doctor Curt Shirlington. In the front passenger seat, Katrina dropped her head back on the headrest, closed her eyes hard, and sulked, "This nightmare just won't go away. Well, it will go away! I will make it go away! She glanced at her blue turtleneck sweater and brown corduroy slacks, much too heavy for Georgia's heat and humidity. In her hand that rested on her lap was her ruby-eyed spider pin. She handed it to Curt. "Wish I never had to wear another one of these filthy things, but it won't be long before Meredith gives me another one."

Curt held the pin above the steering wheel. His vision jounced between the pin and road ahead. "Perfect time to act like a basket case."

His flippancy aggravated Katrina. She pursed her lips and gawked at him. Her silence stirred him to glance at her. "When handed another pin," he explained, "put it on thick and heavy. That will stall Aranea and buy precious time on this end."

She heaved an all-consuming breath. "We are going to rip this spider web to shreds, aren't we, Uncle Curt?"

"That we will." He slipped the pin into his jacket pocket then gripped her hand. "You must keep the mind-set that no matter what, everything is going to work out."

"Why can't the FBI find Dad and Mom and Addie?" she asked.

"The key words are 'can't find,'" he said. "The FBI *can't find* them. So the only conclusion is Aranea lied about their being dead."

"But what if he does have them?" insisted Katrina.

"I'll not be thinking in that manner," said Curt, while steering the car to the far end of the terminal. He put it in park then took her by the shoulders and looked into her eyes. "Wee one, your eyes are bluer than a New England sky after the rain. Never lose hope. Trials make us strong; sorrow keeps us human. Happiness lives in those who cry, those who hurt, and those who search and try, because they, and only they, can appreciate the importance of others who touch their lives. Put yourself in the shoes of others, even your enemies, because if it hurts to wear their shoes, their shoes probably hurt them, too. On the other hand, find out the source of Aranea's pain and make it excruciating!"

She half-giggled, but then grew serious. "But what if I can't?"

"Do your best," said Curt. "Nobody expects more." He kissed her forehead.

"I expect more," she said, getting out of the car. She opened the back door and jabbed Brita. "Wake up, sleeping beauty."

"Bring her around with this," said Curt, offering a hypodermic needle.

Katrina pushed down one side of Brita's pants, took the needle, and jabbed it into the thickness of Brita's hip.

"Where am I?" Brita mumbled as Katrina handed the used needle to Curt.

"For crying out loud," grumbled Katrina, towing Brita out of the car. "If you'd lay off the drugs, you'd know where you are! Come on, we'll miss our flight!"

"Be careful, wee one," called Curt.

"I can take care of myself," said Katrina, "most of the time."

Brown leather hiking boots clunked as the girls trudged to the terminal, winter parkas slung over their arms and backpacks over their shoulders. Katrina shot a glance at Curt driving away. *How easy it would be to flag him down and run back to Bert.*

Wind and high clouds sped unhindered across the tarmac, making for a rough takeoff. Katrina was grateful when Brita finally stopped blathering about Vic's demise and started to blow gum bubbles and pop them. *Some things never change,* thought Katrina while staring out the window. *Yet everything has changed. Bert's not a bad guy after all. Oh, I hate myself for thinking that. I should've known it the first time I looked into his eyes. Gosh, when is the FBI going to find Dad and Mom and Addie! What am I going to do without them? Whew, the fights Dad and I had over me being on my own. Stop thinking that way, Katrina! They'll turn up. Everybody says so. Just wait until Dad and Mom hear about Uncle Curt showing up at Fort Stewart. He never should've left Brighton, but I guess it was a good thing. He was there when I needed him. Interesting how Vic murdering Joe turned out to be the breakthrough Uncle Curt, Bert, and Don MacPhallon were hoping for. A crack in the granite walls of Jonathan's evil empire is how Bert put it.*

Uncle Curt was so funny when he walked in on us making out in that hospital room where MacPhallon hid us. Gosh, I felt like Dad just caught us. Katrina toyed with the band of gold on her left hand, picturing Curt blustering in his Scottish-English way, *"Oh, pardon me!"* He cleared his throat the same way fuddy-duddy comedians do.

"Nothing's going on," Bert tried to tell him. *"Look. Our feet are touching the floor!"*

Things really heated up after Uncle Curt left. But Bert called a halt to it. "I want you, Trina. You know I do. But not like this. Not here. I want it to be special— because you're special—because we're special."

"I don't care," I told him. *"You might not make it back to me, so why not grab a little happiness while we can?" Wish I knew where Bert is. All he could tell me is that he's part of a specialized support staff. I understand. Oh, how I understand. But understanding doesn't comfort me much.*

"Please, don't worry," he told me. *Oh, I can almost feel his hand cupping my chin. I can almost see his eyes looking into mine. "I'm*

prepared to do whatever needs to be done," he told me. "I decided that
a long time ago when Jonathan snagged me in his web."

"I know you have to be the man you have to be," I told him, "but
I can't help worrying—and I'm not going to cover it up." It was so
hard not to cry.

"If we get through this," he said, "we can get through anything."

"What's ahead for you and me?" I asked.

His face squinched and then he said, "Loving each other will keep
us going even when we think we can't. No matter where you are when
this is over, I will find you, and you better believe there's no way I'll
let you go again. I intend to wake up each and every morning and see
you next to me."

The loudspeaker of the plane clicked on. "This is Captain B.
J. Griffin. We will be landing in Portland in about twenty
minutes. The weather in Portland is clear. The temperature is
twenty-five degrees."

Meredith Aranea was a lot colder than twenty-five degrees
when she picked up the girls. Not one word passed between
them. *That's okay with me,* thought Katrina as Brita popped a
bubble. She gazed out the passenger side window and toyed
with the wedding band on her left hand. *Too bad I left that picture
of Bert and me back at Toffee Castle.*

By the time they drove beneath the granite arches, the
campus lights were on. Katrina headed straight to the kennel in
the clearing.

⌒

Inside the warren, she got into bed and shut off the light. She lay
there, overtired. *Wish I was in Bert's arms tonight instead of in this
dreadful place. I have to be tough, not only for me, but for Dad and
Mom—and for Bert.* "Watch your back," Bert told me. "Never ignore
or shrug off anything. Be quick on your feet and master of your fate..."

Katrina awoke with a start.

"Don't react," pleaded a low, nervous voice. Hazel eyes
signaled first over one shoulder and then the other, warning of
the ever-present cameras.

Katrina glanced at Mickey Blue Eyes unmoved by what was going on.

"We have to talk," whispered Alice. Her hand moved over the blanket and onto Katrina's hip.

"Are you nuts or something?" squealed Katrina, squirming up against the headboard. *Act like a basket case,* she told herself, *just like Uncle Curt said.*

Alice smiled seductively. "Something you have to know," she purred while slithering into bed.

"Get out of here!" shrieked Katrina, pointing to the door.

"You got your opinion of me," cooed Alice. "Hard to change that, but..."

"Impossible to change is more accurate," snapped Katrina.

"Keep it down, will you?" said Alice, offering a nip of Jack Daniels.

Katrina shoved it away. "Get that poison away from me!"

"I was a shy kid," whispered Alice in between nursing on the bottle. "Aranea thinks that's why I started boozing. It relaxes me, you know, so I fit in? Can you keep a secret?"

Katrina eyed Alice. *Something tells me I should squash the basket case charade.*

Alice blew in Katrina's face. "Notice anything?"

Katrina turned her head, anticipating the stench of booze. There wasn't any. Her brow furrowed as she looked at Alice.

"It's a façade," murmured Alice. "The nips in my left pockets are the real thing, but in my right pockets? Hey, how about that—tinted water! You never considered that, did you? ever wonder how I perform so brilliantly?" Her left hand cupped Katrina's cheek as her right hand wedged a small vial into Katrina's hand and compressed her fingers around it. "This vial contains antibodies. Make sure your brother gets them."

Katrina gasped. "Addie?"

"Get him out of here tomorrow night," murmured Alice. "Far, far away."

Katrina tightened her grip on the vial. "Is this some kind of trick?"

"I'll see to it that you escape clean," whispered Alice, drawing near in a sexual manner. Katrina put up her hand, and Alice dropped onto the pillow eyes deceptively bright as she stared at the ceiling and hummed "Mary's Song."

Katrina's jaw dropped.

Alice turned to Katrina and winked. "Jonathan and Meredith mess around while watching the Tonight Show. By the time it ends, booze or drugs, sometimes both have put them under. Security guards know about it—because I told them, of course. So by 12:35, the guards are having themselves some z-time."

"Where's Dad and Mom?" ventured Katrina.

"Not in the warren," cooed Alice, snuggling into the pillow.

"You sure?"

"I have access to video tapes, remember?" said Alice. "I also wired rooms that don't have cameras in them, so like I said, 'Alice sees everything!' Even the Araneas' bedrooms. Sweet, huh?"

Katrina's fist that contained the vial shot to her mouth to squelch a gasp.

"Leave your dog in the kennel in the clearing tomorrow night," said Alice. "I stashed a plastic bag under the watering trough. Money is in it and papers divulging the locations of Jonathan's assets, associates, and names of kids alive and dead. Whatever I could get my grubby paws on, I copied." Nervousness came through her hands that massaged Katrina's thigh, harder, faster. "Winds are blowing our way. Tomorrow night, this place is toast."

Chills shot through Katrina. "What are you going to do?"

Alice shrugged. "When life hands out lemons," she whispered, "choices are: one, turn sour, two, make lemonade. I squeezed lemons for a long time. Tomorrow night, I will add sugar and water and drink to my heart's delight!" She got up on an elbow and faced Katrina so the camera couldn't see. "Now listen. We have to look as though we're getting sexually acquainted."

Katrina squinted at Alice.

"You have any other bright idea how to get your brother out of here?" whispered Alice.

Katrina tilted her head to one side. After a moment of thought, she gave a tentative nod and scooched down.

Alice kissed Katrina's forehead and then her cheek and then pulled the top sheet over them. Her words were soft and low, but cutting. "Jonathan and Meredith are addicted to watching pube jumping. The pathetic predators won't guess in a million years that we're faking it or the world as they know it is about to come crashing down on their slimy libidos."

"What's going on?" whispered Katrina.

"Know all that brilliant work you did to screw up the computers around here?" murmured Alice.

Katrina felt her stomach flip-flop. "You knew that I've been…"

"I added bugs you never thought of," said Alice.

"Listen, Alice, I don't think…"

"Priscilla," said Alice.

"Huh?"

"My name is Priscilla. Priscilla Hamilton."

Katrina's eyes skittered across the face next to her.

"I know what you're thinking," said Priscilla. "Why didn't you find my file when you did the others?"

Katrina gasped. "You knew that I…"

"Like I said," whispered Priscilla, seeming to talk outside herself. "Alice sees and hears everything. A long time ago, I set in motion a series of events that led to my high mucky-muck father's death. Shanked him myself with a two-foot sword, part of his civil war collection." She looked away, snarling, "I was invisible to him, worthless. I tried to talk to him. Sometimes, he faked listening, but I knew his mind was on something else. I always hurried home from school, but when I called out to him, he never answered. It's like I was in this black hole, a pain in the butt to him. It's said that the loser in a divorce is the first side to run out of money, but the real loser is the kid. He kept telling me I'm just like my mother, stupid, I'd never amount to anything— just like Brita said that day on the trail." Alice flipped up her middle finger as if every person that had treated her badly stood before her. A smile broke on her face. "But you hollered back, 'that was a terrible thing to say.' Nobody ever stood up for me. For sure, that rich old bastard father of mine never did. I know what I did and I'd do it all over again. I never worry if I did right or wrong. Just like I'm not worried about what's going to happen to Aranea and his evil repression. What does he expect, anyways? Every ten seconds he's hollering at somebody: "You're horrible! You're evil! You're wicked!" Well, nobody's ever controlled me! It's not like Aranea can kill my family, so I have nothing to lose. Death doesn't faze me at all, only the thought of Aranea on top of me again. That makes me want to puke. He picks and chooses the innocent and vulnerable and doesn't ask permission. Well, piss on him! I'm not going to be invisible much longer!"

Chapter 35

L osing prized spiderlings at Fort Stewart pushed Jonathan over the edge. He talked to himself constantly. "Finding replacements takes valuable time. I must cash in additional assets, much more than anticipated. Such tasks are difficult to accomplish with infidels on the alert. Meanwhile, my power erodes beneath me. My inner circle, spiderlings, that wife of mine—they all plot against me! Moro needs to control them. And where is he? Detained at Fort Stewart! Only a matter of time before base security discovers Moro is not who he claims to be. Spells trouble all the way back to Granite Mountain." Jonathan shook his fist. "Moro? You better keep your mouth shut! If you don't, I will hunt you down like a dog!"

Too much time inside Granite Mountain exacerbated paranoia, making fear as real as taking in air. "Nothing is safe," he blathered. "A simple bee sting, to which I am deathly allergic, planted in a drawer...it will kill me! Even touching a speck of dust might prove lethal. Dying in ways like that will not gain me martyrdom. I keep my arms folded beneath my aba, always armed, always on the move to avoid being tracked."

His build and veneer had made finding a body double impossible—even plastic surgery could not enhance that much. He ate little; and what he did, Meredith sampled first. Then again, he didn't trust her.

He lacked sleep, because those he had tortured, raped, and eliminated besieged him at the threshold of slumber. If he made it past that, nightmares of ruination from an unknown but catastrophic mistake accosted him. Such happened the night Meredith picked up Katrina and Brita at the airport. He got out of bed and set about cleaning his gun. Shortly thereafter, Meredith entered the bedroom and announced, "The grieving widows are safe and sound in their cubicles." He grunted and then looked down the gun barrel to inspect its cleanliness. "Will you put that thing away?" she snapped, taking off her coat and hanging it up in the closet. "You've become a madman!"

"I am no madman," he spat. "I am realistic. Cunning. Ruthless."

She rolled her eyes. "Plans for the Day of Judgment are going to have to be postponed."

"Over my dead body," he blasted. "Operatives around the world await my signal."

"We need time to regroup," she argued, unbuttoning her blouse. "This thing that happened in Georgia must die down."

"The last time I regrouped was after my father's assassination," he growled. "Rashid did the regrouping then. Regrouping means failure. I will not admit to failure!"

"It would be a tremendous loss of face," she added while taking off her blouse, "to seek support from the Middle Eastern powerbrokers we have snubbed."

"It shows weakness," he said. "If I show weakness, my spiderlings will crumble."

"Brita already has," said Meredith, "and Kitty refuses to give me the wedding ring. She went bonkers when I tried to take it. She bit my hand!"

"Judgment Day goes off as scheduled!" shouted Jonathan.

"Okay, okay," she puffed while stuffing her blouse into the hamper inside the closet, "but only half is ready here."

"Half is sufficient," he barked. "Chemical and bacteriological weapons are my trump cards, the be-all yet end-all of what Jonathan Aranea is about."

"I suppose," she agreed, unzipping her slacks.

"All Kitty and Brita need is another brainwashing session," he said. "They will settle into the mold. Now that I have the

Waters cub in my clutches, I have the leverage to get Kitty to finish computer prep…"

"Will you look at that!" exclaimed Meredith. "Our favorite skanks are finally coming together!"

He glanced at the monitor just as Alice's leg slithered over Katrina. "This is going be good," he lathered, flicking on a second monitor to pick up another angle of Alice straddling Katrina. "Yes, the cameras are getting all of it."

"Great idea for a TV show," commented Meredith, taking off her slacks.

His right eye twitched. *Ah, Alice,* he mused. *Those amazing hands of yours work magic. You made me so furious about having to yank you from the Georgia assignment. Still it turned out for the better. Losing you would've been the straw that broke this camel's back. Despite your addiction to bourbon, you have been nothing but reliable from the moment I brought you in—so easy to rob of innocence. I taught you everything and you learned so well. Now, you are the main spoke in the wheel for pulling off the Day of Judgment.* He adjusted the volumes, craving to hear. "Damn speakers!"

"That voice enhancing system Alice installed is a real dud," muttered Meredith while stuffing her slacks into the hamper.

Lust enveloped Jonathan as Katrina stretched out. A look of sleepy pleasure plastered her face. He rotated more dials. "Can't get close-ups either!"

Meredith stood in her underwear. The blue floral-print caftan she was about to put on was draped over her arm. "Easy, Alice," she rumbled. "Don't be an idiot and rush it. Kitty's not a loaf of bread. Okay, get her turned around. Gently. That's it." Alice's hands went beneath the covers. As a grin rippled Katrina's lips, Meredith slapped her thigh, boasting, "Just as I thought! Those two are one of a kind. It always happens when that kind get off on a rocky start. Come on, Alice, sweet talk Kitty. Get her into position. You know we want to see."

After a few moments of what looked like stroking beneath the blankets, Katrina sprung up and slapped Alice across the face.

"Damn it, Alice," barked Jonathan. "Whatever you did back-fired!"

Fire burned in Katrina's eyes as her knee came up and cata-pulted Alice off the bed. A hand appeared and yanked Katrina off the bed and out of camera range.

Imagining the catfight in the throes of hormones and instinct, Jonathan had no intentions of satisfying himself with his own hand. *Virgins in paradise be damned,* he thought. Turning to Meredith, he cooed, "Come here, my luscious doll…"

Meredith gawked at him.

"A little massage for your hunk-of-burning-love?" His seductive smile implied satisfaction, though his true intentions were to be satisfied. He removed his aba, revealing a holster crossing his bare chest and a loincloth.

Her jaw dropped. She cocked her head. A half-smile grew. She dropped the blue floral-print caftan and tore off her under-wear.

He turned his eyes. *Her ugliness will not interfere with my fantasy of romping with Alice and Kitty.* He tore off all the bedding, expecting to see a poison adder. Finding nothing, he flattened on his stomach. A moment later, thighs straddled his flanks and a soft underside warmed his rump. Hands kneaded his shoulders, making him feel like a mass of bread dough. He closed his eyes and wallowed. *This wife of mine, daughter of the dog, believes she gives herself to me, but I will take her and relieve these weeks of absti-nence. I take her like I take Alice—and soon Kitty. I take everything that is coming to me!*

Chapter 36

S o the knight in shining armor is off to save his damsel in distress," said Penny, setting down her briefcase on the coffee table. "You just can't wait and go with me in the morning."

Her jasmine perfume sweetened the dreary barracks cooking in the noonday sun as Curt zipped up the suitcase. "Listen, Penny, I…"

"No need to explain," she cut in. "I knew all along this day might come. I've known you're in love with Julie since Ken was hospitalized after falling off that cliff in Cohasset. I saw in his room. You were looking at Julie sleeping, soaking up everything about her. I knew right then I didn't stand a chance."

His face felt as stiff as his utterance, "I…I…"

Again she cut in, "You're a prisoner in your head, and you've made Julie Waters your jailer. You thought running away would preserve your friendship with Ken, but you lost it anyway. Too bad you didn't tell Julie, so she could've rejected you for real. Fantasy would've been dead and buried. In time, you would've gotten over it. By now, you'd be standing here, realizing you're in love with me."

The bottom fell out of Curt.

"Don't look at me like that," she said. "Of course, you love me. I know it and you know it, but you're too thickheaded to admit it."

He turned, paced to the wall and stopped at the colorless wall. No magnolia designs like papered to the living room walls back in Atlanta. *Atlanta? I'm homesick for Atlanta? But I'm homesick for New England!* He rolled his eyes and let out a long self-pitying sigh. "What if she's de... How..."

"How can you possibly let M'lady go?" said Penny, finishing his thoughts. "M'lady is in your blood—in your soul from that first moment you set eyes on her."

Curt stood there. He could have said so many things, but his thoughts were too fragmented to put together a single word.

She snagged his hand and tugged him around. Looking sad, yet so strong, she held his hand to her cheek.

He tried to conjure up the image of M'lady, but all he could see was Penny. All he could smell was jasmine—not honeysuckle.

"Destiny decreed that we be together," she said. "Why else did I find you at the CDC? You needed a friend. I thought I could help, but the fever burning inside you made me cry inside. So many times, I've wished I was Julie." Letting go of his hand, Penny turned away. "And now she's out there...perhaps without a husband...guess your soul is lost." She gazed at the third finger of her left hand where no gold band had left its mark. "I never expected to be the center of your universe, but you know, sometimes, the one you need you need the most—the one you really want—is right under your nose." She heaved a sigh and ran her hands up and down her arms. "I feel so lonely when I'm with you. Even with you lying beside me, the bed feels so empty. But if I could change these years of having you in my life, I wouldn't."

Curt squinted at his suitcase then shook his head. "I'm a bloody twit."

Penny heaved a sigh then seemed to reset herself. Turning back to him, she said, "I'm not going to watch you traipse off to your fantasy and be here when you get back. No way. You're going to save yourself this time. Find yourself another soft heart."

He stared at her. Hands hooked on her hips. *She looks so strong, so beautiful... like she says, the one I need the most.* He took her hands off her hips and enwrapped them in his. Looking into her eyes, he said, "This fool needs your soft heart. I don't know why you're still here, but I'm so glad you are."

She smiled. "My Dad once told me, 'No person is worth your tears; and the one who is won't bring you tears.' Those I've shed are of my own making. I love you like Julie never can—like she never will."

"But I turned a blind eye to you," he said. "I refused to let go of…"

"M'lady," said Penny. "Even dreamt of her while lying next to me."

He let go of her hands and gawked at her.

"You talk in your sleep," she explained.

He scratched his head. "I've contributed nothing to our relationship. We're childless, the only offspring at the ends of family trees."

She ran her hand across his back. "We're supposed to meet a few wrong people," she said, "so we'll be grateful when the right one comes along."

Curt swung his head in agreement just as the telephone rang. He picked it up. "Shirlington here." He listened for several moments. "Thanks, Holt." He hung up and glanced at Penny. "MacPhallon heard from Peter Blair getting back to Brighton after a sailing trip. Adriano came up missing from the day care. Police dogs tracked his scent to the Charles River and his shoe. It is presumed the tyke fell in and the current took him—quite possibly all the way through Boston Harbor to the Atlantic. Julie left a note. She was unable to get in touch with Ken, somewhere around Granite Mountain. He's checked out of his lodgings. She was afraid to contact law enforcement up there, so she's off to find him Pete's worried—she's got another in the oven—bad weather's predicted. He put pressure on MacPhallon and Thornton to send out a search chopper."

Masking her pain, Penny picked up her briefcase and rummaged through it. Her tone was changed, terse and professional. "Lots to do before we head up to Granite Mountain. We must formulate a precise plan ASAP and get it to Katrina, so she can get those kids away from Granite Mountain before General Thornton lays waste to it."

"Might not be time to execute a plan," said Curt.

"Bad weather plus the mountainous terrain could be a key to get them out undetected," said Penny. "Here's the lab results for tests I ran for antibodies to the chemical and biological agents that Pomoroy told us Aranea's developed. Haven't had a chance to study them…oh…this envelope came for you."

Holding the envelope, Curt flapped it on the palm of his hand, thinking, *Another can of worms.*

Penny eyed him and then the envelope.

"Blood work," he said. "The wee one and the Ol' Chap."

"Oh, come on," she groaned. "Verifying paternity now?"

"Slimy, 'ey what?"

Penny snapped up the envelope and stomped to the stove. She turned a dial. Flame swooshed around a burner. She lit one corner of the envelope then another. At the sink, she let twisted soot drop. She glanced at Curt. Flame reached fingers. She dropped the remains. "Back to work." She gave him a sheepish look. "When we're done, we'll have a go at our family trees, 'ey what?"

Chapter 37

"How much farther?" panted Ken, catching up to Gus at the juncture of Davis Pass. Each trail, boulder, ledge, and crook in the trail had a name, and if it didn't Gus gave it one. Then Tank christened it in that special way dogs do.

"Ever get a hankerin' to own all of this?" asked Gus while his hand swept across the vista shimmering in the liquid heat of the noon sun.

Ken leaned on his hiking pole. The back of his arm swiped sweat off his brow as he squinted at the sky that appeared to go on forever above woods tinted in greens and yellows by early budding leaves. A waterfall tumbled out of a nearby ridge. "If not for attracting attention," he said, taking the cap off his canteen, "I'd cup my hands around my mouth and shout at the top of my lungs, 'I claim all this in the name of God and all the Waters family.'" He took a swig of water from his canteen and raked moisture off his chin with the back of his hand. Tank yipped. Ken glanced at Tank sitting on his haunches, tongue drooping, and tail whipping. Ken bent at the knees then poured water into his cupped hands. Tank lapped up the water. As Ken poured some more Gus got a big kick out of the newfound friendship.

"Aranea's got to vacate the premises," said Ken.

Gus nodded. "Better get a move on. Weather's goin' down-hill fast. Mackerels headin' out of the west."

As the two men and dog followed a scalloped trail, black-capped chickadees and other songbirds, not due back for

another month, serenaded them. When Gus and Tank veered off
to the left and down a steep talus slope, Ken paused. *One misstep
on those sharp-edged rocks means a sprained ankle, bruised shin—
worse, another broken leg.* Half-closing his eyes, he went to run a
hand through his hair, but the hardhat Gus had made him wear
got in the way. *Don't tell me I have to break another leg again before
I can save my baby girl?*

"No time for serious mullin'," hollered Gus from the bottom
of the slope.

Ken hitched up his britches then took a cautious step then
another. Sweat trickled down his face and back and pooled in
the small of his back. His shirt was soaked by the time he got to
the bottom, but it didn't matter as sensations of success, power,
and lightheadedness overcame him. Hitching up his britches
again, he shot a toothy grin at Gus who merely shook his head
and grunted, "City slickers."

A short time later, they intersected a gurgling brook. Insects,
known more to summer than March, accosted them while they
knelt to drink. Having his fill, Ken leaned back on his ankles and
eyed his surroundings. "I couldn't find my way out of here if
my life depended on it."

"Don't go sellin' yourself short," said Gus, his hand swoosh-
ing away insects. "Times I felt like a greenhorn in Nam. Be
surprised wha'cha can do when need arises."

They crossed the brook then tramped along its flow that
steadily increased then unexpectedly vanished. Gus studied the
ground. "Hear that?"

Ken listened. "I don't hear anything."

"Open your ears, man," said Gus.

Ken peeled an ear then gawked at the ground. "Sounds like
spilling water."

"A cistern's 'neath us," said Gus, squatting then pushing
aside small boulders. Tank was right there, sniffing and pawing
at the debris.

"Water supply for inside the mountain," said Ken, studying
the stream rushing down the steep gradient. "No need for a
pump and runs too fast to freeze up."

Gus stood up and swiped his hands together. He eyed the ground. "More 'n one cistern's brimmin' with water down there. Lots of ants." His eyes narrowed and wandered along the ground. "Somebody took great pains to make this road look unused."

"What road?" Ken asked.

"Stick close, Tank," said Gus. The dog glued himself to Gus' leg as the three started down the invisible road. "Somethin' mighty heavy got hauled up here." A short while later, a pile of brush stopped them. "Will ya looky here."

"Another mine?" asked Ken.

"Too coincidental to my way of thinkin'," said Gus, giving a whole body tug on a bow. The pile of brush collapsed. Gus let out a great groan and Tank kiyiked.

Seeing Gus splayed out on the ground, Ken chuckled. "You okay?"

"Got a tickle outta this did you?" said Gus, his oxen-like eyes fixed on Ken.

"Is kind of funny," said Ken, offering his hand.

Gus pushed away Ken's hand. He got to his feet and stomped into the shaft. Tank followed. Then Ken, zipping his jacket to his neck. At a granite barrier, Gus said, "Seen the likes in Nam." His eyes traced the granite. "Magic button's around here somewhere."

Ken ran his hand across the icy surface. "This another diversion?" Pressure on an odd blemish caused a rumble. Then the wall retracted to the left, exposing a dark tunnel. The two men turned on the lights attached to their hardhats. Their brows shot up to their hairline. "Well, cut my legs off and call me Shorty!" puffed Gus.

"A-a m-missile silo," stammered Ken.

"Behooves us to get your girl out, real quick like an' hightail it to authorities," said Gus, shutting off the light. "Douse your light, man."

Ken didn't have to be told twice.

At a small promontory overlooking the campus, Tank growled. So did Gus. "Not another word out of ya, Tank, 'ntil I give the word."

As Gus and Tank settled onto a soft spot beneath a pine, Ken jammed his hands into his pockets and groused, "It's getting cold. How long we staying here?"

"'Til dark," said Gus. "Count your stars this ain't no ordinary March in these here hills." He opened his backpack and took out a sandwich. "Grub time."

Ken used his foot to brush together a nest of pine needles and leaves then sat down and looked at Gus taking the first bite of a sandwich. Only a third of the sandwich was left to give to Tank.

"You been inoculated?" asked Gus, between chews.

"Inoculated?"

"Ayeup."

"Biological weapons?"

"Ain't puttin' it past Aranea, what with that silo an' all," said Gus while pouring water from his canteen into Tank's raised and gaping muzzle.

Waiting for darkness to fall was hard on Ken. The sandwich he ate sat on his stomach like a lead weight. The chill got into his bones. Trees and rocks creaked as thoughts of missiles and biological weapons spooked him. An owl hooted, but he wasn't about to swear that's what it really was. An icy mist shrouded the shadows when at last Gus announced, "It's make or break time." He crept toward the campus. Tank and Ken stuck close. Halfway there, Gus' hand flew up. "Freeze!"

Ken and Tank flattened on the ground.

"Somebody wanderin' about," whispered Gus. "Hunker down." He wedged his bulk into a narrow place, unbent yet half-buried.

Ken did his best to do the same, thinking, *Again the waiting game.* Lights flickered then stopped. Minutes later, the same thing. The third time, he whispered, "What's up with the lights?"

"Peculiar, ain't it?"

"With all the high tech bells and whistles Aranea has," whispered Ken, "peculiar is an understatement."

Chapter 38

*A*ll evening, the electricity flickered on Granite Mountain, wreaking havoc on computers, monitors, and the like—even worse, on Jonathan's nerves. Ramming his hand into the desk, he bellowed, "Great! Just great! Just get the computers booted up again then out goes the power!"

"What is going on?" bellowed Meredith, stomping into the office.

"Alice is tracking it down," he shouted, pacing like a caged animal.

"Too bad we lost Bert and Vic," sneered Meredith. "*They* were our electrical experts. *They* would've gotten us up and running a long time ago."

Jonathan whipped his turbanned head around. His black eyes shot daggers at her. "Rub it in, why don't you?"

An hour later, Aram O'Mara telephoned.

"Bacteria vials are missing in the lab?" shrieked Jonathan. He charged to the door and yanked it open.

Chas was about to knock.

"What do you want, midget?"

Chas stood there, trembling.

"Out with it!"

Chas gawked around Jonathan to Meredith. She up and downed Chas then heaved, "I'll check it out and join you in the lab in a few."

Jonathan converged on the lab, shouting, "Where's the roster?" He yanked it out of O'Mara's hands and scoured the

315

names. "Isolate all these people!" He rammed the clipboard against a guard's chest. "Don't let any of them speak to each other before I have a chance at them!"

Alice raced in, pulling on a lab coat. "Kitty Star and Brita Fry are the only ones who have authorized access to those vials."

"And you," spat Jonathan, his eyes narrowing into a slit. His jaw tightened beneath his beard.

"And me." She adjusted the madras bandana Katrina had given her. "But I've been tracing electrical lines. O'Mara was supposed to be keeping an eye on things."

"I-I," stuttered O'Mara, white as a sheet.

Alice smirked.

"I saw that," snarled Jonathan, grabbing her arm. "You're in on this, aren't you?"

Yanking her arm free, she snapped, "Don't you dare pin anything on me!"

"How dare you speak to me in that tone?" he hollered, grabbing for her. All he got was the bandana and strands of hair as she twisted out of reach and smacked into O'Mara who then flattened against the door. Jonathan hurled the bandana and strands at her. "Habitual liar, that's what you are—into things for your own purposes!"

Nastiness spread across her face. "You see me so much better than I see myself."

Her words jerked Jonathan back as if he had been slapped.

She snuggled up to him and patted his chest. "I'm just what you desire in a spiderling," she purred, "and therefore believable."

He eyeballed her. "Is that bourbon souring your breath?"

She smirked as her hand circled downward, lower and lower.

"You drunken slut," he seethed, but then unexpected pleasure made him wheeze. "Like waves upon the ocean, my spiderling Alice comes back for more."

The door burst open, shoving O'Mara into Alice. She rammed into Jonathan. All three crashed into the workbench. Petri dishes and tools flew into the air. Glass shattered. Fluids rained. Metals clanked. As Jonathan regained his equilibrium, he didn't see Alice pick up the bandana. He didn't see her putting it on as security guards herded spiderlings into the lab. He didn't see the looks she and Katrina exchanged or the smiles that lifted their lips ever so slightly.

Circling spiderlings like a buzzard ready to feed on putrefying flesh, Jonathan growled, "Vials have come up missing. Somebody better come clean, real quick."

"Yeah, Brita," said Alice in a sing-song voice while picking at a fingernail. "Come clean."

Jonathan got in Brita's face. "You?"

"I didn't do anything!" cried Brita. Terror filled her eyes as her head thrashed side to side.

Alice fingered the bandana and tilted her head, hiding the wink she gave Katrina.

"An accident," cried Katrina, nodding. "Brita told me it was an accident!"

Brita stamped her foot and screeched, "Liar!"

Jonathan leered at Katrina. "Accident?" His right hand made a circular gesture that called for details.

Alice stepped in. "Not to worry. I cleaned it up before anybody got contaminated. Still had my gear on. Brita, too. Nobody else was in the lab. Isn't that right, Mr. O'Mara?"

O'Mara's apprehensive eyes zinged back and forth between Alice and Jonathan. He would've agreed to anything right about now. "S-she speaks the truth!"

Jonathan weaved in and out of spiderlings. He stopped in front of Katrina. His right eye twitched.

"You want a piece of Kitty," said Alice. "So do I. And I intend to take my time—have a real nice time, which means ménage à trois has to wait."

He leered at her seductive grin. He grunted and gave a hand signal. "Get these spiderlings back to their cubicles! O'Mara!"

"Yes, Mr. Aranea!"

"Get all the codes and locks changed around here!"

"Right away, Mr. Aranea!" O'Mara backed out the door, head bobbing.

"I'll block all computer access until you reassess personnel," said Alice.

"Good idea," said Jonathan, smiling at Alice with evil satisfaction. "Truth comes out when one's butt is on the line, even if it means turning in a friend."

"Friendship's overrated." She stroked his arm. "Did I tell you I have been working on a new project in chamber one?"

"Is that right?"

Her voice was silky as Alice looked up at Jonathan with bedroom eyes. "Old ways must be eliminated before new life can begin."

"Ah, my spiderling Alice," he said. "You are my greatest prize."

"Want to see my project?" she asked.

"Lead the way." He gave a chivalrous half-bow and sweep of the palm.

She guided him to the north side of the warren. At the control panel outside chamber one, she pressed a button. The curtain slid to the side. Chas was gagged and strapped into the primitive electric chair. His eyes were as large as eight balls. "Ah," said Jonathan with sinister pride. "I see you have acquired your very own guinea pig."

"Can't make an impression without one," she said. "You will see results beyond your wildest dreams."

"You do me proud," he said.

"If you will, sir," she said, her palm coaxing him, "press the red button."

"You sure you want me to?" he asked, eying Chas who thrashed his head side to side. "Won't the end come too quick?"

"Have you ever known me to be quick?" she murmured, a glint in her eye.

"Good point," he said, stepping to the control panel. He pressed the button she pointed to. His eyes bugged out. His body convulsed. Then he crumpled to the floor.

Chas jumped out of the electric chair and ran to Alice. They stared at Jonathan for a long moment. Then their eyes met.

Chapter 39

*A*n hour after guards herded spiderlings to their cubicles, Katrina flattened on the floor then maneuvered a dentist's mirror under the door. She scanned the hall to the left. Walls, floor, ceiling, closed doors, cameras, florescent lights. *Nobody around.* She flipped the mirror. *Nobody.* She pulled in the mirror, got up, and slouched against the door. *Doesn't make sense. Somebody's always around until Jonathan and Meredith hit the sheets. That happens at one.* She glanced at her watch as the enormity of leaving the cubicle to rescue Adriano and the consequences of getting caught overwhelmed her. *Not even midnight.* She sucked in a breath. *But Addie's alive! Alice can't put on a show like that and it not be true. I have to get him out of here before she does...whatever. Hope Jonathan lied about Dad and Mom. But if he lied, where are they? Alice says they're not inside Granite Mountain. Gosh, Uncle Curt's supposed to get a message to me about how to get the kids out of here, but I won't be here. Wonder who the messenger is now that Bert's out of the picture?* She sucked in another breath. *Calm down, Katrina. You've been spooked since Fort Stewart. Get Addie out and worry about everything else later.*

She flattened onto the floor again and maneuvered the dentist's mirror under the door. *Nobody.* She pulled in the mirror, got to her feet, and stuck the mirror into her pocket. Adrenalin charged through her as she cracked the door, squeezed through it, and closed it without making a sound. She tiptoed to the staircase and down a level to the cubical, which Alice had described. She punched into the keyboard the sequence of numbers Alice had given her. The door snapped open, and the noise rattled along the empty hall. She glanced over her shoulder. Everything went quiet. She nudged open the door. "Addie?" Spotting him lying on the bed, curled in a fetal ball facing the wall, she was torn between the euphoria of finding him and the paralyzing fear that neither of them would survive the night. She stepped into the cubicle, pulled the door to almost latching, and hurried to the bed. "Addie?" When he didn't wake, she turned him then touched his cheek. She lifted his right eyelid. "My poor Addie. They drugged you." A smile rippled her lips. "They couldn't control you, huh?" She kissed him on the forehead and then studied him. "You're getting so tall. Time passes too swiftly—too swiftly to be hanging around here!" She took the vial and needle Alice had given her out of her pocket and prepared the needle. "Sure hope this stuff is antibodies like Alice says." She took a deep breath. "Gosh, can I really jab this needle into him?" Her heart felt like it was beating a million miles an hour as she pulled one side of his sweat pants down to his thigh. "Sorry, Addie." Gritting her teeth, she jabbed the needle into him.

Leaving spent materials on the bed, she slid one arm under his shoulders and the other arm under his knees then lifted him. "My Addie's just a featherweight. Haven't eaten in a while, huh? Hunger helps conversion. Guess it's a mixed blessing. Carrying you will be a lot easier. But have no fear—big sis will fix you up."

She peered through the crack in the door. *All clear.* She adjusted Addie in her arms then slid out into the hallway, along the wall, and up the stairway. Passing cubicles with tacky stickers, she fretted, *It's much too quiet.* In the parking garage, not one guard was in sight. Usually three, appearing to be students, wandered about. *This is too easy.* She glanced at her watch. *Jonathan and Meredith will be going to bed soon.* She stepped over the cement chock and hurried to the exit. Hiding behind a column, she scanned the shadowy campus. *Wish I knew what I'm up against out there.*

The lights flickered. *Alice is messing with the electricity. Turn them back on, Alice. I can't see anything but silhouettes of trees.* Katrina peered over her shoulder. *Can't stay here all night.*

Icy mist fanned her cheeks as she rushed down the ramp and onto grass that crunched under her steps. The lights came on, startling her. She stumbled into a bush, scaring up birds that had taken refuge there for the night. Her elbows saved her from crushing Addie. Leaving him where he lay, she sat up. *My footprints are sunk into the lawn! Anybody with half a brain will know I'm here!* She gasped. *Somebody's coming!* She ducked and pulled Adriano to her. After a time she got to her feet, picked him up, and half-ran half-stumbled down the gravel path. A shadow sent her into a crouch against a privet hedge. *Footsteps!* She wedged her body against the hedge much too thick for concealment. *Don't move,* she told herself. *Don't make one tiny sound.*

Chapter 40

*L*ights stopped flickerin'," said Gus. His breath hovered about him a moment then dissipated. "Guards are hunkered down for a snooze."

"Sleeping?" asked Ken through chattering teeth. No amount of clothing or hugging himself kept him warm with the temperature below freezing.

"They've come to know this is a reliable time to kick back," said Gus. Raising his hand, he pitched it forward. "Move in."

Ken dug his walking pole into the ground and pried himself to his feet. His joints creaked from an eternity of ground fusion. "I can't see a blessed thing," he griped.

"Put a sock in it," whispered Gus in a loud whisper.

"Who goes there?" somebody shouted.

"Hit the deck," snapped Gus, throwing an arm across Ken's back and pulling him down flat on the frozen ground. Tank flattened on top of both of them.

Chapter 41

"Who goes there?" barked a male voice.

Katrina's heart skipped a beat. *A guard! I'm cornered! What do I do? Stand up? Lay low? Surrender?*

"Hey, man."

It's Chas!

"What's going on?"

Where is that guard?

"Can't sleep," said Chas, pulling a black fedora over his eyes. He stuffed his hands into the pockets of a black overcoat.

He looks like a miniature hit man.

"You know better, wandering around this time of night," scolded the guard.

"Dorm's closin' in," bellyached Chas. He lowered his voice. "Got a light?"

"Since when do you smoke?" asked the guard, coming into view.

"Since I lost my virginity," muttered Chas.

The guard chortled. The lid of a butane lighter flicked open and the flame lit their faces—and hers. She looked down to avoid detection. The lid closed with a click. She looked up as Chas expelled a cloud of smoke and said, "Quiet, ain't it?"

"Everybody's at the meeting in the conference room," said the guard, lighting a cigarette.

"How come you didn't go?" asked Chas.

"Same old, same old," said the guard. "I won't be missed."

"Creepy being out here alone," said Chas.

The guard snorted. "Just the way I like it."

"Me, too," said Chas, tossing the cigarette onto the ground. His foot crushed it. A flurry of movements followed and then the nauseating sound of bone snapping.

Katrina struggled under Adriano's weight to get to her feet as Chas came toward her. "I saw what you did," she said.

"Told you I'd get you through stuff," he said. "A safe-house has been set up in Jackson. Take your brother there. After you pass that ice cream stand Bert took you to during summer camp, take Mountain Road to the end."

She shifted Adriano's weight. "You know that for sure?"

He put a finger in his ear and wiggled it. "Like Alice, Chas knows everything."

"Where is Alice?"

"I'll go with you," he said.

"I can't take Addie there," she said.

"You have to," he insisted.

"How many others—good or bad—are there?" she asked.

"Can't tell who's good or bad."

"If only one is still loyal to the Araneas…" she argued, "…if they find out Addie and I are alive… No, it's safer if nobody knows."

"Where are you going?"

"I'm not sure."

"Where will I find you?" he asked. "Me and Alice need your help to deprogram everybody when this is over."

"When this is over?" she belched, never conceiving of this nightmare being over. *When this is over, what's left for Addie and me if Dad and Mom are dead? What if the Araneas catch onto Chas and Alice? What if the Araneas and all the bad guys get away like some did in Judgment? What if…* "Oh, I don't want to think anymore!" she moaned then ran full bore into the moonless night, Adriano in her arms.

Chapter 42

*J*onathan exploded out of unconsciousness, thrashing and cussing. He scowled at the chains ensnaring his wrists, chains stretched tight by his weight, chains stretched tight all the way to ceiling hooks. Gritting his teeth, he kicked the air with one foot then the other then both, defiant, as if that might shake him loose. Exhausted and heaving for breath, he swung like a side of beef, several feet above the floor. He leered at his aba, loincloth, keffiyeh, agal, and sandals strewn across the floor. Unfazed by his nudity, he growled, "Where in hell is Alice?" Turbines hummed in the otherwise silence. "Alice!" he barked. "Alice!"

"Shush," she scolded, sliding through the curtain, wine bottle in one hand and remote in the other. "You'll wake the dead."

"What is going on?" he demanded. "Where's the midget? What are you doing with my remote?"

Loathing filled her eyes as Alice said, "I figured missing vials were going to trigger your interest, but not so soon. Really had to scramble to make this happen." A smile grew on her face like that of a sailor rescued after years of seclusion on an uninhabited island. "When you announced March 19th is your Day of Judgment, I had to speed up my plans."

"Cut the crap," he snorted. "Get me down!"

Brittle excitement laced her voice. "I'm trying to be nice. Don't spoil it."

"Spoil what?"

Her eyes went wide. "You haven't figured it out?"

"Figured what out?"

"My new, state-of-the-art torture method," she extending her hands that gripped the wine bottle and remote. "I call it, snaring the tyrant in his own trap!"

"The joke's wearing thin, Alice," he warned. "Get me down."

Her fingers toyed with buttons on the remote. "But you haven't analyzed the effectiveness of my methodology," she argued. "It's vital in revealing my true self to you. The images I put forth are so far removed from reality."

"What in hell are you talking about?" he demanded.

"Hell," she echoed, her voice pouring out disgust. "Ironic you bring up that place—you about to go there and all." She held the remote at eyelevel. "This is the same remote you used to murder Camille and others in the conference room."

"Could be," he said. "I have several."

"I know," she said, pointing to remotes on a nearby crate.

"Get me down!" he hollered.

She pressed a button on the remote. The side wall retracted. Stepping into chamber two, she pressed another button. Water streamed out the showerhead. Steam rolled upward as she pressed another button. He swung toward the scalding torrent. "You've had your fun, Alice."

"Priscilla," she said. "Priscilla Hamilton, remember? And Priscilla wants you to come clean." She pointed to the cameras. "For your audience."

"About what?" he hollered.

"The torture, brainwashing, terror," she said. "The atmosphere of lies and hopelessness."

"Whore!" he howled as water sheeted over him. "Your days are numbered! You will suffer for this for years!"

"Years?" she asked as he emerged the other side, his skin blistered and red. "You will take into account the years I have already suffered, won't you?" She pressed another button and the curtain to the third chamber slid open. "Surprise!" she squealed, clapping with delight.

His eyes bugged out at Meredith shackled in the shallow tub—what was left of her.

"Isn't she lovely?" asked Priscilla, gazing at the corpse with the sweetest demeanor. "Our darling Meredith has had the latest chemical peel! Sweet, huh?"

"Arachnophobia!" he howled.

"Not going to work," sang Priscilla, pressing another button. "Brainwashing doesn't work on everybody, you know." The curtain to the fourth chamber slid open. "You might be wondering what I intend to do with this total-immersion tub. As one who has been there, I call it hell. Oh, you thought I wouldn't remember? Well, surprise! Thought about doing the same to you, but..." She pressed a button on the remote. The hooks in the ceiling halted abruptly; so did Jonathan. She watched him sway and then heaved a sigh and shook her head. Stepping to the wall of cards, she asked, "Who are these kids? Bet you don't even remember their names. Strays you stole. Guinea pigs."

"Don't think for one minute you're getting out of here," growled Jonathan. "Security will..."

"You ordered security, O'Mara, and all your other cronies for an emergency meeting in the conference room," she said. Turning to him, she shook her finger. "Absolutely no exceptions!"

"I issued no such order," he countered.

Her eyes twinkled. "How long have I been doing your bidding?"

"You have one last chance to get me down from here!"

Amused, she gazed at her watch. "Right about now, those computer outlets in the conference room should be opening. Featherhead spiderlings should be plopping out..."

"I give you a pass this time," he bargained, his voice laced with mounting stress. "Leave the warren. Go wherever you want. Do what you like."

"That calls for a celebration," she said, holding up the wine bottle. "Buy you a drink?"

"Don't you ever lay off the booze?"

She chuckled. "I must dress for the occasion," she said, setting the bottle on the floor in front of him.

"Where you going?" he shouted. "Alice? Alice!"

Chapter 43

*H*ey, man," said a youthful male voice.

"What's going on?" demanded a second male voice.

Ken lifted his head; Gus shoved it down. Ken frowned at Gus; Gus frowned back.

"You know better than to wander around this time of night," scolded the second male voice.

"Dorm's closin' in on me," bellyached the youthful male voice.

Silence. A butane lighter flared. Silence. Another flare. Silence. A snap.

"One of 'em just got his neck broke," whispered Gus.

Ken's eyes filled with questions.

"Heard snappin' plenty of times," explained Gus, "hunkered down in Nam. "Mornin' come. Sure 'nough, corpse turns up, neck broke." He brought his wrist up to his eyes and squinted at his watch. Unable to read the time, he twisted his wrist toward campus lights. "Fifteen minutes," he whispered. "Then we'll make another go at the place." He peered at the sky. "Ugly-looking clouds." At regular intervals, he checked his watch. Finally, he started edging down the mountainside on his belly with Ken and Tank sticking like pilot fish to a shark. Nearing the area where the male voices had come from, he paused. They listened. Gus got to his feet. So did Tank and Ken.

"Size six-and-a-half tennis shoes came out that garage this way and headed that-a-way," said Gus, his finger pointing out the route. "Heavy into the grass. Size nine hiking boots exited those bushes and followed. Veered off from six-and-a-half there and met up with size eleven combat boots over there." His eyes narrowed as he went to the meeting point. "Nine took down eleven. Grass ain't torn up. Eleven didn't know what hit him." Gus followed ragged grass toward the woods. "Nine dragged off eleven to the trees."

Ken went to run a hand through his hair. Again, the hardhat got in the way.

"You comin' or what?" Gus called from the edge of the woods.

Ken swallowed hard. He hitched up his pants then took off after Gus.

"Nine went off that way after dumping eleven," whispered Gus. Stopping a couple yards into the woods, he used his hiking pole to nudge aside some pine bows.

Ken took a quick step back. A teenaged male lay on the frozen muddy ground, glazed eyes staring into eternity. Ken steadied himself on his hiking pole as Gus bent at the knees, eyes roaming the corpse and then fingering the teen's neck for a pulse. "Dead as a door nail. Neck's broke."

"Missile silos. Biological weapons. Broke necks," Ken sputtered. "What's next, for crying out loud? Let's get my baby girl and get out of here!"

"Keep your voice down," snapped Gus, standing up and glancing around. "More of these here fellers sure to be wanderin' about. Let's see what six-and-a-half is up to." Exiting the woods, he pointed. "Six-and-a-half ran into nine over there then hot-dogged it to the kennels—alone. 'Fore we go trackin' six-and-a-half, I want a gander at that garage. See the way it's jammed into the mountain?"

"Yeah," said Ken.

"Intuition tells me," said Gus, "an entrance to the mountain is in there."

Inside the garage, they walked along a line of cars, scrutinizing each and also the structure of the garage. They came to a door painted with the words, Authorized Personnel Only. "Here's the entry we expected," whispered Gus.

"Aranea's onto us," warned Ken, pointing out a camera attached to a beam above their heads.

Gus squinted at the camera. "If he ain't, only a matter of time till he is. He'll be siccin' his dogs on us. Get a move on."

Hurrying after Gus, Ken muttered, "At least my baby girl's got that dog to fight off Aranea and his thugs. Still, a kid her size...with a dog...can't..." He stopped in his tracks. "Size six-and-a-half? Hot-dogged to the kennels?"

Gus pulled up and glanced back at Ken.

"My baby girl's size six-and-a-half!" exclaimed Ken as his hiking pole clunked onto the cement floor. "She's headed to get her dog at the kennel!"

Chapter 44

*O*ut of breath, Katrina stumbled to the kennel where in the furthest pen, red eyes glowed as the husky yelped a mutated greeting. "Mickey Blue Eyes, stop," commanded Katrina, heading for the converted wagon. After placing Adriano in it, she shook numbness out of her arms then unsnapped the halter from the wagon harness.

The husky jounced about as though riding a pogo stick, launching exhalations that billowed like that of a pipe smoker lighting up. "Settle down," said Katrina, opening the chain link gate. She put the halter on the husky then hitched the halter to the wagon harness. As she went to close the gate, she spotted the watering trough. *Alice says she stashed money under there in a plastic bag containing papers about where Jonathan's assets are, who's working with him, information about kids, alive and dead.* Pointing at Mickey Blue Eyes, she said, "Sit. Stay," then stepped into the cage. She dragged the trough to one side then poked a finger into the mud. At knuckle depth, she struck an obstacle. Driving her thumb into the mud, she clamped onto the obstacle and pulled. Fighting the urge to open the plastic bag, she hurried to the wagon and wedged the bag under Adriano. She patted Mickey Blue Eyes on the head then commanded, "Heel." Sprinting into the woods, she avoided looking over her shoulder even though Bert's words echoed in her head, *"Watch your back. Never ignore or shrug off anything. Be quick on your feet—master of your fate."*

But, she wondered, *what if I'm forced to defend myself against an enemy that only hours ago were fellow spiderlings? I understand what they've been through—been there, done that, twice in my life. It's not their fault if they want to kill me. After I get Addie to safety, I have to come back. I have to help Chas and Alice deprogram them.*

The trail west was cemented in her mind and heart after numerous rehearsals, so darkness meant little. Dipping temperature wasn't a factor either. So far, it had kept sweat at bay. Twenty feet or so before the first fork, she said, "Whoa." Taking hold of the halter, she guided Mickey Blue Eyes into the woods to the shallow stream. It was still running, though ice jutted out along the edges. She had to pull the dog into the water where sneakers and fur provided no protection. Hearing Mickey Blue Eyes whine, Katrina said, "I know. It's really, really cold. So hurry up; or we'll freeze to death."

A little ways upstream, Katrina let go of the halter. The husky needed no help to pull the wagon up the rock embankment. As Mickey Blue Eyes shook off moisture that failed to penetrate her winter coat, Katrina glanced back at the scratched embankment and noticed flakes of snow landing on it. Looking skyward, she said, "Come on, snow!"

They rejoined the western trail just beyond the log bridge that she and Chas had helped to build over Webster Brook. A short distance later, she gave a hand signal, and the husky stopped. "Sit, stay," she commanded while stepping off the trail to the left.

She rummaged beneath the base of mountain laurel bushes for the supplies she had left wrapped in plastic bags. She pulled her down jacket out of one bag, slid her arms into it, and for a moment snuggled its warmth. Then she tore off her frozen sneakers and hurled them into the woods as far as she could. She pulled a pair of dry socks and sweatpants out of a backpack then put them on. Sitting on the ground, she took boots out of the backpack and put them on. She hooked her arms into the straps of the backpack, snapped the breast harness, and grabbed the other two backpacks and the rest of the plastic bags.

Back at the wagon, she took a rolled up blanket out of a plastic bag and stuffed it underneath Adriano's head. He didn't stir. She felt his cheek. "A bit cool," she mumbled. "Nothing to worry about—I hope." As she took another blanket out of a plastic bag, a flashlight dropped on the ground. She picked it up. *Wish I could use this, but somebody might see the light.* Sticking the flashlight back into a backpack, she noticed a black strap. She tugged on it. "Night vision goggles. A paper is attached to them." She took out the flashlight, covered her head with the blanket, and turned on the flashlight. *Good luck. Your friend, P.H.* Katrina stared at the water-smudged initials. Alice's voice filled her head, *My name is Priscilla. Priscilla Hamilton. Friends in thish god-forshaken plash? He kept telling me I'm just like my mother, stupid, and I'd never amount to anything—just like Brita hollered at me that day on the trail. Nobody ever stood up for me like you. I'm not going to be invisible anymore!*

"From now on," grumbled Katrina, shutting off the flashlight, "nobody's invisible." She yanked off the blanket and looked up into the snowy heavens. A smile broke on her face.

Chapter 45

*P*riscilla Hamilton returned, shrouded in protective gear. If not for the orange color, she would've looked like Darth Vader. Breathing through the stubby snout, she sounded like Darth Vader. Gloved hands grappled the wine bottle then held it up. "A drink to old times?"

"You disgust me," spat Jonathan.

"Oh, come on," she said. "I prepared this cocktail just for you. I could've left the contents of those missing vials in their original concentration. One single breath would've killed you. No. I diluted them. You must have time to suffer, you know, experience what you put others through?" She twisted off the cap then held the bottle at arm's length. "Breathe deep, my tyrant. Oh, my, you're trying not to." She waited. "There you go." She took a step toward him. "Another breath. Feel it going deep into your lungs? Spreading into your bloodstream? Into your brain?"

"We will meet Satan together!" he shrieked as his foot came up and struck her mask.

The impact sent Priscilla reeling into the wall. She steadied herself, adjusted the mask, and focused on Jonathan. Spasms wracked his body. His arms and legs flapped. She clenched her fists, breathing in, out, steady, but his suffering and screeching went beyond anything she had ever imagined. *This is his brand of justice,* she told herself, but somehow, she felt unconvinced. She fled from the chamber. At a safe distance, she ripped off the mask. Air chilled her sweaty face and then the rest of her body as she peeled off protective gear and raced to the kitchen. She soaked her head under the tap then turned her mouth to the stream and drank. Raising her head to the heavens like a wolf in the wild, she howled, "Granite Mountain is contaminated!" She dashed into the hall. "Run for your lives!" Her head throbbed as she banged on cubical doors. "Get out! Granite Mountain is about to blow!"

As pandemonium broke loose, her eyes stung as if acid had been thrown in them. Her chest tightened as though caught in a vise. *The first symptoms of nerve agent poisoning! Jonathan kicked my mask! He busted the seal!* She gripped the madras bandana. In a voice devoid of self-pity, she wheezed, "Didn't bring me as much luck as we hoped, Kitty Kat."

The killer stalked her body, replicating, spinning her world. Coughs wracked her body. Nauseous, she gagged. Bending over, she vomited. She raised her head. Foam oozed out her mouth. Her eyes narrowed. Straightening up, she shook a fist in the direction of the torture chamber. "You are not in control this time, Aranea!"

Gritting her teeth, she staggered out of the warren. Limbs stiffened with each passing second. Muscles turned to mush. Another round of vomiting. She swiped the foamy dregs away from her mouth. Her feet moved as though cast in lead. Doddering along, she looked like the Creature from the Black Lagoon. *Monsters are not victims! They control situations! They make victims!*

In the unlit parking garage, she caught the toe of her shoe on the cement chock. Her legs buckled. As she collapsed in a heap, bones snapped. Her lips pulled back against the pain. "I will not die like this!" she stormed then hauled her broken and dying body to the exit. She got up on one elbow and squinted at the gray dawn spitting snow. *Pure, sweet snow.* She breathed in the chill that did her fevered body no good.

Grunting with effort, she crawled down the ramp to an isolated section of lawn where daylight hadn't reached. As she crumpled, her thumb depressed the red button on the remote. Alarms blared, but the sound comforted Priscilla Hamilton. It was soft. It was like Katrina humming "Mary's Song."

Chapter 46

*T*he atomic self-destruct device is armed!" cried Katrina as sirens screeched, evil sounding, like mythological harpies—like Regina.

Mickey Blue Eyes bristled. Pointing her muzzle to the heavens, she emitted a mutilated bay.

Katrina grabbed the reins. "It goes off in a half an hour! Mush! Mush!"

The husky pitched forward. The front of the wagon came up off the ground. Adriano jounced about.

A reasonable pace wasn't restored until they reached the Webster Cliff Trail. Arriving at the Webster Jackson Trail, they were covering ground efficient enough to achieve maximum endurance. But at Bugle Cliff the going got tricky. Katrina slipped on a dislodged stone, twisting her right ankle. Luckily, she caught herself from falling. Shaking off the pain, she climbed onto the converted sled and rode until reaching Bugle Cliff Boulder, which blocked half the trail. "Whoa," she commanded. Holding the reins, she waddled to Mickey Blue Eyes and knelt down. Night vision goggles allowed her to see into the darkness below the boulder, but not around corners. *The bears might be out foraging. Wish I had thought to pack bear mace.* She listened. *The sirens aren't so loud way out here.* Within the sirens she thought she heard, "Friendship means nothing!"

"Alice?" she puffed, squinting toward Granite Mountain. "Friendship does mean something, doesn't it, Priscilla? That's how come you told me about Addie, but you're one of the spiderlings Jonathan programmed to arm the automatic destruct device. Did he give you the right word? Or did you do it on your own?" A shiver raced through Katrina. "Priscilla! What did you do to Jonathan?"

Mickey Blue Eyes yipped.

Katrina looked back at the husky. "Not much time left before the device goes off. I think we're still too close. The safe house in Jackson is too close, too. Priscilla and Chas better hurry and get everybody out of there. We better get out of here! Talk to me, Mickey Blue Eyes!"

The dog put her nose high in the breeze and drank up the scents. She sniffed the ground. She looked at Katrina and wagged her tail.

"Good girl." Katrina took hold of the halter. "Come." Wary eyes stuck to the dark hollow as they stepped around the boulder. Halfway past, Katrina let go of the halter. "Hike!" Making a mad dash for the other side, they didn't stop until reaching the southern shoreline of Saco Lake. A skim of ice was broken, forming a trail from shore halfway into the middle. At the end was a bull moose standing shoulder-high in the water. An unconcerned eye took in the newcomers while huge jaws masticated aquatic plants. Then the equine-looking head crowned with antlers plunged into the depths.

"Mush," said Katrina.

A hundred yards to the west, a pair of loons dove underwater. Moments later, they bobbed to the surface. They kept a safe distance from shore as Katrina took off the night vision goggles then released Mickey Blue Eyes from the harness. "Let's get a drink."

Thirst quenched, Katrina fell back on her elbows and backpack and watched the husky lap. An owl hooted. She turned and studied the silhouetted tree line. Hardwoods creaked, bending to the whispering breeze. Coyotes yapped in the far distance. Half-smiling, she mused, *Before I came to Granite Mountain, I only heard owls on TV.* She rolled onto her side and braced her head on her arm. *I love eavesdropping on nature.* Her eyes closed to the music of water caressing the shore. *So tired.*

Have to save my strength. Make it to the phone...call Dad...Curt...
And she was dancing with Bert.

Mickey Blue Eyes snarled a challenge. Water surged. Loons took flight. Snowflakes peppered Katrina's face. *"Mommy says snow is angels pillow fightin'*," said Adriano. *"They fight so bad, feathers fall out all over the place and turn to snow!"*

"If Mommy says so..." muttered Katrina.

Mickey Blue Eyes yowled.

Katrina opened her eyes and turned over. The husky was bristled to twice her size and leaping about between the wagon and a bear cub that let out a squawk. There was a roar, and all eyes shot to the tree line and a charging mother bear. "Addie!" shrieked Katrina, bolting upright. The mother tacked and came at Katrina.

Mickey Blue Eyes turned from the cub and leapt. Jaws sank into the mother bear's neck. Then husky and bear flopped onto the sand and rolled into the lake. Meanwhile, the squawking cub high-tailed it for a tree line perch.

Katrina skittered on all fours, crablike, to the wagon and grabbed the harness. She looked back.

Mickey Blue Eyes and the mother bear rose out of the water. Heads cocked as they eyeballed one another. The bear woofed. The dog growled. Incisors gleamed. The bear reared up, and so did the husky. Ursine roars. Mutilated canine curses. And the racket echoed across Saco Lake like an obscene rap song. As the bear and husky sidestepped out of the lake, Katrina got to her feet. "I have to do something! No, I can't! I'll put Addie in jeopardy. Wait! There's that word! She sucked in air then hollered, "Arachnophobia!"

Energized, the husky snapped, dodged huge black paws, and circled the bear. The bear rotated. Mickey Blue Eyes dove for a leg. Canines sank into flesh. Then the husky threw everything she had into reverse, tugging, snarling, and wrenching her head side to side. Blood spewed.

Katrina tugged on the wagon harness and lit out on the trail west. She glanced over her shoulder. The husky was jack-knifing out of the way of the huge black paw, but then another huge black paw made contact. Mickey Blue Eyes soared through the air, twisting, then came down on the snowy ground. Thud! "Kiyike!"

Chapter 47

*R*unnin' 'round like a chicken with its head cut off won't get your girl back," chided Gus upon catching up to Ken.

"The pens...empty..." wheezed Ken, circling the kennel. His breath followed him like steam from a train. "Where's...my baby...girl..." He swiped beads of sweat off his brow with the back of his hand. "What's she...doing...way out here...in the middle of...the night?"

"Set on down on this here rock for just a minute," said Gus. "Give me time to reconnoiter."

"No time..." wheezed Ken.

"All the time in the world," countered Gus, his massive hands pressing on Ken's shoulders. "Set yourself down an' catch your wind."

Ken buckled. His teeth clack, clack, clacked from anxiety-riddled cold.

Gus shoved a hiking pole into Ken's chest. "You dropped this back at the garage."

Ken wrapped his arms around the pole and held it as though it was his missing child. Barely able to get words out between chattering molars, he moaned, "Terrorism separated my baby girl and me once before, and it's done it again." He gaped at the heavens. Snowflakes burned like acid on his face chilled by plummeting temperatures.

"Your girl's picked up a wagon 'n' dog," said Gus, eying traces of tracks.

"Mickey Blue Eyes," said Ken.

"Whatever weighed down your girl, weighs down the wagon now," said Gus.

"I'm so inept at all this stuff," moaned Ken.

Gus rolled his eyes and sat down beside Ken. "Massatusitts greenhorns like you ain't got a lick of sense." He glanced at Ken. Getting a leer, he quickly added, "When it comes to these here woods, that is." He squinted at Tank flopped at his feet. "Fact is, backwoods hicks like me ain't up to speed on tech'log'cal gadgets, neither. Don't see 'em in my mansion, do ya? Uh-uh. Wouldn't know what to do with 'em. Might set a plant or somethin' on 'em." With his left foot, he stroked Tank's back. Tank rolled over for a belly rub. "In Nam I learnt relyin' on fancy gear and gadgets backfires at the worst moment. Take your GPS satellites. That dense canopy of trees up there obscures the moon and stars—worse when there's leaves—blocks out GPS. Communication gets limited by range and batteries. If that happens, be some scary moments when Tomcats duel with Aranea's missiles. 'Tween these steep mountains, only way to use laser guidance without obstruction is flyin' in slow and direct fire. On the other hand, knowin' what you knowd about computers and such got you to piecin' together this mess way back when. You never would o' knowd your girl's gotten herself tangled up in that Aranea feller's spider web. So don't go cuttin' yourself down. We're all good at somethin' and clueless on somethin' else. Bottom line: what you knowd and what I knowd we put together. We'll come up with that girl of yours."

Ken gave the offbeat dissertation thought as his hand went to run through his hair. The hardhat got in the way. *Never knew I scratched my head so much.* He took in a deep breath that exited in a cloud of steam that surrounded his head.

Gus stretched his arms up and wide and squinted skyward. "Can't wait on a moon that ain't about to show itself this night." He slapped his knees and got to his feet. Tank jumped to attention.

"Snow's covering her trail," said Ken, eyeing the ground.

"Works to our advantage," said Gus, following tracks high-lighted by snow. Tank glued himself to Gus. "Heavy stuff is another thing, but that ain't comin' for another hour or so."

"My baby girl needs me...er...us now!" cried Ken, leaping to his feet.

"Got your wind back, I see," grumbled Gus, shaking his head.

"But at this rate," argued Ken, starting to pass Gus, "snow will cover up everything in no time. We'll lose her for sure."

Gus put out an arm. "Don't be getting' ahead of me, you hear me? Got enough trouble makin' heads an' tails of things without you botchin' 'em up. And don't be goin' off half-cocked again—lose us the trail that way."

A few yards into the woods, their eyes shot back toward the campus as floodlights cut through the trees and sirens screeched. Chills zinged through Ken. "What in the world..."

"Hair spikin' my neck tells me alarms ain't goin' off on account of you and me. Let's get after your girl, quick-like!"

As campus lights faded behind them, the two men snapped on the lights attached to their hardhats. Not long after that, Gus glanced to the left. His hand flattened on Ken's chest. "Hold on a sec'. Branches got broke on them there trees." He stepped into the woods. Tank followed and then Ken.

"Hauled her dog and wagon into this here stream," said Gus, analyzing the riverbank. He plodded upstream and stopped at a rocky embankment. His hand swept off the snow. "Rocks got scratched up."

Tank and Gus scooted up the embankment, but Ken slid backward, again and again. Driven by determination, Ken climbed sideways, crawled on hands on knees, even took baby steps. Nothing worked.

"Send up your pole," shouted Gus.

Ken tossed his hiking pole.

Gus caught it then stretched out on his belly and hooked his foot around a good size birch sapling. His arm with the hiking pole in hand extended down the embankment.

Ken snagged the pole then hand over hand, pulled himself up to Gus. He paused.

"Ain't got all day, man," grunted Gus as blood rushed to his head, bloating his face and turning it red.

Ken grasped Gus' arm and dragged himself up, along Gus' torso and leg. Then with the aid of the sapling, he scrambled onto the embankment.

Gus stood up and gave Ken a look.

"What?"

"I saw you struttin' 'round like a cocky rooster."

"Rooster?" Ken tried to visualize himself as a chicken. He looked up. "Gus? Hey, Gus, wait up!" He picked up his walking pole and scurried into the dense canopy of pines. He stopped. He held his breath and listened. Dark, weird noises surrounded him. "Gus?" His heart thumped.

"This-a-way," hollered Gus as the beam from his hardhat light showed the way.

Just beyond a footbridge that spanned Webster Brook, Gus stepped off the trail to the left. Several yards in, he stopped and studied the ground surrounding mountain laurel bushes. "You got some smart girl there."

"Whaddaya mean?" asked Ken.

"Stashed supplies. I s'pect she made daily runs with her dog."

"But why?"

"Same thing ate at her as you 'n' me." Gus eyed the ground back to the trail. "She's been plannin' a quick exit. Wearin' hikers now." He glanced over his shoulder. "Bet we'd find sneakers off in those trees. Your girl's a lot warmer—that's a load off my mind."

"I'm so cold," said Ken, "I don't even feel it anymore."

Gus circled wagon tracks nearly invisible in the snow. "Diddled here with the wagon. Got herself a flashlight."

"And you know that how?"

Gus bent at the knees and pointed to an imprint. "Dropped it here then picked it up. Ain't usin' it though. I'd'a picked up the beam."

"You think she's got night vision goggles?" asked Ken.

"That's my way of thinkin'," replied Gus, standing up and hooking his hands on his hips. He squinted up the trail and down the trail then lurched into nearby rhododendron bushes. Branches shimmied and shook. Then a handgun flew out and landed at Ken's feet. Gus exited the bushes, dragging a miniature teenager by the collar. "What's Chas Riley waitin' on?"

"I thought you was out to get Katrina!" bawled Chas.

Gus up and downed the black overcoat Chas was wearing. "You figurin' on shootin' us?"

"I...I didn't know it was you, G-Gus. When I recognized you, I ducked in the bushes!"

"Where's Katrina going?" demanded Ken.

Chas wide eyed Ken. "I-I don't know!"

Gus shook Chas. "'Fess up, boy!"

"She wouldn't tell me! Honest!"

"You wrote those love songs I found in her bedroom!" exclaimed Ken.

Chas stiffened. His eyes bulged worse than ever.

Gus snorted and reached down for the gun.

Chas shook loose and bolted down the snowy trail.

"Why on earth would anybody go back there?" asked Ken.

Chapter 48

*T*he ursine roar that echoed against the mountains turned Katrina's stomach as she hauled the wagon away from Saco Lake. If not for the overwhelming fear of a pursuing bear, she would have stopped to vomit. The harness cut into her shoulders as she avoided the ranger station. At an out-of-the way shelter that was rarely visited, especially at this hour, she squirmed out of the harness. The dank, weatherworn wooden shelter was so much emptier without Mickey Blue Eyes. *A true saint among dogs,* thought Katrina. Sore and sleep-deprived, grimy and grieving, she collapsed on the bench. *How many days did we travel together, rehearsing for this?* She put her hands to her face and sobbed, "And now Mickey's dead! Nothing's turned out the way I wanted it to! I didn't tear down Jonathan's evil empire! I didn't rescue the kids—only Addie...I did rescue Addie." Her hands fell away from her face. "But I don't know if he's ever going to wake up! I don't even know if Dad and Mom are alive! And Bert... Oh, Bert. I'm such a rotten person for thinking you were a kingpin in the Araneas' web of deceit." She swiped away tears and massaged her arms. "My muscles feel like they're going to fall off my bones. All the exercising and preparing didn't stop me from getting tired and making mistakes—mistakes like that stupid bear!" She rolled her eyes and peered up. Snow peppered her face. "And this weather is getting nastier by the minute! No snow all winter long and now that spring is right around the corner—here comes winter! Mind boggling." She massaged knotted calf muscles. "The sky isn't so dark. Dawn's coming. Gosh, I must've dozed off quite a while. Hey, I'm not wearing goggles!" She squinted at the wagon. "Where are they?" She looked in the direction of Saco Lake. "They're back there." She tucked her hands into her armpits and shivered. "Can't hear those sirens anymore." She got to her feet, stretched her legs, and swiveled her neck. "There's such a long ways left to go."

Bert's voice rippled in her head. *Take it slow and steady. Like the turtle. Slow and steady gives the edge.*

She swayed to thumps of a train lumbering over tracks on the other side of Route 302, too far and steep to maneuver a loaded cart. Its whistle, soulful within the eerie silence, reminded Katrina of Chas and the day she patched up his bloody ankle. His soulful eyes had peered into hers as he pleaded, "Don't trust anyone with your secrets. I heard you tell Bert. You're the only one who ever treated me like a person." She raised her wrists to eye level and stared at them as if Chas were gripping them. "Don't let them take me! I did this to myself!"

"Wonder if Chas is okay," murmured Katrina. "Priscilla doesn't care what happens to her. What about Brita and everybody else? What about Addie?" Katrina smoothed her stepbrother's chestnut locks in a motherly fashion. "Gosh, that drug sure was strong to keep you down this long. What if it's too strong?" She grabbed his hand and slapped the back of it. "Come on, Addie, wake up!" He showed no signs of waking. She dropped his hand, hopelessness festering. "Your color's a little better. Wish you could tell me about Dad and Mom. Priscilla says they're not inside Granite Mountain. I want to believe her. Oh, if only to be back in Toffee Castle, safe and warm in Dad and Mom's arms like when I got back from Mississippi."

Katrina adjusted the blanket around Adriano. Her fingernail caught on the plastic bag. *Money,* Priscilla's voice echoed in Katrina's head. *Papers. Locations of Jonathan's assets. Who works with him. Names of kids, alive and dead. Copies of everything. This place is toast.*

"Toast," said Katrina. "I should eat." She picked up a backpack and took out a bag of banana chips. "Potassium will help my muscle cramps." She stared at the chips. "I really don't feel like eating." She put the bag back into the backpack and tried to slough off fear and fatigue of which she never knew existed. She twisted the gold band on her left hand and hummed "Mary's Song."

Bert's voice rippled in her mind. *To survive, reduce weight and preserve energy.*

She consolidated necessities into one backpack and tossed aside nonessentials. "Snow's coming down harder, Addie." She could almost hear his squeals of delight. She could almost taste hot chocolate topped with whipped cream that followed sledding outings. "Better get going."

She picked up the harness and stumbled along, uncertain that she was following her planned escape route. She tripped over a hidden tree stump and ended up in a ditch. Blood oozed from a nasty gash on the side of her head and down her cheek, but went unnoticed owing to fatigue and numbing cold. Alone and scared, she brushed off snowy grime. The warmth and security of Granite Mountain seemed to be calling her. "No!" she hacked. "I'm not going back!"

The wagon creaked, teetering on the edge of the ditch. "Addie!" Coughing, she doddered to her feet, hooked the harness over her shoulder, and pulled. Around the next bend, she paused and tried to say, "The terrain's getting too rough for the wagon," but every time she opened her mouth, coughing accosted her. She blotted her runny nose on the back of her hand and squinted at the highway skimmed with snow. A critter was ambling across it. *That's going to be Addie and me,* she thought, *future road kill.* She glanced over her shoulder. *The sky's brightening real fast over Granite Mountain. No helicopters, flashlights, nothing. But for how long? Addie and I haven't been missed yet, but any time now, they'll be their on the way to breakfast. Then Aranea's spiderlings will be after us.*

With great effort, she dragged the wagon onto the highway. Loping along, she kept her eyes peeled at trees, boulders, any shadow in which she might hide at a moment's notice. Light streaked across the landscape. She glanced over her shoulder. *Headlights! I have to hide! There's a culvert!*

She dropped over the side of the road and slid down ice-slicked rocks that gave way under her and the wagon's weight. Somehow, she managed to keep the wagon upright. At the bottom, she pulled the wagon against the bars of the culvert, one of those heavy metal kind made to stand the strain of spring freshets and time. The bars kept out debris. The bars kept out her and the wagon, too.

Headlights haloed the snowy grayness overhead and then disappeared. The whir of tires faded.

Katrina stuck her head up and looked up and down the highway. She struggled up the embankment and headed west again. She fretted about the openness of the road and the half-light of dawn, but the great peaks of the Presidential Range, standing like proud patriots, urged her on. Coming to the Golf Course at Breton Woods, she nearly had a heart attack when a flock of grouse flushed out of the bushes. As the birds disappeared, snow resettled on the bushes.

The Ammonoosuc River closed in on the highway, not a big river, but too big to cross if a car appeared. A quarter mile after the entrance to the Mount Washington Hotel, railroad tracks crossed the highway. The wagon joggled over the trestle bridge that spanned the river, but rocky terrain on the other side forced travel back to the snowy highway. "We're sitting ducks again, Addie," she hacked, glancing over her shoulder. "What's that? A pinpoint of light! No, two!"

Chapter 49

*G*us balanced on a stump and gazed off to the west. "I'd say she's got about half an hour on us."

"Half an hour?" gagged Ken, stopping to catch his breath. "Is that a train whistle? Where in the world are we?"

"Webster Jackson Trail," said Gus, jumping down." Your girl and her dog cover ground quicker'n cheetahs. Keeps to the woods, so's nobody sees her from the road. Might've lost her if she took to the pavement. Tank would've had her though." He crossed a man-made wooden bridge then stepped over a rock of considerable size that had dislodged from a nearby ledge. Ken tripped over the rock, going head-over-teakettle. Gus gave Ken a one-eyed squint. "Footin' is gettin' a bit dicey."

"I broke my leg to get my baby girl back the first time," blustered Ken, getting to his feet. He hitched up his britches. "If I have to again, so be it!"

Gus tisked. "Had 'nough of greenhorns yet, Tank?"

The dog yipped.

"Got me the very same feelin's," snorted Gus, shuffling off, Tank prancing at his side.

Ken grunted. He wedged his hiking pole into the ground and pried himself to his feet.

Nearing an enormous overhanging boulder that blocked the right half of the trail, Gus stopped and pressed his hand against Ken's chest. "She pulled up here."

"How come?" asked Ken.

Tank snarled.

Gus pointed to the dark hollow beneath the boulder. "Black bear hang out there."

Ken's eyes popped.

Gus took a can out of his pocket and shook it.

"What's that?"

"Bear mace. Better safe than sorry." Can at the ready, Gus took cautious steps around the boulder, eyeballing the dark hollow. Sticking close, Tank sniffed the ground. On the other side, Gus straightened up and gestured. "Coast is clear. Get a move on."

Ken swallowed hard then ratcheted himself up and stepped around the boulder. A roar echoed against the mountains. "What was that?" he cried, charging for Gus.

"Bear," said Gus, stiff as a statue.

Tank snarled, fangs glistening in the low light.

"Now what?" Ken asked.

"Lower our voices," warned Gus. "Be vigilant. Above all, don't panic."

Nearing Saco Lake, a gush of water caused them to focus on the middle of the ice-skimmed lake where a bull moose stood shoulder-high in the water. One very large, dark brown eye locked on Ken. "That there moose is decidin' whether he's got concerns over you," whispered Gus.

When the moose stuck its head back into the water, Gus followed wagon tracks. A hundred yards later, he said, "Your girl's on her own."

"What?"

"This sand's been torn up, and over yonder…" Gus pointed to Tank sniffing a dark form skimmed with snow.

"Katrina's dog!" cried Ken, running to the husky.

When Gus caught up, his eyes wandered blood-clotted wounds. "Bear smacked the dog for rilin' up her cub." Using his hiking pole, he nudged the husky then bent down and fingered its neck. "Gettin' the wind knocked out was a lifesaver."

"Why's that?"

"Didn't get up when mama bear came to finish her off." Gus handed Ken the can of bear mace. "The claw marks mama bear's way of findin' out if the dog's dead. Got nothin'. Hauled off for her cub treed in the timberline."

"Cub?" asked Ken, jittery about holding the can yet ready to use it.

"Ayup," said Gus, picking up Mickey Blue Eyes and hooking her around his neck like a boa. "Cub was too far for mama's comfort."

"Not enough for mine," said Ken.

"Somethin' mighty important in that there wagon for her to be hauling it herself." said Gus. "Night vision goggles half-buried in the sand yonder." He gestured with his nose.

"Katrina has no protection," said Ken. "Can't you make Tank go and look after her until we catch up?"

Gus shook his head. "You know very well Tank don't take to folks without me introducin' 'em first."

Chapter 50

*P*riscilla Hamilton dreamed of being a great bird, rising above streams, trees, and power lines. Soaring in the bluest of sky, for once in her sorry life, problems no longer bogged her down. Her entire being was free. She skimmed a hillside of wildflowers. Sweetness swelled her breast.

Then a violent seizure struck and left her twitching. Sweat iced, chilling her to the marrow. Almost too weary to draw breath, she strained to lift her head. Her eyes lolled at the chaos. *This is all wrong! It's not what I planned on for so long. The Granite arch is still standing. So is the Administration Building.* Her head plopped onto the ground. *One last option.*

Finger muscles twitched, straining to depress a sequence of remote buttons. Priscilla Hamilton smiled weakly and waited. Alone. Friendless. Unloved. Nobody comforted her. This was the bed that Jonathan Aranea had made for spiderling Alice Milton.

Chapter 51

Wheels bogged down in snow as Katrina steered the wagon into the parking lot of the convenience station. She tugged, strained, and coughed. Muscles mutinied. When at last she got to the telephone outside the station, she released the harness and picked up the receiver. She reached in her pocket for a coin, but her grip was tenuous as she slid out the coin then fed it into the slot. Hearing a dial tone, she hit the bottom key.

"Operator."

"I need to make a collect call," said Katrina between coughs.

"The number, please, and your name."

Katrina gave her name and the number at Toffee Castle.

One ring…two…three…four. "Can't take your call, right now," said her father in a recorded message. "Leave your name and number. We'll get back to you."

Tears flooded Katrina's eyes.

"Nobody answers at that number," said the operator.

Shoving away tears, Katrina choked out a second number.

A woman answered, and the operator said, "I have a collect call from Katrina Waters. Will you accept the charges?"

"Absolutely," said the woman.

"Go ahead, Ms. Waters," said the operator.

Through a coughing fit, Katrina said, "I have to speak to Doctor Curt Shirlington."

After a slight hesitation, the woman said, "Katrina. This is Penny."

Fear rippled through Katrina as she hacked, "His wife?"

"You might say that," said Penny, humor lacing her voice. Her hand muffled the phone. "It's Katrina."

"I'm here, wee one," said Curt.

Katrina cleared her throat. "Addie and I are in real trouble."

"You have Adriano?" asked Curt.

"Yeah," she sobbed. "He's been drugged."

"Hold tight," he said. "Penny and I are heading your way in less than an hour."

"But I need you now," Katrina half-screamed, half-sobbed. "A bear got Mickey Blue Eyes! And I see flashlights. The Araneas are after us! I can't call the police. I can't trust anybody! Jonathan controls everybody!"

"Take a deep breath, wee one," said Curt, "and calm down. Tell me where you are."

Katrina sucked in a breath and shook off adrenaline and fear. "At a convenience station a quarter mile west of the Mount Washington Hotel entrance. I don't know any place to hide. They know every square inch of these mountains."

On the other end of the line, there was muffled conversation. Penny came on the line. "Curt will register you at the Mount Washington Hotel. Nobody expects you to go there. He'll tell the manager he's your father and there's been an accident. You and your brother called him from the convenience station and he told you to go to the hotel and wait for him there while he gets help for your mother."

Curt got back on the line. "I must use my credit card, so claim you are Katrina and Adriano Shirlington. I'll tell the manager you and Adriano are terribly frightened, so give you your privacy and don't let anybody know you're there."

"Gosh," said Katrina. "I don't know if that's a good idea or not."

"Penny knows what she's doing," said Curt.

"Guess it's better than hangin' out here in the cold and snow," said Katrina, looking around for shelter. "It's awful open here. Hiding behind this building is out of the question. Daylight's coming and somebody's after us."

"Kat," whimpered Adriano.

"Addie! You're awake! Uncle Curt! Addie's sitting up! He's looking straight at me!"

"I wanna get out," whined the disoriented boy as his fingers spread wide at her.

"Stay in the wagon," she said. "I'll give you a great big hug in one second. Addie, no..." She dropped the receiver and swung Adriano's leg back into the wagon. "You have to stay put or the bad people are going to find us and take us again!"

Fear immobilized Adriano. His eyes bugged out. He started to whimper.

Katrina picked up the receiver. "Addie's awful groggy and scared."

"That's to be expected," said Curt. "Great news anyway. Now, I want you to..."

A kaleidoscope of light flashed across the valley. Ba-ba-ba-boom! Echoes erupted as the ground shook and then surged like a tidal wave.

"Kat!" squalled Adriano.

She dropped the handset and scooped him into her arms. He clung to her like a monkey, head buried in her chest, as the thump of concussions penetrated her feet. The building creaked. Windows rattled. She scanned the countryside. The clamor was coming from everywhere. To the east, a black cloud mushroomed beyond Mount Webster. The cloud blocked out the dawn. No houselights. No streetlights. No pinpoints of lights. *Granite Mountain's gone! Chas! Priscilla!* More to calm herself, she whispered, "It's okay, Addie." Despite muscles that cried out from a night of exertion, she rocked back and forth, thankful to be holding him. She heard somebody hollering. It was coming from the receiver swinging below the callbox. She strained to stand up then snagged the receiver. "Uncle Curt! Granite Mountain just blew up!"

"Good Lord," winced Curt. "The WMDs! The cloud—what's it look like?"

"Humongous," she cried, "but it's not the same as I've seen in books or on TV, you know, like the ones set off in the desert a long time ago. Addie and I are safe, I think, because Mount

Jefferson's between us and Granite Mountain. I don't know why, but the snow's turning to rain."

"The heat of an explosion can do that," said Curt. "The rain will turn into snow soon, but for now, get to the hotel straight away. Don't answer the door for anybody other than Penny or me. We'll be there…wait! Do you have anything to eat?"

"Granola bars," said Katrina.

"Great," said Curt. "You won't need room service. Under no circumstances let anyone trick you into saying they'll take you to your family or the police."

"Those lights are really close, Uncle Curt," whined Katrina. "They're attached to hardhats. I see outlines of two guys. One is carrying something around his neck; and it makes him look big—like King Kong. They have a dog! And it's tracking us!"

"Be strong now, wee one," said Curt. "Make way for the hotel. Penny and I will be there directly."

Katrina put the handset on its cradle.

"My belly's hungry," whined Adriano.

"Mine, too," she said, setting him in the wagon.

Behind the building, she squirmed out of the backpack then took out two granola bars. Her fingers struggled to open the wrappers. Handing one bar to Adriano, she took a bite out of the other bar. *I used to feed Mickey Blue Eyes pieces of my food. Oh, why didn't I think of bear mace?* She brushed away tears. *Addie can't see me cry.* She took a bottle of water from the backpack and stared at it. She remembered Bert. She remembered that island.

Adriano grabbed the bottle and sucked down half the water. Suddenly, his face lost color. His lips barely moved as he whispered, "What's that noise?"

Katrina listened. "A lamb, Addie. It wants its mother."

"I want my Mama, too," he whimpered.

Chapter 52

*R*anger station ahead," said Gus. "Ten to one, your girl steered clear of it. Ayeup. Looky here. She cut the angle to a shelter off the beaten path. She's been this way before, planning a quick exit. Knows her stuff, that girl."

"She didn't get any of that from me, that's for sure," spouted Ken while doddering across a slimy log.

At the weatherworn shelter, Gus eyed clothing and supplies. "Tossed extra weight. She's pooped and knows better than to be bogged down."

Hardwoods creaked. An owl hooted. In the distance coyotes yipped. Ken's veins iced. "Let's get out of here!"

"Aw, come on," teased Gus. "Let's set a spell, sos I can tell you about the Eastern coyote, an evolving subspecies of wolf what hunts in packs or families for bigger prey."

Ken gave Gus the hairy eyeball.

At Crawford Notch, Gus stepped onto the highway, prompting Ken to ask, "Thought she was avoiding roads?"

"No choice, what with mountains closin' in tight," said Gus. "Can't go north or south. Bet your life she ain't about to turn back from where's she come."

"Good point," said Ken with an uncertain degree of confidence.

"Got a sense of her thinkin' and what she's up to," said Gus, "but I'm keepin' my eye on the edge of the road. Don't want her to trip us up. Tell you this: Her insides don't match her outsides."

"Huh?" asked Ken.

"Smarter than her age would have you," explained Gus, gawking at the sky. "Day's comin' on. Makes trackin' easier." A mile later, he peered over the side of the road. "She holed up next to that culvert." He glanced at the highway ahead then behind. "Waitin' on a vehicle to go by. Came back up over there an' took off." He adjusted Mickey Blue Eyes on his shoulders then slogged up the highway. "She'll stick to the Breton greens and the line of trees what runs alongside the Saco River—that be my guess."

Ken opened his mouth to speak just as an explosion rocked the countryside. Covering his head, he dropped to the snowy ground. When the retorts died down, he uncovered his head and scanned the area. Gus was sitting a short distance away, his arm around Tank, both staring off to the east. Following their line of vision, Ken spotted a black mass rising on the other side of Mount Webster. "What the heck happened?"

"I s'pect Granite Mountain is no more," said Gus.

Hearing a mutilated whine, Ken looked over his shoulder. Mickey Blue Eyes struggling to get to her feet. Gus offered an open hand, saying, "Sorry about droppin' ya the way I did, girl, but first instinct sent me to the deck."

Ken got to his feet and clapped grime off his hands. "We gotta find my baby girl!"

Gus twisted the cap off his canteen, took a quick slug, then poured water into his palm. Tank and the husky lapped. "Soberin' yet impressive what mankind does to itself."

"We're wasting time," protested Ken.

Gus twisted the cap onto the canteen. He got to his feet and picked up Mickey Blue Eyes. The husky offered no resistance as Gus slung her across his shoulders.

Fifteen minutes later, snow turned into sooty drizzle. "Take a gander at the cars haulin' butt out o' the Mount."

"Don't blame them from running away from nuclear fall-out," said Ken. "I would, too, if I had my baby girl."

"Wasn't a nuke," said Gus.

"You're also an expert on explosions?" asked Ken, glancing back at the ragged darkness hovering over the eastern peaks.

"Seen ammo dumps blow in Nam," said Gus. "This one's classic ammo. Looky there, I believe we caught up to your girl."

"Where!" cried Ken.

"Gas station ahead," said Gus.

"Katrina!" hollered Ken, waving like mad and charging up the road. "Katrina, stop!" He was chucking coins into the phone on the outside corner of the store when Gus caught up. "Why didn't she stop?"

"Voices don't carry over the ruckus them there vehicles put out," said Gus, eyeing the muddy ground. "Got the feelin' she was in the middle of a call when the mountain blew. Hit the dirt here."

Ken dialed home then watched Gus follow tracks around the back of the store. The answering machine in Brighton picked up. He listened to his recorded message, his fingers tapping the receiver. At the beep, he spouted, "Hey, Julie. Gus and I tracked down Katrina. Get back to you as soon as I can." He hung up. The hardhat stopped him from running his hand through his hair. He spun around and stopped. "Gus?" He ran behind the building. He looked left and then right. "Now where did he go?" He looked down. "Footprints!" He followed them into a stand of pines. Locating Gus entering a clearing split in half by a road clogged with cars, Ken groused, "You sure can cover ground." The Mount Washington Hotel loomed ahead. "She's headed there?"

"Ayeup," said Gus.

Ken sucked in a breath and his cheeks ballooned as he blew it out. "Wow. I promised to take Julie and the kids here for a winter getaway."

"Some getaway," snorted Gus. Trudging up the knoll covered with grimy, waterlogged snow, he pointed with his nose. "She's off that a-way."

"Valet parking?" asked Ken. Then he spotted two young men in hotel uniforms stashing a sled-like wagon into an outbuilding. Animal rage broke as Ken charged at one of the young men. "Where's my baby girl?" he demanded. Grabbing the man's jacket, he shook with all his might. "Where is she?"

The terrified young man glanced toward the hotel entrance.

Ken released the jacket and raced inside. A mass exodus engulfed the lobby. He snagged the first uniformed person he saw and bawled, "You see a blond girl?"

The uniformed stranger looked shocked at first. Then his brows came together. "Lots of blonds around here."

"Where's the reception desk?" demanded Ken.

The stranger pointed.

"Hey!" shouted some woman above the din. "No dogs allowed in here!"

"Put a sock in it!" barked Gus, setting down Mickey Blue Eyes. Tank licked the husky's right ear as Gus took off his hard hat and rapped it against a high back chair. An icy glaze scattered across the floor like broken glass.

Ken elbowed through the surging crowd. "Cripes, I'm a salmon swimming upstream! There's Katrina! Katrina, wait!"

About to enter an elevator behind a bellboy, Katrina turned. "Dad!"

Ken stopped in his tracks. "Addie?"

"Daddy!" cried Katrina and Adriano, scampering to Ken.

Ken scooped Adriano into his right arm and wrapped his left arm around Katrina. Pressing their heads against his breast, he whimpered, "Oh, thank you, Lord!"

A cold, slimy nose nudged Katrina's hand. She looked down. "Mickey Blue Eyes! You're alive!" She dropped to her knees and dissolved into tears, hugging the husky. "We made it, girl! And we're all alive!"

Epilogue

A steady whoomp-whoomp woke Katrina from an uneasy slumber accosted by blurry visions of the last twenty-four hours. Outside the large paned windows, helicopters were heading east, but swaddled in the queen-size, four-poster bed, she felt safe. Warm. The world outside that window couldn't touch her. *Like the time Bert held me in his arms at sunset.* As the noise faded, she heard her father and Gus snoring on the pull-out sofa in the adjoining sitting room. She heard soft breathing and looked at Julie, asleep next to her, arms wrapped around Adriano. A helicopter had located Julie and her minivan with a flat tire near the Old Man of the Mountain then airlifted her to the Mount Washington Hotel.

Katrina rotated the gold band on the third finger of her left hand. *Wonder where Bert is?* She scanned the room: clean, pretty, antique furniture. Guilt overwhelmed her. *Here I am safe and warm in my family's arms—what about Chas, Priscilla, and the others? Did they make it to that safe house? I owe them. I have to go back. Doctor Edie helped me to keep demons of the past at bay. Maybe she can do the same for the kids at Granite Mountain.*

Katrina slid her legs over the edge of the bed and sat there, feeling light-headed, arms and legs weak. Her toes nudged Mickey Blue Eyes asleep on the braided rug. The husky let out a small yip then labored to sit up. Katrina offered her hand. The husky licked it. Traumatized blue eyes lolled. "My poor love. You've been through so much—too much in your two years." Katrina slid out of bed and knelt beside Mickey Blue Eyes.

Cupping the snout in her hands, she rubbed her cheek against the fur. "I promise you, nothing will ever hurt you again. I'll get you the best veterinarian in the whole wide world to erase that dreadful word from your brain. But I have to go back to Granite Mountain first. Those kids need all the help they can get."

Injury stifled Mickey Blue Eyes from showing the usual on-the-ready mannerisms. Mutated panting was strained.

"Easy, girl, you need to lie down. Stay here and heal. I'll be back soon."

But Mickey Blue Eyes stuck to Katrina all the way to the kitchenette and watched as Katrina took a sandwich off the room service tray, tore the sandwich in half, and chucked half into her mouth. She tossed the other half of the sandwich to Mickey Blue Eyes then poured water into a plastic cup and set it on the floor. The husky lapped it dry as Katrina poured another cup and gulped it down. She spotted the canteen her father had left on the table next to Alice's plastic bag. She grabbed the canteen and filled it with water. As she stuffed another sandwich into her pocket, she felt Mickey Blue Eyes worm between her legs. She looked down. Tank was licking the husky's mane.

"Sneakin' off?" asked Gus.

Katrina spun around and pressed her index finger against her lips. "Sh-sh. I'm going back to Granite Mountain."

"Didn't get much rest," said Gus in a low gravely voice.

"You either," she countered.

"S'pect folks like us are used to a couple hours on the run," he said.

"What's going on?" demanded Ken, slogging into the kitchen, eyes heavy-lidded. He ran his hand through his matted locks.

Katrina gave Gus a now-see-what-you've-done look while answering, "I'm going back to help the kids who survived."

"Uh-uh," said Ken, shaking his head side to side.

"I'm going, Dad," she insisted. "I want to help deprogram those kids then organize and train whoever wants to become fighters like me against terrorists who just won't quit recruiting innocent kids. Terrorists think they're so untouchable, yeah, well, they got another thing coming!"

"Can't unring a bell," sputtered Gus.

Ken squinted at Gus. "What do you mean by that?"

"Wise to let your girl be what fate intended," advised Gus.

"Fate my butt!" snapped Ken. "I looked fate in the eyeballs and allowed my baby girl go to that Ecology Camp! I should-n't've let her go to that summer camp! And I damn well should-n't've let her go to that academy! I won't make anymore wrong choices!"

"You didn't make any wrong choices," argued Katrina. "My life wouldn't have turned in the direction it's destined to go unless I took that first step. So stop obsessing over me. Whatever path I choose, no matter what happens, I'll figure things out."

"Our daughter's headed for greatness," said Julie, stroking Mickey's head and then Tank's.

Katrina telegraphed Julie a silent thank you. Ken telegraphed aggravation.

"What a sweet puppy," oozed Julie as Tank licked her cheek.

"That *puppy* almost ate me for breakfast," spouted Ken.

"Oh, come on," said Julie. "This is the sweetest puppy in the world."

Gus chortled. "Think me and Tank'll go scare up some grub."

Katrina caught herself twisting the ring on her left hand. She linked her hands behind her back.

"Katrina's going back to Brighton with me," snorted Ken, "and that's final!"

Her blue eyes iced as Katrina cried, "I'll run away! I want my own identity! My own destiny! Not what you want! Not what terrorists want!"

"Lower your voices," scolded Julie. "You'll wake Addie."

Ken hitched up his pants. "I will not allow you to go back to that mountain. Besides, it's not there anymore!"

"I'm going," insisted Katrina.

His hands jounced at his sides. "Haven't you learned anything from all this? You're a target for terrorists. Regina and

Jake made you one. Terrorists will hunt you down the rest of your life."

"If that's true," countered Katrina, "I'll be ready for them. You know, you and I were torn apart by madness, but madness brought us together again, and here we are again in the same boat. I for one am determined not to let that happen again. I can't change the past, but if I don't get a handle on it, I'll never get on with my life. That's the only way to make the future brighter, not only for me, but for Addie. See how easy they took him? I hated Mississippi. I hated Jonathan. I wanted to go home every second of the day and feel the arms of everybody I love around me. I survived in Mississippi by turning inside, but not at Granite Mountain. While I didn't do the things I really wanted to do there, I feel triumphant. But it's different for other kids. It's hard for them to run away from programming. I could've run to you about it or the cops or FBI, but if I did, what about the other kids? What about other places like Granite Mountain and Judgment? How many are there that nobody knows about? I can't let the evil continue."

Julie spoke up. "Emma always says, 'In every life, there should be somebody who believes that wrongs must be fixed or at least be driven away.'"

"Okay, okay. You two made your point," said Ken. His hand ran through his hair. "I have to admit I am a proud father, seeing my daughter born a second time—a miracle born of a wicked woman, a champion of children everywhere."

"That means more to me than anything else," said Katrina, putting her arms around him. As she laid her head on his chest, a knock came on the door.

Julie tiptoed to the door. "Who is it?"

"Gus, ma'am."

Julie opened the door. Tank pranced in. Gus followed, carrying a tray of coffee, juice, and pastries. The telephone rang. As Julie ran to get it, Katrina brought dishes to the table. Gus, too accustomed to eating alone, wolfed down a couple of donuts while tossing pieces of another to Tank.

"Katrina and I are going back to Granite Mountain," said Ken. "I want you to stay here with Julie and Addie."

"Ain't cowerin' like a frightened schoolboy," said Gus with a mouthful. "My expertise of the area, your computer skills, and your girl's background, we'll straighten the situation real quick."

"Addie and I will be okay," said Julie, returning to the kitchen. "That was Curt on the phone. He and Penny are on their way to Granite Mountain, but wanted to make sure we're okay. I told them yes, not to stop here. We should hear their helicopter go over any second now."

"Nice of Curt to show up," sputtered Ken.

"Don't judge Uncle Curt until you hear the whole story," scolded Katrina.

Ken ran his hand through his hair. "Can't win for losing around here."

⌒

Greasing palms secured the hotel courtesy van that Gus drove east on Route 302. He turned on the radio.

"This storm's a complicated one," said the announcer of a Portland, Maine station. "Depending on location, it's a mixed bag. Rain along the seacoast has not changed over to snow as expected after the explosion at Granite Mountain. Higher elevations could get a backlash of one to three additional inches of either rain or snow. Improvement is not expected until day after tomorrow when highs go back into the forties. Meanwhile, slushy inland road surfaces remain slick, especially in the vicinity of Granite Mountain where authorities are keeping mum on exactly what took place in predawn hours."

Katrina watched trees layered with sooty ice pass by the backseat window. Branches bent to the ground, stressing tree trunks and making the trees look like tired old men.

Conditions worsened the closer they got to Granite Mountain. The sky darkened despite the mid-morning hour, casting eerie half-light as if slanting rays of the sun might never again reach this ground or set clear and bright upon the Presidential Range. Grit thickened the air near Saco Lake. A

black-and-white cruiser passed, headed in the opposite direction. Blue lights sliced the darkness. A siren began to wail.
Katrina looked over her shoulder. Headlights blinded her. "He's
after us!"

Gus jammed on the gas. He kept glancing in the mirror.

"He's closing in," cried Katrina. The cruiser came up on the
bumper. "Make like there's no place to stop."

Gus flipped on the right directional signal and began to
slow, moving his head as though searching the shoulder for a
place to pull off the highway.

"See those mountain laurel bushes, Dad?" said Katrina,
pointing to the left side of the road.

Ken squinted. "Yeah?"

"Gus is going to turn around and speed off the other way,"
said Katrina. "The cop will chase after Gus. So when I say, 'go,'
open your door and roll into those bushes."

"No way," said Ken.

"I'm going with or without you," she said.

Ken ran his hand through his hair. "Why should we risk our
lives? Those kids might not want help."

"Look," she said. "I'm terrified. I admit it. Wish I never got
caught in terrorism in the first place. But I did; and those kids
need me. They need us. Just like you and I needed each other a
long time ago. I intend to help them!"

"What's the plan, girl?" asked Gus while drifting off the
highway.

"The Sam Willey Trail to a cross trail that'll get me back to
the campus."

"I'll catch up soon's I can," said Gus.

"You agree with this?" asked Ken, leering at Gus.

"Freedom's worth fighting for," said Gus, slowing to a stop.
"Went to Nam over it. Here I am again—in my own country—
warrin' against terrorists bent on annihilation."

"Now, Gus!" shouted Katrina.

Gus spun the wheel then jammed on the gas.

"Get ready, Dad!"

"I don't think we should…"

"You told me once, Dad, that you had pipe dreams about becoming a dashing Tom Swift. Here's your chance." She opened her door and rolled out. "I think you are a dashing Tom Swift!" She ended up beneath the mountain laurel bushes. A car door slammed as Gus accelerated. Another car door slammed. Thump. Groan. Ken rolled up next to Katrina.

Cruiser lights rotated and lit up the roadside as blue lights streaked and the siren wailed. The black and white zinged past. Ken and Katrina's heads popped up. "Gus will give those cops one merry chase," said Ken.

"You okay?" asked Katrina, getting to her feet and offering her hand.

He smiled up at her then took her hand and pulled himself to his feet. Dusting himself off, he said, "Didn't break anything for you this time."

"Yet," she added.

About the Author

K Spirito has always been a history buff. She loves to browse through microfilm of old newspapers, especially at the Boston Public Library. Noting human interest articles, she later weaves them into fiction that explores the human condition.

New England born and raised, K later traveled throughout the United States, having also resided in California and Kentucky. She has also traveled to Canada, Mexico, England and Germany. She believes she was born of gypsies (although she was not) because she wouldn't mind one bit living a year or two in New York City then moving on to Montreal then San Diego then Rome then London then …

K Spirito holds a Bachelor of Science Degree from Franklin Pierce College in New Hampshire and also an Associate in Arts for Interpreting for the Deaf from L. A. Pierce College in California. In the '60s she built power supplies that now sit on the moon in the Lunar Excursion Module. She transcribed *Five Little Firemen* by Margaret Wise Brown and *Edith Thacher Hurd* into Braille for the L. A. Public Library. She was a licensed Cosmetologist and owned a hair salon.

K is a member of the New Hampshire Writers' Project and the Maine Writers and Publishers Alliance.

She and her husband of forty years raised four children and are now blessed with two granddaughters and four grandsons. She enjoys traveling, in-line skating, sailing, kayaking, and Mexican Train dominoes.

K Spirito's goals are to continue her education and become the best storyteller she can be.